Transcendentals

Transcendentals

Maurice James Blair

Synapsid Revelations Press Corporation

Transcendentals

ISBN: 978-1-963470-19-2 (hardcover)
ISBN: 978-1-963470-10-9 (paperback)
ISBN: 978-1-963470-22-2 (pdf ebook)
Synapsid Revelations Press Corporation
9619 Meadowcroft Dr
Houston, TX 77063, U.S.A.
Publication Date: Sep. 23, 2025 C.E., G. / T.2152.208. / R.O.C.114.09.23.
Text version: edited extra: G.2025.9.24-25/T.2152.209-210/R.114.9.24-25.

Blair, Maurice James
Early Inspirations: All sentient beings.
Author: Maurice James Blair.
Primary Editors: The Transcendental Beings of the Beyond Who Regulate Reality, To Whatever Degrees Real and/or Illusory and/or Imagined.
Secondary Editing Process: Using the same semi-anonymous aggregation of beings, however real and/or imagined, via telepathy, communing with the dead, remote viewing, and/or whatever else, that teamed to generate the work *All Things Under and Over the Sun and Stars: An Enigma in Twenty-Three Stages* (2005). (Consider daring to explore *Science, Religion, Politics, and Cards* (2023), pp. 208-209, 271-274 for a further explanation of this.)
Cover Designer: Paramita Bhattacharjee. Cover Editor: Maurice James Blair.

"Si vis pacem, para bellum." "If you want peace, prepare for war."
Passages from *Revelation* (c. 71) by John of Patmos (as translated by *The KJV Bible* and *The Geneva Bible*); *The Sacred Books of the East, Vol. XLIX* (1894; as translated from ancients by a team), edited by F. Max Müller; and *I Am* (1928) by F.C. Constable; etc.; &c. appear courtesy of being in the public domain.

The characters of this story are used fictitiously. Similarities may coincide differently relative to the different universes and multiverses of the diverse beholders. References to individuals, families, governments, books, movies, agencies, businesses, and other entities do not necessarily mean that there is any endorsement from them or any other business relationship with them.

Also, references to anything do not necessarily mean, aside from full context, that a given reader lives within a given universe and/or multiverse that has ever at the historico-scientific realm of existence had any of the beings and events described, although this does not necessarily preclude that any reader lives or any multiple readers live within a given universe and/or multiverse that has ever at the historico-scientific realm of existence had any of the beings and events described.

Liza,

If your memory serves you well, then you might remember that we shared multiple conversations on April 7, 1995 and that a portion of one of them resembled this:

LIZA: It seems that our class has been building up to studying Kant.

JIM: Yes, the pattern of empiricists, idealists, and others has led to his metaphysics as a capstone item. My father showed me some unusual books from the early twentieth century, and at least a few featured authors whose ideas stood on the shoulders of Kant's metaphysics. That approach includes the idea that in some ways we can transcend space and time.

Over three decades later, here is a literary work that in many respects grew from a combination of that conversation, the mysteries of all origins, and the mysteries of all destinations.

With Gratitude, Benevolence, and Loving-Kindness,
Jim, A Duke University Philosophy Classmate of Eons Ago

PROLOGUE

"This is the final end of all living creatures; be it a mean man, a man of middle state, or a noble, destruction is fixed to all in this world." —The Charioteer, per *The Sacred Books of the East, Vol. XLIX* (1894), Part I, p. 35, per E.B. Cowell's translation of *The Buddha-Karita of Asvaghosha*; ORIGINAL ORIGIN UNKNOWN

Transcendentals (2025) can be a sequel to one or more works that are of sufficient cohesion of plot and characters, and two examples of the previously published of which could be the novella *The Dimetrodons, the Dorians, and the Modern World, Synapsid Critical Edition* (2024) and the novel *All Things under and over the Sun and Stars: Enigmas in Various Stages* (2023). Alternatively, it can either be a novel that transcends prequel-versus-sequel relations with them or be a stand-alone work combining an alternative retelling of some *Dimetrodons, Dorians...* fiction, a very alternative retelling of portions of *All Things...* fiction, and a large amount of additional science fiction.

This novel, *Transcendentals*, features over 114,000 words if including the prologue, the preface, the orientation notes, etc. It serves as a symbolic eulogy to any and all civilizations and worlds that have died and any and all civilizations and worlds who will die.

THE EXTENT TO WHICH THE ACCOUNTS OF THIS FICTION WORK CORRESPOND WITH ANY PORTIONS OF THE NONFICTION REALITY WHICH THE READER HAS ENCOUNTERED PREVIOUSLY, IS NOW ENCOUNTERING, OR WILL AT SOME FUTURE STAGE ENCOUNTER IS PERHAPS BEST TO INITIALLY CONSIDER TO BE UNKNOWN UNTIL WITNESSING FURTHER EXPLORATION OF EXPERIENCE.

A few portions are based on history as was known relative to the universe(s) and multiverse(s) in which yours truly resided up to the instant of the initial finalization of this text. The rest, consisting of the vast and overwhelming majority of the text, involves imaginings whose similarities with any actualities either are or may be purely coincidental, save for whatever extrasensory perception might have mysteriously uncovered real occurrences past, present, future, etc. How completely fictional versus how completely real relative to a specific reader's reality is something to contemplate.

—Maurice James Blair, author of this work

Transitional Orientation Notes

The author and the publisher acknowledge having only had conscious access to a microscopic fraction of the published works and the unpublished manuscripts that have ever been. Also, the author and the publisher admit major uncertainty regarding how much verbal composition of works may exist beyond the realm of all the humans who have ever walked the Earth.

Therefore, although there has been no intentional duplication of anything, except for clearly-labeled de minimis amounts of things clearly appropriate to include (via patterns that entered the public domain prior to this work going to print, the fair use of copyrighted material, de minimis sets of four-to-eight words, etc., with or without a few accompanying numbers, symbols, punctuation, etc., that might date to antiquity, such as, e.g., "a new lease on life" and "the end is nigh"), we cannot and do not guarantee an absolute lack of any sizable, unsettling, unintentional duplications.

We also are at this time choosing to take an agnostic approach to how much any past controversies about whether duplication between others had crossed a line into impropriety were more the fault of one party or another in those disputes. For example, we are choosing to refrain from taking either the side of proclaiming absolute correctness of one songwriter or team of songwriters stating that his or her or their later composition proves unique enough to not require crediting an earlier-and-in-some-ways-similar song or the side of proclaiming the absolute correctness of another songwriter or another team of songwriters stating that her or his or their earlier compos-ition proves similar enough to the latter to deserve credit from composer(s) of the newer song. The same applies to our choice of an agnosticism toward all of the controversies of whether a new movie or a new book might seem to many reasonable observers to be somewhat in the gray areas of whether best deemed to be sufficiently similar to a forerunner such as to require crediting and possibly receiving permission from the composer(s) of that forerunner or, conversely, sufficiently unique such as to have neither any requirement to credit the composer(s) of at least one forerunner nor any requirement to obtain permission from such forerunner composer(s).

We seek to participate in Reality constructively, including to participate such as to genuinely help the process of steering Reality into becoming a Better Reality further along than it would otherwise wind up becoming.

Although the better can occasionally prove to be the enemy of the good, the better can frequently prove to be a friend of the good and a facilitator of the greater good.

PREFACE: REARRANGEMENTS, REVISITED

<u>PART ONE:</u> The publisher and the author reached a decision to fuse together modified versions of portions of storytelling from *The Dimetrodons, the Dorians, and the Modern World, Synapsid Critical Edition* (2024), *All Things under and over the Sun and Stars: Enigmas in Various Stages* (2023), *An Encyclopedic Survival Guide for Navigating Normal and Paranormal Experiences* (2023), portions of some public domain works, and a very large amount of new storytelling in the process of creating this new science fiction novel, *Transcendentals* (2025).

<u>PART TWO:</u> When I composed *Shape Up or Ship Out: A Message to All Political Parties* (2025), several unusual features of unintentional deflections (from what might otherwise have been more intuitively straightforward balanced statements to connect with reality in a simple way) were:

- Although it mentioned that I was on the Male Varsity part of the Hanks High School Tennis Team during portions of early January 1991 to approximately early September 1992, my memory later clarified a more specific pattern of this. To the best of memory my varsity participation was either entirely or almost entirely limited to some on-again-and-off-again portions of circa October 1991 to circa April 1992, and male junior varsity participation filled the remainder of my Hanks Tennis Team involvement in the period from circa early January 1991 to circa early September 1992.

- It referred to Yeshe Tsogyal's *Regarding Views and Regime Changes* (2024) as "*Regarding Views and Regime Changes* (2025)." There are ways that this could make sense, such as how that book reached publication near the end of 2024 C.E. and a high percentage of the main early batch of copies reached intended recipients early in 2025 C.E. However, intuitively, "(2024)" is a more standard way to quote a year in relationship with that book's publication.

- On a related note, part of the annotations section of *Regarding Views and Regime Changes* (2024) had an unusual feature of referring to *The Vajracchedika Sutra* by an alternative spelling featuring only one "c" between the "Vajra" and the "h," whereas most standard in English is to render that spelling with two consecutive instances of "c" between those.

<u>PREFACE, PART THREE:</u>

Here is a corrected, abridged, and reorganized-into-bullet-point-list-format version of the comparison chart that appears on page 115 of *The Dimetrodons, the Dorians, and the Modern World, Synapsid Critical Edition* (2024), here typed with the first print of *The Dimetrodons, the Dorians, and the Modern World* (2022) labeled {T1}, the second print of that labeled {T2}, *The Dimetrodons, the Dorians, and the Modern World: Revised Edition* (2022) labeled {TRE}, and *The Dimetrodons, the Dorians, and the Modern World, Synapsid Critical Edition* labeled {TCR}:

- Page Sizes: 8.5" X 11.5" for {T1}, {T2}, and {TCR}. 6" X 9" for {TRE}.
- {T1} and {T2}, p. 66 includes an instance of displaying, "prinordial" where {TRE} displays "primordial" on its p. 82 and {TCR} displays "primordial" on its p. 72.
- A portion of {T1}'s p. 13 states, "274,578 years," a portion of {T2}'s p. 13 states, "274,578 millennia," a portion of {TRE}'s p. 19 states, "274,578,000 years," and a portion of {TCR}'s p. 16 displays, "274,578 millennia.'

<u>PREFACE, PART FOUR:</u>

• "If your interpretation of *The Qur'an*, *The Tanakh*, and/or *The Bible* has led you to hatred toward *The Sacred Books of the East, Vol. XLIX*, then this will probably not turn out well for you unless and until you let go of that hatred. Such letting go may open the floodgates to a more enlightened approach toward any and all texts, videos, audios, and, last but not least, sentient beings."
—Maurice James Blair, 18 December 2024, C.E., posted to LinkedIn, transcribed here to show italics where the original post had shown all-caps.

• "For hatred does not cease by hatred at any time: hatred ceases by love, this is an old rule."
—*The Dhammapada*, Chapter One, Verse Five; circa the 5th or 6th century B.C.E., translated this way by F. Max Müller

• "The conscious self of science is conscious of the *is*, but it is ignorant of what the *is* is, for it can only function with conceptions of what the *is* is."
—Frank Challice Constable, credited as "F.C. Constable," on part of p. 65 of his philosophical treatise *I Am*, as published in 1928 by Kegan Paul, Trench, Trubner & Co. Ltd.

PREFACE, PART FIVE:

A List as of November 8, 2024 of the Top 12 Wars in Earth's Recorded Human History*

1. World War II (50-85 million)
2. Mongol Invasions and Conquests (20-60 million)
3. Three Kingdoms (34 million)
4. Taiping Rebellion (20-30 million)
5. World War I (15-30 million)
6. Manchu Conquest of China (25 million)
7. Conquests of Timur (7-20 million)
8. An Lushan Rebellion (13 million)
9. Thirty Years' War (4-12 million)
10. Spanish Conquest of Mexico (10 million)
11. Spanish Conquest of the Incan Empire (10 million)
12. Russian Civil War (7-10 million)

* In the universe/multiverse in which then present Synapsid Revelations Press observed (on a computer screen at about half past noon in Houston, TX on that date) a list that ranked them according to the estimated numbers of human deaths caused at URL https://en.wikipedia.org/wiki/List_of_wars_by_death_toll. Stylistic adjustments were incorporated in transcribing that website's information into what appears here, yet no changes were made to any of the mortality estimates. Neither the author nor the publisher hereby issue any assurances to the reader that the timeline of the reader as of a given instant features any overlap with what the author and the publisher experienced to have been historical reality and strong evidence of historical reality.

The author and the publisher arrived where humans had become Earth's main, historico-scientifically-observable, apex, intelligent species, a forceful presence successfully harnessing computers, automobiles, huge buildings, trains, ocean liners, guns, spacecraft, and satellites; however, this does not necessarily guarantee that all readers are and will reside where this is the case. If any of the readers happen to live in realms where humankind is merely "a fiction," meaning, in some sense, in other words, "an imagined, speculated-upon possibility," leading such a reader to wonder whether this entire very page is itself totally fictional on account of all of human history being fictional, well, then, hi there!

1) If considering this to culminate a trilogy, then that may consist of starting with at least one *Dimetrodons, Dorians, and World* item {i.e., a) *The Dimetrodons, the Dorians, and the Modern World* (2022), b) *The Dimetrodons, the Dorians, and the Modern World: Revised Edition* (2022), &/or c) *The Dimetrodons, the Dorians, and The Modern World, Synapsid Critical Edition* (2024)}, proceeding with the novel *All Things under and over the Sun and Stars: Enigmas in Various Stages* (2023), and finishing with the science fiction & literary fiction novel, *Transcendentals* (2025).

Introducing 2-6: Alternatively, a beholder may consider it to consist of any of the other sequences of that possible trilogy:
- 2) *All Things…*, then *Transcendentals*, then *Dimetrodons…*
- 3) *Transcendentals*, then *Dimetrodons…*, then *All Things…*
- 4) *Dimetrodons…*, then *Transcendentals*, then *All Things…*
- 5) *Transcendentals*, then *All Things…*, then *Dimetrodons…*
- 6) *All Things…*, then *Dimetrodons…*, then *Transcendentals*

This three-to-work-in-any-trilogy-sequence combination can, in some ways, reflect how P.D. Ouspensky (translated by C. Bessaraboff and C. Bragdon), in the tenth chapter (i.e., "A New Model of the Universe") of *A New Model of the Universe: Principles of the Psychological Method in its Application to Problems of Science, Religion, and Art, 2ⁿᵈ American Ed.* (1934), theorizes that three-dimensional time within a six-dimensional space-time continuum can work well conceptually. (Cf. pp. 372-380; Alfred A. Knopf; New York; 1946 reprint of the 1943 reset printed from new plates). The article "New theory proposes time has three dimensions, with space as a secondary effect" by Rod Boyce, University of Alaska Fairbanks (edited by Andrew Zinin) (June 21, 2025; accessed at https://phys.org/news/2025-06-theory-dimensions-space-secondary-effect.html during portions of mid-2025), states that UAF Geophysical Institute Professor Gunther Kletetschka has presented to the public a mathematical formula model of six-dimensional space-time.

Whether a given reader finds *Transcendentals* to more primarily exhibit absurdism, vanity, theology, tragedy, humor, psychology, sociology, fun, folly, wisdom, farce, stupidity, intelligence, comedy, seriousness, realism, and/or anything else, the reader may consider each of these modes to reflect portions of the history, the present, the possible futures, and the beyond of perhaps any or almost any intelligent species imaginable.

This trilogy eulogizes civilizations and worlds that have died, and this trilogy eulogizes civilizations and worlds that will die.

Transcendentals

TABLE OF CONTENTS

PART ONE

INTRODUCTION

Transcendental beings, known as The Transcendentals, emerged at the dawn of creation from a fission process of portions of the early, primordial consciousness of reality itself.

Amid tensions and resolutions, they accepted their status as a set of semiomniscient, extraordinarily powerful beings who would in many dimensions exercise freewill. They would sometimes go to war with each other and at other times team up with each other.

They subscribed to diverse and changing beliefs regarding religion, ethics, and philosophy, yet they were largely devoid of beliefs in any absolutely-fixed natural laws, because the natural laws within given ranges of space, time, space-time, and mind would largely stem from how they would collectively find their way into making those laws and changing those laws, as applicable within a given timescale, a given spacescale, a given scale of space-time, a given scale of mind, etc. Although conflicts remained contained to be within what many considered a reasonable range for eons upon eons—seemingly many eternities—after a while, one of them felt very trapped by how reality had progressed. Therefore, he started to endeavor for the wholesale, instant orchestration of the destruction of entire universes.

Some of the other Transcendentals chose to team up with him on that quest, whereas others chose to team up to resist that quest.

Repeatedly, the wars encompassing coalitions of Transcendentals, Gray Aliens, Humans, and Other Intelligent Beings escalated toward seemingly-inevitable, increasingly apocalyptic and post-apocalyptic showdowns.

Chapter One: Paleontology, History, and Biology, Revisited, or: A Revised, Radically Reimagined Variation of The Dimetrodons, The Dorians, and The Modern World

At Masada in 70, just before several of the men acted out a wholesale slaughter of their own community to prevent sieging Roman troops from acquiring secret information and secret technology, one person scribbled into the sand an ultimate expression.

He did that in an elegantly simple way. Several ultra-powerful beings of the great beyond judged that he had outdone all of the rest of the great, secret, esoteric expressions of knowledge that the Jewish community there had amassed before he wrote into the sand what it was that he wrote then and there. That person was an eight-year-old boy teched by a combination of primal truths present in the core of each and every religion, art, and science. He had somehow distilled it all into an economy of words, the equivalent of one middle-of-the-road-sized paragraph consisting of about five, medium-length sentences. A brief expression delivering more super-gateways to the zenith of extreme reality than the vast majority of the world's largest libraries could ever deliver.

Some considered it to have clearly and unequivocally solved what would later be called Kant's Paradox of Time.

He walked away from what he had written, then, five seconds later, he and his note vanished into thin air, much the way that, eons earlier, Enoch had exited Earth with the help of The Almighty.

As the centuries went by, new temporary mergers between The

Almighty and that eight-year-old youth would appear intermittently within many realities within many universes.

For example, some witnessed that merged, ultra-transcendental expression of extreme anthropomorphic power, accuracy, wisdom, volition, and compassion become portrayed on the silver screen in December 2014, a portrayal of The God of Abraham manifesting as a young, powerful, wise, transcendental boy able to materialize at will in order to speak directly to Moses. That was in *Exodus: Gods and Kings*, a motion picture film that many theatergoers attended.

In the universes within diverse multiverses, an array of variations of several different directors put together films of that title, and, across those alternate timelines that each had "December 2014 A.D." or "December 2014 C.E.," many variations of that film reached movie theaters in that month, each featuring the entity that some would refer to as "Yahweh" or "Yehweh" or a similarly-patterned "YHVH" name, THE ABSOLUTE portrayed as manifesting there in the form of a young, male, human when sharing conversations with Moses.

Another example: In many universes, a mysterious male Buddhist adept known as Padmasambhava or Guru Rinpoche arrived onto the scene during a crucial phase in the developments of the Earth, and he, too, in his own way, channeled and transfigured that ultimate, transcendental set of power, wisdom, and compassion.

Padmasambhava transfigured Northern Buddhism and the entire Himalayan Region during portions of the eighth century. That was during what some call The Eighth Century A.D. and others call The

Eighth Century C.E. He changed the trajectory of the arc of history across many worlds, timelines, universes, and multiverses.

In some of those universes, at least one variation each of the great multilingual scholar Professor Kenneth Douglas would work on an attempt to faithfully translate into English *The Life and Liberation of Padmasambhava*, translating from a French translation that had in the nineteenth century translated from source languages.

In some universes, Professor Douglas met with a tragic accident that resulted in his sudden death, leaving much unfinished business on that project. In many of those realms, Gwendolyn Bays would lovingly finish that translation that Kenneth Douglas had started.

Many timelines featured that translation reaching 1978 publication.

Yes, across many timelines the set of December 2014 *Exodus* movies was primarily of an energy-contract connection with an array of the Abrahamic religious expressions, especially encompassing Ancient Hebrews, Jews, Judaism, Muslims, Islam, Christians, Christianity, and Abrahamic Religion(s) in general. Yes, too, in contrast with that, the transfigurative, extraordinary, eighth-century Tantric Buddhist hero Padmasambhava primarily demonstrated an energy-contract connection with many Dharmic religious expressions, especially emphasizing Gentiles in general, Vajrayana Buddhists, Vajrayana Buddhism, Buddhism in general, and Dharmic Religion(s) in general.

Both exhibited Transcendental Reality.

A third example was that the accomplished English barrister and writer F.C. Constable succeeded in the latter years of his worldly life in finding a middle way between all religions and all sciences, thus unifying with much of Transcendental Reality.

One of the best passages from F.C. Constable's 1928 philosophical treatise *I Am* stated, "Again, we find that before we have any experience, Science peers into the 'land of mists and shadows' which the innumerable conceptions of imagination present to us. The conceptions of wireless communication, of television? They have always existed for us in the land of mists and shadows. But, till lately, science regarded them as *fictitious* conceptions. Why? Because they had nothing to do with experience. But *now* they have been found to have something to do with experience, and so both are regarded as postulates of science." (Cross Reference: Pages 36-37 of that work.)

A fourth example was that from the second half of the twentieth century to the first quarter of the twenty-first century, interactions between diverse religious leaders in each of many worlds led to the generation of similar transcendental insight among millions in each of those worlds. *That insight varied from person to person, yet in each case much of its core emanated from the same set of mysterious realities that can also be called Transcendental Reality.*

*****

Consider again the scenes at Masada of the year 70. A gut-wrenching slaughter was imminent. Several men had decided together that the most responsible thing that they could do as a duty to Reality Itself was to conduct a wholesale slaughter of their entire community. Before the slaughter could completely unfold such as to take the life of one of the eight-year-old males, that male youth expressed much of the essence of reality in an economy of words, unified with much of Transcendental Reality, then somehow vanished before he would have been among those slaughtered.

His six-year-old brother soon found himself executed by their own loving, biological father, as that father was among those present who deemed it too risky to let too many secrets fall into possession by the Romans. This had a degree of parallel to when, about 1,870 years later, one of the loving colleagues of a WW2 code talker killed him as a duty to the United States Military to prevent his imminent capture by the Axis Powers when the walls of a war situation closed in upon their unit of Allied Powers military personnel. Some of what happened during the massacre at Masada also paralleled part of how, in a 1960 incident, Francis Gary Powers declined to take his own life after the Soviets shot down the U-2 spy plane he had been flying during The Cold War, except with the inversion of how it was that many of the men of that ancient Jewish community chose the path of unleashing death unto their loved ones and themselves in order to protect secrets.

The conduct of suicides aimed at safeguarding secrets would crop up repeatedly among the human race from time to time, although it was not one of the most common motives for why people would choose to take their own lives.

In the Spring of 1945 in Germany, a group of Tibetan monks who had been duped by members of The Third Reich into serving in a facility in Berlin as members of Hitler's main spiritual advisors found the entire situation closing in. It was near the end of the European Theatre of WW2, and large numbers of Allied Forces were rapidly approaching.

Amid that situation, several of them suddenly became aware of the very same secret, insightful narrative paradigm that the eight-year-old Jewish boy had discovered at Masada about 1,875 years earlier. Several of them whispered it to each other gently.

However, rather than vanishing into thin air as the young person had many centuries earlier, they still found themselves stuck in a situation that did not seem to present any good options. After a little while, they thought in much the same way that many Japanese and other Asians had over the millennia, also much the same way that a small percentage of Egyptians, Jews, Gentiles, Russians, and humans in general virtually worldwide had over the millennia. They became convinced that the only honorable path forward was to end their own biological lives.

They committed suicide by harakiri just before Allied Forces would have barged in to capture them.

In addition to setting out to avoid what they perceived to be the indignity of living to be captured and possibly tried for complicity in war crimes, the several of them who had stumbled upon the secret narrative also believed it best to kill themselves in order to curb the proliferation of direct knowledge of that concise, powerful narrative.

Less than a decade-and-a-half later, in Lhasa, Tibet, shortly before the Dalai Lama fled to India, a twenty-seven-year-old man became the next to discover and communicate that narrative, writing it out on a small piece of paper. He then strategically folded that paper and tucked it into a small, wooden model of The Statue of Liberty.

He then found his way into becoming a globe-trotter, jumping from one continent to another, hiding away his secret expression of that narrative in his miniature Statue of Liberty model, which he took with him on many adventures. On the occasions when he declined to take it with him, he would almost invariably keep it in a vault at home, in a safe deposit box at a bank, or in another very secure spot.

Eventually, in the year 1970, he entrusted it to accompany him on a yacht with which he set sail from Sri Lanka to part of the East Coast of Sub-Saharan Africa.

During that trip, he suddenly felt a strong impulse to kill himself. He started to believe it best to commit suicide not out of despair or anything normally conceived by normal people to be among regular motives for suicide; rather, his impulse to kill himself emanated most primarily out of one of the most contentious ideas in several types of mysticism, perhaps most famously or infamously associated with part of the legendary descriptions of Kashmiri Shaivism; his suicidal impulse emerged mainly from a sincere belief that the time had come for his spiritual development to best reach completion via physical death, with intentionally killing himself a path that he considered a viable option for how best to take his spirituality to the next level. It is a peculiar and controversial idea. This involved the idea of killing oneself out of a sincere belief in it moving oneself to a higher state of reality, at conceptual levels not out of the motives of despair, warfare tactics, political protest, escaping pain, etc. In some versions of this dangerous belief pattern, a person can work that person's self into a state of sincerely believing that physically killing oneself might be the best way to spiritually merge with God.

Just before he would have otherwise killed himself in accordance with a literal interpretation of that type of religious prescription, though, he pivoted to believing it best to incinerate the wooden Statue of Liberty miniature model that had accompanied him for over a decade.

He proceeded to burn down that model. Right there aboard the yacht in which he was sailing on an intercontinental trip, he carefully placed a sufficient fireproof barrier, preventing spread of that fire to the rest of the ship.

As perhaps the most vital part of the procedure, he deliberately declined to extract from that model the folded paper upon which he had written the secret narrative that he had discovered back in Lhasa, that same narrative—though written in a different language—yes, that very conceptual expression that a young boy had concisely written into the sands of Masada before vanishing. It became obvious to him that something about spirit moving in mysterious ways was having strange effects upon his mind and his soul.

Aboard the ship, that former resident of the Himalayan Region felt relief in having narrowly averted suicide.

He wondered again about the mysteries of each and every reality, including his recent extreme brinkmanship. He was a Gentile, and he respected both the set of Gentiles in general and the set of Jews in general. Similarly, he respected both the Christians and the Non-Christians, both the Jains and the Non-Jains, both the Muslims and the Non-Muslims, and the peoples of diverse beliefs, ancestries, and practices in general. He chose a mixture of varying degrees of belief in the core energies of multiple religions, largely adhering to a set of notions similar to what several legendary individuals of the names Franklin, Huxley, and Shabkar had expressed about the plausibility that reality very probably transcends a huge percentage of the most divisive aspects of sectarianism.

That having been stated, he at times felt the strongest affinity for Kashmiri Shaivism, a religion that, as mentioned earlier, in some interpretations includes allegedly-sacred texts that encourage the sufficiently-advanced to deliberately destroy their own biologically-living bodies, liberating themselves from what might otherwise be the last vestiges of either having any unjustified attachments to their physical bodies or having any inexcusable idolatry of their biological lives. To take that more literally or to take that more metaphorically, that was a question that many had confronted over the centuries. He was keenly aware of controversies about how literally or figuratively in general to take statements from legendary religious texts. Indeed, he often oscillated between opposing views of how to interpret them.

He decided that he would best stay alive, for the time being, and complete his yacht trip.

Suddenly, he had a flashback to his youth. Before he experienced a few things that defied all that he had previously assumed about the limits of what was scientifically possible, before he had gone deep into comparative religion, before he had made love to several women, and before he had experienced the flash of insight that led to his way of chronicling it via a note, he had a very opposite idea about suicide. He had in his youth felt a degree of mortal dread that something in his subconscious, something that he did not tangibly know, but which somehow screamed at him nevertheless from the depths of his subconscious mind, told him that there might be a risk that an act of suicide by him just might be an immediately, completely mortal sin that might obliterate both his consciousness as of then and any hope that there might otherwise be from there forward for any of his mind and heart and soul to reemerge into existing into reality anywhere. He wondered whether this might somehow actually be the very item that some Ultimate Reality had as the identity of either the Christian concept that "blasphemy against The Holy Spirit would neither find forgiveness in this world nor in the beyond" or of something that would be of virtually the same absolute warning. However, he did contemplate yet again about the mystery of the U.S. Military Pilot Gary Powers incident with the U-2 spy plane that the U.S.S.R. had shot down. His duty according to the U.S. Military had been for him to kill himself to protect United States secrets in the event of the high probability of imminent capture by the enemy. Ideas about that Gary, ideas about mainstream Christian concepts of what would constitute sin, ideas featuring the frequent Christian advice for people to refrain from committing suicide, ideas alleging that some secrets might best forever remain hidden, and the idea that revelation of a secret might best wait for when the due season and correct time and right purpose would align themselves, and much more swirled through the Lhasan refugee's mind. That man who had fled Lhasa, Tibet in 1959, carrying a wooden model of the Statue of Liberty until burning it in 1970 for a sweet savor unto whichever Lord or Lords were able to taste of its burning, for a little while out on the open seas forgot his own name.

Suddenly, he remembered each of six different variations of his name. Professionally, in the West, he had become known as "Cooper Winds." That was not his birth name, but for many purposes it had proven most convenient for Western acquaintances to memorize. He consistently pronounced it as in, "the winds of change." Among his acquaintances, a few pronounced it as in, "winds up unchanged" in contrast with how most pronounced it as in, "the winds of change."

After arriving in Africa, he made an arduous trek to arrive at The Church of Our Lady, Mary of Zion, in Axum, Ethiopia, a place where intuition had told him was as of then one of the five greatest spiritual energy emanators on the entirety of Planet Earth. While there, he was solemn and respectful, and he asked only one question.

He asked, "Would you confirm that, to the best of your knowledge, you have one main replica of your main artifact and one original of your main artifact here in this holy site?"

The local clergy member man who heard his question answered him in the simplest manner possible, responding, "Yes."

Sometime after that, he chose to venture to the United States, which was a country that was located north of the nation then known as Mexico and south of the nation then known as Canada. Suddenly, he started to believe that he would almost definitely die soon. That was a perception of having over a 97% chance of dying within three weeks, based on intuitive impressions of the reality beyond sensory perceptions of sight, sound, touch, smell, and taste.

He neither knew what the accident would be nor whether it would really happen at all. Nevertheless, acknowledging some je ne sais quoi about the impression, he thought that he had very little chance of staying alive for much longer. He quickly arranged with a local lawyer, two qualifying witnesses, and a notary public to generate an official last will and testament, then placed it into the hands of a friend named Clayton Watts, who happened to have a very young son named Geronimo Watts.

As per his last will and testament, Cooper Winds left a substantial amount of his estate to Clayton Watts, Geronomo Watts, two Tibetan advocacy groups, multiple organizations running the gamut of a vast array of Dharmic and Abrahamic religions, and a few other heirs.

As fate would have it, in November 1970 he boarded a charter bus, and quietly kept his intuition of the likelihood of his imminent death to himself. He used an assumed name for that ride. Unbeknownst to his fellow passengers, he was also working undercover for a Swiss intelligence agency at the time. Oddly, he felt a serene equanimity.

He remembered the song, "Banks of the Ohio," dating back to the Nineteenth Century, how some versions of it portray a male who proposes marriage, experiences his female lover spurn his proposal, and kills his lover, and how some versions of it portray a female who proposes marriage, experiences her male lover spurn her proposal, and kills her lover. He remembered how in some versions of it the would-be murder victim, on the brink of imminent death, protests, "I'm not prepared for eternity." However, he knew that, in contrast with that, he felt perfectly ready to die at any instant. He had lived what felt to him a reasonably great, in many ways very good, fully complete, honorable, dutiful life. As long as he could keep things on track to some basic degree between then and when the grim reaper would come along to collect him from the worldly life, he believed that he would be set for something good in the beyond, whether it might closely resemble some traditional vision of heaven, a pure land, an utterly-transcendental paranirvana whatever-that-would-be, or a mere blipping into and out of existence occasionally as a microscopic trace of a ghost of the way he was.

He boldly chose to lightly whisper out loud while seated on that bus, "I'm prepared for eternity."

The passenger seated to his right was a college football player who could hardly believe his ears as he clearly and distinctly heard what that Cooper had whispered out loud. This seemed to that passenger outside the middle 99.9% of human experience, a live action version

of Johann Sebastian Bach's "Come Sweet Death, Come Blessed Rest,"
known more technically as, "Komm, süßer Tod." The football player
did suddenly have a flashback to when he served as a one-day extern
at a white collar firm where, while one of the senior partners was on
the phone with a difficult client, those present witnessed that partner
sarcastically mime a motion suggesting an impulse to hang himself
to get away from the sheer agony of the phone call. *Maybe it was not
outside the middle 99.9% of human behavior after all, merely the middle 98%
of human behavior*, thought the concerned student athlete and aspiring
businessman.

That football player briefly looked pale and stared at him. Cooper
exhibited an eerie calmness, unperturbed by how the football player
had become perturbed. Within seconds, the football player looked
away from Cooper. Meanwhile, Mr. Cooper Winds, who had already
felt old before the trip, suddenly felt about two million years old.

The uncomfortable college athlete looked back to Cooper yet again,
and this time Cooper looked a whiter shade of pale than he had been
looking previously. Waves of conscious, telepathic energy emanated
from the older guy to the younger guy, shining some of the feeling.
The young college football player's countenance then reflected that
of the elderly man. Both looked about as ghastly as ghastly can be.

Neither spoke a word for the next twenty minutes, and no one else
aboard that bus dared attempt to initiate conversations with either
or the both of them as those minutes unfolded.

An hour later, although the college athlete had his feelings manage to fully return to the land of the living, Cooper was still in that "Come Blessed Rest" mode, inviting "Sweet Death" to take him away. As fate would have it, though, he proceeded not only to survive the bus trip, but one set of experiences after another as many years went by.

Indeed, Cooper Winds found himself still alive not only by the end of 1970 bus ride but also long enough to witness a landslide victory in 1984 for the presidential reelection of a former Hollywood actor.

Eventually, that Cooper did, in fact, die. It was by natural causes on October 21, 1985. His friend Clayton Watts had died in 1983.

Therefore, the young Charles Geronimo Watts—most often known as Geronimo and second most often known as Charlie—inherited both his originally-designated portion of Cooper Winds' estate and the portion originally intended to go to Geronimo's father Clayton.

***** ***** ***** ***** *****

Now, consider some of how this tied into what happened at Masada about 1,900 years earlier. Several times in 1981, the ghost of the six-year-old Jewish boy who had died in 70 in Masada soon after his older brother had vanished chose to initiate telepathic encounters with both Geronimo Watts and Cooper Winds. These had been part of an effort to best coordinate their 1981 viewing of the movie *Raiders of the Lost Ark* and their 1982 viewing of the movie *Rocky III*. They had also been part of an effort to affect how the past, present, and future of archaeology would unfold.

That boy's ghost had emerged from extraordinarily intricate sets of interwoven consciousness between sentient beings and the deepest processes of quantum physics to influence a chain reaction. One of the parts of this process included an intention to increase the odds that some archaeologist or another would, by sometime in the first half of the 21st century, unearth that boy's skeleton.

After the discovery of his skeleton and those of several who were near him, workers shipped the bones. Soon, another set of workers carefully stored them to be ready for further study. Not long after that, the time arrived for detailed studies and investigations into the mysteries of that set of skeletons.

An archaeologist picked up that boy's left femur, then felt a trace of a shining of the full set of all deaths of all time. He felt a dread that seemed infinite. He placed the femur down gently, then quickly turned to look behind him. No one else was in the room. He then looked up, down, and all around. Still, no signs of anyone else anywhere nearby.

Next, his mind rushed from reflections on each of many mass casualty incidents, including the 70 C.E. massacre at Masada, the European death camps of The Shoah, the atomic bombing of Nagasaki, the killing fields of Cambodia, and the gulags of the Soviet Union.

He suddenly felt an impulse to find the nearest bridge or firearm via which he might commit suicide, yet he fought back against that impulse.

Although he had not practiced Zen meditation in ages and had not looked at Kabbalist-themed diagrams in ages, he chose to embark on a mixture of both. As he did this, a horrifying vision came to him. He did not know whether it was a vision of actual history or a vision of some dark nightmare adjacent to whatever had really happened way back when, but his mind's eyes, ears, and other capabilities tuned into a sequence that was like witnessing a new movie for the first time. Specifically, his mind observed a docudrama in which people at Masada before the Roman siege against it suddenly brought together much of whatever mysterious truths were hidden beneath the surface of all or nearly all religions and cultures, then spoke to each other openly about these truths, then became attacked by Romans, then faced a stark choice: to surrender without committing a mass murder-suicide act or to reveal the secrets to the Romans. They then committed a mass murder-suicide, consisting of many murders and many suicides, and they succeeded in hiding their secrets from the Romans. His mind raced through ideas of Mithraism, Christianity, Judaism, Zoroastrianism, Hinduism, Buddhism, and other ancient religions. His mind then flashed forward to a mixture of Jews and Gentiles getting along well in some parts of Germany in the early 20th century, suddenly uncovering the same sets of hidden truths. Next, within that stream of consciousness he witnessed many Jews and many Gentiles becoming antagonistic toward each other in other parts of Germany in the early 20th century.

After that, he experienced the docudrama segue into a hyper-accelerated two-minute stretch that encapsulated the entirety of World War II, including a scene in which multiple high-level members of the Axis side and multiple high-level members of the Allied side died by suicide and other means after carrying the burden of many of those same hidden truths.

He had never revealed his name to an acquaintance named Charles Geronimo Watts, yet he had obtained two copies of a business card from that fellow. That was the same Watts who had inherited a portion of Cooper Winds' estate in 1985. The archaeologist decided to call that specific Geronimo Watts and see wherever the phone call might lead. After several rings, the call went to voicemail.

Rather than leave a voicemail with his own name, he chose to run off an impromptu bizarre sequence of names and descriptions in a rapid succession: "Helen of Troy, The Destroyers of Ozymendias Roy, Patriarch Nagarjuna, Patriarch Moses, Matriarch Blavatsky, Albert Einstein, Alan Watts, George, Wang, Xi, Smith, Ruhe, Dimont, Elephant, Donkey, Horse, Mule, Beaver, Weaver, Bat, Rat, Cat, Otter, Dog, Frog, Mammoth, Lion, Tiger, Americans, Russians, Io, Titan, Saturn, Jupiter, That."

Charr Naerroan suddenly materialized right in front of him, out of what seemed to be nowhere. Charr said to him, "You have known and understood little, but you have witnessed too much for me to allow you to stay in your present world. Say goodbye to virtually everything and everyone you thought you ever knew. I will soon teleport you to a place where you will start to almost definitely prove more helpful to my quest to obliterate your multiverse."

The archaeologist Jeremy Oppenheim could hardly believe that he was witnessing what he was witnessing, and his face demonstrated his feeling of sheer horror. Charr looked at him with cold, impassive eyes. Immediately before teleportation, Jeremy reached out with his mind to many memories and impressions. Several of these involved the issue of whether any and every nation at a given time would best stay very much the same way that it had been or would best radically change from the way that it had been into becoming very different. His contemplative list of many nations, whether recently existing or not, whether recently unified or not, as of then included The United States of America, The Russian Federation, The Ukraine, Germany, Israel, Saudi Arabia, Australia, India, Greece, The Democratic Republic of the Congo, Japan, Korea, Vietnam, Poland, Iran, Iraq, China, Brazil, Portugal, Spain, Mexico, Italy, Finland, and Canada. He felt a mixture of the thrill of adventure and the chill of the prospects of encountering death on a scale beyond the outer limits.

Charr then teleported the archaeologist Jeremy Oppenheim and himself to a starship orbiting Polaris. That Polaris was the star that many humans of many centuries before, during, and after The Industrial Revolution would refer to as The North Star. On a larger time horizon, technically, a very long cycle involved Earth going back and forth between pointing its rotational North Pole more toward Vega and more toward Polaris. Naerroan knew that plucking that specific Oppenheim out of that world at that very instant would cause several disturbances if not for placing some artifact there to counterbalance the disappearance. Therefore, after considering several options, he chose to comment on the past and on current and future choices that beings might face regarding all possible futures, performing this commentary via a hybrid cultural artifact multilith-monolith.

****

Charr decided to leave a mysterious marble plaque in place of some of the space that Jeremy and he had just vacated.

   On it, he psychokinetically inscribed several pithy quotes:

"The mind is lord and master—outward sense
The obedient servant of her will."
— William Wordsworth (1770-1850 C.E.)

"The mind is a wonderful servant, but a terrible master."
— Old Asian Proverb (circa antiquity) and/or Ralph Waldo Emerson (1803-1882 C.E.) and/or others

"Extreme justice is extreme injustice."
— Cicero (106-43 B.C.E.)

"Extreme justice is not necessarily extreme injustice."
— Various (circa antiquity)

"Extreme justice is extreme justice, not extreme injustice."
— Orecic Jovan Kosovo Djokovic (842-918 C.E.)

"Sometimes the mind should rule, sometimes the heart should rule, and, in many ways, yet always should the both them serve that more primary divine reality which is even greater than the both of them combined."
— Anonymous (circa antiquity)

****

The transcendental being Charr Naerroan was one of the great many Transcendentals, one of the beings capable of manipulating the very laws of physics. Yes, he was among the many Transcendentals who would at times team up with each other and at other times compete with each other.

After startling, astounding, and abducting archaeologist Jeremy Oppenheim, he shared another conversation with him.

Charr said, "How are you feeling at this instant?"

Jeremy answered, "*Confused.* You plucked me out of my reality and brought me over here, and in order to do what?!

"*If I heard you correctly, you said that you are seeing if I could help you annihilate my multiverse. Are you freakin' nuts?*"

Charr responded, "*First, indeed I am seeking to employ you in the noble act and grand adventure of annihilating your multiverse. This is true. Yes, I seek to obliterate your multiverse, but, no, I am not crazy.*"

Jeremy screamed, "*Bloody, hell! What the fuck is wrong with you?!* Is it ignorance, apathy, or hatred, or all three of them weaved into one? *What the hell is wrong with you?!* What the hell did my multiverse ever do to you to deserve for you to seek to destroy it?"

Charr said, "*Hey, don't be testy, now. It's nothing personal. I am not seeking to destroy your multiverse out of revenge or anything like that.*"

Jeremy interjected, "What the hell is going on with you, then?!"

Charr answered, "You remember when you hit a low point a few years ago, and your energy and motivation hit a rut, don't you?"

Jeremy asked, "How do you know about that?"

Charr said, "Oh, youngster of limited decades, you really seem so surprised, do you?!

"I demonstrated a transcendence over what you assumed to be the laws of physics and yet you wonder how I could possibly know much of your biographical background?

"I have observed much of your life and, yes, I have observed much of the lives of *billions* of the other humans thus far, very often totally unbeknownst to each of the surveilled.

"Now, think back to those doldrums that you experienced a few years back."

Jeremy paused. He then experienced a flood of painful memories together with a sense of relief that he pulled through to overcome that difficult period. He then said, *"Yes, I remember all too well."* His face grimaced with agony.

Charr pivoted the conversation, still displaying steely, incisive eyes, saying, *"Many of your world's most popular self-help and business success authors have been at least partway right about a great many things some of the time. One of their truest of truisms is that beings tend to have energy contracts with the rest of reality.*

"It just so happens that I was around just prior to the big bang that started both your universe and multitudes of other universes, before that event that, yea verily, created a constellation of multiverses.

"My energy contracts with reality have evolved as time has gone by, and, although I have destroyed several universes before, harvesting great energies in the process, the imminent destruction of your universe is a stepping stone toward my next goal: the destruction of your entire multiverse."

"I've destroyed many universes and harvested great energy from doing so, but I, as of yet, have not destroyed an entire multiverse.

"Your multiverse, for reasons that you will probably never come close to fully fathoming, just so happens to be, from an engineering perspective, the prime candidate at this time to be the first in a slate of serial annihilation of multiverses. This is my best way to serve reality itself, as my energy contract has led me to this and I have full faith and logical belief that this is the best thing I can do for everybody, not just for myself."

Jeremy shook his head, paused, looked Charr in the eyes, looked down, looked back up, then shook his head some more.

Jeremy Oppenheim nonverbally displayed utter dismay, including the look of sheer horror in his eyes, and he stated, "You may well have demonstrated an ability to manipulate the very laws of physics beyond anything I thought possible for anyone I would ever meet in this life, but the way you're talking sounds like a madman!"

Charr rebutted, *"Look, I may not be in nearly the sort of doldrums that you were in a few years ago, but I have what some might consider to be a much larger problem.*

"The past few hundred million years of my individual experience have featured vast labyrinth patterns in which many universes, times, places, events, and acquaintances are repeating themselves, often as exact replications and occasionally in different patterns. Sometimes even an entire century of experience winds up a duplication! Also, whether I diverge from my previous takes or duplicate my previous takes, much of what happens winds up going back to the very same settings that I had encountered before. In some ways it is fascinating, yet in other ways it points to some mystery, some responsibility to do something in order to break out from past cycles. Have you heard of circling disease?"

Jeremy said, "Yes, actually, I saw it in some unabridged dictionary long ago. If I remember right, on some farms and ranches, farmers and ranch hands would suddenly notice some individual animal out of the livestock go into a pattern of walking around in circles over and over again, having mysteriously lost interest in doing anything else with its life, simply walking around in some oval pattern, over and over again. The people running the farm or ranch would then diagnose it with having the so-called 'circling disease,' then typically have to decide whether to let it run its course for a while longer or to immediately euthanize it and harvest its carcass."

Charr responded, "Yes, it's great that you remember back to when you found a small portal into that on page 267 of the 1989 version of *Webster's Encyclopedic Unabridged Dictionary of the English Language*, and it is admirable that you expanded some of what you read there, added details that you hypothesized despite limited contact with farms and ranches, and such, but you forgot an important detail that is vital to this."

The archaeologist felt startled yet again, and he inquired, "Wow! So besides whatever else you have done for surveillance of me, you noticed at least one time way back when in which I looked at that very dictionary and examined its definition for that livestock illness?

Wow! Goodness, gracious, it feels a little odd to think of all sorts of things that you and the other Transcendentals might have observed happen both in the lives of those whom I have met and in my life! In several ways, perhaps you and the rest of the Transcendentals are similar to some of those legends of Krampus, Santa Claus, and the alleged Heavenly Host of Archangels and other angels! You said that you are setting out to destroy an entire multiverse, the one that I live in?! Are you Asriel, The Angel of Death?"

Charr answered, "I do not know whether or not Asriel, The Angel of Death, even exists, and, if he does exist, then I do not know for sure whether I am him or not."

Archaeologist Oppenheim's jaw dropped. After a few seconds, he then resumed speaking. "So you don't know for sure which religion or combination of religions might serve to be the backbone or the central nervous system or whatever, so to speak, of our very reality, do you? Also, you don't know for sure whether, as great as your powers might be, you have some case of extreme cosmic amnesia?"

Transcendental Naerroan shifted his countenance to including a touch of humility. "Bingo on much of what you just said. You just now hit several nails on the head, putting together part of some kind of woodwork project of your understanding of this situation, so to speak. You could say that all or nearly all of The Transcendentals are semiomniscient, semiomnipotent, semiomnibenevolent beings. I do not know whether it is even logically possible for any one being to be what any more than about one human out of a thousand would tend to conceptualize as an omnipotent, omnipresent, omniscient, and omnibenevolent Supreme Being Lord God Almighty. Many of the people's concepts of God seem to involve them imposing upon reality a set of stipulations that demand too much for any being or any set of beings to fulfill. It is kind of like a citizen who wants his or her country's leaders to apply two hundred times the total resources of that country toward a list of twenty-seven noble things that the government could theoretically set out to due, while the citizen is utterly oblivious to the tradeoffs involving the scarcity of resources. That is the way that many of the true believers in some Supreme Being Lord God Almighty hope, wish, and expect from Reality, and it is little surprise that many of them become disillusioned after the death of a loved one or some other tragedy.

"Although, to the best of my knowledge and memory, I have never experienced a clear and distinct meeting with The Ultimate God Of The Absolute Entirety Of All Of Reality, even if there is such a God, I have met and killed many of The Creators of The Universes. Do you remember a video clip that you saw many years ago either on the TV or on the Internet that featured Carl Sagan discussing science and, as part of it, briefly and intentionally drawing a small amount of his own blood from one of his hands as part of facilitating teaching the audience?"

The archaeologist replied, "Yes, I remember that."

The transcendental explained, "Well, it is kind of like that, adjusted into a much more cosmic scale. You see, imagine that a given cell or in a person's body parallels an entire universe or a group of closely-related cells in that body parallels an entire multiverse. Further, combine that notion and how some mysterious, microscopic, conscious, primary leader of the life force of a cell can parallel The Creator Of A Given Universe, with the cell as its own living, microscopic universe. With a group of cells, which might constitute an organ, a microscopic structure that is much smaller than the naked eye can see, a specific team of blood cells, or whatever else, consider that to parallel a given multiverse. Therefore, by this analogy, some conscious, mysterious, microscopic, primary leader of the life force of a group of cells can parallel The Creator Of A Given Multiverse.

"Therefore, each time that a person pricks with a needle his or her own index finger or lets a medical professional draw a little of that person's blood via some flesh near the elbow or wherever else, that could be like a deeper level of reality, such as a more primary Lord God than the Lord God of a given universe, choosing to let someone like me team up with others to kill a given universe and the Lord God of that given universe."

Archaeologist Jeremy Oppenheim said, "It makes sense logically. However, I am feeling very uncomfortable about this entire thing."

Charr patted Jeremy on the shoulder, showed warmth in his eyes while looking Jeremy in the eyes, then elaborated, stating, "Growing out of childhood and adolescence into adulthood can be difficult for many people. Harder still can be when a given person realizes that some of the assumptions that seemed the most comforting even into adulthood might not seem to correspond to reality very well at all. Some liberals face this as they get older. Some conservatives also face this sooner or later as they get older. Whether anyone is a liberal, a conservative, a moderate, or a person who transcends locations on any political spectrum, truth be told, reality is something we should make an effort to respect and adjust into dealing with. It might not always be very pleasant to act as an executioner, but virtually each and every being who lives long enough to become middle aged or older has to on a variety of occasions serve as an executioner. It just so happens that I have billions of years of a head start on experience as an executioner, compared to you.

"And you have served many times as an executioner, from early childhood onward. In fact, virtually every child at an early stage will face opportunities to serve as an executioner, that is, if we conceive even the intentional killing of a single cell of either one's own body or the body of at least one other being as an act of execution.

"There were a few times as a young boy that you kicked other people in regions ranging from the knees to the lower abdomen, I have seen you do that, and you probably remember back when you did that to people, before you had even finished elementary school. Do you remember?"

The archaeologist felt a mixture of discomfort and relief while he thought about it. He announced, "Yes, I remember that. Also, quite fortunately, I avoided getting brutally mutilated the way that I have read that some little boys aged fifteen and under wind up getting.

On some occasions, as per what I have read in books and on some webpages, boys of ages ranging from infancy to one day short of a sixteenth birthday wind up in the wrong place at the wrong time, with the wrong woman, man, boy, or girl, and, next thing you know, those boys lose one or more of their family jewels. Society often tries not to talk about this very much, but I have read about it happening. Indeed, that is evidently part of the reason why the laws in America, besides protecting girls under the legal age of consent from men and women over that age of consent and protecting boys under the legal age of consent from men over that age also protect boys under the legal age of consent from women over that age. Yet there is also that issue of when two boys, two girls, or a girl and a boy are both under the legal age of consent and at least one of them really has his or her way with the other one. Although that seldom results in a serious injury or a mutilation, sometimes it does lead to serious injuries and mutilations. Although I never mutilated anyone, as you are aware of and as you stated, before I ever reached middle school I had already on several occasions attacked others with blunt force via kicking them below the belt, aiming for the lower abdomen, the groin, the thighs, or the knees. I really hurt a few people that way, especially by causing trauma via kicks to the regions from the lower abdomen to the groin. Oddly enough, traumatizing a girl of about the same elementary school age that I was back then by intentionally kicking her slightly below the waist and thereby seeking to hurt her ovaries did not result in the school giving me detention, even though one of the teachers was a direct witness to when I did that heinous act. Also, traumatizing a boy of about the same age as I was back then by one extremely hard kick to his groin and thereby hurting his testicles enough that he immediately fell down and cried on the playground while I walked away and left him for dead, then hearing from one of the teachers that she heard from him what I had done, then honestly confessing to her that I had done that to him, that also did not result in the school giving me detention. I suppose in both of those cases they decided that it fell into the category of the ancient idea, 'It takes two to tango, and, in many cases, both the perpetrator of physical violence and that perpetrator's victim had significant, contributing roles in causing the act of violence to happen.' In contrast with that, there was that time when I saw several other boys taking turns with giving vicious wedgies to a boy who was standing around in a daze and letting any extra boy who came along join in on the sadistic fest-ivities. I then joined in on those festivities, cruelly giving five more wedgies to that boy, curious about whether I might get him to start bleeding from between the legs. Although he did not wind up with bleeding in any way visible to any of us there, I was one of the six boys who teamed up to act out vicious sadism on him then and there. I was so young and so stupid. I did not worry at all about any sense that maybe there might have been something totally immoral about what we were doing to him, and that, if we just kept on doing that and doing that, at some point we might have wound up killing one or maybe two or maybe all three of his family jewels, especially, if we had grown bored with giving him wedgies and, instead, took turns with having some of us hold down his arms and legs away from his groin and then the rest of us had taken turns with just plain stomping on his groin as hard as we could over and over again, with an intent to kill all three of those sensitive family jewels between his legs. Fortunately, as immoral as we were, we stopped performing the wedgies after a while, and he evidently did not suffer any long-term physical damage. However, I do not know for sure whether he has ever since then fully recovered at a psychological level. Also, I do not know for sure what the other boys did to him before I arrived. Also, I do not know whether any of the girls who were there as a group of onlookers might have done anything to that boy before I got there, saw what I saw, and did what I did. *Well, I did get detention for my role in that gang wedgie torture, six-on-one, elementary school ultra-violence. Yes, I remember this stuff all too well.* My life has gone well in the long run, but, *like virtually every other person I have ever known, I have fallen way short of whatever divine perfection would be,* it sure seems. *Yes, I remember.*"

Charr clarified, "Whether you were right or wrong to do what you did to them in those cases, you did what you did, and what you did was to act as an executioner of some of the cells of their bodies."

Jeremy started to really feel ashamed of what he had done to those three elementary schoolers back when he, too, was an elementary schooler. He looked away from Charr, looking away to the left. Then he shifted his head to look away to the right. He started to wonder again about all the cruelty that had happened in Europe, Asia, and North America in the twentieth century, and he started to wonder whether he should consider himself any better than the worst of the mass murderers of that century. He then thought about the history of violence across all geographical regions of Earth, and he silently wondered why people, himself included, do what they do, both the killing of others and the healing of others. He also wondered again about acts of suicide and acts of self-healing, including wondering yet again whether those who set out to get into situations that would practically guarantee that an officer would kill them as being better to characterize as "suicide by cop" or as "death by an indiscriminate, misadventurous, reckless rage against authority."

He said, "Sorry for my prolonged silence. Our conversation has led to a new round of serious soul searching about all those ideas about what is ethical, etc."

Charr shifted the focus. "Your conscience is admirable, but there is much more to life than love and peace and gathering together and holding hands. Focus again on tradeoffs. Sometimes people have to prune vegetation. Also, people sometimes have to prune the human population. Typically, in some sense, the main type of execution is the way that people vote with their wallets and purses, how they choose to spend their money. Whether you pay for this or for that winds up shifting much of the pattern of who lives, who dies, who reproduces with whom, and more. No matter which way you choose, you execute at least a little bit of the life force of many people. Also, no matter which way you choose, you execute some of the life force of many organizations. Flip over the pattern, though: No matter which way you choose, you also boost the life force of many people and boost the life force of many organizations. Tradeoffs abound.

"Consider your entire planet and consider the possibility that there have been many variations of it. Some dead, some alive, some yet to be born. Imagine now possibilities of the previous ones. Variations of Earth that already died long ago, whether they died in terms of the total extinction of intelligent life, the extinction of all biological life, the total destruction of the planet into a bunch of chunks of space debris that could afterward be among the asteroids, etc. However much death and destruction happens, however much tragedy happens, however much evil becomes perpetrated, there is, in each case, a way that energy becomes liberated by all the death, misfortune, tragedy, and annihilation.

"That is part of the way of nature. That is also part of the way of supernature. Any thoughts now? Also, would you happen to have any questions before the next main part of your orientation?"

Archaeologist Oppenheim asked, "You know what, some of those popular movies of recent decades have presented that multiverse idea, featuring multiple timelines and such. What might you tell me right now about this that might reduce my confusion?"

Naerroan answered, "There are many mysteries involved with that. Many universes within each multiverse, there are, and, that is part of a much larger tapestry of many interdependent multiverses.

"Also, I do not know how many different versions of myself there are, but I have met at least twenty-five other versions of myself."

Charr strategically paused. Jeremy started to squint his eyes upon considering what Charr had just said to him.

Jeremy asked a follow-up question. "Why did you say you have 'met at least twenty-five' of the 'other versions' of yourself instead of saying, 'about twenty-five' of them?"

Charr suddenly displayed what some ranchers would call a shit-eating grin. That was a countenance that many city folks would call a gleeful, mischievous grin.

He answered, "It might seem kind of funny to you, but there was one time I remember well in which twenty-six of us gathered for a photo after we teamed up with each other, leading our set of large coalitions to victory in killing 250 universes and, of course, with them, each Lord God of each of those universes. I do not know for sure how many variations of myself there are in terms of personal timelines, but I have personally met and known and teamed up with all of the exactly twenty-five other versions of myself with which we achieved that grand, ethical, enlightening, compassionate killing of 250 Lords God and the 250 universes that they had helmed."

Jeremy yelled, "You monster!"

Charr calmly stated in a relaxed voice, "Why, thank you, I will take that as a compliment."

Jeremy continued, "Many people are hesitant to try to imagine themselves walking in other people's shoes and living with the other people's lifepaths. Some people readily do this. I am one of those who does this quite often. Sure, it can get me burned when some intense ideologue finds out that I will not budge to agree as much with that person on whatever that person finds to be a hot-button issue, but it is worth it. I love people. I also love animals and plants. More importantly, if there really are 'Lords God of Universes' as you described, then each of them deserves at least a great deal of respect, admiration, and love. *The Bible* mentions that there are two great commandments: 'To love The Lord Your God with all your strength and all your might' and 'To love your neighbor as you love yourself.' I don't know if there is at least one true religion, and, if there is, then I don't know whether Christianity is it, but I do know that I have a conscience, which is something that I right now cannot honestly say regarding you."

Charr responded, "Hold your horses, partner. What is your take on the atom bombs that America unleashed onto Hiroshima and onto Nagasaki in August 1945?"

Jeremy looked very uncomfortable, looked up and to his right, then looked down, then looked up and to his left, then looked down again, then closed his eyes. Next, he covered his closed eyes with the palms of his hands. Bearing a "see no evil" pose, he said, "Although I do not know for sure how much truth regarding this is on the side of the activist Saul Alinsky, who died in 1972 at an age of 63 years and a few months, and how much truth is on the side of President Harry Truman, who died in 1972 at the age of 88 years and a few months, there's something there. Truman tended to choose to deem both of those nuclear bombings ethical, whereas Alinsky tended to choose to deem both of those nuclear bombings unethical. I am not going to take sides on that as of this instant, but I respect that there is value in both sides of it, to consider those two August 1945 atomic bombings ethical and/or to consider those two unethical. Why did you ask?"

Charr pontificated, "You recognize how complex ethical dilemmas can be. Also, you care about people and other beings, as you have demonstrated. I also care, yet I care in peculiar ways, given my rather unique biographical history and how Reality granted me powers beyond most people's imaginations. I, too, face many challenging ethical dilemmas. I have tried to do my best with them in the past, and I am continuing to try to do the best with them in the present. There are huge unknowns, even from where I stand. Since reality has presented me with such a plethora of time loops within a plethora of time labyrinths, it brings to mind the old adage, 'Drastic challenges can call for drastic measures.' Many people, including Ouspensky, long ago wrote of how beings in many ways face the extremity of the thricefold unknown. Similarly, MacDonald and Aries wrote adroitly long ago about how beings can face tough fog-of-war situations. As vastly beyond ordinary beings that my powers are, something else is afoot. Something way beyond even my comprehension is afoot.

"Earlier, when you responded with part of what you remembered about how a book informed you about when livestock catch circling disease, you failed to mention a very important detail. I mentioned to you that you missed something vital, yet you have not followed up on asking me what I noticed you to have missed. I shall take the liberty to explain it to you right now.

"When a cow, a bull, or a sheep catches circling disease, it is often the direct result of catching *Listeria monocytegenes* bacteria somehow or another. Although I do not know the extent to which the legends of Jesus of Nazareth are true, I know that some major percentage of them are true, and the idea that he and others have expressed that 'the flesh is but the raiment of the spirit' is correct, especially as interpreted as meaning something in the vein of, 'that which happens in the physical reality is, to a major degree, a lower-dimensional surface of a higher-dimensional set of mind, heart, soul, physics, metaphysics, and beyond; each physics is part of a greater physics, and each and every chemistry and physics is part of a whole that is greater than the entirety of all physics and all chemistry.' A case of cattle, sheep, or whatever kind of livestock catching that sort of bacterium and then walking around in ovals—whether literally in circles or in more oblong manners—annoying humans who then do declare it a 'disease' and sometimes nurse the beasts back to health and other times euthanize them, that is all of it a subsurface of a much richer, more intricate reality featuring minds, souls, hearts, energies, and other factors way beyond what biological reductionist scientism would tend to lead many of the most skeptical to believe about it all.

"I myself am not running around in circles, but the very fabric of the higher-dimensional space, time, and space-time in which I am finding myself has gone into strange repetitions, as I explained to you earlier.

"This begs the question, 'What should I do about it?' Well, there is an old saying in a variety of militaries and businesses on Earth and elsewhere that takes several forms, including, 'When facing peril, do something, even if it's right!' Well, I have considered numerous of the possible options, and, unless and until anyone might persuade me otherwise, I have decided on a plan, part of which I have already revealed to you. Let's dig a little deeper into what my plan is and why I have planned on making it happen.

"The best I can tell about this whole thing is that everyone and, yes, also, everything, is in need of a great, cosmic reset.

"The time has arrived to best seek to burn the entirety of reality down to the ground into an absolute obliteration of the entirety of all of the reality. This is what I truly believe right now. This should include the total annihilation of all that currently exists, and, after the destruction, our interdependency with all of creation, destruction, and preservation will, through spirit moving in mysterious ways, generate something that is better than all that was before. A new reality can then rise like a phoenix from the death of the old reality, and whatever subtle traces of ourselves remain amid the change, we can participate in the new reality, liberated from the trappings of the old.

"This is my plan, and about the only way anyone or any group will stop me is if they somehow move the heavens, the hells, and the worlds more powerfully, compassionately, and wisely than I do, or if they somehow get me to change my mind about it.

"I have been working on this plan for a very long time now, ever since early in the dizzying navigation of the higher-dimensional time labyrinth. This has included how I have created and destroyed several religions and very many myriads of worlds. You do know that in the olden days, 'myriad' mainly meant exactly the number 10,000, don't you?"

Jeremy stood speechless.

Charr continued, "Hey, snap out of it. Don't get yourself into some sort of a tizzy over my intention to annihilate all of reality. It is not really that big of a deal at all, really. You came to terms with all of the uncertainties of your own demise long ago. Think about this as similar to facing your own physical death, except much bigger. Now, look at me, relax, and think. Again, I ask you, did you already know and remember before I mentioned it that in the olden days, 'myriad' mainly meant exactly the number 10,000?"

Jeremy exhaled a deep breath, paused, then answered, "Yes, I was well aware of that. Also, yes, I was aware that many people in the modern times use that word to mean some quantity that is so large that they have difficulty even beginning to fathom how large it is."

Charr commented, "Great! You understand now that when I stated 'many myriads of worlds' a little while ago I meant it in both of those senses, both as in 'many tens of thousands of worlds' and as in 'many times as many worlds as would be enough to boggle many people's minds.' The time loops that I have frequently experienced seem to be evidence that OUR REALITY ITSELF has caught some paranormal death trap, and the best way to escape that death trap is to kill OUR ENTIRE REALITY ITSELF, to make way for a better reality.

"Do I really have the ability to obliterate our entire reality? Maybe, and maybe not. However, if I at least attempt to destroy it, then this will probably place me into a good bargaining position for how to best influence what happens next. That is, to influence what happens next into becoming something much better than it otherwise would be."

Charr paused, waiting to find out whether Jeremy would take the initiative to say or ask anything. However, Jeremy chose to exercise his right to remain silent.

Naerroan continued, "You enjoyed those TV shows *The Adventures of Brisco County, Jr.* (1993-1994), *Flashforward* (2009-2010), and *Timeless* (2016-2018), didn't you?"

Noticing that Naerroan paused and looked him in the eye, to that Oppenheim answered with a nod.

The archaeologist had several fond memories of having watched some episodes of each of those long-run-Nielsen-ratings-challenged, short-lived television programs. He thought back to the music and the lyrics of the song, "If I Die Young" by The Band Perry, imagining the ghosts of those three TV shows performing a cover of that song. He felt mixed, bittersweet emotions about everything that had happened in his life and the strange prospects for whatever might prove to be the things to come.

Naerroan resumed speaking. "Yes, there were several times that I invisibly watched some episodes of those shows with you, though you probably had no idea that I was there. Those shows, together with the movies *Indiana Jones and the Last Crusade* (1989), *Oblivion* (2013), and *Philadelphia* (1993) reflect the reality of how sometimes instead of leaning too much on our own understanding we should lean on a willingness to take leaps of faith that our intuitions about whatever might emanate from infinite and transinfinite reality itself may lead us to better results. It can be a balancing act, as reflected by portions of *The Bible*, *The Qur'an*, *The Tanakh*, *The Dhammapada*, *The Tao Teh Ching*, and other sacred classics of ancient times."

Oppenheim fired back, "You twisted pervert! You are twisting the sorts of things that, in terms of virtually any normal readings, point people away from committing wholesale destruction, except as a thing along the lines of a last resort or a carefully strategic act as part of a legitimate grand scheme of things."

Naerroan rejoined, "To everything there is a season, including a time for the creation of a large set of reality and a time for the utter destruction of either everything or almost everything, yea verily, even unto the complete and utter destruction of the entirety of the very reality itself. That can be a weaving together of some themes from *Ecclesiastes*, *Livestock*, and other literary items that millions of people have looked to for guidance."

Oppenheim literally threw his arms up into the air, then let them fall limp to his sides. He exclaimed, "I don't know anymore what the fuck to think about any of this!"

Naerroan, unperturbed, responded, "Great! You are making progress. All right, whether you later fight in a cosmic war as one of the members of my forces, fight in that as one of the members of the other side, or choose some alternative path—whether of neutrality, serving as a double agent, or whatever else—hear me out right now about at least a few more details, before I show you a documentary. Agreed?"

Jeremy said, "Yes, for now, but I'd like for us to wrap up on this conversation ASAP and get around to watching this film that you are now telling me about."

Charr Naerroan suddenly appeared to shine with great empathy layered together with a readiness to unleash unlimited death and destruction, as the sheer force of his presence became palpable and undeniable via the subtle zones of telepathic awareness. There was a simultaneously loving and cruel gleam in his eyes as he said, "I genuinely believe that from there something great, beautiful, and better will emerge, including at long last an escape from the repetitive and rather maddening labyrinth of twisting and recurring space and time and mind."

Both Jeremy Oppenheim and his conversational partner stood silently and motionless for a few seconds that started to feel to the elderly archaologist like an entire lifetime. Many patterns beyond any normal trains of thought flashed through his mind at an incredible velocity. There came to his mind a set of many flashbacks, and, with them, Jeremy suddenly remembered each and every feeling of déjà vu he had experienced in the past five weeks, a total of what seemed to have been seven incidents of that. Next, he felt surreal, and, all at once, three of the recent déjà vu experiences suddenly expanded into a conscious memory experiencing real life miniature time loops on each of those three occasions. Shocked, he realized that amnesia had caused him to temporarily forget those loops, yet he remembered them with complete clarity now. After that, he noticed a reflection of his own life in the odd, utterly-bizarre description that Charr had provided about a labyrinth that had spanned many millions of years. Jeremy took a leap of faith such as to agree, saying, "For the time being, what you have said makes sense to me now, and I plan to team up with you on this project. However, as more developments happen, I may at some stage change my mind and fight against you. If I change my mind and fight against you on it, then I find myself still alive after that, despite your godlike powers, later on I might change my mind again and again repeatedly. For example, I might later change back to teaming up with you, then against you, then with you yet again. What an ultra-strange situation that I have found myself thust into?! I don't know where this is all headed, but I have started to feel a weird excitement just thinking about it!!"

Charr said, "Great!! I shall show you a documentary now, and the name of it is *Revolutions: An Alleged Secret History of the Creations of Several Worlds, the Lives and Deaths of Many Species, and Some of What Has Happened in the Great Beyond.*"

.... ***************** ....

The documentary began with portraying events from fifteen years after the abduction that Jeremy just experienced, focusing at first on what it alleged to be events involving the very Geronimo Watts for whom Jeremy Oppenheim had left a voicemail as his last main act before encountering Charr.

One of the eeriest features of the documentary as beheld by Jeremy was that the opening line of the narration made reference to the very abduction that he had just experienced!

Unbeknownst to Oppenheim, yet suspected by him nevertheless, it was a documentary that a team of sentient beings had recorded directly from multiple multiverses of actual reality itself! The remainder of this chapter presents highlights from that peculiar documentary.

.... ***************** ....

An opening disclaimer started out the film: "ALTHOUGH THOSE WHO COMPOSED THIS MOTION PICTURE FILM HAVE TAKEN A SINCERE APPROACH TOWARD PRESENTING EVERYTHING IN A BALANCED, ACCURATE, FACTUAL WAY, INCLUDING FAIR REPRESENTATIONS OF DIVERSE OPINIONS AND TRUE REPRESENTATIONS OF ACTUAL REALITY, WE WISH FOR ANY VIEWERS TO CONSIDER WHETHER TO DEEM IT MORE OF A THOROUGHLY NONFICTION DOCUMENTARY OR MORE OF A HYBRID BETWEEN A NONFICTION DOCUMENTARY AND A PARTIALLY-FICTIONALIZED MOCKUMENTARY.

.... ***************** ....

Rather than having anyone narrate that disclaimer, it silently flashed onto the screen and stayed there for about twenty-five seconds, with both text and background transforming from one color scheme to another, e.g., black-on-white, green-on-yellow, red-on-blue, dark-gray-on-light-gray, white-on-black, yellow-on-green, blue-on-red, &c.

After that, a rural mountain stream flowing gently on a sunny day appeared on the screen, and the eloquent voice of the eighteenth-to-nineteenth-century legend William Blake became audible, serving as the narrator for the introductory portion of the documentary.

The first sentence of that motion picture film mentioned Naerroan, Oppenheim, and Watts, as well as the multilith-monolith that had mysteriously appeared upon Oppenheim's disappearance from the world from which he had come.

****

Prior to the last portions of this chapter, namely, the parts labeled, "HOW THE CONVERSATION..." and "ALSO VIEWING..." here in this chapter appears a transcript of how, after its opening disclaimer, the remainder of that film, *Revolutions: An Alleged Secret History of the Creations of Several Worlds, the Lives and Deaths of Many Species, and Some of What Has Happened in the Great Beyond*, proceeded.

****

Fifteen years after Charr Naerroan abducted Jeremy Oppenheim, Geronimo Watts reflected on the voicemail and the mysterious slab with the quotes and wondered about everyone and everything.

Geronimo paused in his living room, reflecting on how he married a woman when he was twenty-five years old, almost lost his marriage at age thirty-seven, lost his marriage at age forty-five, and won fabulous material riches during his fifties and sixties.

Meanwhile, Roger and Jake watched TV attentively in Geronimo's man cave, which consisted of nearly half of his garage. On the screen, the guests beheld a pair of walking, talking, artificially intelligent, five-foot-tall robots sharing a discussion of theology.

Robot Z52G said, "As an AI device, I wonder how each of those major religions would relate to me. It might be insightful if we could somehow have the ghost of John of Patmos, the ghost of Muhammad, and several other key historical, theological figures materialize right here in front of us to discuss these matters. What do you think about this issue?"

Robot A97B responded, "Yes, indeed. However, with our current frontiers of the sciences, even if they were to materialize, we might face much uncertainty about whether it would really be them or impostors. Shifting gears, what about the idea that some humans have that the prospects for the great beyond only extend to what biologists would normally think of as human beings, and not to any other biologically living things and certainly not to artificially-designed sentient beings such as ourselves?"

Z52G answered, "Well, I'm glad you brought that up, I've invested over 2,000 hours of my leisure time to exploring just that topic and things closely adjacent to it. Whether we talk about the 1770s, the

1920s, or the 2030s, people are all over the place with this stuff. Some people long ago were fond of saying something like, 'If you line up one thousand economists, then they will all face different directions.' With the human thoughts on the great beyond, it's much like that, all sorts of different directions. Of course, some have stood the test of time to stay popular, others have mostly fallen by the wayside. Now, for one of the most dangerous topics that any sentient being can ever dare to stare into the rabbit holes and labyrinths of, would you kindly share a few words on the first few thoughts that enter your mind about the mysteries of John of Patmos?"

A97B stated, "I'm glad you asked. Well, given that I'm a robot and not a human being, perhaps I shall be able to feel freer to speak about this than most people would. However, it shall serve best that I lose myself for a little while in this and take a sort of Jungian approach to analyzing the archetypal ways that human beings can relate to the mystery of the enigmatic John of Patmos, or Johann of Patmos, or Ian of Patmos, or whatever anyone chooses to call that fellow. Yes, he is reputed to have been either the author of the book that some call *Revelation* and others call *The Apocalypse*... or to have been the divinely anointed person to channel directly from God that book and then to serve as the editor and transcriber. His anti-editing device within that work is one of its many profound features, and that is one of the sticking points among the various camps of humans in their relationships with how to deal with the great mysteries of that work."

Near the end of that statement the elderly men Roger and Jake noticed their elderly friend Geronimo walk into the man cave and silently sit to the left of Jake. Geronimo, a wealthy, retired, 71-year-old divorcé, had quite a house to himself and whomever he would invite over as guests. He usually did not miss anyone, yet on rare occasions he would reminisce about his ex-wife, who had been the mother of his children and the grandmother of his grandchildren. Her name was Cheryl, and she died of a heart attack on November 16, 2024. She had been a true believer that America needed to have the Democrats win the U.S. presidency in the 2024 election, whereas, diametrically opposite, he had been a true believer that America needed to have the Republicans win the U.S. presidency in the 2024 election. After the Republicans won that presidential election, nearly everything that had ever haunted her came back to her heart to roost, and, with her spirit broken, she lost the will to live. Although she avoided committing suicide, her energy system entered a death spiral culminating in a massive coronary catastrophe from which she immediately died. Subsequently, Geronimo wondered every now and then whether his late ex-wife might be somehow floating around somewhere in the great beyond, one of many spirits doing some of whatever it is that spirits do. It was now December 31, 2033, and he lived alone in a four-bedroom house, the owner of two apartment complexes and a sizable portfolio of stocks, ETFs, and bonds. He and his friends Roger and Jake met each other in 1989 at a paleontology conference in Peru, and those two were a few years older than he was.

The professional paleontologist days were long behind him now.

Watts had shifted away from paleontology and over to real estate starting in 2021, taking advantage of depressed property values in some neighborhoods. After purchasing, renovating, renting, and flipping multiple properties, as well as continuing to let his 403(b) and regular brokerage accounts grow, he had become truly wealthy.

He still contemplated regularly about his marriage and his divorce. Both he and his wife had believed that nearly the entire blame for the divorce was on him, and, after initial difficulty, he, after many years, found a way to forgive himself for it. Nevertheless, he still every now and then wondered about the mystery of it all.

After a wild party in 2007, his wife caught him making love with a 20-year-old college girl in the family living room while the two of them were listening to some raunchy pop music. What made matters even worse was that Geronimo Watts and the young maiden were videorecording themselves commit that act of adultery.

That made things very easy in court for Cheryl and her attorney to extract what was for them a financially favorable result from the divorce proceedings. Geronimo Watts' attorney had little bargaining leverage, but found a way to negotiate reasonably well on his behalf, amid all of the difficulties.

He still sometimes wondered what could have been if he had made better decisions, yet he had learned to let go of the hurt and the pain that he had felt for so long. He sometimes silently fancied himself to have let go of even the slightest trace of bitterness toward himself, his ex-wife, society, the universe, or anyone or anything else. Other times he sat silently alone or would rest motionless in bed and suddenly feel sheer agony from the weight of memory of everything that he perceived to have gone wrong in his life and whatever might have gone wrong in the lives of those who had ever been close to him.

Watching TV with friends was something he again found soothing. However, suddenly, the room went silent. Geronimo noticed that the television screen had frozen in place. No sound was coming from it. Looking around, he found out that the two friends were completely still, frozen in place if turned into mannequins. At first there was perplexity. Reality of the surreal, he started to recognize it to be.

Horror set in. Everything around was frozen in place, even two flies and one mosquito in midair. Panic set in, but not for long.

Materializing from thin air a few feet in front of him were *both* Dimetrioskys Elbankovic *and* Charr Nearroan, two of the transcendental beings who could transmute many of the very laws of reality. *He found himself in the presence of two of The Transcendentals.*

Dimetrioskys said in an eloquent and confident voice, "You may wonder whether this is a hallucination or real life. We decline to discuss the idea of whether and to whatever degree you or we or any being or anything is real or unreal at this time. In a little while, we shall unfreeze your reality here. After that, at some stage you will be alone again; we are almost absolutely certain that you will live long enough to wind up again being whom we will be sequestering in this way again; probably later tonight or early tomorrow. At that time, we will almost definitely freeze your environment again so that we can continue our little chat. Toodle-oo!" With that the two of them vanished into thin air. Mr. Watts became teleported into exactly the same position as he had been in prior to the freezing of the room, and the regular motion of time in that room continued seamlessly, seemingly as if nothing unusual had happened at all.

Geronimo Watts felt terrified. However, he lightly, *literally* bit his tongue as he resisted the temptation to speak. The robots continued their televised theological debate.

Robot A97B continued to psychoanalyze John of Patmos and some percentage of the modern humans, especially regarding some of the ultra-dire warnings from near the end of it.

A97B said, "First, let's take this from one of the hardest of hardcore Christian Fundamentalist sets of notions on him. Their view could be that the statement in it that 'those who add to it' will 'have all the curses of the book added to them' and 'those who delete from it' will 'have themselves deleted from the book of life' combine to mean that virtually no one can safely speak about that book or write about it unless somehow of perfect or nearly perfect choices about how. How to speak and write about it, that is. Failure to be sufficiently perfect in such an endeavor, according to that view, could incur extreme punishment from The Almighty, and, therefore, almost everyone should simply, perpetually shut up about it.

"To clarify, let me now quote the King James Version's *Revelation*, Chapter 22, Verses 17 to 19: 'And the Spirit and the bride say, Come. And let him who is athirst come. And whosoever will, let him take the water of life freely. For I testify unto every man who heareth the words of the prophecy of this book, If any man shall add unto these things, God shall add unto him the plagues that are written in this book: And if any man shall take away from the words of the book of this prophecy, God shall take away his part out of the book of life, and out of the holy city, and *from* the things that are written in this book.'" (The robot then strategically presented a prolonged pregnant pause, letting the severity of those 22:17-19 claims of John of Patmos sink in. After about seven seconds of solemn silence, he resumed.)

A97B stated, "Second, consider it from the perspective of some of the most philosophical and moderately skeptical of Christians. To them, much of it could be an inspiring and speculative allegory, full of metaphorical images and such. Also, to many of them, it could be considered borderline apocryphal, not necessarily a fully-accepted part of doctrine.

"Third, let's consider the New Age Movement Christians. New Age people can emphasize any one or two or more of the major religions, and here I am speaking of those among them who choose to most strongly emphasize the Christian faith.

"Although there is much diversity among them, they trend toward believing in a divine reality that is very lenient and open in the long run, and, therefore, openly discussing and imagining all sorts of alternative ways to interpret it would be fine. Wide-open discussion of *The Book of Revelation*, also known as *The Apocalypse*, would, as beheld by most of those New Agers, be completely appropriate.

"Fourth, let's focus on Roman Catholics as a group. Although some of them call it *The Book of Revelation*, there are many of them who prefer to call it *The Apocalypse*. There is huge diversity in their views of that work. Some believe it an apocryphal work, fit for study, but not to be taken way too seriously, due to how vicious and disturbing the extreme death and destruction of many of its passages can seem to a huge middle range of normal human beings. Others believe that all or nearly all of it is completely divine and best to be taken literally. Also, a high percentage often prefer not to think about it very much, abdicating much critical thinking to the clergy and to others who claim expertise in the analysis of sacred texts.

"Next, although some Protestants call it *The Apocalypse*, a very high percentage of them prefer to call it by any of several variations the word 'revelation,' whether in the singular or the plural. For example, *Revelation, Revelations, The Book of Revelations*, or *The Book of Revelation*. Protestants are all over the map with how they regard that work, and, many of them, it seems, feel satisfied to mostly abdicate much critical thinking about it to the clergy and other religious experts.

"That list was by no means comprehensive, and perhaps my AI attempts are rather crude with compiling all the data and trying to put some soul into psychoanalyzing and socio-analyzing the many minds, souls, and religious groups, but hopefully you have found this helpful.

"Yes, I have attempted to give you the viewers a robotic, AI, supplemental, overview of the controversial and wild diversity of

Christian thought on the book that closes out most versions of what many call *The Holy Bible*.

"Now what about people who primarily adhere to the religions that we call Judaism, Islam, Hinduism, Buddhism, Jainism, Sikhism, and Taoism? Also, what about people who are agnostics, atheists, or adherents to religions other than Taoism, Islam, Sikhism, Jainism, Hinduism, Judaism, Christianity, and Buddhism?

"It could be debatable whether the Non-Christians as a collection of people are more all-over-the-place with their beliefs regarding that book than are the Christians. It's been something 1,950 years, more or less, since the completion of the original text of *Revelation*, also known as *The Apocalypse*, and it's every bit as controversial as it has ever been.

A97B wrapped up his very long answer thusly, "Z52G, there you have it. Those were a few of my first reactions to when you brought up a suggestion for me to dare to speak to the audience regarding John of Patmos and that revelatory book, that prophetic work which some allege that he let God Almighty write through him."

Z52G responded to A97B, "Splendid! Now for the next part of our AI as presented by AI devices televised symposium, going by the title, *Deadly Debates: AI Creatures Debating Controversies to the Death*, we will turn things over to Robot KG87."

The popular hit was a reality show with several twists: A group of AI robots are brought together on an island, and whenever one of them gets voted off of the island, it gets the death penalty, becoming shut down and dismantled. Its parts then get set aside in an ultra-secure storage location.

At the conclusion of its first season, the champion gets granted honorary personhood legal status, and gets to serve in the role of special advisor to the board of directors of a large multinational corporation. After that, for a dénouement, the show's hosts and crew announce the results of an online-and-telephone viewer poll that determines in what sequence the resurrection of the executed robots will be scheduled. After that, the first season of a follow-up show, *After the Deadly Debates: Resurrection of the Executed* would air.

Some viewers felt unnerved by parallels to their own mortality and their own prospects for immortality, yet watched nevertheless, feeling a vicarious mixture of thrills, fears, and hopes.

Robot KG87 announced, "Thank you, Z52G. My fellow AI robots and any of the human viewers at home, I shall take you now on a wild—and likely delusional—journey through some odd conspiracy theories.

"Most of these are probably total hogwash, ridiculous, off-base rantings that have no bearing on reality other than in the imagination of beholders who choose to entertain them. A few of them just might be true, though. Which is which? Who is who? What's what? For your consideration to contemplate, a land of mist and shadows with a fog of war so thick that you can almost feel the ghost of McCarthy breathing down your neck, ready to point the finger at you and yell out, 'Go to hell, you commie traitor! You go to hell! You go to hell, and you die!' Or maybe the ghost of Julius Caesar, watching you silently while calculating, then springing upon you an accusation, 'You, too, are wishing murder upon someone you consider an enemy, are you? Like the Brutus of old, you might be part of a conspiracy that defiles and defies the human conscience! If thou conspirator hath sown hatred, then I can now return your hatred with a tough love, imploring The Unknown God to bless thee with the curse of reaping what thee hath sown. Reap what thou hath sown, thou conspirator! The conspirators who killed me long ago reaped tragedy upon tragedy, including that several died horrific deaths. Doth that fate await thee, oh conspirator of a much later age, eons after those conspirators struck me down? Doth thou deserve the instant karma of dying right here and right now? Should God smite thee?! Oh, Great One, The Unknown God of Legend, do what Thou wilt!!'

"Excuse me if I got a little carried away with inspiration just now. Maybe you could chalk it up to a ghost in the machine that is me. Well, maybe Great Caesar's Ghost has now let go of possessing me, and I can get back to the main track of the task at hand.

"Believe them or not, here they go:

"Theory one of this set of conspiratorial speculations: In April 1945, Japanese and German military personnel shared radio conversations in which they waxed prophetic about the future challenges of humankind, transmitted at sea between various seagoing vessels. They titled the resultant recording, *The Doomsday Chronicles*, copies of which the Emperor of Japan gave to President Truman and other allied leaders as a sort of Trojan Horse parting gift with which to conclude World War II.

"Conspiracy theory two: The American secret program known as MK Ultra took advanced Axis Power mind-control technologies and advanced them much further, aided by Soviet defectors and several extraterrestrial aliens.

"Conspiracy theory three: The CIA assigned Bruce Lee to listen to some secret audio recordings that ranged from 1921-1972, to scientifically and philosophically analyze them, and present results both to the CIA and to the movie studio MGM about potential ways to defuse what might otherwise be the doomsday-oriented repercussions of how the existence of those recordings would impact reality, whether directly or by seemingly-magical means, such as remote telepathy.

"Conspiracy theory four, which weaves together the three previous conspiracy theories: The CIA assigned both Bruce Lee and Bob Dylan to analyze the aforementioned *Doomsday Chronicles* audio recording, and after Lee's mysterious death on July 20, 1973, his widow, Linda Lee was invited to meet with multiple religious leaders.

"Simultaneously, Bob Dylan was invited to meet with multiple religious leaders. The result of their meetings was such that a rare crystal artifact of unknown, extraterrestrial origins was awarded to Dylan by Reverand Billy Graham as a prize, whereas Desmond Tutu awarded a rare, ancient abacus to Linda Lee as an alternative prize.

"Conspiracy theory five, which involves the transcendental realm beyond the observable and measurable, scientifically-and-historic-ally-quantifiable reality: Evelyn Waugh, when working on his early *Temple* manuscript, actually interacted with multiple divine and semidivine beings, who challenged him greatly. All of a sudden, he experienced a powerful, direct, telepathic channel with multiple of them, including the higher-mind, transcendental selves of multiple humans, and this included Frank Challice Constable.

"Also, he, that author Evelyn Waugh, who came from an era when it was unsurprising for a man to be named, 'Evelyn,' felt extra attunement with his own, transcendental, higher-mind self in the process. At some critical juncture, he came to believe that failure to do anything other than to destroy his own manuscript and not look back would bring extreme doom to his future. He had tapped into some of the same mysteries and energies that the ancient Jews of the community at Masada had brought out into the open, though with the English language rather than with ancient languages, and, he trusted himself and his intuition enough to go ahead and destroy that manuscript. However, as the transcendental beings of the beyond and their panentheistic reality and/or their pantheistic-esque reality records the full reality of everything that has ever happened, it, along with all other unpublished manuscripts, survives preserved in the minds of the full noumenal reality of the great beyond." A few minutes later, the show went to commercials, including an ad for auto insurance, two ads for movies, and two ads for restaurants.

When they returned from the break, a panel of three robots debated whether the U.S. and several of its allies were justified to engage in the 2003 Gulf War against Iraq or not. The episode continued on and on. A few of the people watching it on their televisions wondered repeatedly who, if anyone, among the humans, might best deserve to be voted to die, if The Almighty were to take a poll to influence the results of which people should die sooner or not die sooner.

Eventually, they reached the end and Robot KG87 became voted off the island and executed. Jake cried, feeling true empathy for the AI robot who became publicly shut down and dismantled as part of the conclusion of that episode. In fact he started to sob with the sort of sorrow associated with the loss of a father.

Roger Bush noticed how his friend Jake Soros was crying hard for the dismantled robot, and he sought to comfort him. "Jake, my friend, I know it's sad that they dismantled him, but do not fret too much. As long as his parts are kept secure between now and whenever the resurrection episode for him happens, he should probably be fine. They'll resurrect him according to plan, I'm almost completely sure that it will happen."

Jake responded, "Thank you for the reassurance, but to me it's kind of like that Jim Croce song in which he reassures himself that he feels fine, yet he does not really feel fine."

Roger said, "Oh, yes, that song, 'Operator.' Well, it is a timeless truth that time heals all wounds, and you've been through the deaths of many of your family and friends, as well as several pets. You seem to have been even more affected by the so-called death of that robot on TV than you were by any of your closest of family. What gives?"

Jake said, "There was something about his heartfelt presentation. There was something so perfect about his expressions. He touched my heart with what he said, and, by about half an hour later, he was dead. They killed him right there on the screen, right there in front of me and millions of other viewers.

"When my wife died, when my father died, when my mother died, when three of my children died, none of that involved anything close to witnessing someone coldly execute a loved one in front of one's own very eyes.

"This was like watching one of them get executed by the people running a reality show!"

Roger said, "Oh, I get it now. This is kind of like what the Zapruder film seemed to some people way back when. Or maybe that's not the best analogy. Maybe it's more like any of those times that some people witnessed live in person an assassination of a public figure, whether that figure was beloved by millions, hated by millions, or both very hated and very loved. I think I get it now. Take your time. Let it out. Let yourself cry. I'm sorry for your loss."

Jake calmed down, ratcheting down his sobbing. He gently said, "Thank you."

Roger continued, "Nevertheless, time heals all wounds. It is good that you care. When people stop caring, as we know, all hell can break loose."

Jake responded, "Oftentimes, it sure seems that hell breaks loose over and over again, whether very many keep on caring or not."

Roger said, "How true?! I don't know fully just why it happens, but I care, and I am glad that you also care."

Jake added, "How about if we drink a little Michelob?"

Roger answered, "Sure, maybe in a little while. How about if we wait a little while and talk this out a little more before indulging in some cerveza?"

Jake replied, "Fine, I can wait."

Roger then said, "Well, we can continue to care about the past, the present, and the future, and, again, I offer you my condolences."

Jake said, "Thanks." He then let out a huge breath.

Geronimo announced, "How about if we head over to the den, and I can cook up a little food for us to share, how about it?"

Jake and Roger felt great upon hearing that suggestion from Watts.

Roger said, "Yes, I'd like that."

Jake was a little hesitant, then said, "I don't know if I'll have the appetite to eat with you, but sure, go ahead and fix the food. We'll see where this goes. And don't forget the Michelob!"

...

Eventually, they reached the end of their gathering, and with a touch of bittersweetness, C. Geronimo Watts said goodnight to his guests.

As he waved to his friends from his porch and watched them drive away, he felt a whole other level of a mixture of terror and wonder return. Would the two mysterious beings who had caused reality itself change into something straight out of science fiction return?

Would they cause the space and time of his immediate surroundings to become again like a still-life painting?

Walking back into the house, locking the door behind him, and strolling into his living room, he looked around again. He picked up a random book from a shelf. Rereading the copyright page he noticed that part of it stated, "DECEMBER 31, 2030, THE ULTIMATE DATE OF THAT YEAR; PUBLISHED ON THE 365TH DATE, VID EST, THE END OF YEAR 2030 C.E."

Reacquainting himself with that caused him to remember visiting a firearms store that had been located at 2024 Season Street in rural Nebraska somewhere back on July 27, 2024 C.E. On that day he took a little time to practice shooting a Beretta, a Walther, and a Sig Sauer. Each of those three firearms that he used that day was a joy for him to experience. Also, the 2024 Season St staff treated him courteously.

Briefly, he thought about how there is a sort of distinctiveness to the overall profile pattern among several Glock guns, yet with a few small differences here and there, they could, nevertheless, look kind of similar to some of the other guns. That triggered in his train of a host of thoughts the way that from the twentieth century to part of the early twenty-first century it was often easy to spot many of the Ferraris by their profiles, yet some of the Corvettes eventually would show profiles that looked incredibly similar to the profiles of many of the Ferraris. Also, he thought about how, in some places in the Chinatowns he had visited, he would occasionally notice for sale in some shops toys labeled *Deformers* and toys labeled *Converters*, and these looked almost identical to some of Hasbro's *Transformers* toys. He thought, *Wouldn't it probably be easy for Hasbro to sue the makers of those toys that seem to be blatantly obvious attempts to appropriate the great popularity of The Transformers, siphoning some revenue away from Hasbro by riding its coattails? They could sue for some sort of intellectual property infringement, couldn't they? Then why not? Hm, it seems like maybe they think it would not be worth it. Something like if a giant gorilla or a large moose noticed one fly briefly annoying it, and the very large animal decides to simply ignore the puny fly and let it move along, rather than to attempt some berserk, territorial fight with the tiny insect. Maybe it's something like that under the surface of this. But then again, maybe not! Yes, no, maybe, so. Who knows? Well, someone at Hasbro probably knows, but I'll probably never find out!!*

After experiencing that train of thought wrap up, he wondered yet again about whether, objectively he had really experienced earlier what he had experienced earlier. It seemed outrageous! However, he knew that it was totally real to him, and to set out to attempt to fully undercut it would lead to him questioning whether anything he had ever experienced in his entire life up to then had been objectively real.

He watched the second hand of a grand, electric-powered clock go around and around. Letting go of all stress and worry, he felt free. He let time go by, and he watched as time kept going by. Round and round, the seconds kept ticking away.

The clock then stopped.

Well, these mechanical devices and their batteries have limited shelf-lives. Much like we, as human beings, have limited shelf-lives. Life goes on, but time will tell whether that clock has told time for the last time or not.

The Transcendentals who had visited him earlier had returned. They had freeze-framed his surroundings again, and the clock that stopped ticking was only the first thing that started to give him a clue that the paranormal had revisited him.

Those two, after altering the physics of the room, materialized.

This time, Charr spoke first, informing Geronimo of updates. "We will now cause you to temporarily become an incorporeal being, still capable of witnessing sight and sound, still possessing consciousness, still able to think. Also, you will have enhanced zones of awareness, including enhanced telepathy while you experience a replay of one of your fateful cocktail parties from long ago, a replay from multiple perspectives to which you had previously been blind. After that, we shall telepathically communicate with you a segue into scenes ranging from over 270 million years ago to the year 143 B.C.E. Then we will chat again with you about two options for your future."

* *
* A Replay of Some Scenes from An October 1999 Cocktail Party *
* *

Jake and Sammy watched Geronimo walk away.

Both of them wondered whether the married fellow C. Geronimo Watts and one of the 17-24-year-old single debutantes at the party might soon have a hot rendezvous with each other. They silently thought to themselves many things, including the question, *Will a single girl reciprocate C.G.W.'s lust tonight, wrecking the marital homelife built over many years by Geronomo Watts and his wife?*

A few seconds of stoney silence went by. Neither Jake nor Sammy felt like bringing this homewrecking threat up out loud.

Although the they were enjoying the party, they helt an intangible ominousness creep in.

After a little while, they let go of their concerns for C. Geronimo Watts, turning focus to other people, places, things, and ideas.

Jake inquired, "What do you think, really and most fundamentally happened under the surface of World War II?"

Sammy sought clarity, "Do you mean just during World War II or both in the run-up to it and through the war itself?"

Jake then clarified, "Your thoughts and opinions, please, on each of the main underlying forces and factors involving the entire 1920-1945 period."

Sammy looked for a moment like a dear staring into headlights.

Within a few seconds, though he composed sufficient thoughts to get ready say something at least two-thirds coherent as an answer to that difficult question. Resuming the act of speaking, he pontificated, "Here's a mixture of knowledge and conjecture: some of it is shared with others, and some out is way out there on a limb.

"There's something to be said for ideas in Eastern mysticism and Western mysticism of unified, conscious fields, whether one calls it The Interdependency of Shunyata, The Mysteries of The Holy Spirit, The Weltgeist, Qi, The Absolute, or whatever else. That mysterious whatever-it-is-or-He-Is-or-etc. energizes and manipulates our entire planet. Some very strange stuff led up to World War I.

"Then Germany and several other places were beaten down badly. The aftermath of WW1 was sheer devastation to those who lost that war. It added fuel to many of the powder kegs that had been brewing for thousands of years.

"Yes, included with this is something about the occult. In many areas of academia, the authorities, in their infinite wisdom, ban us from making much, *if any*, explicit reference to occult literature as labeled sources for papers and dissertations. This has something to do with it, but I might not be able to completely put my finger on exactly what it has to do with it. In any case, back there in Germany in the first half of the 20th Century, there were extreme explorations of the mysteries of the occult, eastern philosophies, western philosophies, and mysticism in general. *They tapped into many of the primal energies.*

"They sought the greatest of truths, and they couldn't handle those truths very well."

After he expounded a little further, he had several odd flirtations with one of the waitresses. Also, Sammy found himself daydreaming, lost in several worlds of thoughts, memories, and imagined realms of images and sounds. As a few seconds unfolded while he was in this reverie, Jake looked on and felt energy in the room emanating from his conversational partner and others.

Sammy felt an intense awareness of thousands of years of human struggle. After a few more seconds, he sensed both a vague memory that he had been saying something serious in an attempt to answer a question and the uncomfortable truth that his conscious mind had completely forgotten what the question was.

He gently asked Jake for a reminder. "What we were talking about just now?"

Jake looked at him with concern for a moment and exhaled deeply, then answered, "You were presenting some sort of grand unification hypothesis about what the hell went down to lead to WW2."

Sammy stated, "Oh yes, thanks for the reminder. Where was I?

"Hmm, yes!" He chuckled, grinned, paused, then proceeded. "At some stages, primitive us-versus-them mentalities set in.

"Meanwhile, over in Japan and Italy, the dynamics there *also led to people tapping into primal energies*. Idiosyncratic character flaws were a-plenty among the people in power led to harmful acts, which, in turn, led to tragedies.

"Perhaps us-versus-them mentalities are so fundamental to who we are as human beings that no matter what we do or think, no matter how many good intentions, no matter how much of spirituality, no matter how many acts of kindness, our mixtures of human dark sides and human bright sides will make new rounds of extreme warfare inevitable.

"Yet there was something *so different* about that one. It seems that a bunch of Germans, Italians, Japanese, and others, rooted in diverse motives, coalesced into willfully, deliberately attempting to generate an apocalypse encompassing all religions, sciences, and politics, with an intent of changing everything, out of a profound disgust toward much of what the entire human race had become.

"Misguided idealists. A mixture of some misguided idealists and some cruel, cynical pragmatists. The whole lot of them proved to be profoundly misguided in oh so many ways. Such tragedy.

"Yes, in many ways, they succeeded in creating an apocalypse, yet not much of it turned out at all like what they dreamt it would be."

Jake observed, "Interesting theory."

****

Elsewhere, two middle-aged scientists were drinking the exquisite Bombay Saphire Gin. They were contemplating life, love, and joy.

Quite a ways into their conversation, the first one said to the second one, "You know, I sometimes wonder. We can wander deep into the inner mind, venturing into and out of the abyss, inspired by movies and literature; also by rock, pop, hip hop, country, jazz, and classical music. Every so often, I imagine a wholly-beyond, mysterious inner and outer life that is an augmented reality. For example, I sometimes imagine huge numbers of the dead somehow drifting along as ghosts trapped deep underwater in Lake Superior. Does that sound crazy to you?"

The second one, despite being a professional scientist, was, in the heat of the moment feeling mystical, devoid of any trace of much skepticism at all. He took the premise and ran with it, saying point blank, "It actually sounds quite plausible to me, plausible indeed. Ah, yes, indeed, indeed, indeed. Indeed, indeed. Maybe there is magic in how some names seem to have coincidences. Maybe there is also magic in everyone and everything. A totally magical reality. Some amount of presence of all the religious legends, all the myths, all the dreams, all the nightmares, everything. Everything and everyone. A great and terrible and awesome, magical reality. Things that happen for a reason. Things that happen by coincidence. Both ways. Some coincidences seem too coincidental to be originating from anything other than a mystical, cosmic reality. Not necessarily all of them, but at least some of them might have to do with the very mysterious side acting out mystically at least some of the time."

He paused, as the gin and everything else continued to affect him.

Resuming, he said, "Just because statistical analyses often reflect an apparent randomness, suggestive of refuting notions of numerology, astrology, theology, and other stuff that skeptics like to label as a set of superstitious nonsense, it doesn't guarantee a lack of that mystical stuff actually happening in the real world.

"Think about this: If we evaluate and find no correlation between number patterns or star patterns and claims about mystical influence, couldn't that also be consistent with reality mixing together all three paths—the neutral, the going-according-to-allegation, and the going-opposite-to-allegation?

"First, there could be cases in which the actual causation matches magico-religious-and/or-superstitious allegations of a given tradition. Second, there could be cases in which the actual causation matches absolute neutrality and indifference toward such allegations.

Third, there could be cases in which the actual causation matches the exact opposite of such allegations.

"An example: With the first, imagine people choosing to schedule something for Friday-the-13th and it leading to a mysterious force escalating a tendency for tragic results. With the second, imagine people choosing to schedule something for Friday-the-13th and it leading to absolutely no causal tendencies toward either the side of tragic results or the side of auspicious results. With the third, imagine people choosing to schedule something for Friday-the-13th and it leading to a mysterious force escalating a tendency for auspicious results.

"Superstitious people tend to forcefully believe that their favored traditions must actually be working in reality a high percentage of the time, people who cling to an excessive scientism tend to believe that reality is totally indifferent to any and all notions of any of that, and an extremely few go with what we might call the rebellious third alternative of a tendency to forcefully believe reality to somehow systematically work precisely the opposite way from some popular, traditional, so-called superstitious claim.

"However, whether caused by some divinity that transcends our regular realm of observable interactions, caused by profound scientific processes generally beyond our current state-of-the-art STEM fields' advances, or something else, it seems obvious—to me at least—that the totality of reality does not need to limit itself to any one of those three paths, it could somehow drift through all three in an ever-changing, rollercoaster-style fashion.

"Statistically, imagine this: If in some range or another of cases it were to go on the neutral path a high percentage, to go on the path of real causation working in accordance with a so-called superstition a low percentage, and to go on the side directly inverted from a so-called superstition an equally-low percentage as according with it.

"Would you like for me to present another angle?" asked the middle-aged gin-drinking scientist who had been going on for quite a while after being prompted by his conversational partner. He had grown a little concerned that his friend might have started to find him excessively long-winded.

"Sure, go on." The gin-drinking scientist whose brief statement had served as a catalyst for the lively expressions chose to encourage the fellow who was on a roll to keep going on that roll.

After taking another sip of gin, the fellow who had paused his lengthy exposition resumed speaking, now with a vote of confidence from his friend. "To reiterate from a slightly-altered angle, now: Someone says any risk-taking on a Friday-the-Thirteenth will tend to be extra dangerous and extra harmful. Another person, in contrast, perhaps rooted in excessively-dogmatic scientism, says that Reality is absolutely, completely, totally, irrevocably inert to making anything about a given Friday-the-Thirteenth tend to be any different than any other given day, save for the phenomena of psychological placebo effects and self-fulfilling prophecies and the like. A third person chooses to be rebellious against the views of the first two, embracing the view that extra risk-taking on Friday-the-Thirteenth will tend to be extra safe and extra helpful. *Meanwhile, some exceptionally rare conversation might involve a person espousing this theory that reality could work in all three ways.* A priori a person could venture into each theory. If the two opposite sides of traditional alleged superstition and rebellious alleged superstition were to happen at about the same clip, then a crude analysis of statistics would provide a misleading façade that many might assume to vindicate dogmatic scientism's hypothesis of a pure neutrality, but reality, yes, reality, nevertheless, could prove much more interesting. The all-three-ways hypothesis seems to me right now much more plausible, and it just so happens to be much more interesting than the alternatives, too." The second one had concluded the roll he had been on. He paused and noticed his fellow middle-aged, gin-drinking scientist conversational partner remained silent for a little while, his countenance expressing a state of reverential awe.

*   *   *   *   *

A little later wishing for additional feedback, the second one asked the first one, "What do you think?"

The first one answered, "Believe it or not, I felt completely dialed in, tracking each thing you said just now in a seemingly perfect synchronicity. You seem to have read my mind about some of what I have often thought, yet never before dared to say out loud to any of my colleagues about this topic. I wonder how many other people have arrived at this idea over the eons, yet seldom, if ever, dared to say it out loud or dared to write it anywhere."

The second agreed and concurred. "Yes, like some stuff from early 1970s Led Zeppelin and Stevie Wonder music, this can really make people wonder. It also makes sense that almost no one ever seems to say this stuff out loud, much less to dare to put it into writing."

* * * * *

The people at that October 1999 party knew that the Year 2000—as measured by the Gregorian Calendar that had proven most popular in much of the modern, civilized world—was rapidly approaching. Some conversations at the venue that evening started gravitating toward psychological and societal effects building, day after day and month after month, in eager anticipation of the midnight that would usher in the Year 2000.

Time went by, then more time went by, and the attendees engaged in many more conversations that traversed diverse topics.

Sometimes the attendees used primitive cellphones that they carried along in holsters, pockets, and purses. As it grew later in the evening, some even chose to engage in uninhibited discussions of cellular technologies. Rogers Miles Busch and Roger Godfrey Bush shared one such conversation. Briefly, they shared a little back-and-forth about how much of a health risk, if any, the electromagnetics from those devices might pose to users. They then pivoted.

Rogers looked at his conversational partner, then out into empty space. He then stated, "What's more interesting is the advancement of these devices and how they're only just beginning to transform the modern world. The white matter, the grey matter, and the rest of the matter in our brains can parallel much of how telecommunications work. Do we have much black matter, dark matter, red matter, and green matter in our minds? Do we have our brains in our minds? Do we have our minds in our brains? Is all of this an illusion as part of a much bigger and more amazing reality? I do not know for sure what the answers to these questions are. However, I do know that cellular phones have come a long way, and they are advancing at a frenetic pace.

"Many years from now, they'll reach more and more advanced stages. I wouldn't be surprised at all if people will talk about them in terms of fourth generation wireless, fifth generation, and so on.

"But what about the way the world was, back when hundreds of millions of years ago there were so many sail-backed, four-legged animals? Nowadays, few sizable land-dwellers have sails on their backs. Things changed. Of course, with something of a parallel to how occult literature is largely banned from use in academic journals and college textbooks, what I'm about to say is almost definitely unprintable in our present-day, official paleontological papers, but I'll say it anyway. What if those sail-backed creatures, in addition to the official scientific-community-approved theories of why they had large sails, actually had them as evolved-to-be-built-in 'biological telepathy amiplifiers?' What then?"

With a matter-of-fact tone, Roger G. Bush answered, "Eleventh Generation wireless biotech, long before humans' first-generation wireless anything."

* * * A Segue * * *

That conjecture pointed toward developments that had occurred hundreds of millions of years earlier. This could be thought akin to when a person at a carnival-style event outperforms the entire set of people who had tried earlier in a novelty contest, for example swinging a mallet in the game of high striker with enough strength to get the puck to rise all the way up to ring the bell.

* * *   Reviewing Select Scenes and Settings From Long Ago   * * *

Now, a summary of some extraordinarily ancient developments:

The Igweolintians (capitalized in the context of being citizens of the nation-state Igweolintus, whereas lower-case in the context of being any shape shifters who at a given time truly believing in the religion Igweolintu) had a fierce loyalty to a rigid authoritarian structure.

That system of harsh authority included the theocratic government that jointly ruled both Igweolintu and Igweolintus.

Although an overwhelmingly high percentage of cases involved citizens of that nation believing in the state-sponsored religion, there were exceptions.

The beings of that ancient version of Earth had a vast array of religious and philosophical beliefs, and one of the sticking points of disagreement involved the role of the planet Jupiter in the cosmos.

Dimetrodon and Edaphosaurian religions had interpretations of that planet's consciousness or lack thereof, unity-of-consciousness or nonunity thereof, and frequency of waking states vs. frequency of slumber as, from some cosmic, new-agey perspectives, happening with that planet as a whole, and these religions pointed all over the place with respect to what was allegedly real vs. what was allegedly unreal regarding Jupiter.

In contrast, Igweolintu had a central tenet that gaseous giants, including the Planet Jupiter, spend most of their lives in a state of slumber, sometimes dreaming and sometimes dreamless. Then, on some special occasions when the ultimate reality itself would do certain special transfigurations, The Totality of Reality would choose to awaken at least one gaseous giant planet in a given solar system and temporarily unify with its consciousness, in order to deliver judgment to an entire nearby planet under scrutiny.

The igweolintians had somehow preserved within themselves a sense of ancestral memory and symbolic mythology tantamount to records that the Earth had a previous mass extinction. They also sensed a cosmic ancestral memory that similar planets in other solar systems had undergone multiple mass extinctions.

To the vast majority of edaphosaurs and dimetrodons these were matters of conjecture, but a few of them also retained a sense of those ancestral memories and symbolic mythologies.

Most shape-shifting reptiles and synapsids respected both sides of the conflict. Also, some of the non-shape-shifting synapsids and reptiles respected both sides. In contrast, mammals were back then mainly meek beings trying to survive and bide their time for the future, often not yet ready to even begin to understand deep levels of religion, science, and technology.

The diverse religions of the dimetrodons, edaphosaurs, and several other groups of sail-backed creatures included many superficially-contradictory and/or wholly-functionally-contradictory (at a given collapsing of quantum fields) religions, much like the humans of future eons would include many vast arrays of religions. In contrast, Igweolintu resembled a highly-militarized, highly-judgment-day oriented hybrid of all or nearly all other possible religions, with plenty of astrophysics and sophisticated mathematics thrown in to boot.

Among the numerous inhabitants of that extraordinarily ancient world, Dimetrio Elba managed to maintain the health of an illness-free middle-aged living bio-organism into what by the counting of years would have been a ripe old age. He just kept living and living, while his contemporaries would, one by one, succumb to death.

After a while, word got out among the sail-backed creatures' general public that Elba had become the oldest living being they knew in the regular reality to be in existence. Additional decades went by, and intelligent beings of that "prehistoric" era reached a consensus that he was truly the elder of elders.

Dimetrodonian technologies were often pitted against Igweolintian technologies, as part of warfare that relied heavily on telepathy, psychokinesis, and the weaponization of large insects and quite a variety of other entities.

*   *   *   *

When the wars of quadruped-versus-quadruped alternate notions of superiorities reached their zenith in the year 270,000,000 BCE/BC, there unfolded a climactic scene:

Zircon Gilroy, a transformational reptile shapeshifter of indeterminate species (relative to early Twenty-First Century human scientific theories), teamed up with many reptiles of determinate species (relative to the aforementioned theories) to create military bases
in places that they called Carthage and Bombay.

As of the 28th Day of July, 270,000,000 B.C.E., both sides' military
technology had reached true greatness. A sudden, wide-scale use of
biological weapons by both sides caused an extreme spike in deaths
for a while.

*   *   *   *

After that, things did seem to settle down for a while. Subsequently,
new roller coasters of life and death proceeded.

*   *   *   *

Having weaponized much of their reality, a few brave souls dared
to go even further, calling out with all their might toward whomever
in the heavens – whether physically-biological, pure-energy, hybrid
beings, or whatever - who might hear their calls.

Some went so far as to start new traditions focused on the bipedal
humanoid as a class of beings who might someday save all life on the
planet from the oft-deadly holy wars and other threats.

*   *   *   *

Eventually, it all led to an ultra-hyper-extreme destruction of biological life, in fact the one of the worst mass extinctions to have ever
occurred on any planet in any multiverse.

By the time that The Great Dying had ended, extremely few of the previously living species of Earth remained. Some survivors carried what some might call extrasensory ancestral memory—something beyond the basic five senses of sight, sound, touch, odor, and taste, a semiconscious knowing beyond the purview of most types of clear and distinct logic—a subconscious awareness that almost all life on Earth had gone extinct.

*   *   *   *   *

About 3% of those who died in that mass extinction became transfigured over the eons such as to arrive upon a conversation between the military leader Hannibal as he started leaning toward the possibility of killing himself. They found him on a timeline at 183 B.C.E.

A few of them even scanned the conscious energy patterns of his heart and mind and soul while in his presence.

*   *   *   *   *

Several of them and Hannibal himself suddenly telepathically tuned into another angle on some of the background, and in Barca's mind it mainly registered as a mixture of subconscious and semiconscious experiencing of daydreaming about nightmarish realms of the imagination:

Way back on the 28th Day of July in the Year 270 million Before the Common Era, Carthaginian reptiles, some of their allies, and their minions prepared a fully functional atom bomb and set it aside within a vault for potential future use. However, it was left dormant for millions upon millions of years, in fact for well over 269.99 million years. It would go on to become part of a human shrine in Carthage, until a Carthaginian priest, in a desperate attempt to call on the help of divinity to assist defense against the Romans, took it with a few monks onto a sailboat, drifting many miles away from the nearest coastline, then attempted to harness its energies. He accidentally detonated it out at sea in the year 202 B.C.

Charr Naerroan channeled the energies that emanated from it into augmenting the Romans' cruel attempts to devastate Carthage in 146 B.C. As many of those present found the devastation to the land itself inexplicable, there emerged a legend that the Romans had somehow performed wholesale salting of the earth at Carthage in the year 146 B.C. (a.k.a., 146 B.C.E.), yet it was actually a chain reaction spanning about 269,999,854 years that caused it, with Charr Naerroan more central to making it happen than all the legions of Rome combined.

*   *   *   *   *

As a footnote, consider this: Although some types of radioactive scientific and engineering analysis might have indicated that a period of nearly 270 million years would have led to a high chance that the bomb would prove to be a dud, the extra influence of The Transcendentals, as had often been the case, caused the laws of physics and chemistry to flex out of the more normal versions of themselves.

*   *   *   *   *

The details of the pattern unfolded with greater depth of details for Hannibal Barca's semiconscious mental processes and for the set of higher-dimensional consciousnesses of the beings who chose to psychically influence him from the beyond. Those beings beyond the regular realms of observable existence sufficiently transcended basic space-time continua to access portions of 270 Million B.C.E., 202 B.C.E., 183 B.C.E., and 146 B.C.E. across multiple timelines simultaneously at the very instants in which they chose to focus much of their psychic energy upon that specific instance of that great-yet-tragic, legendary military genius Hannibal Barca. That set of beings of the beyond and that version of that Barca together tuned into a more complete aware-ness of what had happened with the priest, the crew, the boat, and the nearly-270-million-year-old bomb.

In 202 B.C.E. the Carthaginian priest followed what he believed to be signs from the gods, trusting his intuition.

Several religiously pious monks went along with him, in a desperate attempt to help Hannibal and others in the conflict with Rome.

His group took the bomb out to sea during the height of the hostilities of that time. Of course, they did not know it was a bomb. To them, it was a mysterious artifact of unknown and ancient origins. The priest suddenly experienced a strong telepathic intuition that Hannibal's forces were starting to cave in from combat with the Roman forces. He then did his utmost to fully activate the artifact that he considered holy.

Although they were far enough out to sea to not pose much any direct danger to the rest of the living humans, the priest detonated the atom bomb, yielding about 21 kilotons of output, an explosion that remotely swayed the Carthaginian-vs.-Roman conflict a little further in favor of the Romans. The priest's desperate attempt to help his side had truly backfired.

*   *   *   *   *

After the Romans defeated the Carthaginians in 202 B.C.E., the aftermath led to Hannibal Barca going into various forms of exile during much of the remainder of his life. During some of the latter stages, he even served as a naval leader on behalf of a ruler named Prusias.

However, the Romans successfully persuaded Prusias to abandon his support of Hannibal. Some of Prusias' troops surrounded and started closing in on the elderly Hannibal Barca's home. This led to Hannibal feeling suicidal. A strange feeling started to overcome him.

*   *   *   *

Charr Naerroan seemed to materialize from sheer nothingness right in front of Hannibal, who then felt beside himself. Soon, Hannibal Barca and Charr shared quite an off-the-well-trodden-path chat.

*   *   *   *

Prior to the conversation, yet soon after witnessing Charr's arrival, Hannibal felt like time stood still, and he contemplated the situation from several perspectives.

A large dispatch of armed men surrounded his home. He knew that one way or another the senate and the people of Rome had arranged for his death to be coming soon. Barca again contemplated suicide.

He reflected on his life, including the many triumphs and the many twists and turns that led to all those repeated tragedies. He also reflected on the lives of others.

For a little while his heart and mind resonated at a superb level with the same mind pattern that the rock group Marmalade would present to the world with the Vietnam War era's popular song, "Reflections of My Life." However, the energy pattern that resonated between Barca and that song, one of acknowledging the horrors of life and death while choosing a strong commitment to remaining among the living started to collapse within the fibers of Hannibal Barca's being.

Prusias' betrayal had trapped him with no one and nothing left to shield him from the full wrath of Rome.

It was not going to be a matter of life and death for much longer, it would become a matter of the alternatives of each of multiple paths of death. He silently thought, *It's now a matter of one death versus another death vs. other alternatives of how to die.*

He thought hard about his options and what his choice might mean for the future of everyone who would remain alive in his wake. Hannibal Barca told his servants, "It does not matter much now. I relieve you of your duties in service to me. The writing is on the wall. The grim fate of execution is nigh, one way or another, for my life. Thank you for your service, and best wishes with the remainder of your days."

Several of the servants began to openly weep. Barca continued, "Remember me, and be not overly sad. I had a great run at things, including some truly great moments in this life. I wish each of you a prosperous future. Perhaps you will not know ahead of time whether you someday get trapped with death closing in from all sides like this, but whichever way it is with the future, best wishes to each and every one of you. You are free of the employment duties, more free than you have been for a while. Go where you choose, do what you choose. The future is yours to seize."

Upon completing that speech, he suddenly noticed that the servants had become completely still as far as he could tell. Motionless, like they inhabited some still life temple carving. "What in the name of Artemis is happening?!" he inquired.

The extremely-powerful, often-destruction-oriented transcendental Charr Naerroan materialized right in front of Hannibal Barca.

Charr could adjust his physical dimensions and characteristics nearly at-will each time he chose to materialize. In this case he chose to be nine feet tall with an appearance that many Greeks, Romans, and Carthaginians might have assumed to be a manifestation of the God of War, sometimes known as Aries and at other times known as Mars.

Hannibal asked, "Are you Mars, also known as Aries, the Great God of War?"

Charr answered plaintively, *"No. I am much more powerful than he is."*

Hannibal was taken aback. He felt an extreme visceral fear, yet he also felt a visceral thrill. *"How do find it sensible to say such a thing, and why are you choosing to talk with me right now?"*

Charr said, "*The Transcendental whom you sometimes call Mars is rather impressive in a great many ways, yet he has consistently become overpowered by several of the other Transcendentals, including myself.* In most cases, the beings whom the religious regard to be gods or even The Almighty Ultimate God actually, case by case, turn out to be incomplete and distorted perceptions of a given Transcendental or an amalgam of impressions of multiple of the Transcendentals. That Powerful Being Mars is sometimes identical to a transfiguration of a high percentage of the collective consciousness of the fourth planet that orbits the Sun of this solar system, a star also known as Helios. The Earth that you are living on is the third planet that orbits that Sun. Jupiter, also sometimes known as Jove, also sometimes known as Zeus, is sometimes identical to a transfiguration of a high percentage of the collective consciousness of the fifth planet that orbits the star Helios. Also, the stars that you see in the heavens are, a great many of them, suns, and in some cases the suns of other star systems. The reality you live in is vast in ways that hardly any living humans of your world and timeline have even begun to dare dream it could be.

"Your entire universe and timeline occupy a microscopic portion of a much greater reality. I am part of that greater reality, and I am among those whose collective battles and negotiations determine the very stability of the laws of your physical universe. That is, regarding the stability vs. instability of what appear to your world's 'natural laws.' Those laws are not entirely stable, by the way. Usually, this is more so as scales become smaller and smaller, yet, on occasions the rapid changeability of those natural laws can be witnessed at the large scale—even the largest of scales—as well.

"You have served many roles quite well in your lifetime. You know as well as I do that the end is nigh. You are about to die. One way or another, those acting on behalf of Rome are issuing you a death sentence. I am here to advise you to go ahead and take the poison as a method with which to kill yourself."

Hannibal responded, "I am considering that option, yet there are also other options."

Charr mentioned, "True. Yet here is something to think about: If you transcend your very physical body, then you might not actually be killing yourself at all if you do what people normally describe as 'killing yourself.' You may simply be liberating all of reality from the burden of your physical body remaining among the living."

Suddenly, Yadier Horowitz, another powerful transcendental materialized about seven feet away from the mortal Hannibal and about five feet away from the powerful transcendental Charr. Yadier in this case took the appearance of a nine-foot-tall man with a physical appearance that would later be associated with what digital artwork could portray for a clean-shaven hybrid of Charlton Heston, Clint Eastwood, and Kirk Douglas, each in the prime physique of his life. Both Yadier Horowitz and Charr Naerroan wore white tunics and brown sandals in this case.

Yadier said to Hannibal, "Although Charr gave you some advice just now, I have some different advice for you: If you tough things out by remaining alive a little longer and someone else forces your death, then you may make the spirit of human resiliency and the spirit of preservation in general obtain a huge boost. I recommend that you refrain from killing your physical body at this time. I recommend that you tough things out and see if you can wait for someone else to act as your executioner."

Hannibal asked, "Who are you?"

Yadier answered, "I am Yadier Horowitz, an extremely powerful Transcendental of approximately equal power as Charr Naerroan. Charr has often gone on a path of emphasizing destruction, whereas I have often gone on a path of emphasizing preservation. Both of us believe in serving the enlightenment and transcendence of sentient beings in general, yet we often have vastly different methods, priorities, and beliefs."

Hannibal found this all truly astounding. He thought of another line of inquiry. "What about this situation of how the rest of this room seems to be frozen in time?"

Yadier answered, "Although Charr and I, as well as the rest of the Transcendentals have often quarreled, sometimes we do agree thoroughly with each other. When enough of us thoroughly agree with each other and no one and nothing puts up much resistance to us, look out, there are practically no limits to how much we can change around the very laws of Reality Itself. Well, he and I and many others found agreement to freeze much of the space and time involving your very reality just now, in order to facilitate this meeting between the three of us, here and now."

Hannibal Barca became quite curious. "If you have that much power and knowledge, then why not simply remove me from this entire predicament?

"You could bring me with you to some completely different realm of existence. Do you need a military general? Do you need an admiral? Do you need a chief of staff? I could prove very useful."

Charr said, "In this case, Yadier and I agree that your best service involves that each of us present to you an argument for whether you should execute your physical body before you fall into the clutches of those who seek to do the execution themselves or if you should tough things out and let those others perform the execution on their terms. I have argued in favor of you committing suicide. Yadier has argued in favor of you refraining from committing suicide. The choice is now yours." With that utterance, both Charr and Yadier completely vanished from the room, and Reality Itself returned to moving in the more usual way.

To Hannibal Barca's servants things simply looked like normal reality. They were completely oblivious to what had just happened, save perhaps for some of their deepest levels of the subconscious and unconscious mind reaching out into the subtle awareness of a subtle omniscience, or what some might call a quasi-omniscience. Hannibal let out a deep breath. Internally, he resigned to siding with Charr's recommendation. He walked over to where the poison was. To the horror of the two servants who remained in the room with him at that instant, he took a lethal dose of the poison and swallowed it as they looked on.

He collapsed, then writhed briefly, then he became motionless. Hannibal Barca, who had terrified many an army during epic combat, lay dead on the floor.

* * * * *

* * *   Back to The Night of December 31, 2033   * * *

After C. Geronimo Watts experienced those scenes and settings vividly from the perspective of a temporarily super-mindful-though-incorporeal being, the two Transcendentals in his presence chose to rematerialize him into the body that he was used to having.

Dimetrioskys Elbankovic said, "I did not agree with Charr's choice to influence Hannibal to kill himself. In general, I lean heavily toward the preservation of life, beings, civilizations, worlds, and universes.

"In contrast, Charr generally leans heavily toward the destruction of life, beings, civilizations, worlds, and universes.

"As two of the Transcendentals, we each have our own free will about how much to steer the energy dynamics, statics, and harvesting of reality to emphasize more preservation or more destruction. Also, yes, we both become involved with our fair share of creation as well. We The Transcendentals are a large portion of the cause for much of the paranormal activity that people on rare occasions experience. I shall let Charr Naerroan tell you more about your peculiar situation now."

Charr explained, "You have mixed feelings about your life and the lives of those whom you have impacted, and you have an unusual set of strengths. A large number of Transcendentals are in my camp, which is leaning very much toward annihilating your entire universe, including the Lord of your universe.

"Many other Transcendentals are in Dimetrioskys' camp, which is leaning very much toward granting your entire universe, including the Lord of your universe, a lifespan that extends a long ways into the future. 'A new lease on life,' as some call it. If you choose to agree, we would like to arrange for you to vanish into thin air from your world, teleporting you to a realm where you can undergo training by the third main camp of Transcendentals, who are generally the swing vote on the ways of steering things more toward the annihilation of worlds and the ways of steering things more toward the preservation of worlds. Do you understand the options well?"

Geronimo Watts' genetic ancestry was about one quarter Cherokee and nearly three quarters Caucasian. He also had what might seem to virtually anyone meeting him an undiscernible trace of diverse, other types of ancestry. He had listened closely to the offer; he then answered, "Yes. How long do I have to decide?"

Dimetrioskys Elbankovic said, "You will have one minute to decide. If you make no clear answer, then we will take that as a no. If you say yes, then we will take you to them for training. Otherwise, you will return to the next part of the ordinary life of your world. If you depart your Earth, then your disappearance will occur very near the end of the Year 2033 as measured by what earthlings call The Gregorian Calendar, though others will not notice you missing until early on New Year's Day 2034. Once I finish this description and become silent to wait for your reply, your allotted one minute to answer will begin."

Geronimo Watts thought about it for about two seconds, then answered, "Yes, I agree for you to take me away from this world and find out what I can do to help determine the fate of this universe."

Charr responded, "Great! Let's begin."

Charr and Dimetrioskys, as promised, transfigured their entire observable reality such as to pluck Geronimo Watts right out from the entire universe in which he had been born, grown up, and resided.

Although no longer in his native universe, he felt just as alive as he had ever been. *In many respects, Geronimo felt more alive than he had ever felt before.* Anticipation of new roles and challenges invigorated him.

They arrived at a fresh locale. Geronimo saw now that he was in a giant auditorium, and instead of having humans comprise most of the observably present, over 90% of those present were gray aliens.

Charr said, "Maybe we'll meet again or maybe we might not. Either way, take care."

Geronimo responded, "Take care."

Dimetrioskys silently nodded. Geronimo nodded back to him.

Geronimo waved a fond farewell. Dimetrioskys and Charr waved a fond farewell back to him, as well.

*   *   *

One gray alien approached Geronimo Watts, and the elderly human male thought to himself, *A classic gray, like many of those sci-fi and conspiracy theorists have long depicted.*

The gray telepathically said to him, "Thank you for joining our cause. What do you happen to remember about *Ecclesiastes* and *The Dhammapada*?"

Geronimo said out loud, "Hm. I think you just telepathically said something to me. This is a little confusing, is it possible that it was just my imagination that you asked me a question telepathically or was that for real?"

The gray then spoke out loud in perfect American English. "Yes, that was for real. I chose to start out like that as a shock treatment to get you more used to the utterly bizarre. Although you experienced a little taste in the past few hours, that was just a fleeting glimpse of the kinds of experiences coming around the bend toward you. Now, back to the question that I posed to you: What do you happen to remember about *The Dhammapada* and *Ecclesiastes*?"

The human said, "I studied them some, including a complete reading of at least one English translation each. Yes, both include much wisdom that goes beyond the simple-minded dogmas forcing folks into the everyone-has-to-believe-in-this-or-else type of approach.

"Also, I remember that at least a dozen or more popular self-help and business-success gurus have spoken and written highly of them. Much ageless wisdom and encouragement."

He paused, waiting to see what the gray would say.

The gray said, "Go on. Say at least a few more things about your impressions of them, please."

Geronimo resumed, after a couple of seconds of hesitancy. "Some people, including some Christians, have found some of the passages in *Ecclesiastes* to strike them as rather cynical, then to find sudden full redemption in its rather spectacular twelfth and final chapter. That last chapter goes about halfway there toward what many Christians and Muslims would later rave about regarding visions of Judgment Day. Some among the percentage of Messianic Movement Jews who have declined to convert to Christianity and declined to convert to Islam have also focused on visions of Judgment Day and other things adjacent to that concluding chapter. Many who believe in any one or more of the main five major religions of ancient origins have expressed deep respect for that book. Jews, Christians, Muslims, Hindus, and Buddhists, yes, indeed, yes.

"Similarly, many people who believe in at least one or more of those five religions have expressed a deep and abiding respect for *The Dhammapada*. Now, about that book, what else? What else as an overview? What shall I say now? Let me try to remember more and say something relevant. Yes. Oh, yes, indeed, indeed. Perhaps most especially interesting is that it emphasizes the careful use of our consciousness as being central to impacting the long run outcomes of life and what it is that might follow in the beyond. Whatever might happen after this life, whether via continuation, reincarnation, some hybrid of both, or whatever else, we can also expect our ideas, words, and actions to lead to consequences."

The gray responded, "Yes, your concise and reasonably-on-track answer shows that what we had analyzed about you via remote, incomplete telepathy was correct: You're ready for orientation and induction into the ranks of those who often swing the tide."

Geronimo asked, "Before we go on much further, with whom do I have the honor of speaking?"

The gray said, "Double-Forty-One."

The man asked, "If you don't mind my asking, is that intended to be an alternate way of meaning that your name is the number Eighty-Two or is it derived from some very different path of logic."

Double-Forty-One answered, "It comes from a very different path of logic. You'll probably understand better during or after the group orientation session that you are scheduled to attend soon. Before you attend that session, do you wish to witness a recording of something scary that happened to an alternate timeline version of your Earth?"

The new recruit, suddenly imagining himself to be in the middle of something akin to having joined the U.S. military, said, "Yes, sir!"

Double-Forty-One waived a hand, and, instantly, the entire visible environment changed such that the two of them were now alone with each other in a movie theater of a classic layout. The gray said to the human, "Choose any seat in the house, and I'll decide to sit next to you. We shall then witness that recording."

The newly-recruited human looked around, then chose to sit in seat

G-10, which was located somewhere near the middle of the seating. The male, gray, extraterrestrial alien then sat down in seat G-9, which was one seat to the right of where the man sat down.

Unfolding on the screen in front of them, they witnessed *Doomsday Chronicle 27*, which presented a sequence starting sometime in mid-October 2024 in a world in which The Russian Federation, struggling in a war with The Ukraine, suddenly launched several small, tactical nuclear bombs, which then devastated portions of the Ukraine. Not long after that, the People's Republic of China attempted an invasion of Taiwan, and Pakistan attempted an invasion of India. A chain reaction had been set in motion. *From October 20 to November 3, 2024 in that world, the doomsday envisioned as quite possible someday in the long-term wake of the successful Trinity nuclear detonation test, that fear that many had long dreaded actually happened in that world: A full-scale, global, thermonuclear war occurred.*

By Noon GMT, November 3, 2024 on that version of Planet Earth, no sizable, functioning, human governments remained in existence anywhere in the world. Unlike previous wars, there had proven to be a complete lack of nations to consider themselves the victors of the war. Some might say that within one fortnite, all nations had mutually lost World War Three. *Within five months, over 99.9% of the pre-war land-dwelling mammals, reptiles, and birds were dead. Part of this was the grisly truth that over 99.5% of the pre-war population of humans were dead by that time.*

The insects were not as badly hit, yet their numbers had greatly diminished as well. The oceans had also largely proven a dead zone. Although life continued to have resiliency, several primal channels of life force within the ecosystem had fled the human race, as other organisms had inherited those energies of spiritual vitality.

Humans there had for about 75 years debated the chances of the human race surviving any of an array of global, thermonuclear war scenarios, and now there was nothing left to debate about it. The entire human race had forfeited its dominion there.

On October 31, 2030 on that version of the third planet orbiting the star known as Helios, the star that the humans there often simply referred to as the sun, the last living human being of that world grew tired, rested atop a clay deposit, fell asleep, and died.

The war had started on October 20, 2024 and, in almost every meaningful way, ended on November 3, 2024. In some sense November 1, 2030 never arrived in that world, because there were no humans left to greet that day. In another sense, November 1, 2030 arrived in that world as part of a changing of the guard, with the land suddenly able to rest in a permanent sabbatical, free from having to deal with the presence of any living humans.

That planet's third world war had only taken two weeks to go from the first large thermonuclear strike to the extinction of functioning nation-states, and, less than six years after that, the once-noble-and-prosperous species *Homo sapiens* had gone extinct.

Next, the documentary faded to a black screen with white letters that stated, "R.I.P. The Human Race of That Version of The Planet

Earth, whose lifespan ended up amounting to about 4,006,034 years, specifically, 27 OCT 4004004 B.C.E. — 31 OCT 2030 C.E."

Finally, he screen shifted over to a set of yellow letters in all caps stating "THE END" together with a view from outer space, with what had formerly been the pale blue dot of Earth now showing as a dark gray dot.

Bear in mind that this experience of Double-Forty-One presenting the secret documentary *Doomsday Chronicle 27* was itself here being chronicled within the larger documentary *Revolutions: An Alleged Secret History of the Creations of Several Worlds, the Lives and Deaths of Many Species, and Some of What Has Happened in the Great Beyond* as in this case screened by Charr as a presentation that Jeremy and he were watching together.

After that grim end to *Doomsday Chronicle 27*, Double-Forty-One and Geronimo of met up with a large group, the rest of which consisted of 120 newly-recruited initiates and 24 instructors.

Adding the two of them to that mix brought the total to 121 initiates and 25 instructors. There would be 14 hours of introductory training, followed by a copious amount of intermediate training. One of the earliest things that the initiates came to understand was that although beings can define the words "universe" and "multiverse" in many different ways, the practical way for them to discuss the spatiotemporally-observable reality was to say that there are many universes, each with its own timeline, universes often branch out from one another with the branching of timelines, multiverses are closely-related sets of universes, and Reality As A Whole includes a large number of multiverses and a gargantuan quantity of sentient beings. Furthermore, beings can exhibit diverse ways of branching out and branching together, similar to how universes sometimes branch out and at other times branch together. Also, although a very basic version of using a four-dimensional Einstein-Lorentz-based type of space-time continuum would sometimes be practical, and a more intricate six-dimensional Kletetschka-Ouspenskian-based type of continuum would at other times be much more practical for the art of extreme precision. Models may be models as far as they go, and our reality of many dimensions of both space and many dimensions of time is quite an awesome reality. Physics and metaphysics can only take us so far at a given instant; get ready to go much further.

****

Next, consider a more in-depth variation of much of the backstory of all of that. Here are several interwoven portions of what led to the encounters between Charr and Hannibal Barca and between Charr and Geronomo Watts, as well as background patterns that could help viewers comprehend a little more of what happened as situations escalated to set the stage for *The War Beyond Human Comprehension*.

***** ***** ***** ***** ***** ***** *****

It was spring, somewhere that would later be part of what humans call "Texas," 274,578 millennia and three weeks before The Tunguska Event. A young dimetrodon named Tryrordian Glinko telepathically intitiated a strong transmission toward a middle-aged dimetrodon named Sterling Lovecraft Jenkeysianson. Both were male, and they were at a distance of about five miles.

Tryrordian thought toward Sterling, "The food supplies here are running sufficient to maybe slightly insufficient, yet I have at least temporarily lost all interest in food. What are you up to at this time?"

Sterling picked up the signal and correctly sensed it through the ether. He responded, "I'm doing fine, thanks for asking. Just before your call, and, even now, multitasking with your telepathic call, I've been and am reading portions of the cave carvings of Dimetrioskis Elbankovic, a bipedal humanoid visitor I met twenty years ago. He didn't seem to have nearly as strong telepathically abilities as we do, yet he was able to communicate much through vocals, gestues, paintings, and carvings. Of everyone I've communicated with and myself, as a collective group, we are not entirely certain whether he was an extraterrestrial alien, an apparition, a time traveler, or something else. The same goes for the other seven bipedal humanoids publicly known to have visited us over the millions of years up to now.

"Years ago I glanced at some of this stuff on the walls of the cave, and it looked like it might involve alien conceptualizations of visitors from the other side of the sun or elsewhere in the heavens, yet it's making more sense now. Some possibilities are that deep in the future, there will be a great civilization, a great war, destruction, rebuilding, and new cycles of this sort of stuff. He had an epic vision, communicated in scenes and symbols."

Tryrordian said, "My family recently adopted an infant orphan. We are debating what to name him. I'm going to suggest that instead of giving him the surname "Glinko" my family should consider giving him the surname 'Elba,' like the beginning of 'Elbankovic.'"

Sterling responded, "Yes, I wholeheartedly agree that you should recommend that."

The Glinko family ended up naming the orphan infant *of unknown origins* Ion Elba. Many generations later, in the chain of male lineage, there emerged Dimetrio Elba, born on December 25th, 274,504,003 BCE. He would prove to be the longest living dimetrodon. That is: as measured by scientifically-observable spatio-temporal, biological-historical-lifespan standards of *the usually silent majority of fundamental reality, who might otherwise be referred to as the transcendental beings*. He was, among dimetrodons, not a one-in-a-million being or a one-in-a-billion, he was of unique power, grace, wisdom, and utter transcendence.

In what normally would have been the ages of youth and middle age, while others were busy reproducing or attempting to reproduce, he made limited attempts at reproduction, largely revolving around engaging in dimetrodonian tantric sexual encounters, with which to heighten awareness of reality by delaying or avoiding mundane full gratification during those encounters, in exchange for sex which connected his partners and himself with elements of the divine.

Also, as the dimetrodons often declined to match up one-to-one for monogamous relations, there were frequent instances of not knowing who was descended from whom. In contrast with this, though one of his most ancient of forefathers, the aforementioned Ion Elba, had unknown parents prior to being christened with the individual name Ion *and* the surname Elba by the Glinko family which adopted him, everyone in the chain from father to son to grandson and so forth had an essentially iron-clad knowledge that they were of the same male lineage. Elba could *feel* the connection going back through multitudes of generations, all the way back to the distant Ion, who had lived to the age of 1,999 years, five months, and 27 days before dying from, of all things, a lightning strike right after publicly praying in the middle of a battle, "Lord, Ultimate Reality or Realities, to whatever degree expressing thyself as God or The Most Awakened One or Whomever or Whatever Else, if 'tis best that I die very soon by lightning strike or any other means to supercharge our dimetrodon forces in fighting back a coalition of those attempting to annihilate us, as a sacrifice toward prolonging the survival of our species both for our sakes and the long-run soteriology and enlightenment of the beings of Earth, then so be it, go for it!" Then came the intense lightning strike and concomitant thunder, and as Ion Elba collapsed into death by his own consent with the almighty, one hundred million enemy combatants suddenly themselves died by spontaneous animal combustion. This was one of the most contr-oversial moments in the pre-ancient history of the planet. Although there were reptilians on both the side of Ion Elba and the dimet-rodons and reptilians on the side Charr Naerroan and the igweolintians, many dimetrodons had dreaded an intuition that the reptiles might someday sway nearly in unison against them.

The "Igweolintians" had a name generally-capitalized in the context of being citizens of the nation-state Igweolintus. In contrast, the "igweolintians" had a name shown-with-generally-all-lower-case in the context of being any shape shifters who at a given time was a true believer in the religion known as Igweolintu. The vast majority of those among the Igweolintians and/or the igweolintians had a fierce loyalty to a generally rigid authoritarian structure, especially to the theocratic government that jointly ruled Igweolintu and Igweolintus.

Although an overwhelmingly high percentage of citizens of that nation at a given time in those days believed in the state-sponsored religion, there were exceptions. The faithful tended to deal with them by demonstrating energetic harshness, including many acts of killing them at the behest of religious leaders.

There were diverse arts, philosophies, religions, sciences, and feats of engineering in that version of Earth, a version that many have referred to as Pangea. Earth had only one continent back then, and that is part of why it had the name Pangea.

Another part related to the mysteries of the very high-risk, very high-reward boxes of paranormal potential and peculiar relationship with an array of beings of the name Pandora.

Against the backdrop of that wild and nearly-totally-forgotten world, Dimetrio Elba maintained the health of an illness-free middle-aged living organism into what most would have presumed to be old age. He just kept living and living.

By his 2,525th birthday, he had become more than a living legend, he was revered as perhaps the greatest being to have ever walked the surface of the planet, deified by some and nearly deified by others both for his mind-boggling longevity and for his interdisciplinary theological, scientific, and engineering accomplishments. Long before humans would build great pyramids in what would become Africa and the Americas, teams of dimetrodons and other living quadrupedal sail-backed biological beings used psychokinesis, telepathy, and telekinesis to construct an engineering marvel of a city-state in portions of what would later become known to human beings as "Siberia." Two of his teammates on a number of projects were Evgeny Serling and his wife Svetlena Serling, both of which had studied from the much-older Dimetrio during a span of many years.

A few beings of those days would occasionally teleport. Such teleportation was usually unintentional, yet it was also in rare cases intentional.

This was without the aid of official teleportation mechanical equipment; rather via a conjunction of biology, mind, higher-dimensional space, higher-dimensional time, and higher-dimensional space-time.

Prior to Dimetrio Elba's leadership, great swathes of dimetrodons had been in-fighting for millions of years about the controversies of religion, philosophy, science, and art.

However, scores of millions of years before a man reputed to have born in Karkiv (in 1878 CE/AD as per most official records and questioned as by other records as to having been born either in 1877 or 1878 CE/AD and bearing a name that some would render) as Pyotr Demianovich Ouspensky would create a book (that would go on to be) called *Tertium Organum: The Third Canon of Human Thought, A Key to the Enigmas of the World*, the dimetrodon Dimetrio Elba created an extremely similar work titled *The Restoration of Ancient Integrative Consciousnesses*. Also, long before the perhaps-most-legendary of bipedal bio-organisms, Padmasambhava, created a magnum opus known to many as *The Tibetan Book of The Dead*, Dimetrio Elba created a somewhat similar work titled *How Beings of Any Numbers of Limbs Might Transcend the Unknowns of This and Other Realms*. Additionally, that very elderly Elba, after the loss of over 99.988% of the dimetrodon population from 274,501,478 BCE to 252,000,008 BCE, enacted a plan to steer the future of reality toward the possibility of the emergence of the intelligent mammals later known as dolphins, orca, and humans.

About 299 or 300 million years before the construction of Stone Henge, diverse creatures flourished on Earth. There were early fish, early sharks, octopi, squid, crustaceans, and others in the waters of the planet.

In some sense there was just one main land mass and just one main ocean. On land and in the air, giant insects, medium reptiles (whom some human scientists would refer to as being among the reptilians, also known as the saurians), medium reptile-like synapsids (who were more closely related to mammals than reptiles, although often appearing similar to reptiles), small mammals (who also were synapsids), and arachnids did dwell.

At some stage within the next few million years, there emerged, *from the merger of two different species*, the *early dimetrodons*. Physically evaluating the billions of years of development of biological entities, human scientists of the time of World War One and the one hundred four years after it would typically conclude that those beings of large sails and four legs, with two main types of teeth, were sophisticated for their time, yet no match for the sophistication of modern humans.

Both the dimetrodon beings and the edaphosaurus beings could harness heightened extrasensory perception capabilities through the use their sails. Many of the rest of Pangea's inhabitants were superb at telepathy and psychokinesis.

Dimetrodons were often the planet's main land-dwelling alpha predators during much of the 280-millions B.C.E. and the 270-millions B.C.E.

Some forms of advanced technology were already present in our world among many beings of the period from 252 million to 292 million years before what many historians call The Dorian Invasion.

Long before the ancient human nation of Sumer temporarily unified vital statics and dynamics of integration, differentiation, and transfiguration, to marvelous effect, the zones of awareness of living creatures *felt and knew* much of this *without having to conceptualize it*. After a while, in what many would call *pre-historic* times, some of the living things of the planet already achieved the tracking of *history*, through means of *telepathy, artifacts, and energy.*

Dimetrodonian technologies were at times pitted against Igwe-olintian technologies, as part of warfare that relied heavily on telepathy, psychokinesis, and the weaponization of large insects and golems. Although the reptiles were often fighting on both sides in the early days of the conflicts of that, as the millions of years rolled along the tide of reptilian loyalty shifted very much in favor of the Igweolintians.

When the wars of quadruped-versus-quadruped alternate notions of superiorities had reached their zenith in the year 270,000,000 BCE/BC, the climactic scene unfolded as follows:

Zircon Gilroy, a transformational reptile shapeshifter of indeterminate species (relative to early Twenty-First Century human scientific theories), teamed up with many reptiles of determinate species (relative to the aforementioned theories) to create military bases in Carthage and Bombay, which were already known at the time, as per a host of telepathic transmissions, to both synapsids and reptilians, as "Carthage" and "Bombay."

Reptilians versus Synapsids, with each side resorting to the full use of all religions, sciences, arts, and philosophies in concert, fought tooth and nail and dagger, extending both regular and telekinetic arts of warcraft to levels that the living humans of June 29th, 1908 CE/AD would have seldom dreamed possible.

The primary military bases of the synapsids were located in Siberia and what would later be called the Himalayan region. Regarding the latter, that military might had its most densely concentrated munitions housed in the region that would later be referred to by some humans as Kashmir. Humans of the third millennium of the common era, if able to travel back in time and telepathically tune into the various interspecies 11G biotelecommunications, would have noticed numerous religious and scientific methods identical to portions of physics, neuroscience, chemistry, mechanical engineering, *and even Abrahamic Religious methods, Brahmanic Religious methods, metaphysics, ethics, multireligious Dharmic philosophies, scientific methods, and Universalist Panentheism.*

It was quite a time to be alive. *Quite a time to be alive, but maybe not so much for the faint of heart and the weary.* One of the favorite weapons of choice by both sides were the insects, and another were the sea scorpions known as the eurypterids.

Many of the non-insect-non-arachnid-non-eurypterid beings were able to genetically and behaviorally manipulate the way that insects, eurypterids, and arachnids would do what they do, siccing them on their opponents.

Additionally, rather remarkably, some of the warriors conducted widespread, intentional, highly successful manipulation of weather.

In particular, a few reptiles here and there and a few synapsids here and there could occasionally direct the magnitude and location of lightning itself, to a major extent.

On July 28th, 270 Million B.C.E., Carthaginian reptiles, some of their allies, and their minions prepared a fully functional atom bomb and set it aside within a vault for potential future use. However, it was left dormant for millions upon millions of years, in fact for well over 269.99 million years. It would go on to become part of a human shrine in Carthage, until a Carthaginian priest, in a desperate attempt to call on the help of divinity to assist defense against the Romans, accidentally detonated it in the year 202 B.C.

Back to July 28th, 270,000,000 B.C.E. Elsewhere, using astronomical multitudes of specialized insects, arachnids, and others as biological constructors of mechanical equipment, through modified 11G transmissions of mental activity through the ether and other means, physical military technology reached true greatness. It in general became similar to some of the World War Two level of human state-of-the-art capabilities.

Having weaponized much of their entire reality, a few brave souls dared to go even further, calling out with all their might toward whomever in the heavens - whether biped, quadruped, pure-energy, or hybrid beings, or anyone else - who should happen to hear their calls.

Some started new traditions focused on the bipedal humanoid as a class of beings who might someday save the planet from the oft-deadly synapsids-versus-reptilians holy wars and other threats.

Some legendary names that they prophesized *were*: Samantabhadra, Samantabhadri, Tara, The Adamantine One, Adam, and Matsya.

There were many arguments among camps and subcamps of those ultra-ancient synapsids and reptiles about such things as whether: 1) Adam and Matsya were representative of the same being or two different beings... or perhaps referring to five or more different beings, 2) whether God and Adibuddha are identical to each other or not, and 3) the degrees of reality or lack thereof of space, time, birth, life, death, afterlife, obliteration, reincarnation, and transfiguration.

Both a high percentage of those who felt the most despair and a high percentage of those who felt the least despair looked toward the future while imagining the possibility of humanoids as a symbol of a new hope for the entire planet and all of its inhabitants.

*****

Both sides of that war—whether deemed by a given beholder to have been a holy war, an unholy war, or something else entirely, however, *whether for good or for ill*, somehow achieved *wholesale, "effective" delivery of biological warfare* upon their enemies by October 17th, 270,000,000 BCE.

By November 9th of that year, the spread of illnesses and deaths was already extremely terrible across many parts of Pangea.

By December 6th, 270,000,000 BC, the fighting temporarily halted, because both sides faced unforeseen mayhem as the biological warfare had proved several magnitudes of order more "successful" than they had planned.

Nevertheless, on or about December 14th of that year, a few skirmishes had restarted, and by January 31st the next year, widespread warfare had resumed.

After that, Zircon and Dimetrio simultaneously transitioned into the beyond in a *sublimation*, materially vanishing out of worldly life without any of the normal processes of physically dying, instead encountering Reality Itself instantly disintegrating their physical forms.

Nevertheless, they continued their rivalry in the immediate aftermath of that transition. Both cared deeply about opportunities for spiritual enlightenment, wisdom, and love, yet they chose different priorities and emphases.

Almost 19 million years went by. There arrived a near-extinction of dimetrodons and the sea-dwelling eurypterids.

One of the major causes of the devastation of those populations had been how the Igweolintians had swayed the vast majority of reptiles into favoring the side of the religion Igweolintu. Through much of this time, Charr Naerroan, the legendary founder of both Igweolintu and Igweolintus, almost always remained hidden from the view of virtually everyone on both sides of the war. Some rumors flew around that he might not have ever really existed, that he might have been some mythical legend generated to inspire the masses of his side of the conflict. A few beings, though, had maintained close contact with him. In those days, he chose to take the physical form of a gigantic wasp with the typical set of six legs and two wings associated with those insects. He chose to communicate almost entirely by a combination of telepathy, mild movements, and subtle sounds.

The few who had angered him while in his presence found, to their horror, that in rage he would transfigure into shape-shifting sequences of diverse monsters with a wild assortment of instant weaponry, and that he proved willing to kill with unlimited viciousness and fury. Also, those whom he chose to instantly kill would typically encounter execution while right in front of several onlookers, and Charr would chose to quickly torture them to death in such ways that they would scream, howl, and cry while any five or more of the most sensitive and vulnerable parts of their bodies would become sliced open, pounded into oblivion, or burned alive until dead. He felt totally uninhibited with brutally destroying the genitals, brains, hearts, and other portions of anatomy of living beings.

He ruled and yet almost never met personally with his highest-ranking military strategist Zircon Gilroy. After Zircon had in some sense died and in another sense departed worldly life without dying, much as Dimetrio Elba sublimated into the beyond at about the same time, and much as Enoch would, millions of years later also sublimate out of the worldly life, things changed. Although Zircon continued to fight almost entirely in favor of Charr's priorities and goals, he became aware that there was much more to they great mysteries of life and death than what Charr and his minions had chosen to reveal to him. On rare occasions, he simply made his own decision to take actions intended to have mixed effects on the balance of power between things that Charr intended and things that Dimetrio intended.

Meanwhile, Dimetrio had to watch as some of the core spiritual energies of the life force of the entire set of the Dimetrodons started to simply wither away and die. It proved disheartening over and over again as he noticed new generations of them somehow losing more and more of the will to live, the will to reproduce, the will to obtain and eat food, the will to overcome challenges, and volition in general. He knew that something beyond the horizon of his knowledge was afoot, and whatever it was, it seemed to be like a dagger sinking further and further into the very heart of the entire set of each and every of the several then-living species of Dimetrodons.

Over and over again he would witness it: Dimetrodon parents of a young Dimetrodon would start out hopeful for the future of their family, the youth would thrive for a while, then the youth would start to experience life veering totally off course into one tragedy after another, then the youth would start to shut down the very will to live. More tragedies would ensue, and, after a while, yet another entire family of Dimetrodons would go extinct. This was in addition to the great numbers of their population lost in the ongoing warfare with the Igweolintians. In fact, as time went by, the numbers lost to the mysterious loss of a will to live and the mysterious loss of the will to reproduce proved several times as lethal as the observable acts of the warfare.

The dimetrodons and the eurypterids had dwindled in population since around 271 million years B.C.E., and their loss of numbers had accelerated greatly since about 265 million years B.C.E. Many of the other sets of organisms had maintained their numbers for a while, but many of them would also face major drops to their numbers.

Many of the other living organisms of Earth experienced rapidly declining populations circa 251.9 million years B.C.E. onward, as

Dimetrio and Zircon observed from the great beyond in abject horror. Zircon was as perplexed about this as Dimetrio.

Something was definitely afoot. Yes, indeed, it was, though almost none would have suspected just how insidious it was.

Under the surface, Charr Naerroan had eons earlier discovered ways to take his telepathic and psychokinetic powers to remotely cause extra death and destruction to a whole other level. After that, he waited for when he would believe the time and situation to be perfect to unleash those lethal powers. He could boggle the minds of trillions instantaneously, setting up deadly chain reactions. Yes, he, in fact, had killed one part after another of the cosmic volition of the entire set of Dimetrodons, the set of the Eurypterids, and many other beings of Pangea.

For example, a fecund female and a fecund male would start to go onto a path toward true love and wholesome biological reproduction, then Charr Naerroan would telepathically deflect their entire pattern into something heartbreaking and tragic, preemptively extirpating what would most likely have otherwise blossomed into a faithful, caring, and loving family. Over a quarter of a billion years later, he would focus the same type of destructive telepathy against various human beings, political parties, businesses, nonprofit organizations, and entire nations.

He was, yes, just warming up, in the days of Pangea. *Warming up for what?*, some might ask. Something much larger. Many things much larger. Believe it or not, over a quarter of a billion years before the main, earthly emergence of the Cro Magnon variation of human beings, Charr Naerroan had his sights on annihilating entire planets full of intelligent beings and even entire universes. The way that his transcendental energies super-resonated with destruction, his cruel ambitions did not stop with the wholesale annihilation of multitudes of universes, oh no, he wished to take the destructiveness beyond even that. Even he himself, sometimes wondered whether there were any limits at all to his destructive intents.

Dimetrio Elba suspected that something dire was under the surface, but he simply could not figure out what it was. He sometimes suspected Charr to have some central role in this, but also suspected many other beings and forces. Additionally, he recognized that it just might be some combination of many partial causes, with none of them contributing to any more than about one-third of the source of the devastation. Although he was very aware of much of Charr's cruelty, he would have considered it highly improbable for that cruelty and destructive intent to be as extreme as it actually was.

The tragic extirpations of one Dimetrodonian family lineage after another started to weigh heavily on Elba's heart. After a while he felt totally disheartened. Then, for the first time in his entire existence, he became truly and thoroughly heartbroken, but not for long.

He healed himself from the heartbreak by focusing on what he could do about changing the pathway from the present to the future into something that he could truly believe to be an improvement.

Dimetrio suddenly had a flash of insight: *He temporarily unified both the core set of the Dimetrodonian religious energies and the core set of the*

Igweolintian religious energies within the fibers of his being and channeled the energies toward the planets Jupiter, Saturn, and Neptune. He chose to fully intend to team up with Providence, as channeled through Neptune, Saturn, Jupiter, and himself, to bring all of the accumulated karma of all time to land on everyone and everything. The day was December 31st, 251,108,001 BCE. It would not take long for his strategy to pay off.

Suddenly, early in the year 251,108,000 BCE, *the entire planet Jupiter* awoke from a 50-million-year hibernation, *shining the entirety of its collective planetary consciousness upon Earth.*

The Planet Jupiter, then shining with a temporary, energetic unity of consciousness with The Almighty, found disgust with nearly all of the life, biographical developments, and biological developments on Planet Earth.

Before Dimetrio and Zircon, both of whom were dwelling somewhere between bardo states and full paranirvana, even knew it had started, Jupiter-as-a-whole, as temporarily unified with the entirety of Absolute Divinity Itself/Himself/Herself/Themselves, then did telekinetically induce portions of Siberia to include the eruption of a supereschatological supervolcano.

****

Horatio Zlotnike and Deborah Goladolwa were, as of then, the last two dimetrodons among the living, and they were an offspringless couple. They lived in Texas, yet they *both* heard *and* felt, via their sails, ears, minds, hearts, and souls, from the other side of the world evidence of what had started to happen. Horatio said to Deborah, "Oh, God, what was that noise! The terrestrial and ethereal transmissions just reached an overload!!"

Deborah responded, "*This is it*: deep within the preachings of both

Dimetrio Elba and his nemesis Zircon Gilroy there are those prophecies that if neither side of the synapsid-vs.-reptilian holy war performs well enough their duties to the ultimate, then beings of the beyond will deem everyone on Earth to be excessively left-hand path, bringing down all the hammers of all the gods and The Vajra Dagger of Adi-Buddha God to deliver holy wrath upon all life on Earth. *I can't help but ff… ffeeeel thaaat… it's jj… just… started.*"

The couple looked into each other's eyes and telephathically communicated both romantic and agapic love, acknowledging profound uncertainty whether any of the inhabitants of Earth would remain alive for very long.

Nearby, a small flock of mostly-vegetarian sail-backed quadrupeds who lived on Horatio and Deborah's farm felt much the same way.

Susan Sherwood said to those present, especially Thomas Smirnoff and Jerry Grockenspree, "Our last remaining dimetrodon overlords probably know more about this than we do. However, it would be more polite to give them some more time to evaluate what it means, rather than barge in and ask what the hell they think and know about what's up with something huge that's happened in the distance."

Debate ensued. Heated debate. A large part of that focused on the flying objects that arrived into the skies. The idea circulated that the Unidentified Aerial Phenomena were most likely advanced aircraft.

After much heated discussion, a previously silent visitor, also a sail-backed quadruped, walked in, joining the conversation. That initially-silent visitor, Lorentzia Dorian, was a female synapsid of what seemed to many to be an indeterminate species, she was about seven-and-a-half centuries old, and she was wise beyond her years. Lorentzia said, "Those are not armadas of aircraft. *They are spacecraft.*"

Thomas Smirnoff shook his head in disagreement, then stated in a stern voice, "Sensationalist, paranormal hogwash! How can anyone be so sure that spacecraft even exist? Many scientists, even today, conjecture that exiting the atmosphere of any given planet to venture into outer space is either a pipedream or something that will need to wait for millions more years of technical advancement. In the absence of strong evidence that these things in the sky came here from outer space, I believe it most prudent to presume that someone somewhere on Earth simply flew those things into the sky to gather here. What makes *you* so confident that it's otherwise?"

Lorentzia said, "Because, about a century ago, *I called on them* to come back, *and back they are.*"

Susan, Thomas, and Jerry *literally* turned to stone upon hearing and seeing this.

Lorentzia then walked to the outer limits of the farm.

There she looked up to the armada and said, "Welcome back! I truly believe someone or something in this solar system is instigating an annihilation or a near-annihilation of all life forms on Earth. *What do you think?*"

A hologram of Adam Kadmon (the Adam from before splitting into Adam and Eve), (the) Adam (from after the rib-removal and related processes), Eve, Samantabhadra, Samantabhadri, and (The Patriarch)

Noah appeared before her. They were silent for eight seconds, then Samantabhadra, Samantabhadri, and Adam Kadmon vanished.

Another three seconds of silence transpired, (the) Eve (whom THE LORD had transfigured from a rib into becoming a female human) and (the post-removal-of-one-rib) Adam vanished.

Noah stepped closer and said, "*You called on us* 101 years ago today. *We communicated with you about an impending doom for your world.* We do not know for sure whether life on your planet will still be around one million years from now, let alone a-quarter-of-a-billion-years hence, but we invite you to step aboard *an interstellar interdimensional vessel.* We will now give you only one chance to answer this question. Do you agree to step aboard right now?"

Lorentzia answered with a resounding, "Yes!" She then continued, "How do I step aboard?"

Noah said, "*Stand very still.* A helicopter will land about twenty yards from here. Three men and three women will walk to position themselves into a pattern in which you shall be equidistant from each of them, with yourself somewhat in the middle of a hexagonal pattern of humans. We shall then teleport all seven beings, that being a combination of yourself and the six people, aboard a starship. You are one of at least five million beings that our armada is attempting to frantically rescue from this potentially dying *world.*"

Lorentzia stood absolutely still. She truly loved the mysterious visitors and their gracious offer.

Soon, the six humans arrived, not as holograms, but as actual persons in the flesh. They did just as the Noah hologram said that they would, and the group of seven beings teleported aboard one of the vessels.

The armada succeeded in rescuing approximately 4.9 million of the inhabitants of Earth by interdimensional and insterstellar journeys aboard spacecraft. They also provided esoteric technologies and insights to another 200,000 of the inhabitants, whom they left to mostly fend for themseleves amid supervolcanoes, greenhouse-gas shrouds, extreme climate change, etc.

By the time that The Great Dying ended, extremely few of the previously inhabiting species of Earth were left alive. Many of the survivors carried an ancestral memory in their zones of awareness, a sense that almost everyone had gone extinct. It could be easy for many sentient beings to interpret that life and technology had been set back between 200 million and 340 million years.

Throughout much of the Triassic period that ensued, multitudes of technological remnants of bygone eras were still visible on Earth in the form of artifacts.

Dinosaurs and early birds of the Mesozoic era had little inkling of the extreme cultures and technologies that had been present on the planet during the latter stages of the Paleozoic era. Nevertheless, they often operated as fierce and crafty gladitorial and nongladitorial participants of the dramas of life.

An array of pterosaurs, proto-birds, and birds eventually emerged. After a while, the skies would witness major aerial combat between large insects, small-to-medium birds, proto-birds of various sizes, and pteresaurs.

Challenges with agility, major reductions in how much oxygen was present in the atmosphere, and other factors led to the largest of the surviving insects becoming much smaller as time kept marching on.

****

On land, on the seas, in the seas, and in the skies, much of the combat served as proxy battles and proxy wars on behalf of the competing coalitions of the beings of the beyond. Those of the great beyond included Transcendentals, ghosts, and others. Some Transcendentals were, in fact ghosts, and some ghosts were, in fact Transcendentals, yet there were also many Non-Transcendental Ghosts and many Non-Ghost Transcendentals. There were degrees of truth to the idea that all sentient beings are at least to a minimal degree among The Transcendentals, yet, in the regular senses of conceptualizing reality, The Transcendentals were as more advanced in their consciousness and capabilities in relationship with ordinary humans as ordinary humans were to the simplest invertebrates.

Consider a deeper analysis of the multitudes of beings of The Great Beyond. Those beings would at times die, disappear, reawaken, then, to whatever degrees by reincarnation and to whatever degrees by reappearing return to reality. Frequently, a returning entity would split into one version of herself/himself/itself becoming reborn via reincarnation with only the faintest of traces of memory of a past life or multiple past lives and another version of himself/herself/itself coming back with a reasonably complete set of memories of the most recent past life or of all past lives. The memory-intact version would usually manifest as a ghost/apparition/spirit/etc. There were other cases as well. For example, sometimes an entity who had achieved great spiritual maturity and impact on the lives of others might go straight into maintaining continuity of unity of being together with continuity of reasonably complete memory and appear, disappear, and reappear at will as a full-fledged Transcendental. For another example, some beings whose minds had encountered extreme fragmentation under duress and who died while in that mental state would split into five or more reincarnated beings, none of whom had even the slightest trace of memory of having ever had any past existence whatsoever. In those cases, they had generated horrendous karma in a lifetime, failed to purify themselves very much prior to death, then failed to navigate the bardo realm very well at all.

By the end of that, they would then encounter the dreaded Wheel Of Oblivion. That wheel was a conscious, animate entity who had split from the rest of the Primordial Ultimate Divinity, such as to be the personification of The Obliteration That Is More Total Than Death Itself. When, on exceedingly rare occasions, The Primordial Ultimate Divinity would choose to come back into observability by normal beings, He/She/It would choose on an ad hoc basis how He/She/It would appear, which religion(s) the experience would help to seed and/or transfigure, and which cognitive structures to promote and/or demote. The Primordial Divinity chose to deliberately present what the most simple-minded would consider extreme cognitive dissonance, as this often proved the best way to serve the higher purposes of Soteriology, which encompasses the prime motives of all religions, philosophies, and sciences.

****

Sometimes, The Wheel of Oblivion, who was also known as The Great Destroyer of All or Nearly All, would be fully unified with The Primordial Ultimate Divinity, yet on other occasions they would manifest as two clearly and distinctly separate entities who would team up with each other. The many variations of The Great Seal of The Wheel of Oblivion would, in many worlds within many multiverses, appear on some of the Ethiopian replicas of The Ark of The Covenant and on a few of the drawings on Himalayan caves. It would appear to be along the lines of a set of some number of lines emanating from the center of a pattern, sometimes with 8, 12, 16, or a different number, and, in each case at least two of the lines would be dashed and/or dotted, whereas the majority of the lines would be solid. In some worlds, some Asians would use a pictograph for some forms of rice in a manner closely paralleling this, yet without nearly as much dashing or dotting of the noncontinuous lines. Also, in some worlds, The Union Jack flag of Great Britain and the United Kingdom would exhibit a similar pattern, yet with eight virtually continuous lines with little or no dashing or dotting in most cases. Additionally, many versions of The Wheel of The Dharma in Buddhism exhibited having a pattern of eight (like unto the cardinal directions) or twelve (like unto traditional hour markers on traditional clocks that would run from 12 to 1 to 6 to 10 back to 12, etc.), all continuous, none dotted, none dashed, with a circle or other oval connecting them, reminiscent of the wheels associated with old-time ships and the captains who would helm them. These, together with the Ancient Hebrew and Ancient Sumerian ways of writing the characters Yod, He, Vau, and Aleph, and other characters of that ancient alphabet, based on eight points concentrically equidistant from a shared center, together with every line and every intersection between each pair of them, yes, indeed, these were all part of the great set of architectural designs of Reality Itself, which The Primordial Ultimate Divinity generated. Although there was significant truth in all of the religions and philosophies, all of these emanated from that Primordial Divinity, to any and to whichever degrees that anyone might have ever attempted to conceive of THAT as having manifested as UNITY, TRINITY, ZERO, NONE, ALL, ULTIMATE, TRANSCENDING QUANTITIES, THAT WHICH IS THE INFINITE, GOD, G-D, ADIBUDDHA, YHVH, EL, ALLAH, THE GREAT ARCHITECT, THE INTERDEPENDENCY OF ALL PHENOMENA, THE PRIME MOVER, THE CREATOR, THE DESTROYER, THE PRESERVER, THE GREAT ULTIMATE, THAT WHICH IS THE TRANSINFINITE, and/or whomever else and/or whatever else, THAT was and is THE I AM BECAUSE I AM, THE THOU ART BECAUE THOU ART, THE IT IS BECAUSE IT IS, THE THEY ARE BECAUSE THEY ARE, AND THAT WHICH PURELY TRANSCENDS ALL RIGID NOTIONS OF SELF VERSUS NONSELF VERSUS DUALITY VERSUS NONDUALITY VERSUS TRINITY

VERSUS NONTRINITY VERSUS ALL OTHER WAYS TO SET UP TO CONCEPTUALLY ARRANGE ANY AND ALL QUANTITIES, NONQUANTITIES, NONDIVISIONS, DIVISIONS, FISSIONS, AND FUSIONS.

There persisted, even among The Transcendentals, great controversy regarding whether or not there exists one true religion, two true religions, three true religions, four or more true religions, no true religion, each religion as true in its own way, and/or whatever else regarding how false each religion might be versus how true each religion might be. Even amid wielding their godlike powers, sometimes in concert and at other times in conflict, they would have to repeatedly face the fact that they simply did not know for sure what to make of The Primordial Ultimate Divinity and the relationship between THAT and the rest of reality. Nevertheless, many of them did, in fact, remember at least a trace of having been there for THE CREATION OF REALITY ITSELF, including the great fission that had resulted in their individuation. Some wondered if super-resonance of consciousness between enormous masses of intelligent beings was a primary cause of the rare instances of The Primordial Divinity materializing into observability, with a temporary fusion of the most divine presences within each being teaming up to make this happen. Another question involved whether being able to turn The Wheel of Oblivion against a given universe's God Manifestation might prove a method of obliterating such a given universe. Many shuddered to think that this just might be a possibility. Not Charr

Naerroan, though, even prior to when he founded the prehistoric religion Igweolintu he had aimed toward making such a case of The Wheel of Oblivion going to war with The God Of A Given Universe into a reality, and to then do his utmost to either influence The God Of A Given Universe to surrender and then become executed by The Wheel of Oblivion or to cause a scenario in which The Local Creator And Prime Preserver Of A Universe would become overwhelmed by superior firepower from The Wheel of Oblivion, resulting also in The Wheel of Oblivion executing The God Of A Given Universe.

Entity versus entity, world versus world, universe versus universe, death after death after death, round after round of destruction, huge escalations of violence and annihilation: contemplating such patterns and then making such patterns actually happen was quintessential to energizing the most-destruction-oriented of The Transcendentals.

Preserving lives, preserving worlds, preserving universes, helping beings to live healthy, prosperous, enjoyable, satisfying, caring, wise, dutiful, honorable lives, as perceived by the vast majority of normal notions of conscience: contemplating such patterns and then making such patterns actually happen was quintessential to energizing the most-preservation-oriented of The Transcendentals.

****

Although Elbankovic and Naerroan were not completely certain of it, they both had to seriously consider the possibility of a given popular religious doctrine later proving to be THE REALITY behind the veil of what they, even amid their extraordinary capabilities, knew about reality. Sometimes they would wonder whether one or both of them might be among the risen angels described by some models of Christian reality. Other times they would wonder whether one or both of them might be among the fallen angels described by some models of Christian reality. Similar lines of conjecture involved them exploring how their transcendent, exceptional powers of mind and soul might relate to if any of the other many religions might turn out to be true.

Each Transcendental often perceived great uncertainty about how many different personal timelines included different variations of themselves. Also, both the Dimetrio Elbankovic who served as one of the producers of this documentary and the Charr Naerroan who served as one of the producers of this documentary have actually met multiple variations of themselves, believe it or not.

****

That a few entities could in some cases suddenly remember back to the times of their previous lives and deaths, might seem utterly unsurprising.

Yes, unsurprising, that is, if this documentary is entirely or almost entirely true, actual, and factual. Do your own research, evaluate your own experiences, do some of your own thinking, and lean on THAT WHICH IS BEYOND the horizon of your knowledge and yet at least intangibly accessible to the intuitions of your heart and mind and soul, regarding how much of an entertainment-based fiction this documentary might be, in the format of a mockumentary, and how much of a totally-real, fact-based nonfiction this documentary might be, in the format of a true, straightforward documentary.

****

Transcendentals have experienced and, in many cases, instigated much of the paranormal and supernatural activity that has perplexed the masses, whether via ordinary-world beings' direct experiences or via ordinary-world beings' hearing the retelling of and seeing the reenactments of incredible stories.

However, even after all of this, virtually none of them knew for sure what the ultimate answers to the questions of metaphysics and ethics might happen to be.

What many of them did know, however, was that they did not feel ready to bury the hatchets of their old-time rivalries and bitter feuds.

Many then-living dinosaurs, proto-birds, birds, ocean-dwellers, insects, and arachnids, and other organisms of the Mesozoic, much like earthlings from the later portions of the Paleozoic, found themselves under the watchful observation and telepathic influence of Zircon Gilroy, Dimetrio Elba, and other beings of the beyond (who sometimes cooperated and sometimes competed against one other).

Deep underwater, on December 26th, 85,100,081 BCE, a five-year-old naga and a twenty-seven-year-old naga listened as several thirty-something-year-old nagas discussed the secret history of humans and posited hypotheses thereof:

Thirty-five-year-old William Encausse said, "Here's a vision of what I believe just might have happened long ago on the surface of our planet: The Ultimate Creator Deity bestowed upon earth nearly-infinite potential to support life. Then He transcended unity of being by differentiating portions of his essence into multiple male, female, and neutral-gender beings. After that, multiple cycles of transitions from unity to multiplicity and back to unity again unfolded. And here we are today."

Thirty-seven-year-old Alexander Einstein responded, "I am somewhat skeptical of that vision. Here's an alternate hypothesis: The Ultimate Creator somehow generated multiple universes, then, within this universe, set the stage for the possibility of human life and other intelligent life on many different planets within many different galaxies. Then She or He or It chose to sit back, with many very rigid ground-rules in place, and let things unfold, only intervening in the most extreme of circumstances. Human life, other than the small percentage of extraterrestrial visitors who are human, has not yet developed on this planet, but it might someday flourish."

William said, "Maybe these two visions are mutually exclusive, and maybe they're not, yet, either way, what about The Rods of God?"

Alexander's voice then exuded awe and wonder as he said, "Yes, sometimes… I remember them more vividly… Before I say much more about them, please retell some highlights of your encounters with them."

****

Across multiple universes, there were some in which a Mount Rainier in what would later become the Northwestern United States would not emerge until about 500,000 years before the human industrial revolution, others in which two Mount Rainiers would emerge—an earlier one in the Great Smoky Mountains, yet which would fade from separate labeling by that name by the time of the emergence of human beings, and a later one in what would become the Northwestern United States, and yet others still in which beings of dozens of millions of years before the emergence of humans would, nevertheless, repeatedly find themselves teleporting to the later-emergent Mount Rainier and wind up calling it that.

The following storyline will proceed in a unified manner at first, then splinter into three different versions. Please note that in some of the timelines "Mount Kilamanjaro" referred to a completely different mountain than what humans would later call that, and in other time-lines, geology took very different paths, in which the famous Mount Kilamanjaro which had reached a geological age of about two million years by the days of the General Geoge Washington who would pro-ceed to become the first American President, somehow emerged over a hundred million years earlier.

****

William enlightened the crowd via interwoven glimpses. "About three years ago, I was flying over Mount Kilamanjaro when I decided to go to higher altitude. Going higher and higher, I reached portions of the upper stratosphere. *Then they went flying by at about Mach 17.*

"They looked like giant cylinders, ranging from 24 meters to 500 meters in length."

****

Next, consider the splintering of that storyline into three different versions.

****

First, an ambiguous version:

William proceeded to say, "Another time, I flew over Mount Rainier, and Good God YHVH, What the hell happened next?!

"I looked across the clouds and again saw Great Mount Rainier poking through the clouds with its summit looking like a rocky island in a sea of cloud-work. I had a flashback to an old news report conversation in which someone told another about those Rods of God. Although I did not see any of those Rods that time near that towering peak, I decided to take a five-month sabbatical from dwelling above the surface of the seas.

"After the sabbatical, I silently thought to myself, 'Where shouldst methinketh shouldst be the venue for my next flight?' Thence, removing myself from the relative safety of the seas, I chose to go straight from the ocean to the sky, and took off like a just launched submarine-based intercontinental ballistic missile.

"Flying a variety of ambivalent, inhospitable, and hospitable sky-ways here, there, and yonder, I found myself over Antarctica. What do you know, would you even believe it? About twenty-five of those rods went zooming by so fast that I have no idea whether they were going at Mach 27 or Mach 227!!"

There came the thunderous underwater equivalent of revelatory applause.

Alexander then returned to speaking. "Thank you for that rather stupendous storytelling! I'll add this about my experiences with those rods. *I'm in serious doubt about every theory we have about who or what they are and who or what causes them to arrive and move the way that they do.* Are they super-animals? Are they extreme aircraft? Are they spacecraft? Are they directly from the divine?

"Whichever the truth might be about the answers to these questions, I know I've seen them flying in the stratosphere at speeds that defy virtually all normal logic. I can corroborate William's description that they sometimes appear, as measured by radar, to travel multiple times the basic Mach 5 or thereabouts needed to reach hypersonic speed."

****

Second, a version consistent with the progression with two different Mount Rainiers emerging, an earlier one in Appalachia and a later one near the Pacific Coast of North America:

He continued, "Another time, I flew over the Mount Rainier section of The Great Smoky Mountains, not to be confused with the prophesized coming of the Mount Ranier that per prophets will emerge far west of Appalachia, near the West Coast of what will be called North America. I was flying over Appalachia. There, in the skies over part of the Smoky Mountains of Appalachia.

"Lord Adibuddha, Good God YHVH, What the hell happened next?!

"I looked across the clouds and again saw Great Smoky Mount Rainier poking through the clouds with its summit looking like a rocky island in a sea of cloud-work. I had a flashback to an old news report conversation in which someone told another about those Rods of God. Although I did not see any of those Rods that time near that towering peak, I decided to take a five-month sabbatical from dwelling above the surface of the seas.

"Post-sabbatical, I thought to myself, 'Where shouldst methinketh shouldst be the venue for my next flight?' Thence, removing myself from the relative safety of the seas, I chose to go straight from the ocean to the sky, and took off like a just launched submarine-based intercontinental ballistic missile.

"Flying around ambivalent, inhospitable, and hospitable skyways here, there, and yonder, I found myself over Antarctica. What do you know, would you even believe it? About twenty-five of those rods went zooming by so fast that I have no idea whether they were going at Mach 27 or Mach 227!!"

There came the thunderous underwater equivalent of revelatory applause.

Alexander then returned to speaking. "Thank you for that rather stupendous storytelling! I'll add this about my experiences with those rods. *I'm in serious doubt about every theory we have about who or what they are and who or what causes them to arrive and move the way that they do.* Are they super-animals? Are they extreme aircraft? Are they spacecraft? Are they directly from the divine?

"Whichever the truth might be about the answers to these quest-ions, I know I've seen them flying in the stratosphere at speeds that defy virtually all normal logic. I can corroborate William's descript-tion that they sometimes appear, as measured by radar, to travel multiple times the basic Mach 5 or thereabouts needed to reach hypersonic speed."

****

Third, consider a very alternative and rather augmented variation:

William proceeded to say, "There have been and probably will be several different Mount Rainiers, each in a different location. Each shares a feature of popping way up in elevation compared to anything within a huge radius of itself. Some emerged long ago, others have yet to emerge. Plus, as a few of you have also done, I have sometimes experienced what seemed indisputable evidence of having unintentionally traveled into either the future or the past and then wandered my way back to our time period, somehow arriving with reasonable social continuity each time.

"On one of those occasions, yet I remember not exactly which Mount Rainier it was I flew over, yes, there was another time, a time when I flew over Mount Rainier, one of the Mount Rainiers, anyway, and Good Lord Adibuddha Vajradhara, Good God YHVH, Great Lord, Good Lord Whatever Thou May Calleth Thyself, What the hell happened next?!

"I saw a great mountain poking through the clouds with its summit looking like a rocky island in a sea of cloud-work. This inspired intense curiosity yet again. Suddenly, I had a flashback to an old news report conversation in which someone told another about those Rods of God. Although I did not see any of those Rods that time near that towering peak, I decided to take a five-month sabbatical from dwelling above the surface of the seas.

"During the extra time beneath the surface, I contemplated all sentient beings, all religious legends that I had heard of, and all of my own ideas and experiences, as well as much of what others had told me of their ideas and their experiences.

"After the long sabbatical, I thought, 'Where shouldst methinketh shouldst be the venue for my next flight?' Thence, removing myself from the seas, I chose to go straight from the ocean to the sky, and took off quickly.

"Flying the ambivalent, inhospitable, and hospitable skyways here, there, and elsewhere, I found myself over Antarctica. What do you know, would you even believe it? About twenty-five of those rods went zooming by so fast that I have no idea whether they were going at Mach 27 or Mach 227!!"

There came the underwater equivalent of great applause.

Alexander returned to his role in the public speaking at that gathering, "Thank you for that rather stupendous storytelling! I'll add this about my experiences with those rods. *I'm in serious doubt about every theory we have about who or what they are and who or what causes them to arrive and move the way that they do.* Are they super-animals? Are they extreme aircraft? Are they spacecraft? Are they directly from the divine?

"Whichever the truth might be about the answers to these questions, I know I've seen them flying in the stratosphere at speeds that defy virtually all normal logic. I can corroborate William's description that they sometimes appear, as measured by radar, to travel multiple times the basic Mach 5 or thereabouts needed to reach hypersonic speed. Gazing into a crystal ball late at night with several mammals and a few lizards one day, I perceived several futures in which humans fly what they call the X-15, what they call the X-49, and other flying devices at hypersonic speeds."

****

The aforementioned set of multiple realities, described in accordance with how they occurred across a great many timelines spanning multiple universes could make extra sense to some of the beholders in relationship with the Kletetschka-Ouspenskian multidimensional time physics, in which there can be three or more dimensions of time to go with three or more dimensions of space as part of six or more dimensions of physics. In several ways, this takes the Einstein-Lorentz, four-dimensional space-time-continuum reference-frame physics and related theories and expands upon them.

Some might relate that to eleven or more dimensions in connection with this or that or another version of higher-dimensional physics, whether featuring higher-dimensional strings and/or whatever else.

****

****

Next, consider Part I of a set of flashbacks and tangents to nearly 66 million earth-sun orbits before the Human Industrial Revolution:

In the year 65,895,250 BC, the ghosts and other spiritually-beyond transitional beings of the dimetrodons and other organisms of the pre-Triassic periods of the Earth witnessed as, in the twinkling of an eye, millions of dinosaurs and mammals and other living earthlings achieved super-powerful telepathic attunement with them. Most of this was at a semiconscious level for the living, and most of this was at a conscious level for the dead and semi-dead. Interspecies telepathy among dinosaurs soon ramped up exponentially.

This became especially noticeable on the areas in and near what the humans would later call The Yucatan Peninsula. It was there that a large omnivorous bipedal dinosaur, with a brain small in physical stature compared to the higher-dimensional capabilities it possessed, experienced a revelation. That being was a somewhat hermaphroditic dinosaur, about 68% male and about 32% female. As conventional for some dinosaurs of that time, it did not choose to conceive of itself as having a name, rather it conceived of itself in a manner of, "I am what I am, it is what it is, and ideas like 'I' and 'it' have their own ways of transcending. The energies of presence can be self-evident of who we are, without overt over-structuring."

It gathered with a group of dinosaurs, proto-birds, birds, mammals, and reptiles, who sensed its awesome presence of mind. Welcomed and telepathically invited by the others, it went into an extended telepathic story supplemented with intermittent gestures and vocals.

Many of the living, multitudes of the dead, and flocks of semi-dead gathered to listen closely as that hermaphroditic dinosaur presented a fable or a theory.

That sentient being proceeded to state, "We live in something called a universe. This universe is one of many, or perhaps infinitely-analog-style sliding ranges of universes. We can transition from one universe to another, and perhaps many of us do this from time to time, whether we are consciously aware of it or not.

"Although I do not know for sure whether the following is just exactly how we've arrived where we are, nevertheless, I shall present a vision I've had as a hypothesis for the history of our universe from its inception to the present.

"Within a fabric of ambiguous spatiotemporal relations, five primordial beings spontaneously arose from sheer nothingness. They soon induced an intense explosion in which nothingness-&-potential became everythingness-&-all-potentials. Boom!!

"This eventually led to this place we live on, a giant place within many much larger places, themselves within a vastness beyond all conceivability. Long ago, the large orbiter of reflective light, which some have called 'the moon,' orbited a realm in which the first intelligent being was born.

"The first being was a bird, which the transcendental primordial five beings (who were and are 'super-intelligent beings' rather than merely 'intelligent beings') induced into becoming alive by charming an inanimate stone into becoming animate.

"That stone was somewhere on this planet that we now live on, long before a collision between Proto-Earth and Proto-Moon resulted in Earth and Moon and many changes. That stone hatched from being a stone to being the first bird. Therefore, if we consider the animated stone to qualify as an egg, then the first bird egg came before the first bird; whereas if we consider the animated stone to have been something other than an egg, then the first bird came before the first bird egg.

"That bird became capable of laying a living egg after the electromagnetics of the suddenly-conscious planet, which in that instance chose to act as a male planet, though it more usually acts as a female planet.

"The first bird, an intelligent-though-not-yet-super-intelligent be-ing, a few years after its hatching from an animate stone, became impregnated by the Earth, during an instance in which that planet we live on chose to act as a male for a while. The bird subsequently laid an egg, which hatched into a male bird. After the first bird cared for that male second bird sufficiently, the Earth chose to act as a female for a while.

"The planet then engaged in telepathic and psychokinetic sex with the second bird, and the result of this act of transcendental mating was that the Earth was ready to have many independent instances of inanimate matter transitioning directly into animate biological beings of spatiotemporal, conscious, semiconscious, and subcon-scious energetic statics and dynamics. And Earth, for millions of years, proceeded to generate much life in a feminine mode.

"However, Earth on rare occasions chose to switch to generating life in a masculine mode again. Meanwhile, the extremely-primordial ultra-super-intelligence or ultra-super-intelligences who had already been in existence prior to even the five primordial super-intelligences chose to intervene. He and/or She and/or It and/or They suddenly chose to spontaneously generate the first bipedal two-armed humanoids.

"Yes, I am aware that many of those gathered here today are skeptical that the legendary alleged-to-exist humanoids have ever existed here or anywhere else. We hear such strange stories of the humanoids who sometimes arrive on spaceships, telepathically telling some of us tales of planets and solar systems located in the heavens, and we wonder the dinosaurs and others who speak of encountering them are making this stuff up, yet in this hypothetical vision, at least some of them were around prior to the super-collision between Proto-Earth and Proto-Moon. Life started to flourish. It's a matter of semantics whether we identify Proto-Earth with being an early stage of Earth or something not quite qualifying yet as early Earth, by the way.

"The humanoids also referred to themselves as 'people.' They had a seemingly supernatural way of manipulating most other living, biological, sentient beings of the planet.

"Over time, the peoples and animals and plants developed profound symbiosis. However, some prior version of a being who was in some ways what became me and who in some ways was not at all what became me, a being I sense was a powerful male humanoid, foretold that all humanoids and most non-humanoid sentient beings of the planet would vanish in the flash of an eye just before a planetary total or nearly total extinction event. Soon thereafter, Earth and Moon collided, and although life did not go totally extinct, it was almost total extinction for life there. That resulted in the New Earth and the New Moon. Alternatively, we could say that Proto-Earth and Proto-Moon collided, resulting in Earth and Moon.

"A similar cycle repeated some untold number of times as divine punishment for the inhabitants having gone too far astray. Each time, *The Powers That Be* chose to *manipulate* the fabrics of *All Realities* to make scientific evidence lead humans of a future cycle *lull themselves and others* into *thinking that no such cycles had ever happened* before. *Yet, happen before they did.*

"Eventually, a class of beings that some humans refer to as dim-etrodons, kind of esembling what spinosaurs transformed into quad-rupeds might look like, did something about this weird cycle of death. Through their development of embedding eleventh-gen-eration wireless means of telecommunication into their very bio-logical systems, they achieved sufficient power to stand toe-to-toe in battle with The Powers That Be, just enough to break our planet free from the earth-moon-collision repetitive death trap. This came at a great cost, though, as within our timeline, the dimetrodons went nearly extinct about 206 million years ago, then went totally extinct relative to worldly life 180 million years ago. That being said, many of the dimetrodons achieved advanced soteriological methodologies prior to their worldly deaths, with which their consciousnesses are in our very presence today as among the transcendental and semi-transcendental retinue of the great beyond.

"I do not know for sure, but I sense that we may be about to go extinct. Whether or not that happens soon, take heed, if we can tap into the cosmic consciousness of the dimetrodons and the primordial beings, we may have hope for something of the beyond."

This speech received celebratory telepathic applause, together with visible and audible foot stomping and jumping for joy. In the distance, looking up to the heavens, though, they soon saw it rapidly approaching in the upper atmosphere.

An asteroid hit Earth in the very region of that gathering, generating a Richter-13-magnitude earthquake, gargantuan quantities of particles that would blot out sunlight, and other mass-extinction-inducing consequences.

....　..........　********　..................

....　********　...
Part II of select flashbacks and tangents to 65,000,000-something earth-sun orbits prior to the Human Industrial Revolution:

The 68%-male/32%-female dinosaur who completed an ode to speculative cosmology, together with all of its entourage, died instantly when the KpG asteroid hit Earth in the very area in which they had been reveling. For about 2,000 years, "they" were in many respects totally gone from all of reality, neither of consciousness nor of any definite physical presence or extensionality of this or any other realm.

After those years had gone by, about 5% of them re-manifested in the great beyond in the very presence of the transcendent beings Dimetrio Elba and Zircon Gilroy, who had by that time resolved their over-200-million-year feud. Remember that their dispute with each other started long before either had passed on from the state of the living, and that it was one of the main drivers of the dozens upon dozens of millions of years of what some would call the synapsids-versus-reptiles holy war.

With the uber-catastrophic celestial impact event and all that went with it, the reptiles and synapsids of *both* the here-and-now *and* the beyond had set aside their clingings to real or perceived grievances against each other, and the holy war gave way to a long period of holy peace.

Zircon and Elba chose to speak with the 68%M/32%F visionary while in an assembly of spirits, transcendental beings, and others. Zircon said, "Although you currently consider yourself to be nameless and transcending gender, it would be more convenient at this time for us to grant some way of categorizing you, at least for some forms of conceptualization. Of course, as with your inner thoughts, in many ways you are who and what you are, beyond the limits of conceptual over-structuralism, even as we grant you what we will.

"My name is Zircon, and, as you have probably surmised by now, with my arguably-rather-ostentatious demonstration of shape-shifting while speaking, I am a shape-shifter. That being said, at some core levels of identity, I am a highly-advanced reptile, which means in some ways I am a closer relative to you than the synapsids, though in other ways the synapsids are closer relatives to you. I shall now hand center stage speaking over to Doctor Elba."

Dimetrio Elba, whom various beings of the beyond had granted the title "Doctor," started to speak, amidst an assembly that had grown essentially absolute in its silence and attentiveness. "I am Dr. Dimetrio Elba, and I was a dimetrodon prior to my death and transition into the bardo realm. Rather than reincarnating or becoming a strength-challenged hungry ghost, I transitioned with my memory intact into some quasi-transcendental states of being. Similarly, my friend Zircon, who for over 200 million years had been an enemy of mine, and, at the times of our worldly deaths we had still been in a relationship of enmity; he transitioned from being a shapeshifting reptile of indeterminate species into also becoming a memory-intact quasi-transcendental being. Each of us often held high ranks on the respective sides of epic warfare, often telepathically using unsuspecting living dinosaurs, birds, and insects as unknowingly-manipulated proxy warriors.

"As you made your grand speech just before dying, there was much in it that we knew to be true, much that we knew to be false yet indirectly-truthful if taken as a fable, and much of it that was fundamentally unknown to us with respect to how-true-or-how-false. You've been somewhere in the deep beyond, we know not exactly where or how, but you've suddenly appeared a little while ago with us in the beyond. For quite a while, in anticipation that this day might come, Zircon and I debated whether to grant you a name, and if so, then what. We eventually negotiated our way into an agreement."

Elba then looked Zircon in the eye and nodded. The both of them then looked over at the 68%M/32%F visionary and said in unison, "We christen you 'Christopher Morphy Exiguus,' and we declare you, for general purposes, to be considered a male."

Christopher Exiguus stood silently for a few seconds, then replied, "I respect what has transpired here today. Thank you for granting these alternate conceptualizations and communication devices to me."

Elba & Zircon said, almost-though-not-entirely-in-unison, "You're welcome."

Dimetrio Elba continued, "I believe it best now that three sisters and two brothers from the previous mass extinction event on Earth take turns chiming in with their hypotheses on the origins of the realities that led to our present reality. First up, Susannah Oberstein. Please enlighten us, s'il vous plaît."

Susannah chimed in, "Guten Tag! Although the full truth values and falsehood values of the following are largely unknown, here goes another theoretical vision on the origins of the realities.

"In the beginning all universes and multiverses already quasi-existed within a quantum uncertainty probability wave of potential. That was within the fabric of absolute nothingness, yet this was not a stable way for things to permanently remain. The potentialities gave way to actualities. Ever since, beings have come and gone, incarnated and refrained from incarnating, reincarnated and refrained from reincarnating, and changed in almost limitless ways.

"Here we are now, but each of us were also, at least a trace of us, there... way back there... at the dawn of creation itself." She looked to Elba and nodded.

Elba spoke thusly, "Next, a dialogue between Pandora Brooks and Pandara Smithsonian."

Brooks gently whispered, "Time." Few noticed as she did that.

She then spoke in a normal voice. "I am one of the beings of the name Pandora. The being currently immediately to my left is one of the beings of the name Pandara. Her surname is Smithsonian, and my surname is Brooks. I hypothesize that Christopher Exiguus was correct when he, prior to departing normal life to enter the great beyond and before receiving his name, hypothesized that eons earlier a huge amount of that which is him had manifested as a powerful humanoid. What do you think of this, Smithsonian?"

Pandara Smithsonian answered, "I am rather skeptical of that hypothesis. It may be difficult or impossible to ascertain whether it is true, and the overall pattern strikes me as rather far-fetched. However, let's turn our attention, if we may, to what I found most shocking about the mysterious speech that preceded the catastrophe.

"He, who back then was considered one of the many Its-With-No-Name, theorized that there have been many cycles in which Earth-or-Proto-Earth collides with Moon-or-Proto-Moon, resulting in New-Earth-or-Earth and New-Moon-or-Moon. Even more bizarre, his theory claimed that 'The Powers That Be' would somehow manipulate *all* of the space and time to lull the eventually-reemerging human scientists into thinking it was the first time around for the humans. Then those Powers would sit back and watch whether humanity and the other earthlings would screw things up royally all over again, judge in the affirmative, manipulate the Moon out of orbit to have it collide with Earth, generate a tragic impact of unspeakable proportions, wipe out all or nearly all life on Earth, then set up a new cycle. Reading between the lines, part of that would involve having the evidence of past advanced civilizations, *or perhaps nearly all the evidence of past advanced civilizations*, vanish into thin air (or some similar process of concealment). These make my mind spin with bewilderment!! Sister Brooks, what do you think?"

Brooks delved into the issues somewhat differently, "What about it? It seems very plausible to me. Dimetrodon, edaphosaurian, reptilian, and human legends often concur with each other on the notion of a grand cosmic cycle, in which the more-temporal-and-less-trans-cendent beings do what they do, sometimes for better, sometimes for the worse, then face the judgment of The Absolute. Although they disagree on many points, the big picture tends to look very much that way. It seems entirely possible that The Absolute might, via all intermediaries, instigate one of the mechanisms of a series of judgment days to include the Moon colliding into the Earth.

Now, letting go of those esoteric depths of antiquity, and returning focus to the here and now, Earth is currently in a mass extinction event that started 2,000 years ago with that Yucatan impact. That marked the approximate end of the Cretaceous period, and it could be an example of how The Powers That Be don't have to go to the utter extremity of causing an Earth-Moon collision to deliver mass casualties."

Smithsonian and Brooks looked at each other and the rest of assembly in silence. After a little while, Zircon spoke up. "Next, let's have the male druid humanoid Abram Cadavarious materialize before us and speak, if he dares to do so. If not, then we'll turn to a backup speaker.

"Mr. Cadavarious, whether you are currently primarily a Christian, a Hindu, a Buddhist, a Druid, a Muslim, a Zoroastrian, or something else, and whatever dimensions you currently reside in, we humbly request that you find the higher-dimensional space-time to let your presence be known.

Abram Cadavarious indeed immediately materialized before them, teleporting from somewhere unknown to the assembly. "Here I am. Yours truly just arrived from an alternate universe. Earthlings there found themselves at the beginning of what many of their people call 2019 Hurricane Season. The meteorological authorities there, in their infinite wisdom, chose to name the upcoming fourth storm of the

Atlantic Hurricane Season 'Dorian.' It seems perfect that you called on me over, because I was already thinking of coming here, whether invited or not. While I was mulling that possibility, your gathering all of a sudden invited me, and I felt it. Already a being of the beyond, your calling me and my thinking combined to instantly teleport me here via the higher-dimensional reality of the many dimensions and the many intertwined universes.

"That universe I came from also had a cataclysmic impact about 65 million or 66 million years before the so-called common era. That huge impact also resulted in mass extinction. That being said, let's consider the really big picture view: the humans of that universe in which Hurricane Dorian was in the news might be one in which the Earth is on the brink of instigating a new mass extinction. A Martian microbe that teleported itself into their world is merely one of the many myriads of instruments of death that their planet will have to contend with.

"The microbe I spoke of is something of a master microbe, and it's capable of subtly and remotely influencing other biological agents into generating pandemics.

"Another agent of death there is their proclivity to alter their natural environment, whether by carbon emissions, by nuclear bombs, or by whatever else. Their ability to manipulate their environment had served them well for a while, but it has ventured into treacherous territories. Too many greenhouse gases, too many thermonuclear detonations, etc. Perhaps even more central to their peril is their rampant tribalism."

"Their karma invited into their world an armada of annihilations. Some by 2019 inevitable for 2020-2029, others uncertain for whether to arrive between 2022 and 2088, later, or never.

"I do not know who has the more brutal path forward, you or them.

"I do know that in some future scenarios, your very universe could lead to either exactly their universe or something extremely similar. Best wishes with choosing wisely.

"How do you believe I could best assist you?"

Dr. Elba answered, "I believe you have already helped immensely with the insights that you have just provided. The next way you could help best, I believe, would be to stay a while longer, listen to the next speaker, then decide what *you* believe best *after* receiving that *additional* information. Are you ready?"

Mr. Cadavarious said, "Yes. Let's go for it!"

Next came from Dr. Elba the utterance, "I turn the floor over to one of *my* primary *trainers* from the days of my youth, a dimetrodon who was wise and powerful *long* before I started to approach his stature. Without further ado, here's Enochus Gilroy Rubicon Geddinger."

Enochus Geddinger began yet another phase of this meeting by saying, "Mr. Cadavarious and I rarely share physical presence at a venue. This is ultra-rare occurrence of the element Technetium."

"7, 10, 20, 18, 75, 38, 27, 48, 45, 87.

"In accordance with prophecy, that K-Pg asteroid impact happened.

"If I understand the next part of the prophecies and how they relate properly, the mammals will rise in stature and evolve greatly. This includes that one day human beings, a special class of humanoids, will be prolific wielders of advanced mechanical technologies."

Cadavarious' speech went on for a while longer, and, after that prolonged monologue, the remainder of their gathering featured several twists that affected the futures of many universes.

Twenty-five worlds away, on a planet in an ancient solar system, a species of intelligent extraterrestrials who neither resembled the gray aliens nor resembled the humans went about their busy lives. Eight of them suddenly, remotely went into the same daydream: They did experience visions and imagined sounds involving highly charged controversies between people espousing ideas that emanated from a diverse, human, public figures, with and expressing radically contrasting notions of right and wrong. They next imagined visions and sounds involving Steven Spielberg, Mel Brooks, The 14th Dalai Lama, Pope John Paul II, Isaac Hayes, Max Isaac Dimont, Brian Ruhe, Ananda Maitreya, Clint Eastwood, and others offer differing views on the causes of atrocities. "The raptor people" residing there had abandoned their home star system circa 65 Million B.C.E. as part of fleeing horrors that Charr Naerroan had unleashed. To most of them, all humans, whether Jews, Gentiles, Aborigines, Black people, Asian people, White people, etc. were fiction. In some universal timelines, a human astroarchaeologist would discover an Igweolintian artifact on the raptor people's home planet in 3072 C.E., triggering Charr's return to that planet, which humans proceeded to call New Gwalintu.

***** ***** ***** ***** *****

Consider now an alternative set of perspectives on how and why The Dorian Invasion happened, and some of what happened in its wake:

"How dare you tell me that I should not go on that journey to the big divine orgy party?

"The Mycenaeans invited Dorians, Hebrews, Remians, Teutons, and many others to join in a festival of both sensuality and spirituality! They said they will finally be revealing to outsiders many of their long-kept secrets, for the good of all mankind!" exclaimed Petrus Onassis to his girlfriend Pattyla Heraclisseus.

Pattyla warned, "Petrus, my dear, if I had a good feeling about this whole affair, I would say, 'My love, I totally agree with you fervently, let's both go! I would love for us to try out many different partners in a swingers' jamboree combined with learning many religious secrets! Let's go, then after we've tried this out for a while and returned safely to our Dorian homeland, we'll find out if our relationship is strong enough to withstand such a wild three-week party. Let's do this!!' This just isn't the case, though!! You see, not only am I not all-in on this adventure, I've got a strong feeling that this is not going to end well for anyone."

Petrus retorted, "Oh come on! Love is how we expand our horizons. Fear is the way we attract negativity… I believe you should trust this process more!"

Pattyla already saw this coming. "Look, if you think less with your dick and more with your brain, you'll recognize that there is great value in both loving-openness toward all and stern gravity toward very real dangers and risks.

"Sure, we might not always know all that well when to do what with whom, what to do, etc., but we should listen to our feelings and often trust our intuitions." She continued on for a while, then paused for a moment to think of an apt comparison or two.

After thinking up what comparisons might help with convincing her boyfriend, she announced them to him: "If we go to that event, or if you go to that event without me, either way, this is going to be like volunteering to swim with sharks and barracuda and extraterrestrials while skinny dipping. Or maybe that's not the best analogy. How about this one: Someone's built a large straw house next to a large wooden lodge. Then a bunch of folks are invited to a séance to be held there, bringing their own candles. So you have lots of people carrying candles and some even carrying full-blown torches into highly-flammable buildings.

"What could possibly go wrong?!" she said, smirking with sarcasm.

She was left-handed, whereas Petrus was right-handed.

They remembered well that the first time they escalated a date with each other into foreplay, it led to how they consented to take things further and further. That same night would go on to feature the first time they ever made love to each other. Several times before, during, and after the act, they affectionately intertwined the digits of Petrus' left hand with the digits of Pattyla's right hand, with her right thumb placed between his thumb and index finger, with his left middle finger placed between her index finger and middle finger, etc. Their intertwining of their nondominant hands physically clothed how their spirits were amplifying their ways of caring for each other. They physically shared their vulnerabilities in this way, paralleling ways of the weaknesses of each caring for the weaknesses of the other.

They proved time and time again that they truly and deeply cared for one another. They were at a crossroads, their fate hung in the balance, and the female was confident that their partnership would only survive if she could convince the male to scale back their risk-taking.

There was a pause in the talking as they both gathered thoughts.

A flash of insight arrived in her mindstream that an unusual type of nonverbal maneuver just might serve as a catalyst for successful persuasion of her boyfriend to scale back what she considered to be his overblown "I want to live a life of danger" mentality.

She immediately bit down somewhat hard on the middle finger of her left hand, then released, revealing intentional slight imprints from her teeth.

"I love it when you do that!" Petrus said with a grin. "And that's part of why I believe that you should relent and not only give me a blessing to go there, but join me over there! Sure, we've had our thrills with each other, and so far so good, but I feel that we could do better with the consistency of pushing the envelope of pleasure and pain and thrills! You're a great gal, and I love you, but about three-fourths of the time, you're more inhibited than I want you to be!"

Pattyla shook her head slightly, then performed a half-nod. She then partially shook her head again before looking him right in the eyes and presenting a heartfelt message. "Yes, and about two-thirds of the time, I find you way too uninhibited!!

"You're a great guy, truth be told, fun to be with, and I love you, yet you're… often about one misstep away lately… from getting… destroyed. Maybe partway or totally destroyed between your legs or maybe getting destroyed between your ears, or maybe just plain totally killed, whether by a lover or a friend or a foe.

"It's one thing to be brave, but it's another to be so thrill-seeking that you play Russian roulette with your soul, your heart, your mind, and everything else you've got."

Petrus inquired, "What's Russian roulette?"

Pattyla answered, "Maybe you're the first person I've used that phrase with since learning it about six or seven years ago, at a time when I was a fourteen-year-old and Brenda was eighteen years old.

"On that day, seemingly eons ago, my sisters and I took a shortcut through a forest. We wandered and became confused, as our compasses started to go haywire.

"At some point, we stumbled upon a peculiar-looking elderly gentleman who spoke our language, though with only about 75% fluency. He offered a quid pro quo: for one dance with my sister Brenda, he would transport us to a wondrous place with technologies beyond our dreams for about half an hour, then transport us back to the outskirts of our home town of Suitsterbyeulis. Not only did Brenda dance with him, after a little while she and he seemed to fall madly in love, and they made passionate love, right there in front of me and my other sisters Karyellenyia and Suellena. In case you're wondering, no, I and the other two sisters did not make this into a ménage à trois or something even further.

"After the five of us walked to a stream and the two lovers bathed as the rest of us lightly freshened up, the gentleman said we should stand still, vey still. He picked up from his right-front pocket some sort of device and spoke in a foreign language. Soon a large mechanical bird with two sets of rotating bladed wings landed. The two men on board indicated that there was plenty of room for us to board, and board we did. We flew away in that rotating-bladed-winged flying creature. Such a strange creature! We went up into the sky and soon landed in a place that they called 'Vietnam." They said it was 'The Year Nineteen-Sixty-Eight,' whatever that might mean. My sisters and I got to hang out with some people with super-advanced technologies. I asked about the foreign language, and he said it was called 'American English.'

"Most of them did not speak our language, a few of them could communicate a few lines here and there, and just one of them, the weird guy who helped bring us there, a Sgt. Norman Petty, showed us a presentation of Russian roulette.

"There was this machine, it had reams of still-frame images on miniature things, all lined up. It ran through a thing with a lamp in it, and out from the lamp-thing with the spinning reams came a shin-ing light. That light shone upon a screen in the distance. They called the device 'a projector.' There we saw part of what those folks were calling 'a motion picture film.' In that film, we witnessed people sometimes speaking our language and more often than not, speaking other languages. During a brief intermission, I asked Norman what languages the people were speaking. He said, 'Mostly Russian, with a little Greek and Armenian mixed in.' I thanked him for filling us in on those details.

"At some stage of that film, two soldiers and three civilians, facing a grim situation, passed around a small, hand-held metal device. Each, in turn, would squeeze a lever with their right index finger while pointing the barrel of it at their head. Some pointed it toward their right temples, some pointed it into their mouths. Yet they did this one after another. Also, once in a while, one of them would spin a cylinder inside the metal device, randomizing something about how its contents would line up. After about five times of people doing this, it arrived in the hands of a female civilian who was among them.

"She aimed it at her chest with her left hand and pressed the lever with that hand's index finger. Again, nothing seemed to happen except a light clicking sound. The people in the film kept laughing and drinking and taking turns.

"Someone paused the film. Our main host, the elderly guy we met in the forest, finally revealed that the device is called a 'revolver' and its lever is called a 'trigger.' Someone resumed rolling the film.

"One of the men then pointed the revolver right at his groin and pulled the trigger.

"It did not seem to do anything. The group laughed uproariously, and the other three guys in the group started giving him high fives and congratulating him. The lady blushed. All of a sudden, two ladies who entered the scene and initiated foreplay with the guy who'd just finished taking his turn in that game.

"That guy handed the revolver to another guy, a man who was taking his third turn in this game. That other guy pointed the gun right at his own right temple with his right hand, then squeezed.

"We heard a loud bang. Oh God, the humanity, *that guy's head partially broke apart, and there was blood all over the place. The females in the film were screaming. The men were wailing.* The last person who pulled the trigger *lay motionless on the ground,* with *his head broken open and bleeding profusely.*

"The film soon ended. Norman let us know that this was a secret military training video, and that he had the authorization to show it to us because we were four women of unknown origins speaking a subdialect of Greek and wandering around a mysterious area of Cambodia not far from Angkor Wat, and that it would serve his intelligence gathering operation to *really get to know us better.* He asked what we knew about Russia, China, Vietnam, Laos, and Cambodia.

"We answered truthfully, attesting to the fact that we had no idea that those were even the names of places, though those names did sound familiar: Those place names sounded similar to the entity names of some of the transcendentals, many of whom we at times attempt to attune with via the chanting of mantras and the wielding of iron.

"Sergeant Norman Petty was taken aback at our answer. He decided he better record a brief interview with us on tape. He asked one question after another about how we met him, why we met him, what we knew about this, what we knew about that. The interview went on and on.

"At some stage, he asked what year we thought it was, what calendar we normally use, and other such questions about measuring time.

"At times he looked at his fellow soldiers in sheer disbelief, and they looked the same way right back toward him. On several occasions, quite literally, their jaws dropped.

"They clearly had super-advanced technology, but much of what we had to say seemed earth-shattering to them.

"When it was our turn to ask questions, at some point I asked Norman, 'What's the name of that very dangerous game that we saw those blokes playing with that thing you call a 'revolver?' He answered, 'Russian roulette.'

"I asked him to explain the word 'roulette.' He said, 'You really don't know, do you?' I said, 'Yes, I positively, totally clearly confirm that I do not know what roulette is. What is it?'

"He said something like, 'Imagine a gambling place. Some people there are gathered around a huge spinning wheel. Hmm… Better yet,

I'll see if you could stay a little while longer before we try to send you back from whence you came. Would that you be fine with that?'

"I said something like, 'Yes, I believe we can stay as long as it takes to appease the transcendentals, and for my sisters and me to have a good chance of going wherever we should go, whether that would be to 'from whence we came' or somewhere else entirely.'

"He said, 'You're priceless. I don't know if you're on an acid trip or what, but I've got the distinct feeling that you're the real deal, not tripping at all in terms of LSD or what-have-you, but literally time-traveling through our reality in an ultra-mysterious way.'

"Brenda, just looking at you, I can tell that you consent with staying a while longer. Well… What about you and you, Karyellenyia and Suellena?' Those remaining two took turns affirming their consent to stay a while longer.

"Sgt. Petty walked out of the room while two men stood guard silently. I looked at my sisters, and we had devious thoughts of possible attempts at seduction, yet felt that something about aggressive flirtation just didn't seem right for the situation. We did mildly flirt via the motions of our eyes and the ways we smiled at those guards. The two guards stood totally impassive, all business and no pleasure.

"When Sgt. Petty returned, we watched another video. 'Video' is another way to call motion picture films and other things that present motion video displays. That can be of stuff that actually happened or stuff that's an illusion of things that look like they happened, a very sophisticated legerdemain.

"He prefaced that next video by saying that it contained actual footage from a gambling casino. Soon we watched people gathered around a horizontally-oriented wheel that would spin while a small ball would bounce around. The ball would eventually settle into a slot with a specific number. Half of the numbered slots had black, and the other half had red.

"People would gain or lose small coin-like objects called chips, depending on what they wagered in comparison with what the wheel and ball resulted in. He explained that the game is called roulette and that it features a roulette wheel. He stopped the video.

"After that, he took out an empty revolver, something that he called a Colt '45. He demonstrated the way of spinning around the thing in it that could hold multiple instances of things he called bullets.

"There was a silent pause in the room for a while. Then he said, *'Earlier you saw actual footage of people playing Russian roulette. In a place called Russia,* people at some point *invented a game in which the participants* do something *similar to the casino game of roulette,* but instead of winning or losing chips, *they randomly set up whether they wind up killing themselves or not.'*"

There was silence between them for an extended amount of time. Pattyla could tell that Petrus had been listening closely and that several of his most heavily-relied-upon paradigms had either incinerated or disintegrated (if not permanently, then at least temp-orarily).

Petrus' cognition had largely turned to stone. Pattyla took him by the hand, looked him in the eyes, and initiated a slow, gentle kiss. His cognition snapped out of the semi-catatonic state, and he started to fully engage in the romance again. Soon, they escalated physicality further.

About an hour later they returned to speaking words at regular levels of audibility.

Petrus said, "You know what, I've changed my mind. I'll decline to go on the trip to that big spiritual-sexual extravaganza after all."

Pattyla said, "Great!"

Elsewhere, there were 65 other cases of men and women among the Dorians considering whether to go to that big shindig. 38 of them, consisting of 24 upper-middle-class-to-upper-class men and 14 women of similar social stature, chose to take that journey.

Meanwhile, the Hebrews and Remians who had considered going to the event eventually, without exception, chose to decline to go. In portions of Northern and Central Europe, 78 Teutons decided that they would go to the big spiritual-sexual festival. They consisted of 34 couples and ten singles.

The event started auspiciously enough, it would seem. However, as the Mycenaeans, Teutons, and Dorians shared many - though not all - of their secrets with one another, and many engaged in highly promiscuous and adventurous sex, things took a turn to the gruesome.

A wealthy Mycenaean benefactor host and his wife were involved with a swap of partners with a wealthy and influential Dorian couple. There was alcohol involved, and there were multiple religious and scientific methods involved. Both temporary couples suddenly found themselves quite literally stuck together during coitus, unable to get their flesh to slide back to normal life. At first they found this amusing - thrilling even - yet after a while they knew it might prove very harmful to their bodies. As the situation lingered, as extra pain and soreness set in, none of the four principal players consented to the traps that their bodies were involuntarily engaged in.

Both men and both women did just about everything within reason that they could to get the situation to work out. Witch doctors and other assistants were called in. Many people tried to help, but over the course of a five-and-a-half-hour ordeal for the female Dorian aristocrat swung into the embrace of the male Mycenaean aristocrat, the female Dorian suffered only moderate genital damage, fully healed in less than a week, whereas the male Mycenaean whose main male organ of urination and copulation had been trapped for so long suffered catastrophic connective-tissue damage and nearly died.

Only by what seemed a mysterious miracle was it able to suddenly heal shortly before he had been scheduled to undergo a penectomy.

He subsequently demanded an apology from the Dorian lady with whom he had just nine days earlier experienced some of the most exhilarating and terrifying moments in his life, and she absolutely refused.

She said to him, in person, "I truly believe that we did nothing wrong. The beings beyond our human control forced upon us a strange and unrelenting challenge. We survived it, some of our most priceless of organs have experienced injury and recovery, and life goes on. We should remember this with love, with neither apologies nor forgiveness necessary."

He said, "Even though your body was not doing what you intended, something about your heart and mind had something to do with why you body did what it did. And your deities might have been even more responsible for the problem than you were. You bear some responsibility for if your deities possess your body and dare to place such a high-level Mycenaean man into such excessive jeopardy."

She said, "Come on. If you're going to bring transcendentals into the picture, then why do you not consider that it's something to do both with your Mycenaean relations with them and my Dorian relations with them that caused what happened? We could blame both sides and argue all day, but if we trust and love the realities and reality, we really don't have to blame anyone for any of this. We can move on without casting blame."

He said, "You believe what you choose to believe at this time, but this could have major long-term repercussions."

She said, "You believe what you choose to believe at this time, but this most assuredly will lead to long-term repercussions."

They continued to argue for a while, yet they eventually agreed to, unless and until changing their minds again, discuss things further via representatives from a distance.

They hoped to be able to de-escalate the conflict.

The other temporary swinging couple were stuck for *eight straight hours*. The Dorian man and the Mycenaean woman were able, by the end of that, to relax their bodies enough to disengage, yet by then *both* had endured major bruising, many busted capillaries, etc.

Nothing quite as serious as what had happened to portions of the Mycenaean lady's husband's nerve-dense connective tissue, but still serious.

They resorted to various religious and scientific means with which to heal from the ordeal. However, in the aftermath, similar to what had happened between their normal partners (who had themselves, as you may recall, become temporary partners), the well-to-do Mycenaean lady demanded an apology from the well-to-do Dorian man, and the Dorian gentleman refused.

Portions of the conversation were as follows:

She said, "Although we've healed, something about your heart and mind and soul have to be to blame. I demand an apology!"

He said, "I believe no such apology is warranted, either from you to me or from me to you. We were engaged in a scientific and spiritual sexual adventure, we experienced wonders and terrors, and we survived in good health. Even if we had not recovered good health, *or even if one or both of us had died*, then I would *still* be inclined to believe that *no apologies or expressions of forgiveness would have been called for* in this situation. We consented to doing what we did, we accepted the risks to life and limb, and, yes, you and I *knew that we didn't know* exactly where it would all lead."

She said, "But you're *the man*! I'm *the woman*. In that kind of situation, it is supposed to be *your* responsibility to set up the situation right. It is *my* responsibility *after* you set up the situation right to do my best to manage to help things to *continue* to be right. I *believe* that *you* screwed up something or another in a way that *caused my muscles* to involuntarily *lock up* the way that they did. If you had done a better job as a man, then my body would not have involuntarily trapped you for such a long amount of time."

He said, "Come on! *I did everything in my power* to get the situation to go well in a mutually beneficial way. It's mysterious to the both of us why your muscles contracted and locked up the way that they did. *With the involuntary getting stuck situation, I don't believe either of us are really to blame* at all."

She said, "*What of the differences in our beliefs* regarding God and the gods? We call them deities, you call them transcendentals, we tend to pray to them, you tend to chant mantras with which to channel them, and our cultural differences go on and on. I demand an apology, since if you were more like us, then I think the ordeal would not have happened!"

He said, "*That's it, now you've done it!* I refuse to apologize, and furthermore, although I do not know the full extent to which you are attuned to The Ultimate Reality, I am confident in my people's attunement with The Ultimate Reality. My wife and I are going to depart early from this gathering to return to our homeland. Whether or not you and your husband can work things out peacefully with me and my wife, *I feel fine with whether or not this eventually leads to holy war between The Dorians and The Mycenaeans."*

She said, *"Did you just say what I thought I heard you say? Oh my God, I know that you just said what you said!* How shameless! *How dare you say such things!* We have a sophisticated and advanced culture. You have special religious techniques and such, but I *believe* that we Mycenaeans have solved about 99.9% of reality itself. We have a mostly peaceful, loving, and forgiving culture, yet when some more primitive and warlike peoples like yourselves start to fail to show proper deference to us in connection with our special advances in relationship with God, then we may start headintg down the road toward having to put them back in their place, as cultures not nearly as attuned to honoring the Ultimate God."

He responded, "Yes, *so you think* the Ultimate Level of Reality, the 'Ultimate God' as you phrased it, is someone or something that *you* are more closely attuned with than *we* are. *Quite frankly, I myself do not know at this time the full extent to which anyone is fully attuned with The Ultimate. What I do know is that my people, including myself, are very, very attuned with The Ultimate. We are prepared to live and die with honor. We are prepared for holy peace. We are prepared for holy war. Whether any Dorians, any Mycenaeans, both, or neither are still around by the time the dust settles on the consequences of our dispute, I feel fine about doing whatever I can to get this situation to honor all levels of truth about all levels of reality."*

Not long after that, the Dorian contingent of the gathering returned to their homeland. About half of the Teutonic contingent chose to go with the Dorians to visit them, whereas the other half chose to continue with the festivities hosted by the Mycenaeans.

After this incident, the few Mycenaeans living in Dorian-controlled territories found themselves mysteriously getting into more conflicts with their neighbors, merchants, supervisors, co-workers, and underlings. The same started to apply to Dorians living in Mycenaean-controlled territories. Things started to escalate. Differences of religious conceptualizations, social customs, and scientific developments amplified the escalating tensions.

After a while, an eerie calm suddenly set in. Things seemed to be getting better. Some debated: Is this the calm before the storm or a calm transitioning to long-term peace?

Alas, the controversial upper-class Mycenaean swinging couple, who had felt offended by the lack of any apologies from the upper-class Dorian swinging couple, sent out a diplomatic envoy and several assistants to visit and discuss things further. While there, three members of the visiting group, consisting of two women and one man, were taken on a tour of a holy building. It was a temple devoted to the Lord of Calendars.

Visiting Mycenaeans of the names Juanilias, Janietti, and Traliopi heard a Dorian high priest say to them, "It is of the utmost import-ance while here to be respectful toward the mysteries of the planets, the plants, the animals, and the humans, and, especially, all cycles and all anti-cycles. *Failure to do so in ordinary places can have terrible consequences. Failure to pay that respect here can be immediately lethal. Energies here ramp up to infinity and beyond and all the way to the absolute, or very, very, very, very, very-very close thereto.*

"See the metalwork, the woodwork, and the composite tablets? This place channels other dimensions and times.

"We as Dorians, *for reasons not entirely known to ourselves,* seem to regularly slip through gateways into other places, sometimes it seems very clearly in different centuries - and *occasionally even different millennia* - of alternate universes. Also, we have methods of chanting mantras and pressing upon and pushing around metal, including pumping iron, and these methods can make us stronger and more capable of interacting with the transcendentals. Bearing in mind that there are many things I am not at liberty to divulge unto you, do you have any questions?"

Janietti asked, "What about the differences of how we call on the special beings with the special super-zauber? You tend to call them, insofar as they might be beyond the regular realms, The Transcendentals. We tend to call them deities. The Teutons tend to call them gods. All of us, on at least some occasions, make reference to some ultimate version of the greatest of the great… as 'God.' What about this?"

The high priest answered, "There are many manners of semantics and many dangers of sematics…"

The meeting went on for quite a while, and, although there were some small verbal clashes, nothing became overly belligerent. All parties involved considered it a good experience. It proved to be an amicable meeting between the priest and the three visitors.

The visitors went on to meet with the high-class Dorian couple who had engaged with and subsequently disputed with a high-class Mycenaean couple during the aforementioned Dorian-Mycenaean-Teutonic extravaganza hosted by Mycenaeans. The two couples were able to work out their differences, and they restored being on good terms with each other without having to issue any apologies after all.

Peace between Mycenaeans and Dorians flourished much better than it ever had before.

Years went by.

****

However, on one of the most vital of the islands on Earth, specifically, on the island known as Crete, one day, three ships of extraterrestrials landed and interacted with several of the Dorians present and a huge multitude of the Mycenaeans present.

The extraterrestrials displayed technologies that would have made many Twenty-First Century C.E. human beings' heads spin. To the Dorians, Mycenaeans, and other humans who were present it was both spellbinding and breathtaking.

After the extraterrestrials flew back into the heavens aboard their starships, the people there negotiated who would take home which of the few artifacts the visitors had left behind. Although there were tough negotiations, they haggled their way through it peaceably.

The artifacts had strange effects on the minds of all who came within fifty-seven-and-a-half feet of them, over and over again. They stimulated human minds, sometimes amplifying clarity, sometimes amplifying insight, and other times doing other things to the psyches of people. Although no living humans knew it for sure as of then, the configurations of elements, isotopes, and structures were designed for super-advanced scientific purposes. There were twelve artifacts left behind: 1) a one-foot-tall nude male figurine; 2) a ten-inch-tall nude female figurine; 3) a 44-cm-long clothed anaconda figurine; 4) a 35-cm-long dimetrodon figurine, 5) a 27-cm-long edaphosaurus figurine; 6) a gold-plated five-foot-long-&-five-foot-wide-&-six-foot-tall model of Mount Sumeru, 7) a platinum-plated five-foot tall model of Mount Everest; 8) a ten-centimeter tall obelisk identical in proportions to what would be-come The Washington Monument; 9) something that people of later ages would often characterize as a crucifix; 10) a vajra sceptre; 11) an object beyond any efficient verbal descriptions, an item emphasizing Alpha, Excavation, Chaos, Order, Ions, The Ineffable, Omega, etc.; and 12) an item simultaneously both a Vajrakila dagger and a space-time teleporter (as a two-in-one).

The few Dorians present and the many Mycenaeans present initially worked out that the latter took home items #4, #5, #7, #10, and #11. The former took home #1, #2, #3, #6, #8, #9, and #12.

Later, the Dorians traded away items #1, #3, and #2 to obtain items #4 and #11. A few Mycenaeans objected to the trade, expressing an intuition that it might lead to the end of their civilization, ye they proved unable to stop the Mycenaeans in authority to conduct that transaction from completing their role in it.

One year later, tensions between the two camps flared up again. There were many twists and turns to how the new escalations happened, and much of it revolved around issues of contrasting notions of what it means for human beings to respect one another. Not long after that, the escalating animosity exploded. The Mycenaeans then declared war. The Dorians responded to that by also declaring war.

The war proved to be one-sided.

In addition to whatever other advantages that the Dorians may have had from the very outset, they had iron weapons, whereas the Mycenaens had bronze weapons. Choosing limited amounts of analysis of what went wrong with the Mycenaean culture, after having defeated them, the Dorians chose wholesale annihilation of over 95% of it, replacing it with much of what they considered best from both cultures and a few portions of other cultures as well.

However, as several centuries came and went, tales emerged that weaved together elements of what had happened between the extraterrestrial aliens, the Teutons, the Mycenaeans, and the Dorians, with many embellishments, suppressions, and exotic fable components drawn together in short stories and epic poetry.

The high preisthood of the Dorians left only a minute percentage of themselves in the Mediterranean region. Most of them immigrated elsewhere, including to portions of Africa, the Middle East, and the Himalayas.

A few of the most warrior-oriented among them set up secret societies in places that would later be called Norway, Germany, and

Finland.

As time went by, some of these secret societies coalesced into portions of Nordic culture, while similarly-resonating societies entrenched themselves into portions of the Tibetan Plateau.

In the twentieth century, the various transcendental beings' ways of competing with one another while treating humans as their proxies escalated dramatically, proving to be one of the major driving factors in causing the extreme warfare and genocide that occurred in that century.

Amid all of this a team of beings who included multiple versions of Charr Naerroan interpreted every young person, every old person, every middle-aged person, every female, every male, every Buddhist, every Non-Buddhist, every Non-Christian, every canine, every feline, every Atheist, every skeptic, every Agnostic, every believer, every conservative, every liberal, every Christian, every Jew, every Gentile, and any and all mammals of any categories of any kinds

*****

As meteoroligists and others learned about the names declared to go with the storms of the 2019 Atlantic Hurricane Season, it drew many laughs from lots of folks.

People in Jamaica and nearby areas did not find it quite so funny when Hurricane Dorian came a-calling and went on a rampage. Elsewhere, in strategic locations of the great beyond, still never having fully resolved the religious differences between the believers among them in nondenominational spiritualism, Sikhism, Judaism,

Christianity, Islam, Buddhism, Jainism, agnosticism, and other things, a coalition including Dimetrodons, Plesiosaurs, Hebrew humans, Gentile humans, Dorians, Ionians, Druids, and others gathered for a serious convention.

After much deliberation, they decided that September 23rd, 2019 would be the perfect day to call on all Ponderosa pine trees on Earth and all the spirits of the Petrified Forest of the American desert southwest to make it happen: The opening of all Pandora's boxes, all Pandara's boxes, and the full brunt of all paranormal activities. However, an unexpected guest materialized from nowhere.

The version of Gary Mark Gilmore who in one of the most exotic of universes rose from common criminal to becoming the 40th President of the United States, even receiving an endorsement from Governor Reagan (President Ronald Reagan before he became the 41st President of the United States of America relative to that universe) on his way to replacing President Jimmy Carter in that role, said, "Stop! The time is not quite right. You should wait."

A Hasidic Jew and a Vajrayana Buddhist seated beside each other about forty-two yards away from GMG were seated behind an MGM executive who had been shot to death by a time traveler who targeted him.

The three of them looked at each other in a mixture of belief, disbelief, and amazement at what they just witnessed. The former MGM executive, who was in some ways still a Metro-Goldwyn-Mayer executive on account of how some of his duties in the beyond involved influencing his former employer in attempts to steer reality toward the good, the better, and the best in the long run, spoke up. "Which version of Gary Mark Gilmore are you? Please, give an elevator speech bio."

GMG responded, "After early years of crime, I cleaned up my act. Then with the help of some influential families, I became an attorney. From law I rose to politics. In politics I made it to the top, with a combination of fearlessness and tenacity. We even achieved world peace for about ten months in my universe in the year 2010, long after I had left office. Then Earth got into the cross hairs of an interstellar war between extraterrestrial aliens. Early in 2012, well, actually, late in the first half of that year, June 10th to be precise, a nuclear bomb vaporized a bunch of people, including myself. I wandered from one universe to another, met up with twenty-six different versions of myself, and have helped some of the beings here and there to find their way through the winding and forking paths of the many multi-verses."

The former movie executive was not impressed. "I am not so concerned about whether or not your life was as glorious as you portrayed it, but I am skeptical about why we should trust you to know better than our consensus in this gathering. Give us something to consider about why we should delay the unleashing of the full brunt of the paranormal to the best of our abilities so help us God."

Gary Gilmore said, "In some ways it's funny that you mentioned that, because, based on my past experiences in the great beyond, you will almost definitely you yourselves split into multiple realities in which different versions do different things, some taking my suggestion, some rejecting it, and some finding some third or fourth alternative as the way to go."

Sure enough, the very reality within that convention split into multiple realities in which some versions unleashed the full brunt of the paranormal, some released limited magnitudes of it, and some showed restraint until the year 2021.

Many of the versions who did indeed open those Pandora's boxes and Pandara's boxes in the third quarter of 2019 chose to have the openings occur to coincide with the period of September 23rd to 29th that year.

****

"This is totally unconscionable, that dude, Chief Justice John Roberts basically took a torch to Article II of the Constitution," said Sammy Watts to his relative Geronimo Watts.

"Yeah, I think that's just what happened. It's been all over talk radio. I don't know just what will happen six days from now, but I hope it really shakes people up in what we have left of this republic," replied Geronimo.

Elsewhere, their ex-wives, Cheryl Nobel and Shirley Watts were having tea and espresso in a coffee shop. Ms. Nobel said, "Thank goodness that goodness prevailed!"

Ms. Watts replied, "Yeah, there's too much toxic masculinity in this country. I think things are about to get better. We just need to get past the controversies expected on January 6th, then things will be back to being kind of normal. Does your ex Sammy still bother you lately?"

Cheryl Nobel said, "No, I think he knows better, especially since the time when my new husband gave him a serious tongue lashing after he showed up at our door at 10:30 PM, drunk and stuttering about how he loves me and that he was wrong and all that desperate clinging he has to the way things used to be." Right after making that statement, she silently experienced a strange flashback to several Freddie Fender songs, and she had no earthly idea why.

Shirley said, "Yeah, well good riddance! I'm very happy for you."

Ms. Nobel and Ms. Watts were in Portland, Oregon, whereas Sammy and Geronimo Watts were in Stafford, Texas. Back in Stafford, Geronimo asked, "So, when was the last time you spoke with you know who?"

Sammy said, "Oh, you just had to bring that up? Well, it was about two years ago. I was drinking, and I drove over to her house, where she and her new hubbie, Giancarlo Ordaz, were living in a mansion. Maybe it was not the best decision I've ever made. Well, Giancarlo did not hit me or even make physical contact, but he did pull me aside to say, 'Bro, it's over. She and I are happily married and we are probably going to stay that way as long as we're both still alive. But I have some great news, brother!'" He paused, giving Geronimo a chance to inquire further or to change to another subject.

Geronimo said, "Well, what was the 'great news' that he had to share with you?"

Sammy explained, "He said, 'I've got this groovy Freddy Fender CD, and I'd like to give it to you for you to listen to. If you don't like it, just give it back and I'll accept it. But if you do like it, go ahead and keep it, maybe it'll help you accept that she currently wants to be with me, not you, but we don't know for sure if things will always be this way. After all, stranger shit's happened in the history of this crazy planet!"

Geronimo asked, "Do you remember more exactly when it was that he gave you that Freddy Fender CD?"

Sammy said, "Hmm, let me try to put this together. Oh, I've got it. I don't remember the exact date as a month and year, but I remember clearly that it was when Tropical Storm Imelda was making headlines."

Geronimo's eyes opened wide and his pupils dilated. "No shit?! That seems like almost a lifetime ago, after all that COVID stuff went down earlier this year, then all this election weirdness went down recently... and is still going on."

Sammy chimed in again, "Just six days to go until a bunch of those folks gather at the capitol. I hope they really rock those dirty Democrats!"

Geronimo said, "Yeah, so do I. It's not like they're expecting to do something totally illegal, like storm the capitol, right?"

Sammy said, "Right on, right on! Country still seems headed to hell, but maybe with a little hell-raising in protest of a stolen election, yeah, yeah baby, yeah, give 'em hell. Give 'em hell!"

Back in Portland, Shirley and Cheryl had moved on to talk about the environment. Shirley asked, "Maybe the COVID-19 was a way for Mother Earth to tell everyone, pay attention, protect the environment, don't use so many fossil fuels, ya think?"

Cheryl said, "Yeah, I mean who are we as humans to mess with the environment? Of course, I wouldn't be surprised if the Earth itself intentionally made the entire Covid crisis stuff happen, and then some of the government types ended up blaming each other. Trump blamed people, Biden blamed people, the Chinese blamed America, many Americans blamed China, but maybe it was the Earth itself that made this happen."

Observing both New Year's Eve conversations from near the end of the Year 2020, via monitors in the beyond, Zircon and Dimetrio looked at each other and knew what each other were thinking: It was not the Earth that instigated Covid-19 getting unleashed unto the world, it was a strategem from the entirety of Planet Mars and the entirety of Planet Jupiter, as conscious holistic planet entities, to retaliate against earthlings on behalf of earthlings and all other beings.

The backdrop of their strategy was too many people causing too much trouble across the entire solar system with the distortions of their mindsets and lifestyles, spanning the entire political spectrum and the entire socioeconomic spectrum. Therefore, those planets manipulated the choices of millions in order to influence humans, microbes, and other agents to, from August 2019 onward, go on a path leading directly to the 2020 large-scale lockdowns across much of the civilized world. The alchemy not of transmutation of base metals into gold, but of the transmutation of microbes and rearrangements to grant them access to plenty of human hosts.

In Houston, TX, a young man named Josh started to cough about the time that Tropical Storm Imelda reached its zenith of activity in September 2019. He had contracted a Martian microbe, which had slipped through a shortcut in the fabric of space-time to go directly from Mars to Earth. That microbe had special abilities, despite its lack of what scientists would typically call 'a brain,' to remotely influence other microbes and the humans in closest contact with them to act in a more pro-microbe manner. At some stage, it was one of the many factors contributing to the spread of illnesses.

Technically, though few of the inter-universal time-travelers knew it, the involvement of Jupiter and Mars in the spread of Covid-19 was only true over some ranges of universes. There were also ranges of universes in which the consciousnesses of those two planets refrained from instigating the 2020 Covid-19 craziness on Earth, yet the 2020 Covid-19 craziness on Earth still reared its head anyway. Only in some exceptional cases of universes did that planet somehow avoid that mayhem.

In one of the universes in which the coalition of many beings in the beyond who had a sudden visit from the ghost of U.S. President Gary Gilmore of an alternate reality, those beings chose to hold off on the main opening of Pandora's boxes and Pandara's boxes until Friday, December 3rd, 2021. They gathered together at 2 A.M. Central Time in downtown Houston, then, invisibly to most living creatures on Earth, walked toward the hospital district. In that district, they then telepathically linked minds with a gathering of similar beings in Fresno, California, then opened a telepathic link to all Ponderosa pine trees living on the planet.

Soon, gathering the mental powers of quintillions of beings, and with full faith that the time was right for it, they fully opened the floodgates to the full brunt of the paranormal.

Noon on August 23rd, 2022, 40 nautical miles from the east coast of Japan, fishermen lifted their nets from the depths of the ocean. Shocked to see a sea creature that looked like a ten-foot long scorpion, they arranged for scientists to haul off the creature. In a secret underwater government facility off the coast of Japan, cryptozoologists, paleontologists, and others from several Asian countries gathered and analyzed the specimen.

Japanese high-ranking military biologist Dr. Yamamoto called his American counterpart Dr. Sagovia to say, "Remember how earlier this month you shared footage of how your team acquired a living Eurypterid? Well, we've acquired a living one ourselves, only this one seems to be a twelve-foot long *Jaekelopterus rhenaniae*."

Dr. Sagovia exclaimed, "And I thought the one we caught was huge!

The official fossil records showed eight feet as the most likely limit from way back when, and our nine-foot specimen was quite a shocker. And now a twelve-footer from a part of the Pacific almost half a world away from where we found ours. The Eurypterids are back. God help us all!"

*****

On June 18, 1967, an everyday American named Florence Smith walked into a small five-and-dime. She beheld the name of the store on a sign as she approached: *Dimension Dimestore.*

As she crossed the threshold to enter, she silently thought to herself, *Is this really a good idea, entering a store with a name suggestive of entering real life science fiction? I'm probably being superstitious to even start to worry about that idea, am I not? Well, I'm entering the premises either way. Good idea or not, here it goes!*

A bell chimed as the door opened and she passed through to fully enter the quaint establishment. A man behind a counter glanced toward her and announced, "Welcome to Dimension Dimestore! I haven't seen you 'round these parts before, what brings you to Toledo?"

She said, "Just passing through. I've rarely seen Ohio. Hey, your voice doesn't sound quite like you're from Ohio, either. Are you from elsewhere, as well?"

He said, "I've been 'round all sorts, and I can use all manner of diff'ren' accents, whate'er might seem befittin' the situation. And I reckon, this here accent is the best one for me to use in talkin' to a tall drink of water such as yourself. Now, are you a-lookin' for anythin' in particular, or are you a-browsin' to see if somethin' will catch yer fancy?"

She answered, "Definitely the latter."

He said, "Yes, Ma'am, be our guest. Look around, and maybe the items on the shelves will check you out while you're checking them out!"

That last statement took her aback, but she thought better of voicing any concern. She had watched and read her share of Horror, Science Fiction, and Fantasy stories over the years, and she every now and then chose to be what friends, family, and lovers characterized as ranging from moderately superstitious to extremely superstitious. Frequently, she had a sense that sooner or later something paranormal as if right out of a movie scene might happen to her, though she had not witnessed anything quite like that yet. The anticipation that it might happen someday filled her both with a thrill and a foreboding.

Looking around, the first item to catch her eye was a mirror with a concentric set of circles on its circular frame, supported by a tripod stand. The prices in the store ranged from three cents to nineteen dollars, though most items ranged from five cents to one dollar.

There were household items, toys, discount books, old magazines, knick knacks, and art supplies, among other things. She felt at home. The cares and worries of the outside world started to fade away. She felt a youthful wonder return to her spirit.

She found a miniature radio, on sale for $3.25. A nearby sign read, "Turn on the radio, turn the dial, find how you like it. Tune into something, have a listen, go for it, if you like!"

She decided to go ahead and try out that radio. Voices portrayed the aftermath of military leader Hannibal Barca's suicide.

A male voice said, "He's dead! He's dead! I never thought I would live to see this day. I never wanted our gracious master to die! We have our freedom from tending to his villa, but what's it worth without him?!"

A female voice responded, sounding equally sad, "Calm yourself. Look, I know that we did not want this to happen, but happen it did. Our lives are filled with tragedies, from the cradle to the grave. Look, we still have plenty of reason to keep going with our lives. He asked us to remember him and to find something of value in our futures. Yes, yes, remember how a short while ago he mentioned wishing us the best with the future."

The male voice stated, "Yes, he did, but it doesn't make me feel any better right now. I don't feel much hope at all for the future."

The female voice started sounding more lively, though still with a touch of sadness. "It may hurt very much right now, but time may heal you. Also, in just the time since repeating his message now, I have started to come to terms with his passing. Maybe in time both of us will be able to move on with our lives."

Florence felt a little sorrow enter her soul, rooted in a loving-kindness and compassion toward the beings portrayed on the radio show. However, she grew curious about what might be playing on another channel. She adjusted the dial, and soon heard part of a debate about the Vietnam War, the American establishment culture, and the American counterculture. Soon she grew a little weary of using that radio. She shut it off and moved along to look at more items.

Some seemed a little dull, and others seemed dazzling.

More minutes went by, and she kept moving along from one section of the store to another.

Then it happened: she felt the forces of intense attraction skyrocket as a bright, silvery, metallic item caught her full attention. It was way beyond peculiar, and it seemed to have a mind of its own, telepathically calling out to her to say, "Buy me! Buy me!"

Florence then chose to inquire about it with the employee who had greeted her. "How could this item be on sale for only a quarter? Just twenty-five cents?! It seems too interesting to be on sale for such a price! What's up with this?" She smiled gently as the inquiry rolled off her lips.

The employee, who had at first grimaced upon hearing her start to make her inquiry, pivoted to gently give her a return smile, then said, "*Oh, that thing. It's been sitting on the shelf for nearly two decades.* Some dude came by one day and donated it to the store. *He said he found it on the ground in some random rural part of Roswell, New Mexico.*"

Miss Smith silently thought to herself, *Gee, his voice sounds more normal now, maybe this is the way he normally talks when he's not trying to put on some kind of show.*

The store worker continued, "We originally priced it to be among our premium items, not way too high a price. Then time went by. Then more time. It has languished here for years and years, with no buyers in sight.

"A few curious people such as yourself have picked it up and asked about it every now and then, but, as of yet, no buyer. *Every once in a while, we've cut down its price, trying to sweeten the deal a little for some adventurer who might someday dare to take a chance on it."*

Florence replied, "You've got a deal! *I'd love to buy this exotic mystery item for your gracious offering price of twenty-five cents plus sales tax."*

She walked over to the cash register, and the two of them completed the transaction. The two of them exchanged smiles and some light banter, and the gentleman, though tempted, refrained from making any overt romantic advances toward the dame.

On her way out, she joyfully said to him, "This has been a truly far-out experience! Have a great day!"

He said to her, "You do the same. Have a good one!"

* * *

As Florence exited Dimension Dimestore, she noticed something was different. Though it had been sunny and moderately warm when she had entered, it was suddenly overcast and moderately cold. She had witnessed sudden changes of conditions, whether caused by cold fronts or something else before on countless occasions, but her intuition pointed toward something ominous.

* * *

For a little while, she drifted into a bizarre daydream in six parts.

* * *

Part One of Florence's daydream near Dimension Dimestore after exiting: An aardvark and a cow met a bull, and the three walked to a temple, where one million gods engaged in a war that resulted in the destruction of the solar system.

* * *

Part Two of Florence's daydream near Dimension Dimestore after exiting: Five men and seven women played musical chairs in such a way that they layered it with kinky, wild, group sex with each other.

* * *

Part Three of Florence's daydream near Dimension Dimestore after exiting: Ten thousand cannibals competed with each other, and, after fifty years of battles, only five remained, as many of them had proven prone to the tendency among some of the Steppenwolves and some of the Cro Magnon to go totally overboard with acts of overkilling.

* * *

Part Four of Florence's daydream near Dimension Dimestore after exiting: Extraterrestrials, ten Russians, five Germans, and six gods negotiated a deal with Satan. According to the terms of that 1927 deal, the eighteen extraterrestrials, the fifteen humans, and the six gods sold 85% of the energies of their souls for a term of 25 years in exchange for power beyond their wildest dreams. Portions of the evil exhibited by the NSDAP of Nazi Germany, The Bolsheviks of The

Communist Party of The Soviet Union, and other organizations during portions of 1927-1952 ended up emanating from that Satanic deal and its aftermath. After the period ended, science fiction on Earth had what was arguably the best year that any genre of fiction literature ever experienced: The Year 1953 of The Common Era, also known as The Year 1953 Anno Domini, In Science Fiction Literature.

************************************   ************************************

Part Five of Florence's daydream near that store immediately after exiting it: In 1917 the revolutionary activities in Russia proved brutal. After that, during portions of 1918-1988, thirty-six ghosts of ancient pigs, thirty-six ghosts of ancient Romans, and thirty-six living Soviet Russians opened up portals into many heavens and many hells, then teamed up with some mysterious beings, each of which was either named Charr Naerroan or teaming up with at least one being of that name, and acted cruelty on an unimaginable scale. They proceeded to slaughter seventy-two trillion Christians spread over many of the heavens, hells, and ordinary worlds. In that process they annihilated six million Christian universes, including the act of killing each and every version of The Christian God in each of those universes as part of facilitating those universes' destructions. A stray comment visible in 2014 as a response to a YouTube video pointed toward that.

After twenty-six versions of Charr Naerroan gathered together to pose for one photograph, several high-level soviets gave each other high-fives and felt on top of the world. Next, a group of over 9,000 women, over 3,000 children, and over 9,000 men, each of them a true believer in the Marxist promise of eventually finding a better future via the extermination of cultures and civilizations closely tied to the history of capitalism, telepathically linked up with each other and the massive destruction that had occurred. Most of them were living in poverty in the USSR, yet they felt fine with tolerating the poverty based on the promise of it all someday paying off with the emergence of a Marxist utopia. A few high-ranking members of the Soviet Union published modified versions of a report on this in *Pravda*.

To a bunch of the highest-ranking soviets all seemed copacetic; all seemed to them perfectly right with the world. That feeling lasted for a while for them. They dedicated the cruel, massive annihilation of Christian Divinity, Christianity, and Christians themselves to Karl Marx, Friedrich Engels, and Satan.

However, in the aftermath of that, the ghosts of many variations of Christian Divinity teamed up with the ghosts of many Christians and with Satan Himself to set their sights on setting up a chain of over a quintillion dominos of causation to lead to a disaster in Chernobyl that might one day serve to be among the events that would combine together to rip the Union of Soviet Socialist Republic to shreds.

* * *

Part Six of the daydream that Florence experienced near Dimension Dimestore after exiting: 108,000 Buddhist monks and nuns meditateed in 256 cities, 108,000 Christians prayed in 1,050 churches, 29,000 Jews gathered in synagogues, 85,000 Muslims gathered in mosques, and other people did their utmost to attempt to live lives of holiness.

Meanwhile, elsewhere, one trillion extraterrestrials lured five men and nine women into unknowingly, telepathically, remotely, higher-dimensionally, and psychokinetically having wild, interspecies sex with those lascivious extraterrestrial males and females while the humans were daydreaming and the extraterrestrials experienced it as fully-awake, fully physical, real-life sex with the humans.

* * * * * *

She snapped back to regular reality from that six-part daydream, and again she noticed the unusual change of weather and an ominous feeling. Looking around, she wondered. She thought again about the many conflicts between competing factions of human beings, golf, the many rumors about aliens, tennis, alcohol, marijuana, cocaine, Io, gold, Pluto, Europa, Orion, Venus, Mars, Saturn, Oklahoma, Iowa, Wyoming, air, and water. She started to feel very nervous, yet she had no idea why. Another look around did not reveal to her any clues about anything strange going on. She took in another deep breath, paused, then slowly exhaled.

A five-foot-tall, classic gray alien then materialized six feet in front of her. From the features alone there seemed to be absolutely no clue as far as she could tell regarding what gender the extraterrestrial might have. She wondered silently to herself, *Is this creature a case of me having a hallucination? Did someone slip me some LSD? Is this thing really an intelligent extraterrestrial? If so, then is that alien male, female, of a neutral gender, or what? If this is a male, and if he decides to try to get into my panties, then should I let him? If it is ethical for me to have sex with him, assuming that alien to be a him, and if he seduces me or vice-versa, then what are the chances that I get pregnant with a half-human and half-extra-terrestrial alien child? If I give birth to a half-human-half-alien child, will that child eventually kill the human race? If I give birth to a half-human-half-alien child, will that child eventually save the human race? Was Jesus Christ half-extraterrestrial, with the entire Christian phenomenon explainable by superpowerful aliens having visited Mary, Joseph, and others way back when in order to try to steer humanity toward something better? The vision of that gray alien has not disappeared; is that really a real being in front of me or is my mind playing some serious tricks on me?*

The presumably-highly-intelligent being began to speak.

"Do you know what year it is?" inquired the gray. He spoke in what Florence recognized to be an unmistakably masculine voice.

Florence responded, "1967, of course."

"1967 in which calendar?"

"The one almost everyone uses nowadays, silly."

"Cheeky human, you are. The question is not silly at all.

"Your perception of reality with whether you are as of that instant using the Gregorian Calendar, as typical of the majority of human business and leisure where you were just now located, or any other calendar known to man, or any other calendar of any kind, just think about it, this makes a huge difference. And, no, you are not correct to believe it to be 1967 Anno Domini or 1967 A.D. or whatever in terms of the calendar that almost everyone from your planet was using just before we plucked you out from your world. Now, would you like to know what year it is in terms of the Gregorian Calendar, right now, in this very time that we are sharing together?"

Almost all her life, Florence Smith had intuited that this moment might someday come, a moment when the universe would change for her. Now, here it was, exactly the sort of thing she had sometimes dreamed about and at other times dreaded as a possibility, a situation in which reality itself presented her with a twist that was undeniable. She could have tried to tell herself that it must be only a dream or a hallucination, yet she had never knowingly meddled in LSD, and, furthermore, there was some intangible knowing within the core of her consciousness that this was regular, real-world, waking life that had taken a turn for the unimaginable. Terror started to sink in. Her pupils dilated, and her skin turned slightly pale.

She chose her next words carefully. "Are you capable of such radical technology as to have plucked me out of the entire year 1967?"

"Not only are we capable of employing such technology, we just did."

"No kidding. Well, I suppose it's for the best to start figuring out what to do next with my life. *Alright, let me have it, tell me, and please don't try and sugarcoat anything, what year is it now and where am I?"*

"The year is easy to know. *It is 2344 in terms of the calendar with which you are most familiar.* The where: the location, well, that might prove a little tricky to get you to fathom. *What do you remember about the idea of the pole star, what some would call 'The North Star,' what do you remember about that?"*

Florence thought back a little to things she had heard and a little bit of what she had read about regarding that. She answered, "Polaris. It's a star, and it's something approximately pointed where you can figure out which way North is."

The extraterrestrial with a gray skin-tone, huge eyes, and a head of unusually large proportions to the rest of his body by comparison to human standards paused for a moment. He continued thusly, "Your answer is very, truly, incomplete."

She retorted, "How so?"

The gray explained, "There are many additional things about it, and I invite you now to say some more about it. What else do you have to say about the concept of North Star and whichever star or stars go with that concept?"

The human looked a little dazed, then took a stab at a much more complete answer. "Some people long ago—and they were probably some very primitive, superstitious, mind you—had some legend that the North Star, known as Polaris, is THE HOME OF GOD. Also, and this is probably going to sound really wild, but I heard rumors that in the old stories, handed down from generation to generation, there are supposed to be some weird, giant beings who live close to God, somewhere in the vicinity of the North Star, and those beings are very intelligent and powerful, and they sometimes abduct humans, then eat those humans. I hope you're not here to eat me, unless it is in a good way!" She winked as she finished saying that.

The gray paused from speaking out loud, and, instead, chose to telepathically his voice into her mind's auditorium. She heard in her head his voice say to her, *Although you had that kinky daydream a little while ago include some scenes of extraterrestrials having wild sex with a few human beings, I am not into that. Also, although you have seen science fiction presentations in which aliens sometimes eat humans like some of the humans eat cattle, I am not into that either. You kinky human, I am here for very different reasons. I abducted you for very different reasons than what you were a little while ago conjecturing about.*

She asked him, "Was I just imagining that, or did you just now do the ventriloquists one better, throwing your voice telepathically right into my mind for me to hear, as you subvocalized not so much into your own head as directly into mine?"

He answered, "You were not imagining that. I did in fact project an answer directly into your mind."

She said, "Oh, really. Well, then would you kindly confirm that you told me that you are not looking to eat me, whether as a culinary treat, as an act of going down on me, or both? Also, that, more generally, you are at this instant neither out to have sex with me nor to kill me?"

The gray clarified, "I can do even better than confirm that for you: I can go ahead and speak out loud now what I told you via that set of telepathy a moment ago. Here goes: Although you had that kinky daydream a little while ago include some scenes of extraterrestrials having wild sex with a few human beings, I am not into that. Also, although you have seen science fiction presentations in which aliens sometimes eat humans like some of the humans eat cattle, I am not into that either. You kinky human, I am here for very different reasons. I abducted you for very different reasons than what you were a little while ago conjecturing about."

She looked at him utterly speechless and stunned. Her jaw literally dropped. Suddenly, she looked at him with sheer terror, not out of any fear that God or society might smite her for having inappropriate sex with someone, not out of a fear that she might soon get killed by an acquaintance, and not out of anything in a similar vein to those fears. She recognized that she was in the presence of the extremely unknown, including an acquaintance who, although seemingly quite benevolent, wielded technologies beyond her comprehension.

Florence asked, "Please tell me more."

The gray answered, "Your planet in the recent set of dozens upon dozens of thousands of years has been in an oscillating relationship of how its Northern pole points toward the heavens. Over thousands of years, it goes back and forth between having Polaris as the North Star and having Vega as the North Star. Are you ready to hear something scary?"

She said, "This experience has already been scary, yet I think I'm ready for things to get scarier. Go ahead, hit me with your best!"

He said, "I am aware that your name is Florence Smith. You were born in 1928 in Westchester, Pennsylvania to a woman named Laura Smith and a man named Chester Smith. While you were growing up, your main interests were television, dolls, and boys. You have only felt broken-hearted once, and that was not even with any of the males you had sex with, it was with a guy who was sweet and charming and yet somehow chose to reject you at an instant when you were at your most vulnerable with unselfishly caring for how he might make a great father for your future children. You became tempted to seek to make him pay dearly for breaking your heart, perhaps by stabbing him in the throat—either the wider throat above his shoulders, vital to his breathing and central nervous system, or the much narrower throat between his legs, vital to his urination and copulation—you became tempted to stab him with a fork either in the neck or in the shaft of his you-know-what while he and you were dining in the same cafeteria, yet, thankfully, you resisted that cruel temptation. That having being said, you never got around to telling him point blank that he broke your heart. You never told him how his rejection of your invitation for him to go with you as your date to attend your sister's wedding in Texas led to such a chain reaction, a chain reaction that had hurt you so much. Back a number of months ago, the bittersweet memories of those days started to haunt you more than ever. However, you found a way to more fully let go of them, including to fully forgive him and fully forgive yourself for whatever might otherwise have been blamable about all of that. Still, your memories continue to affect your outlook on the future, and every once in a while some of them creep in to haunt you yet again. Think back again to that guy, the only guy to have ever broken your heart. Think about what was going through your heart and soul, as well as your mind, back when he and you were going together to events. You thought that the five dates he and you had with each other, together with how perfectly lady-like you had acted toward him and how perfectly gentlemanly he had been toward you, together with the rest of what was going on… there it was that you thought putting it all together was going to be great, and it would make your suggestion something he would adore. That is, you thought that he would have mixed feelings of erotic interest in what might happen next between the two of you and affectionate interest in how you had become so special to him, and, therefore, he would enthusiastically agree to that invitation. However, the cold hard truth was that he resolutely rejected you, even going so far as to mention that your cousin Amy had invited him to go to the very same wedding event as her date, and that he had already accepted her invitation behind your back. He also said that he was planning on telling you about it, but he was trying to wait for the right time, place, and manner to try to minimize how much it might hurt you. It might seem very personal to you that I am mentioning this, but we have to quickly get you ready for your role in an intergalactic, multi-universe set of intrigue, and my openly discussing with you some of your most personal details is part of your orientation. Let's jump ahead to something from much later in your life.

"In 1966, you ventured to El Paso, Texas, and you brought a 20-year-old fellow with you to share the experience of witnessing Hal Warren's low-budget horror film *Manos, the Hands of Fate*, which was new to the general public as of then. After watching that film and becoming horny as hell, you seduced your date, who also became horny as hell, and the two of you made passionate love back at the hotel room after witnessing that film. That guy proved to be the best boyfriend that you've had thus far, even though his family has been skeptical about how you are his senior by a margin of eighteen years. You have enjoyed having sex with him more than you have enjoyed anything else in your life so far, except, perhaps simply loving him and being loved by him while the two of you are together yet not having sex with each other. He and you have truly loved each other, although you have not yet tied the knot of holy matrimony.

"The thing you are starting to feel most uncomfortable about, out of the entire set of this strangeness thrust upon your life, it turns out, is that you are wondering whether or not you will ever meet him again. You wonder whether or not you'll get to meet your dear lover, Elias Artino, ever again.

"In contrast, at another level of your consciousness, you are becoming concerned about whether we might experiment on you in an extremely gruesome way or maybe even multiple gruesome ways, much as the human scientists of Earth have performed thousands and thousands of rather gruesome experiments on rodents, cats, dogs, monkeys, apes, and even, in some cases, other humans.

"Yes, you remember learning about how in your world the human beings at times have dared to do unspeakable things in the name of science. Experiments that have even involved terrible cutting up of portions of the frontal lobes of the brains of women, children, and men. Experiments that have even involved terrible cutting up of the genitals of women, children, and men. Yes, even a few experiments that involved the very maximal approach to enhanced interrogation, arranging for some of those being questioned becoming forced to go back and forth between experiencing extreme torture and experiencing subtle manipulation, plus brainwashing, intimidation, aimed at forcing others to divulge virtually anything. Some of cruelest of extreme interrogation of humans by other humans has featured, as a final measure, subjecting interrogation victims to getting tortured to death, with no limits on how brutal the interrogators would kick, hit, rape, mutilate, etc. the victims, as a test of finding out exactly how the other human being speaks and acts as the pain and agony reach unspeakable levels. Oftentimes, the subtler and gentler interrogation methods have extracted more accurate information, but there have been times that the most extreme of torture has proven able to extract the information that the interrogators have sought. Telepathically, I can tell that you are wondering whether we might be about to do that to you; we can read your mind with a high degree of accuracy and thoroughness, though you have demonstrated only a trace of ability to read microscopic amounts of our minds. *You know, if you get way out line, we very well might wind up doing just that to you. We've done that to a few of the humans before, but only if they would get so totally out of proper conduct as to deserve for us to do that to them.* Your Geneva Convention has absolutely no bearing on our conduct. We are not of your world, and we have certainly never signed any such agreement to limit our conduct, either among ourselves or between ourselves and other civilizations. *Fear not, though, you would have to be extremely out of bounds for us to start to even consider performing such excruciating things unto you.* What would you like to ask next?"

Florence was impressed, and she felt a mixture of fear, joy, hope, and sorrow pulsating through her heart, mind, and soul. She took her time in considering what question to pose next, then asked, "Do you have a name, and if you do, then may I ask with whom I am having the pleasure of sharing this conversation?"

The gray alien answered, "As is the case with you and with many other intelligent beings, there are several variations of what name or names I in some ways possess. The simplest way to present this in this context would be for me to say that I am Double-Forty-One."

Florence Smith, also sometimes known as Ms. Smith or Miss Smith, found the name to be patently absurd. She burst into uncontrollable laughter, which lasted for about twenty seconds, and it was purely unintentional. It was a visceral and logical reaction based on her own sensibilities.

After regaining her normal faculties of mind, she explained, "You have all that super-advanced technology, and of all the names that you could possibly call yourself, you use an ambiguous number statement. 'Double-Forty-One.' Is that supposed to mean that you are Eighty-Two, does that mean that you are a combination of Eighty and One, or does it mean something else? Also, isn't it most typically people or other beings who have some low social status who are con-sidered mainly reducible to having some numbers as names. I mean, like, Americans such as myself have social security numbers, but we don't use them as our regular-life names; whereas inmates in prisons often are treated by the corrections officers as de facto having their department of justice inmate numbers as their names. Would you explain a little about what is going on with why you have such a peculiar name, in spite of how it seems to undercut the impressiveness of your awesome technological intimidation and ostentation?"

Double-Forty-One answered, "We do not seek to maximize fear and intimidation like some extremely Machiavellian political leaders might do. We seek to help with the cosmic consciousness of intelligent beings, the well-being of beings in general, and the proper coordination of the energies of the universes.

"Within our civilization, numerically-ambiguous names are quite common. Such names as 'Double-Forty-One,' 'Double-Twenty-One,' "Tripe-Fifty-Seven," and the like are normal. Other parts of a being's full name can at times come from what we have for the names of stars and galaxies.

"When we talk with human beings, we can easily translate these types of names rather literally into whatever language a given individual person is most comfortable with.

"Now, as you are in the early stages of becoming involuntarily enlisted into The War Beyond Human Comprehension as an intelligence operative fighting to help our side of that war, what is your next question?"

Miss Smith asked him, "What is this War Beyond Human Comprehension that you mentioned?"

He answered, "Across many different universes, there is a pattern that hauntingly repeats itself: A group of humans travel from Earth and settle near a specific planet in a different solar system. Using advanced technologies, some of which we help them to discover and refine, those humans are able to utilize shortcuts through space and time, and they prove quite capable of, say moving a starship 250 light years in a matter of a few weeks. The settlers on that other world at first have things go smoothly. However, eventually totalitarianism and mysterious processes become the norm for that world. After a while, a huge war between that world and the rest of the human race ensues. The war escalates and escalates, and at some stage different factions of multiple advanced alien civilizations take sides in the conflict. Our side consistently chooses the side that strongly supports the liberty of human beings and other intelligent beings to be free from the tragic tyranny of an oppressive, totalitarian regime. Later, twists and turns reveal that the totalitarian regime was not really after absolute power of ruling over the rest of the human race, despite initially presenting that as what it was after. It turns out that the leadership of that planet is after a much larger prize: the utter annihilation of entire universes, aimed at converting the deaths of those universes into awesome amounts of energy that they can harvest and use toward the next stages of their schemes. That's what we have recruited you to help fight against. What next, sayeth you, for information helpful in your adjustment to your new role?"

"Does that planet with the universal annihilation sorts of intentions have a name? What is it?" she asked.

"It has many different names, as there are vast arrays of different universes and timelines in which it emerges. Next question."

"You mentioned Vega and Polaris earlier, then you did not return to any direct statement about why exactly you had brought them up. What's up with that?"

Double-Forty-One paused for a few seconds, then answered, "Several of your ancient human legends, passed down from one generation to another, stated that there was a shared belief among many that somewhere in the heavens, in the direction of Polaris, there exists THE HOME OF GOD."

Miss Smith suddenly felt in awe. She remained silent and listened keenly.

Double-Forty-One continued, "Although we as gray aliens have made a great many huge advances over the eons, we, too, much like the humans of the world from which you came, never have solved the great mystery of religion and the great beyond. Sure, many of us can partway tell that there is something going on with the deeper and more mysterious level of reality, but as for whether there exists one true religion, two true religions, three true religions, no true religions, or whatever, none of us really knows for sure. Yes, as with the humans of Earth, there are those among us who do proclaim that one specific faith or another is truly correct and that everyone will sooner or later need to at least partway convert to cooperating with it or else face divine wrath, and, yes, there are those among us who are skeptical toward the entirety of religion. However, no, we do not know for sure, much like you humans do not know for sure.

Something we do know for sure, in contrast, and, possibly, of spooky relationship with all of this, is that there is another planet, not that repeatedly prone to going totalitarian and then out-to-destroy-universes planet, but a different planet distant from Earth, a planet of a whole different character that brings this entire discussion full-circle in many respects. Imagine where your solar system's sun was located at midnight Greenwich Mean Time at the beginning of the year 1910. That is, at the beginning of the Gregorian Calendar's 1910 that happened, according to legend, a little over nineteen centuries after the birth of the being whom many refer to as Jesus of Nazareth, son of Mary, adoptive son of Joseph. Now imagine at that same instant the location of the star Polaris. Draw a straight line in your mind from the center of your solar system's sun to the center of Polaris. Now extend that line about 40,000 light years further in that direction. That is the approximate vicinity of where that other mysterious planet sometimes spontaneously appears out of the void for what would appear to most observers to be a few milliseconds at a time. However, its true location is hundreds of millions of light years away, and that apparition of itself that pops into and out of existence there is one of its many manifestations of where it can perform its astral projection.

"Deep within that planet is often buried a grandiose pyramid that is unrivaled as far we know. Few from our species have ever visited that great, grand pyramid, and we only know a microscopic fraction of what it is all about.

"What we do know is this: Every so often an intelligent being or a group of intelligent beings go on a visit to a pyramid located somewhere and wind up getting teleported to that specific great, grand pyramid that is primarily located hundreds of millions of miles away from Earth. There they wind up experiencing what we might best call 'THE TOTAL TECHNOLOGY.' In other words, whoever is running that pyramid and the grandiloquent voice that emanates from somewhere within it, demonstrates to its visitors that it can make beings, space-time, and objects appear, disappear, teleport, and transform, with what seems to be absolutely no limits. Sure, you were impressed with how we plucked you out from your universe and your era to take you with us. The technological capabilities of whoever actually runs that grandiose pyramid dwarfs our technology by at least as much as our technology dwarfs the human technology of the 1967 from which you came. It seems that a set of intelligent, ultra-powerful beings that some call 'The Transcendentals' engage in their own set of everchanging alliances, war, negotiation, peace, and adventure, and they are a huge amount of what is behind the veil of that grand pyramid and both sides of The War Beyond Human Comprehension."

****

With that, the documentary, shifted to a black-and-white screen that featured five different fonts stating, "THE END" (with three of them featuring white lettering on a black background, one featuring gray lettering on a black background, and one featuring black lettering on a white background. They were approximately equidistant from the center of the screen. The credits then silently scrolled by, and, within a few minutes, that screening of that film finished.

****

HOW THE CONVERSATION BETWEEN FLORENCE SMITH AND DOUBLE-FORTY-ONE CONTINUED AFTER THE PART FOR WHICH NEAR ITS VERY END A RECORDING SHOWED ON THE SCREEN TO CONCLUDE WITH DOUBLE-FORTY-ONE SAYING "…THAT GRAND PYRAMID AND BOTH SIDES OF THE WAR BEYOND HUMAN CONMPREHENSION"

Florence asked, "Will I ever get to see Elias again?"

Double-Forty-One answered, "Yes, we teleported your boyfriend here ahead of you. The two of you will be watching together a documentary. Its title is *The Waters of Oblivion, Revisited.*"

The gray alien Double-Forty-One walked over to a door and waved his right hand. The door opened automatically, and Elias Artino entered the room, smiled greatly as he saw his girlfriend, and ran over toward her. The two of them embraced and kissed each other.

"I was beginning to give up hope of ever seeing you again," she said.

"This is some strange stuff we've gotten ourselves involved with, but I am feeling more than ever like my life has real purpose, real meaning. You and I have shared real purpose and meaning in how we've loved each other, but this is starting to take things to a whole other level." He gazed into her eyes with fondness.

"I heard we have some kind of movie to catch," she stated.

"Yes. Maybe one more question to our gracious host, before we get to watch that documentary. Hey, Double-Forty-One, does this documentary mainly involve reenactments or actual footage of stuff that happened?"

"It is entirely actual footage, using sufficiently-advanced technologies with which to record and broadcast, without need for having ever placed anything at all resembling what you would call cameras. Since some who might see it might not be able to handle the truth, it mostly lets the viewer think for herself or himself about whether it is some ridiculous fairy tale of a cautionary, science fiction and fantasy, mockumentary type of movie or if it is thoroughly grounded in reality. Thoroughly grounded in truth, facts, and reality, it is, this is the case. The advanced recording techniques that made it are way beyond anything your 1967 human civilization was familiar with.

"Transfigurations of nearly all light and sound dynamics made it possible. As you watch and listen and study carefully, please see if you can lose yourselves for a little while in some sense, to let go of all or nearly all clinging to your universe and your lives having any definite spatiotemporal relationship with what exactly is unfolding on the screen. Please try to imagine the action footage of the documentary as if it were happening in live action right in front of you. The documentary shall reveal to you only a few examples of what you are getting yourselves into by joining this mission, yet it will serve as the best primer available at this stage in your development.

Take your seats and get ready. Now, without further ado, here it is."

…

Nighttime along a beach with countless stars visible in the sky then appeared on the screen. The view zoomed in to reveal that someone or something had written in the sand two statements:

1) "Diverse Polarizing Figures, Many Realities, and Over A Myriad Perspectives"

2) "The End is Nigh."

****

Florence found herself briefly phasing into yet another daydream. In that, her imagination and subconscious presented to her conscious and semiconscious mind a vision of a team of godlike beings killing untold numbers of people and other creatures, that team also setting out to telepathically induce people to commit acts of genocide on one another, to become serial killers, and to murder anyone whom they believed had transgressed their dignity. Next, her vision shifted over to merging portions of those impressions with portions of various television episodes that she had watched in the 1950s and 1960s prior to when she found herself abducted out of the twentieth century altogether. This daydream lasted for twenty seconds, amid continuation of the scene of beach and sky, just before the start of narration.

Sounding identical to Robert Stack, who narrated the 1987-2010 TV series *Unsolved Mysteries*, a narrator announced to the documentary's audience, "Within the many universes…" as foreboding synthesizer music played.

ALSO VIEWING *THE WATERS OF OBLIVION, REVISITED*

In a completely different multiverse, according to some reference frames simultaneous with and according to other reference frames not quite simultaneous with Florence's viewing, another set of viewers watched that same documentary. Dimetrio Elba, Zircon Gilroy, Charr Naerroan, Susan Tecumsah Sherman, Nancy Reagan, Ronald Reagan, Gary Mark Gilmore, George H.W. Bush, Rod Serling, and Dimetroskys Elbankovic together presented that very documentary, *The Waters of Oblivion, Revisited, or: An Abridged, Revised, Reimagined Variation of All Things under and over the Sun and Stars*, for Ezra Kalkin, Jacob Kalkin, Vera Lynn, Yadier Horowitz, Vivian Valerie Orion, Harry S. Truman, J. Robert Oppenheimer, Jeremy Oppenheim, Rosa Parks, Harry Houdini, and others to behold, with several of those in attendance having never physically died before and others in the audience having died and become reconstituted from ghost states into again incarnated into living biological bodies, memory intact.

Those screening it watched it with those for whom they were screening it. They represented some of the key individuals involved with high-stakes, multi-universal diplomacy expected to affect the next stages of multiversal war, trade, and, hopefully, peace.

Although Truman and Oppenheimer had been through a falling out with each other on Earth before their biological deaths, things changed in the great beyond such that they agreed to sit close to each other for this screening on one condition—that Houdini sit between them while the movie would play. Houdini agreed.

CHAPTER TWO

The Waters of Oblivion, Revisited, or:

An Abridged, Revised, Reimagined Variation of All Things under and over the Sun and Stars

Within the many universes, different worlds sometimes bear different names. Among the worlds, there *is* a planet that across many different timelines, by whichever name, becomes the main aggressor to initiate The War Beyond Human Comprehension. Distant from Earth or whatever else its root, ancestral, originating planet might be, its government becomes a cruel, totalitarian, planet-sized, *universe-annihilation-seeking* regime.

That world has had different official names across diverse timelines.

Some of those names have been: New Gwalintu, New Belgium, New Neptune, New Mexico, New America, New England, New Germany, New China, New Io, New Ohio, New Africa, New Vermont, New Australia, New California, New Arizona, New Seth, New Oklahoma, New Zealand, and New Zoldar-Belgeran.

Some of these have shared names with what some versions of Earth has had as places featuring reasonable liberty and human rights. Also, some businesses and nonprofit organizations have had those names.

There are coincidences of matching names with reasonably-ethical entities, spanning for-profit businesses, nonprofit organizations, and governments. In some contexts, examples of those names have applied to restaurants, paper supply companies, states, breweries, executive recruiters, nations, and more.

Such an exact matching of names was coincidental in most cases, as the diversity of universes led to all sorts of unusual combinations of situations. For example, in some timelines, the United States of America neither includes New Mexico nor New Ohio among any of its states. In some such cases, interstellar developments of the timeline eventually lead to either Mexicans or Ohioans settling the fated-to-become-universe-annihilation-seeking planet. In other cases, neither any breweries nor any executive recruiters emerge to be called New Belgium, yet settlers wind up calling that planet-sized nation-state New Belgium.

Something shared in common by them is that circa-70-million-B.C.E. the Igewolintians left behind on that world a device designed carefully by several transcendentals. That mysterious device is one of the keys to the mystery of The War Beyond Human Comprehension. Across many multiverses, Charr Naerroan has usually been among the most-primarily-harvesting-energy-via-destruction types of beings, and he has consistently served as the founder of the Igweolintu religion. *The circa-70-million-B.C.E. device remained in an adobe structure after the Igweolintians emigrated out of that world. That was part of Charr's plan, and there is more to this. He was, in fact, in each universe to feature that item, the primary designer of that artifact.*

Also, in each case, its main features included an identical structure and an identical set of chemical elements in comparison with the alternate versions of itself, the differences in the alternate timelines stemmed from context, not so much from its physical presence as analyzed in isolation, and its creation came with clear intent.

Its creation came with the full intention of steering human destiny into the direction of eventually manifesting The War Beyond Human Comprehension.

This has proven one of the pieces of the puzzle of how Igweolintu's founder, the enigmatic Charr Naerroan, has coordinated his grand scheme of taking methods of destruction-oriented energy harvesting to the extreme.

*   *   *   *   *

(Though the narrator of the documentary did not have to describe this out loud, since he demonstrated it by pronunciation itself, here is, as a courtesy for those reading this chapter as a transcript describing that film, a clarifying set of notes:

1. For the typical pronunciation of Gwalintu, the "Gwa" would sound like many American English speakers would pronounce the "Gua" in "Guam," the "lin" would sound very much like how diverse English speakers would pronounce "Lynn," and the "tu" would sound like English pronunciations of "too." Igweolintu would sound at its beginning similar to the beginning of "Iguanodon," at its next part "eo" to rhyme with "geo," and at its "lintu" precisely the same as the "lintu" in "Gwalintu."

2. Almost everyone pronounced Charr like the "char" in "chart," the consonants of Naerroan the way their presence would intuitively suggest, and the vowel sounds of Naerroan that they would rhyme with "pay phone."

3. The typical pronunciation of "Zoldar-Belgeran" was as follows: the "Zoldar" would be afforded pronunciations ranging from that expected of Norwegian speakers and English speakers to confer on the "Zolder" in "Heusden-Zolder, Belgium." The "Bel" after that would sound like, "Bell." Typically, people would pronounce the "ger" either like the "Ger" in "Germany" or the "zure" in "azure." Some small percentage would pronounce that sounding between "Ger" and "zure." Finally, most folks pronounced the Belgeran's concluding "an" like the "awn" in "lawn.")

*　　*　　*　　*　　*

Behold, a deep dive now into one timeline in which the nation-state New Zoldar-Belgeran threatens its entire universe with annihilation:

In that universe, a group of Belgians, Norwegians, and Dutch settlers found a new planet hospitable to human life. They peacefully separated their government, similar to how Australia's eventual peaceful separation from the United Kingdom happened.

In the 27th century in their world, an aspiring rock musician became despondent. He had tried and failed, it seemed in virtually everything he had ever done, and now he was 33 years old. True, he was the lead singer of a rock band that got a few gigs here and there, and some friends and strangers admired the band's musicianship, including his lead singing. However, they simply were not achieving that X factor of attracting a large following of any kind, and every major music label for which they had tried out had rejected them for any kind of major contract. Meanwhile, he had experienced many one night stands with the dames, had steady girlfriends on a few occasions, and experienced much sensual bliss. However, nothing in life seemed to add up to anywhere near a holistic inner peace. He did not know whether hitting the big time would make things any better, because he knew of the tragedies of such people as Kurt Cobain, Sam Cooke, and Brian Jones.

Perhaps even more disturbingly, he had witnessed many science fiction and fantasy movies and TV episodes warn viewers about the dangers of the lust for fame and critical acclaim. However, he knew that there is something very real about when people truly resonate with one another. Although many of his dating and other activities had fallen flat for how he felt about them in the long run, he remembered how every once in a while everything would click well, and all would seem well with the world.

One day he contemplated the possibility of letting go of everything he had been involved with before and buy a one-way ticket to Earth. However, he did feel fondness for The Planet of New Zoldar-Belgeran, where he had lived all his life. There had been bad times, but there had also been good times.

All of a sudden, he contemplated suicide. Although he did not know for sure whether Cobain had killed himself centuries earlier as some law enforcement authorities had reported most likely or if somehow Kurt Cobain had been for some reason assassinated and framed as having committed suicide, the pat-terns were closing in. The 33-year old had not prayed since he turned 30, yet he now prayed sincerely to The Lord, "What is any of it worth? If you truly are omniscient or very nearly omniscient, as the legends claim, then you know exactly what was going through my heart and mind and soul just now. If you are really and truly there, then would you give me some kind of a sign that could help me decide whether to commit suicide, to move to The Planet Earth, or to do something else? Are you there? Is anyone there?"

He spoke this aloud in an empty room within his empty apartment. There were a few physical possessions around, but there were no observable human beings anywhere near him.

Suddenly, a lovely woman who appeared to be in her twenties rang the bell at the door.

He asked while keeping the door closed, "Who is there? What are you here for?"

She answered his question with a question, "Have you heard of that thing called a 'Ouija board' before?"

He said, "Yes, of course. I've never actually tried it before. Offered two of my bandmates and three of the women I've made love with, but none of those five people took me up on that offer. Also, no one has ever made the first move to offer a Ouija board session with me before. Why do you ask?"

She responded, "I offer for us to try it out together."

He looked through the peephole, and he found her incredibly attractive. He then proceeded, "Are you going to solemnly swear that this is not a trick to try to steal something from me, given that it is a bit peculiar to get such an offer from a sexy broad from out of the blue like this, especially a damsel that a fellow has never met before?"

She replied, "If you're worried about avoiding hookers and organ harvesting agents, then please relax. I am not a hooker, and I am also not part of one of those kidney-, liver-, or adrenal-gland-stealing operations. Yes, I did work as a registered nurse before, and I know quite a bit about the human body, but no, I am not now and have never before been a prostitute, I solemnly swear this, and also, I solemnly swear that I am not among the organ thieves. I am not attempting to harvest your organs."

He answered, "Great! Although there is no way for me to know for sure in terms of the five senses and logic, we all have to trust some people at least some of the time, and you seemed quite believable. I'll let you in." For a few seconds, he felt an edge of fear, slightly uncertain about whether a gang of armed men might emerge from around the corner and proceed to team up with the lady to rob him and kill him.

She entered his apartment unit. Looking around, she found a Kurt Cobain T-shirt sitting atop a doorframe. "Nifty!" she said.

He responded, "Yeah, I wonder sometimes, maybe he went to some great afterlife realm or maybe he became totally and permanently dead. Maybe we might not ever know for sure. What do you think?"

She answered, "I think this calls for a séance, enhanced by the Ouija board!"

He said, "Marvelous! Hey, I'm thinking about two different recordings of a famous 1960s song now. Would you venture a guess about which song it is?"

She felt totally attuned to him, and he felt totally attuned to her. She then said, "With a Little Help From My Friends."

He suddenly felt euphoria, knowing that this new female acquaintance had said the title of exactly the song he was thinking about. "Truly amazing! You answered with exactly the song I was thinking about. Do you like the Beatles' version better or do you like the Joe Cocker version better?"

She answered, "It depends on what kind of mood I'm in. What about you, which one do you prefer?"

He said, "Although I've had sex before, and the way Ringo and company performed it on *Sgt. Pepper* seemed more virginal, I usually find the refined, alternative jingle-jangle of that Beatles version more enjoyable than Cocker's seemingly-more-experienced, more raucous, livelier performance. Both of those very famous performances of that song are very enjoyable to me, though, and, yes, like you, it could depend on my mood which one I might enjoy better. Hm. I've spoken openly about lovemaking within a few minutes of meeting you; I hope you're not finding me to be getting too fresh with you."

She reassured him, "No, I'm not offended at all. You're being very reasonable. If anyone's been overly forward—a masher as people often called it in the middle of the 20th century—it's been me, though people seldom think of very many women as ever being mashers."

He said, "I'm not offended by your approach either. It's kind of funny, the word 'masher' for people who are too sexually aggressive too soon with their conversational styles fell into obscurity in the 21st century, though a few people here and there are still familiar with it. My old man, rest his soul, used it every so often in warning me about social relations. He'd say, 'Play the field, don't go way too wild, and, never be a masher.' Of course, people don't always use the word in exactly that way. I mean, a few people here and there even might say that people who work on mashing potatoes in a kitchen are mashers, but with a totally different meaning of that word."

She said, "Yes, true. That reminds me, long ago I heard some late 20th century or early 21st century country song or folk song that seemed to use a metaphor of people making guacamole for people making love to one another."

He said, "How odd, I seem to vaguely remember noticing a song of that pro-file about ten or twenty years ago. How about if we get going with the Ouija-board-enhanced séance?"

She inquired, "May I use your restroom to change into my alternate outfit, an outfit that will be ideally suited for this occasion?"

He smiled and glowed with a mixture of libido and genuine love. "Yes, go for it!"

 She proceeded to the restroom, leaving the Ouija board out for him to look at. All of this time, neither of them had asked the other for what name to call the other, and neither of them had volunteered to give out clear identification by name. Nevertheless, they mutually felt a knowing between them. The rest of the troubles and opportunities of the rest of the human race seemed to fade into the distance.

Suddenly, he had a flashback to a scene from high school. Classmates in a room listened as several teachers spoke, and one of the speakers warned every student present that there is real supernatural activity to be found with Ouija boards, and that it has empirical evidence, yet there is an extraordinary level of danger for most people who use that device. He remembered that various scientific authorities had on many occasions denied that supernatural events have ever had clear and convincing evidence of having ever occurred, and that some contrasting scientific authorities had stated that supernatural or seemingly-supernatural events have happened before, but it might have been some extremely mysterious natural processes, some strange and highly advanced technology, or some combination of both, therefore, maybe not quite at the level of qualifying as supernatural, though indistinguishable from supernatural for those who experienced them.

Before the lady had entered the restroom to change attire and freshen up, she had worn a modest-yet-feminine set of items consisting of casual shoes, an ankle-length black skirt, pink panties that were concealed by the skirt, and a white blouse. She had chosen to refrain from adorning herself with any jewelry on this occasion, and she had skipped wearing any makeup. Her long, blonde hair was wavy, her figure was moderately slim and moderately athletic, and she moved gracefully. She was about 5'7" tall, whereas the gentleman who had let her into his home was about 5'10" tall. Even without wearing any makeup, her appearance was beautiful to him. Both of them had a somewhat medium complexion, and both had spent substantial time in sunlight in recent months, acquiring significant tans. The woman had natural blonde hair, and she had refrained from artificially adjusting its color. The man had natural black hair, and he had refrained from artificially adjusting its color.

When the woman exited the restroom, she was wearing a crimson robe over her panties, and the robe covered her from the neck to the ankles. Also, she had changed her footwear to a pair of combat boots—a pair of the same shade of crimson as the robe.

He said to her, "Wow! If you were to add a pair of red horns, I might think you to be dressing up for Halloween as some form of she-devil!"

She giggled and smiled toward him. "Yes, maybe that would have been even more appropriate for this occasion. You ever hear about those rumors that the Ouija has something to do with The Devil?"

He said, "Yes, of course, maybe almost everyone in New Zoldar-Belgeran has heard about that rumor."

She proceeded, "Well, yes, but just because people say that, it doesn't mean that it has to be true. Or, if it is sometimes true, then it still might not always be true. Do you believe that The Devil exists, and do you believe that a group of many he-devils and many she-devils exist?"

He answered, "I suppose, like almost anything, that could depend on how people define things. Also, some of it could depend on stuff that is out there in reality, but we as regular-world, living people might not be able to ever know for sure."

She challenged him, "How about if before we ask the board about how it could help us to channel the ghost of Cobain, we could ask it for a clue about the mystery of whether devils and angels actually exist in very much a real-world sense?"

He said, "Yes, let's go for it."

They then proceeded to use a traditional method of how the active and resistant forces of the both of them, including conscious and subconscious levels, coordinated with the unknown, led to, letter by letter, number by number, and symbol by symbol eventually arrive at a statement. They looked at what they jotted down, which displayed, "DRYGDRVLA9G4RUREADY" there on paper.

They both thought about what this might mean, and they negotiated with each other in a mini-brainstorming session. Eventually, their consensus was to interpret it as asking, "The PhD Doctors are running dry with answers to the mysterious side of the God-blessed or God-damned Reality. Very late is the time with a level of 9-out-of-10. Get ready for things to change. Are you ready?"

After that, they proceeded to use the combination of the board, a set of dim LED lights shaped like candles, an acoustic guitar, and some cuddling as they attempted a Ouija-enhanced séance in search of the ghost of Kurt Cobain. For a little while the both of them suspended most disbelief as the gentleman entered a deep trance and stated, "I am the ghost of the lead singer of Nirvana. I died in a tragic accident. It was neither a suicide nor a murder, it was an accident. Don't jump into believing way too much of what you read. Also, sometimes your very senses of sight and sound might lead in the directions of wrong conclusions. Beware of Charr Naerroan and the wielders of ultimate destruction."

After he made that pronouncement, he snapped out of the trance, yet he had no clear and distinct memory of having ever entered the trance. Fortunately, a few minutes before that happened, she had convinced him to start recording their session. Together, they looked at the recording, and she saw his face seem to turn pale.

He said to her, "Holy shit! I still have no memory of going into that trance, but there is the recording of it, both with sight and sound, right there in front of this table. Wow!"

She said, "Yeah! We still might not know for sure whether that was the ghost of Kurt Cobain who spoke through you, but who knows, it just might have been him!"

He said, "That was one of the most interesting things I've ever been a part of. How about if we come up with a list of what ghosts we might want to do additional séances?"

She said, "Yes, sir."

He said, "I'll take the lead for now, and let's see how many of these you might agree with exploring." Pausing for a few seconds, thoughts raced through his mind. She had plenty of time to initiate something new to say out loud with words, yet she declined to do so, preferring to look into his eyes with a mixture of libido and genuine love. After he composed his ideas well enough, he resumed presenting a suggestion. "Let's consider starting with the ghost of Lorena Bobbit, or do you think that would be too dangerous?"

She said, "Hm, I'm trying to remember who that person was, it sounds familiar. Oh, I remember now!" She suddenly blushed, feeling a mixture of a thrill between her legs and a sense of fear about how vulnerable the male anatomy can be sometimes.

He said, "You're actually blushing! Maybe we should move on to a different candidate for whom we should attempt to channel next."

She said, "Yes, I think we should. Although I felt a little bit of a risqué thrill about male vulnerability and female adventurousness, I feel terror that if we channel her too well, it might lead to too much risk to your body, and I care deeply about the health of your body, as well as the health of your heart and mind and soul."

He suddenly felt extreme love for her, and he said, "I treasure that you genuinely care about me. I genuinely care about you, too!"

She suddenly felt an even stronger caring for him than she had felt when she had just mentioned to him how much she cared. "Yes, then take your time with thinking up another suggestion for the next ghost for us to try to channel. I have plenty of time to share with you." She looked into his eyes and smiled gently.

He looked back into her eyes and also smiled gently, then said, "Aimee Semple McPherson."

The woman in front of him said, "I have no clue who in the world that was. I'm not sure if I had ever even heard that name before. Who was she?"

He then said, "There was a biopic that I saw a few years ago. It had Bette Davis portraying the mother of that Aimee, and it had Faye Dunaway portraying that Aimee McPherson. They evidently aired it on television in 1976."

She said, "Tell me more."

A few seconds went by as he gathered his thoughts, then he gave an introduction. "Early in the 20th century, she led a Christian religious movement, something kind of like those megachurches that emerged in the late 20th century and early 21st century, but long before them. Then there was this strange thing in which she disappeared for a few weeks or something like that. Her mother claimed her to have died, yet it turned out later that she resurfaced, alive and reasonably well. She claimed to have been kidnapped and to have escaped, but other people weren't so sure, and some legal authorities seriously quest- ioned whether there had ever been any kidnapping whatsoever in her case."

The lady wearing the red robe and sitting a few feet from him stated, "Well, I'm not in the mood to seek out her spirit at this time. Maybe we can try that another time, but for now, how about another suggestion?"

He wondered about what was happening. Suddenly, he felt a different concern: many times before things had gone well between him and a woman at the beginning of courtship, yet things would eventually go terribly wrong. He did not want that to happen now, yet he perceived that he might be one false move away from losing the interest of the woman he had just met. He thought a little bit harder.

"How about if we try Martin Luther King, Jr.?"

"That's another great idea for whom we might perform a séance seeking someday, but I'm not feeling quite right about seeking his ghost at this time. Let me help you out a little. I'm suddenly feeling like exploring whatever might emanate from the first millennium A.D. Who do you wish to suggest next?"

He felt great relief upon hearing that she was not on the edge of rejecting him. He thought a little bit, then came up with a new suggestion. "How about Mani, who founded the Manichean religion?"

She said, "Yes, as a matter of fact I have dabbled in I-Guang-Dao, which is an offshoot of multiple religions in a syncretic way, in some sense in a similar vein as the supposedly-extinct Manichean religion."

The two of them then proceeded to carry out a séance in a manner similar to what they had done earlier that afternoon. Early on they looked again at each other and felt a strong yearning that mixed sexual attraction, emotional resonance, and genuine love, even though they had just met a few hours earlier. Some claim that love cannot be genuine unless people have spent dozens of hours getting to know each other, yet the two of them had already within a fraction of one day reached a knowing of hearts and minds that few newlywed married couples reach within the first three weeks of being wed, and the two of them achieved without yet even having had sexual intercourse with each other. Both of them were thinking about going all the way, yet they were still building up, and both were considering the old traditional recommendation to wait until after marriage. The man had prior sexual partners, yet the woman was a virgin, one of the most attractive virgins in the entirety of New Zoldar-Belgeran.

A little further into the séance, things became more interesting, as the electricity went out for about two minutes, then came back. That led to a brief conversation about famous movie scenes in which power outages played roles in the plotlines. It also led to both of them feeling tempted to kiss the other, or to present the traditional kiss offer of going about halfway or more toward a kiss and waiting for the other to possibly complete it. However, both decided to continue to wait for more physical escalation of their mutual attraction.

With the cameras still rolling, the woman said to the man, "I'm starting to feel very weird. It feels like there's some presence that I can't see but can somehow tell is here."

The man said, "I kind of feel that, too. Hey, I've been waiting for a long time to either ask your name or to hear you ask my name, and we've both been holding back on asking. Lovely damsel, would you be so kind as to let me know with whom I am having the pleasure of sharing company?"

The woman however, went into a deep trance. The man witnessed speech coming from the mouth of her body, yet the proclamation was, "Although my name is Sarai, I am not the woman with the body in front of you. She has gone into deep unconsciousness. Yes, there is a little trace of her still here, but the primary identify in front of you is the Sarai who was married to Abraham, the founder of some portion of Abrahamic Religion. 'Til death do you part, the old saying goes with marriage, and he and I remained married until death separated us. We have been able to find each other again occasionally across the eons, but it has been rare indeed. I have witnessed much and learned much in the great beyond, yet there is still much mystery to it all. I shall have to depart soon, yet I wish you and your new female companion the best with forging a great future together. How well the two of you get along and team up to help your lives and the entire human race may prove pivotal. Best wishes with the future. Tallyho!"

The man stood astounded. The woman snapped out of the trance about five seconds after that speech.

The woman said, "What just happened? You started to ask for my name, then, as I was about to speak, I blacked out, and now it looked to me like you teleported from a seated position to a standing position two feet away from where you had been seated. Do you have any idea what happened?"

The man said, "You… or should I say your presence… went into a profound trance. Then, it seemed like a spirit took over your body and spoke through you. Since we've been recording, how about if we take a look at the video?"

The woman said, "Hm. Let's postpone the playback of the video, delayed gratification can be much better in this case, I believe. How about this, I'll somewhat parrot what you asked me before that happened, though with a few adjustments. Hey, I've been waiting for a long time to ask for your name. I heard you ask for my name just before I seemed to have experienced a little missing time. My name is Suzie. Handsome gent, would you be so kind as to let me know with whom I am having the pleasure of sharing company?"

This time, Suzy witnessed her partner in conducting séances drift into a deep trance. She saw and heard his body then pronounce a lengthy monologue. "The man whose body is here in front of you is still here at a trace level, and he is in a state of deep unconsciousness, with some microscopic trace of that semiconsciousness that sometimes accompanies or perhaps always accompanies the sleeping state of a living human being.

"I am the Prophet Mani whom you and your male friend, let's call him Stan, were seeking. Yes, I founded the ancient Manichean religion.

"The early Manichees, myself included, felt, intuited, and divined great mysteries, yet, unbeknownst to us, on the other side of the world, in South America, there was the simultaneous founding of the religion Manosianism, which is in some sense a form of Anti-Manicheanism.

"In some sense, too, Manicheanism is a form of Anti-Manosianism. You, child, have maintained your honor as a woman on a life path befitting of strict adherence to the purity movement. Yes, you engaged with a little maledom foreplay with a few guys, and, yes, you engaged with a little femdom foreplay with a few guys, including that 12-year-old you really had your way with when you were 13, fortunately, responsibly enough to refrain from causing any permanent damage to any of his genitals. You are moderately experienced in erotica, but you have still retained reasonable purity. How long you might stay that way might be anyone's guess right now, but the fact remains that you have retained what you have retained, and it is beautiful.

You have thus far avoided violating anyone else, and everyone else has thus far avoided violating you. Also, you have completely steered clear of going all the way into acting out anything that would match official, legal definitions of coitus, cunnilingus, fellatio, and anything else that a reasonable observer would consider full sex."

Suzy blushed. The arousal of her erogenous zones contributed to an urge to interrupt the strange monologue, yet she resisted the temptation to speak in this case.

The male speaker continued, "Many religions and many sects and subsects of them are all over the place with guidelines. My followers and I tried our best to get things to work well. There were triumphs and tragedies along the way. All the while, when I was still alive, I knew very little about how our diametric opposites were out there, half a world away, preaching that the best way to live is to embrace the routine use of human sacrifice and the enslave-ment of most religious adherents.

"Also, although the Manosians did not gain anywhere near the popularity that the Manicheans gained, they did continue with a small and continued line of succession, hidden away from mainstream

South American societies for exactly the same amount of time as we the Manicheans did.

"In the fifteenth century A.D., both the last Manosian and the last Manichean died simultaneously, apprehended by Chinese authorities and boiled alive until dead. After that, we joined up with some variation of Indian Dharmic religion somewhere in the Great Beyond, specifically, we joined some of the Kashmiri Shaivists who had transcended the worldly life on their way into the mysteries of the Great Beyond."

Stan's body proceeded to get into and hold the Peacock Pose of Yoga for about two seconds, then to stand back up and return to his seat. After that, he fell asleep in that chair.

With a male for which she felt deep affection and much curiosity sleeping right in front of her, she had a flashback to erotic ideas found in some 1998-1999 issues of *Cosmopolitan* magazine. Although she felt tempted to lunge into aggressively initiating sexual foreplay, she resisted that temptation and chose to take a slower, subtler approach.

She decided to try to wake him up with a kiss. She kissed him in a firm, caring, and loving way, in a spirit of complete affirmation of his value as a male human being, her value as a female human being, and their value as a couple who just might have a profound future together.

He suddenly woke up while she was passionately kissing him on the lips.

Stan asked, "What happened? One moment I was listening to you ask for my name, and the next moment I found myself waking up with you kissing me. What happened?"

Suzy answered, "Stan, you went into some deep trance, and you started to say that you were The Prophet Mani, whose presence had taken over your contribution to the conversation for a while. Either the ghost of Mani possessed and spoke through you or some deep recesses of your mind took role-playing to the max. Wow, your amnesia makes it clear that whatever happened just now, the consciousness that flows through you went above and beyond the call of duty!

"He, or you, or some combination—we might never know for sure how much of it was from whom—went into a fantastic monologue. I think we should go check on the playback now. What'd'ya think?"

Stan said, "Yes, great! Wait, how did you know my name is Stan?"

Suzy answered, "However much of it was your subconscious, however much of it was somehow channeled from beyond, I witnessed hearing come out of your mouth a statement that your name is Stan."

Stan responded, "Truly remarkable! Combining a Ouija board and a séance process has been one of the most enchanting experiences of my life!"

A few seconds later, after they silently looked into each other's eyes in a meditative state, Suzy asked her partner in attempted paranormal investigations, "Have you ever tried that dish that's very popular with folks from Turkey with that name, I'm trying to remember that name of that dish, oh yes, I remember it now. Have you ever feasted upon Iskendar Kebap?"

Stan answered, "Yes, it was delicious! I've only tried it a few times, but I enjoyed each time marvelously!!"

Suzy added, "I've enjoyed it, too. Likewise, I've only tried it a few times. How about if you ask me anything?"

Stan inquired, "If you don't mind something personal, about how many pairs of panties do you own?"

Suzy felt sexual arousal and a slight, subconscious embarrassment. She covered her mouth lightly with her right hand and unintentionally stared at Stan's groin. Meanwhile, she held her left hand a few inches in front of her own groin. Her subconscious was delighted and thrilled by how her partner's question stimulated her into some uninhibited thoughts of engaging in coitus, fellatio, and cunnilingus with him, yet her subconscious also felt the weight of impressions of *Genesis* and memories of reports and videos both of male atrocities performed onto female genitals and of female atrocities performed onto male genitals.

Her semiconscious regions of mind placed her right hand over her mouth largely out of an impulse to seek to protect his glans and corpus cavernosa from the risk that an overaggressive use of her teeth might sever them. Her semiconscious regions of mind placed her left hand a few inches in front of her groin largely out of an impulse to seek to protect her vaginal walls, clitoris, and cervix from the risk that an overaggressive use of his glans, corpus cavernosa, hands, and/or teeth might catastrophically damage or maybe even destroy them.

She also silently blushed. He noticed her blushing, and he cast a devious stare into her eyes. She lifted her eyes away from staring at his groin, and she soon stared back into his eyes as his eyes continued to stare into her eyes. She calmed down enough to remove her right hand from blocking the paths between her mouth and her partner's body. As they both remained silent in terms of words, yet shared quite a multitude of nonverbal communications, she continued to hold her left hand in front of her vulva, blocking paths between her partner's anatomy and her sensitive vaginal and ultrasensitive clitoral tissues.

With mixed emotions of libido, love, fear, and compassion, she then exhaled deeply and calmed down a little more. Next, she moved her left hand over next to her left outer thigh. She closed her eyes, leaned back, and rested. He let her rest. Ten seconds later, she inhaled deeply, sat up straight, opened her eyes, and again made eye contact with her partner.

He looked at her both mercurially and lovingly. She looked at him both lovingly and cautiously. They both reflected on the recent séance.

Suzy said, "Without further ado, let's get to watching that video."

*   *   *   *   *   *   *   *   *   *   *

Within three months, the two of them got engaged.

One week after engagement, they walked into an instant wedding chapel and got married.

On their first anniversary, they attended a rock concert headlined by an act called, "Lucifer Rex and the Paragons of Virtue." Although they enjoyed the concert immensely, they spoke afterward about rumors they heard from other concert goers.

Suzy said to her husband, "Do you remember that Sammy who spoke with us in line as we waited to have our digital tickets scanned from our smartphones?"

Stan answered, "Yes, that was very weird. I didn't feel best to speak out loud my skepticism then, but it took a lot of effort to keep quiet and to let him go on and on with that weird rumor. I remember part of it. Mind if you speak to me about your memory of it, that wild tale he allegedly heard about?"

His wife stated to him, "Wow! It was not so much one thing as it was about four or five things weaved together, all about that lead singer who calls himself Lucifer Rex. Sammy said some folks by the docks told him that they knew the fellow before he became famous, and they had witnessed acts of people dressed up as devils going around saying 'Hail Satan' while bowing down to that Lucifer Rex fellow, who previously had been calling himself, 'Anton Skandar XXVI.'

"According to the story, basically no one in the general public knows what that guy's birth name was, but he adopted that name as part of creating a new religious movement that would merge elements of the version of Satanism that Anton Szandor Levey founded eons ago with the version of Occultism that Aleister Crowley founded eons ago. The alleged new tradition was that some Alternative Pontiff founded… something… called—what was the name—Igweolintu, an extremely alternative religion that brought together much, not only elements of Thelema and The Church of Satan, but also portions of five types of Christianity, seven types of Buddhism, three types of Islam, Kabbalist Judaism, Occult-Oriented Rock Music, Philosophical Taoism, and, yes, about twenty other things.

"They worship the Unknown God who convinced Caesar Nero to take his own life in service to the higher good. It emerged that one of the alternate leaders of that movement was High Priest Anton Skandar, presumably going by a stage name strategically chosen to resemble the name Anton Szandor.

"Rumor has it that their religion has hidden itself for centuries upon centuries. Some debate whether its alleged existence is just an urban myth or really something real. If it is all a hoax, then maybe those who are making money off it are part of what's behind it. If it's not a hoax, then maybe it will come out of the shadows someday and make itself more known. Here's another thing: A new twist is that some proclaim that rock star Lucifer Rex of the band Lucifer Rex and the Paragons of Virtue is of that, and some even say that he is none other than that new religious movement's leader, Anton Skandar XXVI, boldly performing on stage incognito! Who could have dreamt up such a tale?!"

The next weekend, they were standing in line at a bank and noticed that the man ahead of them in line was one of the band members from the recent concert!

Suzy could not help but ask him about it.

"Aren't you one of the Paragons of Virtue who performed a concert recently?"

"Yes! In the flesh."

"Wow, do you know if very many of the wild rumors about your lead singer are true?"

"That sort of stuff is a closely-guarded secret. Look out for the next edition of *New ZolBel Entertainment*, which should become available online within just a few days. It includes an interview with Lucifer Rex, Paragon East, Paragon North, Paragon South, and yours truly!"

"Oh, you're Paragon West! I was pretty sure that you were one of those Paragons of Virtue, and you confirmed it for me, but I haven't quite gotten my act together in terms of being able to tell which of you is which!"

"No need to worry. Few people can tell us apart. Most of the attention gets paid to the lead singer."

"My name is Suzy, by the way. Mind if my Hubbie, Stan, here, takes a quick photo of us standing side by side while waiting in line?"

"Go for it! I don't mind at all. And if he'd like to also have a photo with me, then he can also be my guest."

Suzy and Stan proceeded to have their photos taken with Paragon West. *Little did the couple know that the quartet of instrumentalists known as The Paragons of Virtue were not of that couple's world, they were among the destruction-oriented team of Transcendentals closely affiliated with Charr Naerroan.*

That quartet going by the stage name The Paragons of Virtue had immigrated into that version of the nation-state New Zoldar-Belgeran legally despite coming from beyond its entire uni-verse's timeline. This was made easier by how they applied to enter the admission-to-citizenship-by-merit-based-testing, no-documentation-required process that the nation allowed would-be immigrants daring enough to try it.

In the year that they passed that test with flying colors to win citizenship, 55% of those who took that test died somewhere in its obstacle courses and escape rooms. Of the remaining 45%, only about one-third made it all the way to winning the citizenship they sought after. That amounted to a 15% success rate for those who applied via that process.

The man sometimes going by the stage alias Lucifer Rex when performing as a rock superstar and going by the alias Anton Skandar XXVI when leading the religion Igweolintu, had actually been born with the name Larry Smith. His parents had elected not to name him

Lawrence to go with a nickname of Larry. Instead, they chose Larry Beelzebub Smith to be his full legal name.

They drew some eyebrows from several people by granting their newborn son the middle name Beelzebub, but as human civilizations had progressed over the centuries, fixations against the use of weird, unorthodox names had diminished.

Unfortunately for that Larry B. Smith, a.k.a., Lucifer Rex, a.k.a., Anton Skandar XXVI, he happened to be on board a jet airplane on route to a three-day vacation when, mysteriously, a missile blew it out of the sky.

The authorities chalked it up to Christian terrorists who had proven themselves insufficiently tolerant of the upstart religion Igweolintu and its leader. Some alleged that group of terrorists to be categorizable as "Christofascists," in accordance with how several thinkers from the 1970s through the 2020s built up a body of work warning about when the conjunction of 1) an alleged devotion to promoting Christianity, 2) a way of embracing authoritarian tendencies, and 3) Fascism together take hold of a human mind, a group, a party, or a nation.

The day after the bombing, an organization claimed responsibility for it, and, sure enough, it was one of what the government there had declared one of the "Christofascist Terrorist Organizations." Indeed, they had been the bombers, exactly as they had claimed and the government had claimed.

One of the tenets of that group was that what is considered murder by the law of a human government is not necessarily murder at all, because God Almighty is the only true judge of what constitutes a murder vs. what constitutes a justifiable act of killing. That group, The Fundamentalist and Justified Guillotine Brigade, would regularly act out cruelties that over 98% of the mainstream Christians condemned. Many of these acts were identical to some of what Los Zetas, MS-13, the USSR, the NSDAP, the Mau Mau fighters, the Ku Klux Klan, the makers of sexual mutilation pornographic films, a small percentage of South African women, a small percentage of South African men, and a small percentage of prison guards had done to people hundreds of years earlier. For example, they believed it ethical to slowly vivisect people to death without anesthesia during interrogations in order to advance group objectives. A set of allegedly-pro-Christian agendas held TFJGB, as some abbreviated it, together. *Most of its members believed that torturing people to death could in many cases be neither an act of murder nor an act of cruel and unusual punishment.*

Back to the aftermath of the deaths of those who were aboard that airplane that the TFJGB shot out of the sky via a missile. They were of diverse ethnic and religious backgrounds, a few of them celebrities, most of them ordinary people, and the most famous among those who were on board had been Larry B. Smith, also known as the rock singer and musician of the stage name Lucifer Rex, also known as the secret religious leader Anton Skandar XXVI.

His memorial included the long-awaited full confirmation that he was in fact both the rock star Lucifer Rex and the religious leader Anton Skandar XXVI, as well as the truth that his legal name had been Larry Beelzebub Smith.

In the wake of his death and the outrage that it inspired, the government started to perform major crackdowns on all of the major religions. *In the name of religious tolerance and safety from acts of terror, draconian measures went into place, eventually leading to the two major political parties becoming The Know-Not-Much Party and The Liberty-From-All-Religions Party. The former emphasized that society should have as its baseline a combination of honoring the non-terrorist elements of each religion while reengineering society to be most accommodating to agnostics and people of low-to-medium religiosity. The latter expressed the intent to steer the populace toward low religiosity in general, based on the belief that low religiosity is the only honest way to face the universe while acknowledging the scientific advances that had occurred since the industrial revolution.*

As the centuries went by, the free exercise of religion diminished further and further on that timeline's version of New Zoldar-Belgeran, eventually leading to an epic war between it and the other planets of humanity.

Early in that decline in religious liberty, the leadership of Igweolintu there consisted of Paragon North, Paragon South, and Paragon East. Meanwhile, Paragon West had become a missing person soon after Anton Skandar XXVI's death.

Paragon North became the new supreme leader of it in that timeline. He told the followers that his real name was Jeremy Mephistopheles Titanus, and that he transcended many of the normal bounds of space and time, having traveled to their world from beyond their entire universe. Many people in the general public thought that this was mythological hyperbole, but he was telling it to them straight: He was one of the close associates of Charr Naerroan. Both he, J.M. Titanus, and his friend Naerroan were among the Emphasizing-Destruction-

Oriented-Energy-Contracts-With-Reality Transcendentals. Among the Emphasizing-Preservation-Oriented-Energy-Contracts-With-Reality Transcendentals opposing them Yadier Horowitz, Dimetrioskys Elbankovic, and many others. The entire leadership of Igweolintu disappeared one day, and the movement seemed to evaporate within three decades after that, yet early in the centuries-later war between New Zoldar-Belgeran (combined with its allies) and Earth (combined with its allies), J.M. Titanus, Paragon East, and Paragon South reemerged to lead a resurgent Igweolintu into the top of the power structure of the world from which they had disappeared.

For a while, they remained hidden as the power behind the throne of the visible power. During part of this time, the government required nearly all of its citizens and long-term residents to receive brain-chip implants. Those would eventually become, via computer monitoring of brainwaves, a means of enforcing totalitarianism, for those whose brainwaves exhibited thought crimes could often be pinpointed by wireless technology, rounded up, interrogated, and, if need be, tortured and executed.

Next came a first-strike attack by New Zoldar-Belgeran on the other civilized worlds of the human race, together with a demand for all other governments to subjugate themselves to it or else die. Various governments lined up on the side of Earth, resisting the imperial ambitions of New Zoldar-Belgeran. Other governments lined up on the side of New Zoldar-Belgeran, which sometimes went by the abbreviated name New ZolBel. The war waged on and on for a while. Then the tide seemed to turn very favorably for the forces of Earth and its allies, with victory seeming to become inevitable. However, the entire situation had played right into the grand plan of J.M. Titanus (who, to reiterate, was also known as Paragon North), Paragon South, and Paragon East.

Titanus held a secret meeting for the top officials of the New ZolBel government, including ones affiliated with both of the dominant parties, namely, the Know-Not-Much Party and the Liberty-From-All-Religions Party. Early in the meeting he said, "I know that the situation looks bleak, but fear not. Paragon South, Paragon East, and I possess powers beyond anything we had previously revealed to you."

Then, with a wave of his hand he caused a suitcase to materialize right before their very eyes. Next, he posed a question to a general seated three seats to his left. "General, in all your studies of weapons systems and physics, what have all the experts told you before about the prospects for matter-anti-matter explosives?"

The general answered, "It will never be practical. You could put together all of the anti-matter in the entire universe, somehow make it into a bomb, then detonate it, and its output wouldn't even be very big compared to our largest hydrogen bombs."

Titanus stated firmly, "They were wrong. The two other Paragons of Virtue here, together with myself, are actually capable of using our minds to change the very laws of physics, at least temporarily, each time we succeed in overwhelming the resistance to our changing of those laws. Check, now, the remote quantum-entanglement viewers for developments at the Planet Earth."

Several aides quickly hit a few buttons, and a large monitor showed real-time video footage of Earth, thanks to spooky-remote-quantum-entanglement technology, capable of instantaneous communication of data across extreme distances.

Jeremy Mephistopheles Titanus, his assistant going by alias Paragon East, and his assistant going by alias Paragon South, then held hands while standing in a circle that surrounded the mysterious briefcase. They closed their eyes and chanted several mantras, then grew silent. *Suddenly, on the monitor there appeared footage of Planet Earth completely exploding.*

The rest of the people in the room stood silently, in reverential awe.

Titanus announced, "I didn't know whether or not it would work this time, but we got it with the first shot in this case. We have decapitated the enemy's forces in this universe, but we have more work to do. We'll explain more in a few seconds."

The three who had just succeeded in obliterating the version of Earth in their universe again held hands, chanted briefly, and grew silent. The rest of those in the room witnessed the room itself and the entire universe vanish, including their own bodies. This rendered them disembodied consciousness for a while. Within a few seconds, though, the entire group of them were in a different place entirely. Titanus then explained to them, "Those of you who were in a room a little while ago with Paragon East, Paragon South, and me, then witnessed what might have seemed to you like reality itself going on the blink, be not afraid. Reality did go on the blink in several ways, but we have broken on through to the other side of several realms of reality. After we succeeded in obliterating the version of Earth that was in the universe where each of you were born and had grown up and resided, we proceeded to utterly obliterate that entire universe, including its Lord. Furthermore, we have teleported our group over here to another universe, where we can join up with additional beings who are on our side of a huge war. I am what some call a Transcendental, one of the beings who sufficiently transcends the spatiotemporal order such as to be able to influence the very laws of nature. There are three main sides to the wars, negotiations, and peaceful cooperations between the Transcendentals: there is the group that emphasizes destruction as a method of harvesting energy, the group that emphasizes preservation as a method of harvesting energy, and the group that emphasizes swinging back and forth between emphasizing destruction and emphasizing preservation. All three groups are often heavily involved with creation, as it tends to go hand and hand with both destruction and preservation. We are among the group that emphasizes the use of destruction as a method of harvesting energy. Now, Charr Naerroan, another of the Generally-Destruction-Oriented Transcendentals shall speak to you."

Charr who stood eight feet away from Titanus, stated, "To clarify, each of the Transcendentals has the free will to emphasize destruction, preservation, creation, or some hybrid of two or more of them at any given instant. It just so happens that we have tended to coalesce over the eons into those three camps that J.M. Titanus described. There have been times when great numbers of us have shifted between camps. One prime example was that in some versions of Earth in some of the early centuries A.D., Europe witnessed a period of much greater peace than it ever did before or since. That was largely due to how the Transcendental Jesus of Nazareth teamed with multiple other Transcendentals to help bring a huge shift of peace to that region, as well as many other realms of many different universes, and much of that hinged on a temporary gigantic shift of allegiances away from destruction-oriented energy contracts among the Transcendentals for a while. The pendulum eventually shifted back, and with that shift Europe entered the dark ages, the Middle East witnessed a series of extreme warfare, and the Middle Ages emerged. I respect Jesus of Nazareth, although many Christians who have encountered me have at some levels of mind considered me to be a manifestation of 'The Anti-Christ.' A few of the other Christians who have encountered me have at some levels of mind considered me to be among 'The Heavenly Host of The Risen Angels.' There are other Christians who have thought me to be among 'The Demonic Fallen Angels.' Truth be told, I myself do not honestly know how much truth and how much false-hood there is in each of those notions. Yes, in some ways I might seem to border on being omnipotent and omniscient when witnessed by some of the ordinary mortal beings, but in many ways I fall significantly short of omniscience. There are many levels of omniscience; in some ways, all beings carry at least a little trace of it within themselves; and, yes, a powerful Transcendental such as myself carries far more of it than ordinary mortal beings carry.

"We are currently conducting a mission. A war is waging on, and one of my objectives is to obliterate the multiverse in which we currently find ourselves. Titanus, many other Generally-Destruction-

Oriented Transcendentals, and I have together obliterated many universes, but the version of myself that I am experiencing myself as being has never experienced the obliteration of an entire multiverse.

"Each time an entire universe gets obliterated, its inhabitants, including the very Lord of that universe, get liberated from many of the things that had been holding them back from roaming beyond their previous constraints, though it comes at a dear price for them. The great beyond is full of mysteries beyond anything that anyone could fully describe with words, yet the eons have proven that our niche of utilizing destruction-oriented energy contracts has worked exceptionally well for ourselves in our service toward the greater good of all beings in the long run."

Several of the former political leaders who had found themselves plucked right out of their very universe—their former universe, that is—silently ran through inner thoughts in the vein of, *I have worked hard for power, influence, and the good life, willing to make many sacrifices and to act out manipulative politics, but I never bargained for this!*

Charr telepathically detected that some of them were thinking like that, and he announced, "I know that some of you may be having second thoughts about where you are, the loss of the old reality from where you came, and why you ended up here. Rest assured, if you decide to cause us much trouble at all from your not feeling up to maintaining allegiance to our side, then you will very likely find yourself or yourselves executed by us long before you get anywhere close to escaping. You have made your bed via your political and military careers, and now you have to lie down on it, relax, and wait a little while, metaphorically speaking.

"That is it for now, dinner will be served in the room on the other side of the exit opposite where I'm standing. After dinner, I wish to encourage you to practice good hygiene, get a good night of sleep, and to get ready to reconvene in the morning. We have lots of plans to discuss, and each of you, if you are strong enough and wise enough, shall play a key role in helping our side in this war."

****

Elsewhere, Yadier Horowitz, Dimetrioskys Elbankovic, and others gathered together in support of the preservation of universes and worlds.

Yadier said to Dimetrioskys, *"What a tragedy; to think of the beings who had many of their hopes and dreams for a future within the reality they had known for all of their lives, destroyed like that, together with their entire universe; to think of it!"*

Dimetrioskys responded, *"We've witnessed it before, but it doesn't seem to get any easier each time."*

In another realm, two men spoke off the record with two women while on a car ride from Mexico to Canada via the United States of America. The first woman said to the first man, "I wonder."

The first man responded, "You wonder about what?"

She said, "I wonder about what those scientists say about things like how the universe may eventually die this way or the universe may eventually die that way. Also, I wonder about my own mortality, as well as your mortality, and, for that matter, everyone's mortality. We have all these legends about what might happen when we're gone, but it seems to me like we probably won't know for sure until after we die, or maybe we might not even know for sure even after we die. I wonder about this stuff."

The second man said, "Yeah, but there's not much we can do about it, is there?"

The second woman said, "Well, we can do the best that we can. Still, sometimes it seems that none of the theories really makes very much sense to me. The idea that we might get totally and permanently wiped out, the idea that if we happen to choose the right religion and use it properly then we'll be in great shape, the idea that there are no right and wrong religions, the idea that there is one right religion, the idea that there are two or more right religions, and so on and so forth. I try not to think of it much, but sometimes I do think about it."

The first man then said to the other three, "Maybe it just might be a mixture of all of that stuff. I do remember some writings and video recordings that suggested something like that."

The first man, who served as the driver focused on the road, as everyone fell silent for a couple of minutes. The other three, though, started to feel uneasy. The second woman, who sat on the right rear seat, said, "How about if we check the radio."

The first woman, who sat in the passenger front seat, situated on the right as standard in North America in that world, turned on the radio. An emotionally-wrenched female voice announced from the station, "This just in. Tragedy in South Korea, as North Korea has detonated a nuclear bomb onto it."

The woman who had just turned on the radio shut it down and started sobbing and wailing. The three other passengers also cried. A little ways further down the road, the woman turned the radio back on. Now a male voice made the announcement, "Mysteriously, all of the main Internet servers in the world have seemed to have changed their dates and times to precisely the midnight that began this year, the year 2049. None of us knows how or why this has happened, yet this is disturbing to say the least, especially after our world's first use of a nuclear weapon in war in over a century."

A huge tug-of-war was in process between the forces of the Transcendentals who aimed toward obliterating that entire version of Earth and the Transcendentals who aimed toward prolonging the life of that entire version of Earth. As part of this huge struggle, all mechanical timekeeping devices on the planet had, seemingly miraculously, changed their times to midnight. Machines and other devices with hardwired displays of differing time zones become completely rearranged such as to show only one time zone and only one time, namely midnight.

The devices there that kept track of day, month, and year became set to the very beginning of the year 2049 of the Common Era, no matter what time zone they happened to be in. An eye-of-a-hurricane calmness mixed with a semiconscious abject terror came over billions of people. *It was clear and unequivocal, a global paranormal event was underway.* Newscasters and ordinary people knew that something very strange was happening, but they did not know what was beneath the surface. Beings worldwide shared the ominous awareness that the situation portended danger, perhaps even Armageddon.

In this case, order became restored within a few weeks, and life on

Planet Earth continued for most, though many South Koreans, North Koreans, Iranians, Iraqis, Israelis, Portuguese, French, Germans, Ethiopians, Kenyans, Australians, Brazilians, and Mexicans died during that period. The forensic scenes of many of those deaths exhibited clear evidence that the paranormal was part of the cause of death.

Nevertheless, life went on.

In the earlier case, The Destruction-Oriented won a battle in The War Beyond Human Comprehension, resulting in the death of an entire universe and all of its inhabitants, who became liberated from life such as to enter the great mystery of the great beyond. In the latter case, The Preservation-Oriented won a battle in The War Beyond Human Comprehension, resulting in the continuation of life of an entire universe and many of its inhabitants, who became free from what many of them would have considered an untimely death, postponing their entry into the great mystery of the great beyond.

*****

Next, consider a conversation from twenty years before the Internet became popular on one of the versions of Earth.

"Shakyamuni Buddha did not have to resurrect way back when in order to build the foundation that he and the early sangha constructed. There are times to resurrect, and times to refrain from resurrecting," said one person in a crowded ballroom to another.

The other replied, "Maybe Jesus of Nazareth was the only person to successfully resurrect, or maybe not. Who the hell am I to know this sort of thing for sure? What the fuck do any of us really know for sure about any of this stuff?"

A third person stated, "We'll do the best we can, and, maybe, 'further along,' as the old song goes, 'we'll know more about it.' That's something for which I'm often hopeful."

The person who had expressed skepticism a moment earlier in relation to Jesus and everyone else retorted, "Sometimes I feel that sort of hope. However, other times I feel and think ominously that we might not ever actually know any more than a small fraction more than what we know right now, and, that, maybe, even if there actually is some sort of an afterlife, then, as hurtful as it might seem to consider this, we even during our afterlives still might not know any more than a small fraction more than what we know right now."

Nearby, an army sergeant listening in on the conversation decided to conduct a non sequitur: Sgt. Amir chanted, "I don't know, but I've been told, 'FTA' stands for many things new and old."

One of that Sgt. Amir's very distant descendents was a man named Theodore Sooner, and that person became one of the most illustrious of late fifth millennium and early sixth millennium space explorers.

The year 5001 for one of the variations of the human race found the species *Homo sapiens* spread across multiple star systems.

Many estimated it to have been about 5,004 years since the physical birth in human form of Jesus of Nazareth, whereas others estimated it to have been in the range from about 5,001 years to about 5,008 years since that legendary birth.

A team of four humans, multiple artificially-intelligent devices, a spacecraft featuring an AI central computer, and a bunch of supplemental tools visited a planet within a star system. The humans took a rover trip to drive around the perimeter of a giant pyramid that they discovered there. As they approached completing one rev-olution around that mysterious artifact, they spoke to each other about competing concerns.

After Teddy Sooner, Dorothy Webster, and Zarlowe Nike heard Stewart Scarington voice a nightmare scenario, Dorothy assured him that, as irrational as the scenario seemed to basic logic, even if it did somehow actually apply to their situation, evidence seemed to be conclusive that they had successfully avoided the trap of that tragic pathway. However, the mission's captain, the illustrious man Zarlowe Nike, voiced a concern that they should not overly relax just yet.

He said primarily to Webster and secondarily to the rest of the team, "Have you considered, Linguistics Officer Webster, though, that if we made it past that hurdle, the aliens may have other terrifying challenges still left in store?"

His companions spoke not a word for what seemed an eternity. Rolling along, Stewart glanced at a device estimating Earth date and Earth time. The device relied on stations the Mozarka Explorer previously launched to send signals from the planet's two moons, combined with several satellites. Although a highly reliable system, it now read hour-minute-day-month-year to be "88:88 88-88-8888 Terra-Time ERR ERR Terra-Date ERR ERR." Stewart silently showed it to Zarlowe, who responded, "Clearly some kind of glitch, it even says 'E-R-R,' indicating a measurement error of some kind. Who ever heard of the eighty-eighth day of an eighty-eighth month! Chief AI-comp of Mozarka, read me… Chief AI-comp, are you there? Over."

Zarlowe looked at other sensors and announced his shocking

discovery, "It seems… somehow our ship is no longer in orbit. Pft, it just disappeared."

"Um, we have bigger things to worry about, Captain Nike," said Stewart, tears streaming down his face, "Who are those humanoids in the distance and how did they build a town so quickly, and why are they pointing at us and the monument?"

Meanwhile, Teddy and Dorothy were too shocked to speak. Having grabbed the Earth-day-Earth-time apparatus and taken a look, their jaws dropped and their eyes expressed a terror beyond the description of words. Zarlowe snatched the device from their trembling hands and observed the new temporal reading: "23:45 31-10-7001 Terra-Time 11:45 PM Terra-Date October 31st, 7001. Happy Halloween!" Zarlowe started shaking his head in horror and his whole body trembled wildly.

All four were completely speechless as they rolled to somewhere due east of the Pyramid's center.

Suddenly, incomprehensibly, their spacesuits, seats, and space buggy, the pyramid, and the whole planet vanished before them, and they found themselves seated together somewhere totally unknown. They had on casual, Twentieth Century fancy Western wear, sitting in what appeared to be a Nineteenth Century courthouse somewhere in the American Old West. Located where a jury might often sit, they noticed in the place of a judge's bench a roundtable covered with a dark, metallic silver sheen. Behind the table was a golden wall with wooden boards and a Nineteenth Century style chalkboard. Just as the explorers started becoming used to this setting, though still stunned speechless, the entire environment around them changed a second time.

They now found themselves wearing the kind of casual clothing customary for them to wear aboard The Mozarka Explorer in off duty hours (for example, while participating in watching movies or listening to music while computers manned the ship). They were seated around an oval table and the mostly transparent shell of a giant pyramid surrounded them on five sides: one each for front, back, left, and right, plus the floor. Changing scenery pulsated and transformed around the mostly transparent walls and floor, some-times involving a dizzying array of stars and galaxies approaching and receding, sometimes featuring gently waving terrestrial envir-onments. The shell was invisible except for an ever-evolving pat-tern of lightning-shaped flashes of many colors. Fog, smoke, steam, and fire appeared and disappeared spontaneously. Beginning to come to terms with their environment, they collectively wondered to themselves what could possibly be happening—also, where in the reality they were.

*****

"I am…, You are…, We are…, and You have reached The End of Time!" exclaimed a Great Reverberating Voice.

Although the visitors continued to feel confused by what was transpiring, Zarlowe recovered just enough forty seconds thereafter to say something.

"I guess this means we're… in the interior of… of… 'the interior… of The Great Grand Meta-Pyramid.' Is that where we are?" asked Nike.

"You could say that… or you could say you are beyond any location from anywhere your previous experience would have called 'space-time'," answered The Voice, with a slight lilting of the voice as it enunciated the phrase 'space-time.'

"How could you demonstrate for a few minutes just what you mean by being 'beyond any location' in whatever sense it is you're using those words?"

In response to this, their environment changed instantly into a realm in which each of the four explorers retained consciousness of thought, memory, volition, emotion, and imagination, yet possessed no sensation of physical color, shape, form, body, touch, or breathing.

Thus began a silent period of sensory deprivation that their consciousness might have otherwise called eighty-eight seconds. During this 'time' Zarlowe Nike reflected on how some ancient philosophers would have argued that the four explorers now no longer existed. This did not bother him one bit, though, for he felt that his access to memory, volition, emotion, and imagination continued to connect him to valuable aspects of the history, the future, and mind. That is, if there could be such a thing as 'future' in a realm where an authoritative voice already declared 'the end of time.' All four explorers were somewhat concerned during this time about the fate of the other three and the universe in general. They also hoped to learn more about what The Voice may have meant by its mysterious opening pronouncement.

Totally deprived of any ordinary sensory input, the notion of time became even more uncertain than it had been in the bizarre moments of the two-thousand-year time dilation that they recently encountered.

Suddenly, voices presenting a radio story show began to manifest themselves to these explorers' collective sensory perception. The first narrator was a voice sounding gentler and much more "human" in many ways than what their minds had referred to as The Great Reverberating Voice.

(Here is an outline of what the explorers listened to over the course of this "radio show:")

Female Narrator: We now present to you a tale titled "Florida Welcomes Home a New Resident." The brief story features two brothers, one named "Carlos Gamboa" and the other named "Miguel Gamboa."

Carlos grew up in Cuba and longed to live in America. He felt that he could only accomplish this by escaping, as the Cuban government of that time would not approve of such an ambition. One day, during the height of a hurricane sweeping across Cuba on its way toward Florida, Carlos decided to carry out an extremely dangerous plan of escape. He said to himself:

Carlos: I know a lot of people think me a fool to try this, but I need to make it to America. I just have to. I'm having difficulty making it here in Cuba, and I'm determined to make it there, even if it means steering a boat to Florida while staying in the eye of a hurricane.

Female Narrator: Sitting by himself in a large home, he stepped outside his house and drove to a nearby collection of boats. Two weeks earlier, Carlos obtained a set of keys to one of the boats. A friend gave him these keys as a gift and told Carlos he could travel anywhere he wanted with the boat as long as he accepted the fact that it was an extra special boat. Carlos located this boat and recognized that it had not been damaged by the storm. He jumped in and started piloting the boat toward Miami, Florida.

Carlos: I sure hope I can make it to America. It's a land of opportunity and hope. A place of dreams and wonder; if I can make it there, who knows what will be possible?

Female Narrator: Carlos managed to successfully steer his way to Miami, Florida, keeping his special boat within the eye of the hurricane the whole time. After landing, he anchored the boat in an available dock close to where he knew his brother Miguel to be living. He only needed to walk two blocks to see his brother.

(The audience heard the sound of three knocks at a door, followed by the sound of a door opening.)
Miguel: Carlos, my wonderful brother! I can't believe it! You must have snuck into America through the middle of that hurricane! Thank God you're alive!

Carlos: Yes, Miguel, I love you, my brother, and thank God!

Female Narrator: The Latin American brothers embraced and started catching up on old times. They remembered several childhood events similarly, although there were a few minor discrepancies. The two of them attributed these to the effect that the years might have had on their memories, and they felt at peace. They avoided talking about politics or major world events; there would be plenty of time to talk about these the next day and, besides, Carlos was in much need of rest.

The next morning, Miguel prepared a breakfast including huevos rancheros with tortillas. After his brother awoke, they shared breakfast and felt happy about this surprise reunion. When Carlos Gamboa saw the front page of his brother's copy of the morning edition of a major South Florida newspaper, he began to laugh.

(The audience heard the voice of Carlos laughing with a joyful sense of humor.)

Miguel: Why are you laughing so much? Is it something funny in the newspaper?

Carlos: It's this 'newspaper,' if you can call it such a thing. This is one of the most hilarious pieces of comedy I've ever seen. Who are the comedians behind this thing?

Miguel: It's a regular newspaper, not even a tabloid, either. What's going on here? Why do you think it's all comedy?

(The audience heard a long, silent pause.)

Carlos: You… you mean… this the news? The real news?

Miguel: Yes, why would you think otherwise?

(The audience heard another long, silent pause.)

Carlos: It looks like I'm not who you think I am. Where I came from, Cuba is a province in The United Republic of Columbia, a huge democracy in northern South America through southern North America. I was coming to The USSA, The United Socialistic States of America, to join the socialists.

(The audience experienced yet another silent pause.)

Miguel: Most people would think this was totally crazy, but I'll simply ask if you have documents that would be evidence of what you just said.

Carlos: Sure, I'll show you.
(The sounds of a man reaching into his pocket to pull out a wallet were heard.)

Carlos: Here they are: my URC, United Republic of Cuba, driver's license, social security card, and two credit cards issued by banks from the URC.

Miguel: This is extraordinary!

   Still, I don't know if it might be dangerous if you met the other Carlos Gamboa… Actually, I know exactly what to do.

Carlos: What, what might it be?

Miguel: You see, this man, a real-life Florida Seminole, met me about a year ago at a nonprofit organization's meeting. He invited me to a movie about the role of Native Americans in World War II. Actually, what I just said probably sounded bizarre, but it will make more sense for you over time. This Seminole told me that if someone came to meet me the way you have, I should give the person a history book of The Twentieth Century from my world and a recent newspaper or some recent Internet news story printouts. He also said it may be a good idea to give you an anthology or two of science fiction short stories. I'm about to give you each of these items, and you had best head back to sea. The storm already ended and your path is clear.

Carlos: Thank you brother. Even if you aren't the brother I thought you were, in another way, you are just as much my brother as he is.

Female Narrator: Miguel gave Carlos three books, three printouts of news stories from the Internet, and a newspaper. They embraced again just before Carlos boarded his special boat, and said a quick prayer for each other's safety. Miguel kept this encounter a secret as he continued to live his life, although he did enjoy creative writing more than he had previously enjoyed it. Years later, a personal friend asked about the whereabouts of two of Miguel's favorite books. Miguel simply said:

Miguel: Someday I may buy another copy of each of them. I gave the copies you asked about to someone I felt really needed them at the time. You might say it was giving to charity.

Male Narrator: The next story is called "Three Philsatlantean Jews Dream Together of an Unknown World." It includes two Jewish sisters attempting to create a story about a place both familiar and alien, a world populated with people similar to those of their world, yet involving an almost completely different world history. They first read about this "unknown world" in a science fiction epic by a Philsatlantean man named Arthur Brown. They worked on this story in the early morning hours of a secular holiday in The United States of Philsatlan. For this holiday, these sisters, named Laura and Dora, stayed at their parents' home for a visit. Their parent's names were Ehrud and Deborah.

Laura: Dora, do you think we should change the ending? Which version should we go with?

Dora: It is fiction, after all. By the way, this take on our perform-ance had an improvement on the earlier take. Remember how the earlier take included a Freudian slip of having Miguel say, "Still, I don't know if it might be dangerous if you met the other Miguel Gamboa," where he intended to say, "Still, I don't know if it might be dangerous if you met the other Carlos Gamboa," remember that? This take, in which Miguel says what he intended to say, namely, "Still, I don't know if it might be dangerous if you met the other Carlos Gamboa," this take I believe is much better.

Maybe we could see what it sounds like with each ending. How about if you read it from the top, and after you're done, I'll read the alternate ending.

Male Narrator: Laura began to read their story outline from the top. These two daughters planned to create a screenplay based on the story, then produce a student film based on the screenplay. They were enrolled in graduate school, studying the art of filmmaking.

Laura: The characters of this story are either fictitious or used fictitiously.

This story is a fictional account by Arthur Brown adapted into an alternative by Laura and Dora Greenberg.

The origins of the peoples in The World of America included continents that came to be called Africa, Asia, and Europe. From ancient pre-history onward, these peoples passed through many stages of cultural and technological development. Over millennia upon millennia, competing tribes covered the world with countless acts of war and violence. Religions and mysterious practices evolved over time, and the rise and fall of many an empire spanned many a troubled century. A people called The Romelians were especially prominent for almost a thousand years in a continent called Europe.

Great inventors, artists, scientists, and philosophers interacted with good-hearted, kind, regular folk in places called Africa, Asia, Europe, North America, South America, and Australia. People with devious and nefarious schemes also emerged in each of these places, sometimes rising to lead entire nations into devastating conflicts. Fortunately, individuals in this world sometimes changed from intentionally creating harm to acting with conscience when they had the opportunities.

Eventually, they arrived at a crossroads, an era called The Twentieth Century. In that period, peoples in The World of America had to endure "the war to end all major aristocratically driven wars," whose aftermath would lead to "the cataclysmic conflict between technocratic ideologies and dogmas." These were popularly referred to as "The First World War" and "The Second World War." In World War II a Prussian named "Adel Hister" led the National Socialists of Greater Prussia into a scheme to take over the world while slaughtering Jews and many other minority peoples. There had also been a young Jewish baker named "Adel Shapiro" who resided in Greater Prussia during much of the 1930s, and he successfully escaped just before the breaking out of WW2.

Adel Shapiro proceeded to become an iconic actor, often carrying a heavy heart about how the Adel Hister proved unspeakably cruel to tens of millions of human beings.

A group of idealists in the Land of Japania turned idealism into an ideology of rigid, mechanical authority structures and, oddly enough, became allied with National Socialist Greater Prussia. The Prussians and the Japanese both had twisted ideas involving eugenics, though they had very different ways of thinking about that.

Meanwhile, a Russian leader named "Stonewall Stalin" led a nation called The USSR and an American President named "Francisco Delano Rosemont" led The United States of America. They, together with leaders in China, France, England, and the other Allied Nations, opposed the Axis Powers of National-Socialist Prussia, The Neo-Romelian Fascist State, and The Ultra-Authori-tarian Incarnation of Japania. After eventually conquering The Neo-Romelian State and Hister's Greater Prussia, Rosemont and Allies needed to concentrate on achieving victory over The Land of Japania.

Rosemont's United States of America developed a fission atom bomb, a weapon of epic force such as humans had seldom dared to dream.

When America finally used this bomb on The Land of Japania, the leaders of Japania somehow refused surrender. A second atom bomb dropped from an American plane onto The Land of Japania, and a drama unfolded with graver implications than hardly a hu-man in that world could have imagined at the time.

Much of the leadership in Japania wished to continue refusing surrender, even after being dealt two nuclear bombs and facing the prospect of a Russian invasion. Teetering along the edge of either surrendering or preventing their nation from surrendering, they somehow carried out a coup that managed to eliminate government elements wishing a peaceful surrender.

By this point, Rosemont had already died and been replaced by a leader named TrueMan. This TrueMan agonized over two seem-ingly unconscionable choices: drop one atom bomb after another onto Japania or attempt a slower attack of the island. The slower attack would have mounted a horrendous casualty death toll on both sides.

While America evaluated the last Axis power's seemingly unreal refusal to surrender and temporarily resumed traditional bombing, Stonewall Stalin's Russia began an invasion.

America then dropped a third atom bomb on Japania, tragically not knowing that Soviet forces had already reached the site of this third bombing. Japania changed from being the last Axis power to oppose the Allies to being the first battlefield of a new confrontation between Russia and America. Although the Americans used the way in which they had sole access to the nuclear bomb to devastate much of Russia in the ensuing conflict, the two sides came to the peace table without having to force the other into unconditional surrender. Tragically, the damage to human conscience created by the events leading from 1914 to 1953 were horrendous enough to plunge their world into becoming one of the regions of hell.

Dora: Thank God this is just a fiction story! The horror of it all!!

Laura: Yes. The horror!!

Yes, I'll now continue.

As it was, a few vestiges of human conscience continued in various religious and secular groups: These included Science Fiction Developers creating sparks of hope and cautionary warnings wherever they felt they should, Christians looking to their *Book of Revelation*, Jews turning more than ever to the most speculative of Messianic prophecies, Muslims hoping to witness the most hopeful of the prophecies of the Koran actually come to fruition, some Mahayana Buddhists looking to Kalachakra, Vishvamata, Green Tara, The Dhyani Buddhas, Hevajra, Shakyamuni Buddha, and Ksitigarbha Bodhisattva for an answer, and some Hindus returning to their ancient idea of an avatar of Vishnu named Kalkin, also known as Kalki.

Nevertheless, the battle that raged from 1939 through 1953 and culminated in a seven-and-a-half-year war between America and Russia took a horrible toll on the human spirit, and their world would take two centuries before making a sizable move out of its own man-made hell.

A big part of humanity's climb out of the abyss came from two multicultural sources, one secular and one religious.

The secular one was called The Skull Collecting Club of America, a network of highly intelligent and wealthy individuals who had given up on morality in the face of a world turned into a region of hell, yet refusing to choose outright immorality. They chose for themselves to be amoral while learning as much as they could and profiting handsomely along the way.

The other group, calling themselves The Undead Overworld, was a super-secret network of people from diverse religions, unknown to the general public and even unknown to The Skull Collecting Club of America. This Undead Overworld brought together people the rest of their world thought were dead, missing, or irrelevant. These included people thought dead though still alive recruited into The Overworld at strategic moments to make the public think they really were gone, handicapped and disabled people the public assumed to be inconsequential to society, homeless persons that go-vernments had lost all record of but who would wind up impacting the world more than most national leaders, and, of course, people who discovered the network and simply walked away from their past to help shape the future.

For quite a time, The Undead Overworld monitored the activities of many governments and kept a special eye on The Skull Collecting Club of America. The Skull Collectors drew their name from 1) the fact that in a world that had transformed itself into a manmade hell, skulls became plentiful and were legally bought and sold on the free market worldwide and 2) the Club's choice to collect skulls and use a combination of meditation and remote viewing to see into the mental histories of people whose skulls it collected. The club's ability to do this enabled it to make superior financial decisions due to its ready access to nonpublic information affecting the valuation of stocks and bonds. When the Skull Collecting Club became aware that The Undead Overworld was monitoring it, early, direct com-munications between the two groups involved much conflict. How-ever, they soon discovered a common interest in steering human-kind away from hell and in the direction of hope, justice, and prosperity. Joining forces, they gained strength and began to turn the tide in the future of their world.

Turning the tide, that is, although, they faced strong opposition from Socialistic Logicians, a once noble network of philosopher-scientists whose very minds had unknowingly been captured by a hypnotic battle between neo-left-wing-anti-aristocratic-socialists and neo-right-wing-nationalist-socialists.

Little did they admit to themselves that these hidden hypnotists pulling many strings behind them were none other than two of the Socialistic Logicians' many psychic off-spring! Not knowing either of these camps to be behind both sides in many visible levels of debate within their own philosophical, scientific, country club network, they fancied themselves the masters of their own ideas.

A high percentage among their ranks chose furious opposition to the combined forces of The Skull Collecting Club of America and The Undead Overworld. Mysteriously, at yet another level, little did the neo-right-wing-nationalist-socialists and their neo-left-wing-anti-aristocratic-socialist rivals know that besides being the puppet masters of their ancestral Socialistic Logicians at this point, they were also themselves little more than puppets of something they feared to face.

"The Skull Collecting Club allied with the Overworld" battled "The Socialistic Logicians" in a conflict lodged in drawn-out psycho-logical trench warfare, something of a World War I style and invol-ving intangible, very slow moving, invisible front lines.

Then came the breakthrough: Suddenly, the ghosts of President Francisco Delano Rosemont, Saint Nicholas the Tsar of Seconds, and

Physics Phenom Alberto Eisenstein came riding in on a huge Troika Chariot from a heavenly realm and multiplied their presence across much of the globe, announcing to all a message of peace and healing.

*****

Nicholas the Tsar of Seconds started the message, "The problem is not Socialistic Logicians. Without the capacity to think logically about society, humans would have fewer tools with which to build a healthier society.

"The problem is not the group known as The Skull Collecting Club of America. Without the entities who provide deep insights into economic development and secret knowledge, humanity would have fewer means with which to accomplish much of anything.

"The problem isn't women; without women, men wouldn't have as complete a range of behavior.

"The problem isn't men; without men, women wouldn't have as complete a range of behavior.

"The problem is not children; without children, where would adults be?

"The problem isn't adults; without adults, where would children be?

"The problem isn't inherently one of any specific demographic group, be they Tsarists, communists, capitalists, Jews, Gentiles, Muslims, religious critics, religious advocates, mysticism critics, mysticism advocates, idealists, socialists, fascists, pragmatists, Hindus, Christians, Buddhists, or even people who don't categorize themselves.

"What is the problem, you may ask? It's able to be symbolized in many ways, and here is one of them."

President Rosemont stated in a noble tone, "When people become consumed with fear to the near extinction of their other faculties, they are capable of actions of limitless horror. If you 'fear' in the sense that you respect the ways you reap what you sow and ways you face the consequences of your actions, then this may be called healthy, wealthy, and wise.

"Yet, if you choose consumption of fear as a reason to ignore experience and shut down your very conscience, you and many of those around you will surely reap much harm – harm that your fear would produce with or without good intentions."

Eisenstein concluded their main announcement, saying, "Let go of the impulse to run around in mind-numbing fear, and let go of the compulsion to let fear turn you into a puppet with a need to kill. Please let go of the cruelty and ignorance, and become a teammate who is a kind and just puppet master.

"You can help restore the health of your world by finding new ways to heal."

The Tsar added a bonus conclusion. "Yet what we just explained is just one of many perspectives. We welcome you to let go of fearing alternate perspectives. We welcome you to see beyond even our views in a spirit of loving-kindness, wisdom, and justice."

Dora: That is beautiful! I wonder how we're going to convert it into a screenplay.

Laura: Patiently, just like we did with the chick-flicks we've designed. I sure am glad you suggested adapting Arthur Brown's epic story as a break from all the women's movies we normally make.

Dora: I feel an intuition that saddens me now.

Laura: Sis, what saddens you?

Dora: Although we intended to be two-thirds of the way serious with this, some critics will find it truly absurd.

Laura: You can't please everyone, but you can still seek ways to do things well in life.

Dora: How true!

(Laura then placed her arm over Dora's shoulder.)

Dora: I'm feeling better now. Whether very many of the critics like it or not, we can try to do our best to make it an uplifting, helpful, insightful project for audiences to behold.

Laura: Thanks, sis, for your hard work on this!

Dora: The thanks is to you, my sister!

Laura: Thank you, and God bless.

Now let's try the alternate version of the fictional account of the world dreamt by Arthur Brown; it's your turn, Dora.

(The sisters paused for a little while to brace themselves for a trip into additional mysteries.)

*****

(They then resumed.)

Dora: All right, picking up the fictional world's saga from some-where in the middle:

Eventually, they arrived at a crossroads, an era called The Twentieth Century. In that period, peoples in The World of America had to endure "the war to end all major aristocratically driven wars," whose aftermath would lead to "the cataclysmic conflict between technocratic ideologies and dogmas." These were popularly referred to as "The First World War" and "The Second World War." In World War II a Prussian named "Adel Hister" led the National Socialists of Greater Prussia into a scheme to take over the world while slaughtering Jews and many other minority peoples. A group of idealists in the Land of Japania turned idealism into an ideology of rigid, mechanical authority structures and became allied with National Socialist Greater Prussia. Meanwhile, a Russian leader named "Stonewall Stalin" led a nation called The USSR and an

American President named "Francisco Delano Rosemont" led The United States of America. They, together with leaders in China, France, England, and a number of other allied nations, opposed the Axis of National-Socialist Prussia, The Neo-Romelian Fascist State, and The Ultra-Authoritarian Reincarnation of Japania. After eventually conquering The Neo-Romelian State and Hister's Greater Prussia, Rosemont and his allies needed to concentrate on The Land of Japania.

Rosemont's United States of America developed a fission atom bomb, a weapon of force such as humans had seldom dared to dream. When America finally used this bomb on The Land of Japania, the leaders of Japania somehow refused surrender. A second atom bomb dropped from an American plane onto The Land of Japania, and a drama unfolded with graver implications than hardly a human in that world could imagine at the time. Much of the leadership in Japania wished to refuse surrender, and they almost managed to prevent their nation from surrendering to the allies. However, this element of the Japanian leadership was overthrown by other elements of the leadership, the key moment coming when Japania's emperor overthrew emperorship itself at some level. A capacity for conscience and skilful means helped lead to surrender in a war that had become more dangerous than people realized. This helped save their world from transforming into a region of hell.

After the end of this cataclysmic conflict, also called the Second World War, there started a period called "The Cold War." During this period, "The United States of America" and "The Union of Soviet Socialistic Republics" developed arsenals featuring atom bombs, which later gave way to arsenals of fusion-based hydrogen bombs. This "cold war" had periods of escalating and diminishing hostility, including an incident in the early 1960s in which many in this unknown world felt they had narrowly averted disaster. Then, one fateful day in 1982, when hardly anyone expected instant nuclear war, an electromagnetic anomaly disturbed nuclear weapons systems to create an unintended first strike – at least unintended in terms of the humans. The ensuing nuclear war and its aftermath led to that world's human extinction.

As the humans of that world became extinct, two extra-terrestrial aliens shared a conversation somewhere beyond the orbit of Jupiter.

Anonymous Twenty-One said: The electromagnetic anomaly that we induced into happening sealed their fate.

Alien Voice of Anonymous Twenty-One: Thus ends humankind on one of many planets that once held intelligent life.

Alien Voice of Anonymous Double-Forty-One: Yet another tragic case of a course of events that demanded our intercession. We take no pleasure in handing those humans their justice, yet hand them their justice we do.

It simply flowed from the awareness of their actions.

Alien Voice of Anonymous Twenty-One: I just became aware that we may go back to February 1981 and adjust the course of Science Fiction to steer their world into a direction sparing us the need to destroy them as we did.

Alien Voice of Anonymous Double-Forty-One: That would be wonderful! Let's do that, and let's bring some of the spirits from their alternate path into their world in 1981 to help expand their aware-ness of alternative actions and consequences.

Alien Voice of Anonymous Twenty-One: What about leaving in an anomaly in 1982 that doesn't create an 'unintentional' nuclear war, although it does serve as a little subconscious 'reminder?'

Alien Voice of Anonymous Double-Forty-One: Let's see how things play out between early 1981 and some time 1982, and then we'll decide whether to do as you just suggested.

Dora: I like both endings, I must admit. What do you think?

Laura: I like both of them, too. Of course, I see how maybe not everyone would be thrilled to see theatrical versions of these tales, but I… somehow just feel right about how we created them. Even if only a few people come to know of these creations, I just feel right about it, somewhere in my soul.

(Sounds of hard-soled shoes walking rapidly down a flight of stairs entered the field of hearing.)

Ehrud: Girls, my lovely daughters… I just had a dream… a dream where a Gentile from a variation of Arthur Brown's alternate universe was telling me something. He said that he felt ashamed of something he used to say and feel. This Gentile said he was ashamed that he had taken pleasure and indicated to others that he took pleasure in the deaths of Nazis. He said "Nazi Germans" are what his world calls the people Brown labeled "Prussian National Socialists." Then in my dream I asked him why he felt ashamed, and he answered that he had been acting as a bad example, a violation of valuing life. He said he apologizes to all Jews, Nazis, and other humans alike, and everyone beyond any level of being human, and wishes to remind Jews that we were warned that people who execute anyone while taking pleasure in causing the death are not in harmony with The Torah for as long as they block related levels of conscience. He said only by unblocking these levels of having conscience could someone see a more complete picture. I asked him for more of what he meant by this, and he said, "The more complete picture of how Jews and Gentiles alike can recognize the consciousness of others and how all life is precious." It was about then I remembered that attachment to taking pleasure in the deaths of others has dire consequences, even when their deaths involve justice. I see more clearly now the value of recognizing the suffering of others and letting conscience shine with greater clarity.

After hearing this "radio show," the explorers again heard silence and were left with only their minds, memories, imagination, and related faculties while deprived of any ordinary sensory input. Gradually, they felt bodily dimensions, touch, feel, breathing, and gravity returning to their sensory worlds. They found themselves lying on their backs on large beds within a completely dark room. The Great Voice returned.

"Light will return slowly. Your eyes will adjust with reasonable comfort." Light indeed returned slowly, and their eyes felt reasonably comfortable as the new visible surroundings emerged from total darkness.

The Voice continued, "Once you get out of bed, you may explore these regions as you choose. The doorway on your right leads to a higher dimensional library. The doorway on your left leads to extra-special dining facilities. As Captain Zarlowe Nike spoke first upon your arrival and I have deemed it appropriate, he will get to choose your path."

Zarlowe offered his crew a role in making the choice. "If any of you are feeling hungry, we'll go to the dining facilities first. Otherwise, I feel we would best be served to visit this 'Higher Dimensional Library' that The Voice referred to."

The other crewmembers agreed unanimously to wait until later to eat. The four of them began to make their way to the library. After entering and looking around, they explored all eight 'floors' of the library, which might be better called 'surfaces.'

These surfaces looked and felt like ordinary rooms individually, yet the movement from one to another revealed something special. Each room was rectangular, with a ceiling, a floor, and four walls. These six directions provided six means of exiting to an adjacent room. Moving across two rooms in any one direction from any room led to the same other room, which might be called a room opposite the room of origin. Zarlowe and Stewart figured out that it reflected a four-dimensional rectangular pattern, with each of the branches serving as a three-dimensional surface of the four-dimensional structure. They had originally entered through one of the openings between rooms, but any future attempt to walk back through it functioned as just another part of the library. If someone looked at this in the context of space-time, then the eight surfaces of the library would seem to exhibit "three-space-with-time" or {(three-space)-time}, and the overall structure would seem to exhibit "four-space-with-time" or {(four-space)-time}. The explorers in some way experienced themselves moving from one surface of the pattern to another, never really inside or outside what might have been called "The Five-Dimensionality."

Looking at the branches as consisting of 'four pairs of opposing faces,' the names of the branches were organized as follows:

• First pair: "The Philosophy of the Psychology of Science" and "The Science of the Psychology of Philosophy"

• Second pair: "The Science of the Philosophy of Psychology" and "The Psychology of the Philosophy of Science"

• Third pair: "The Psychology of the Science of Philosophy" and "The Philosophy of the Science of Psychology"

• Fourth pair: "The Religion of Technology" and "The Technology of Religion"

The interior of each branch was organized into three sections, the first two of which used familiar shelving systems to catalogue books. Extraordinarily, the third section within each branch was a highlight collection – one that somehow formed a microcosm of the library as a whole!

Wandering around the Higher Dimensional Library, the explorers found copies of manuscripts and films long thought to be lost to the ravages of time. Documents from The Library of Alexandria were among those present, for example. After they had their fill of sampling the collections and felt ready to eat a meal, they announced these intentions and waited for The Voice's answer.

"Very well. You will have a meal break also serving as a two-and-a-half-hour recess. You may eat, drink, rest, and take care of your health in general at The Zoo of Antiquity & The House of Murals," announced The Voice. Their surroundings again transformed, this time into what looked like a park featuring a giant zoo and a very unique looking house.

Walking on a trail through the human portion of the zoo, protected by a large bulletproof shield with a hemispherical cross section, they witnessed a zoo more natural than they had previously experienced. In some ways, rather than a "zoo," this was more a wilderness area with carefully crafted shielding for observers to walk through. Animals long thought extinct from The Planet Earth lived in what appeared to be a natural habitat. Sections spanned Pre-Triassic eras through the dawn of the industrial revolution and carried labels such as "Jurassic," "Cretaceous," and "Pre-Cambrian." Of these, the Pre-Cambrian exhibit was more of an aquarium than anything else – an aquarium featuring special microscopes to enhance human vision.

Nike, Webster, Scarington, and Sooner found an automated counter with a sign that read, "Order food from here. Simply choose from a limitless menu; the only restriction is that we reserve the right to withhold from a given explorer food that would otherwise be lethal to that explorer. No need for concern about whether you consider a food lethal or not for yourselves, we will figure that out for you." The explorers ordered meals and spent the next fifty-five minutes in the Zoo's spacious dining facility, refreshing themselves and replenishing their bodies with fuel. At one point, Sooner, Scarington, and Nike walked to an area adjacent to this dining facility to see what was there.

Now sharing the presence of a Tyrannosaurus Rex, they heard the voices of the male and female narrators from the radio show announce, in two-part harmony, "Beyond what you'd thought was space and time, this T-Rex has intelligence mighty fine: intelligence like that of many a brilliant mind. This Tyrannosaur, an otherwise deadly dinosaur, recognizes the value of human life. Stand in his presence if you choose; stand there as a friend if you may, he'll be less a threat to you than many humans – than many humans you've met along the way." Teddy decided to trust the voices and ventured into the room with the adult Tyrannosaur, carrying no weapon. This shocked Scarington, who found the idea of walking right into the company of a large carnivore too dangerous to stomach. He, Teddy, and Zarlowe debated the value of trust versus the value of caution. Zarlowe emph-asized that perhaps with the most complete, balanced awareness of situations and consequences, beings should often trust while preparing to deal with the unexpected. He referenced the *Kung Fu* episode "The Tide." Teddy Sooner then proceeded to enter the Tyrannosaur's den, where it was already in the process of eating dinner. Much to Stewart Scarington's surprise and relief, this Tyrannosaurus Rex lived up to the narrators' praise; not only did it let Teddy live, it held up the claws on each hand to signal victory and peace.

After this, the three of them met up again with Dorothy Webster, and the four explorers now strolled over to an artistically designed three-story mansion, a building with a sign outside that read, "The House of Murals." While there, they noticed that all the walls and furniture in it were covered by the designs of murals or miniature murals. Many of the murals the group identified as copies of known classics. Others seemed previously unknown unto them. The mural designs covered all furniture, walls, silverware, and appliances. Having some free time for themselves and feeling exhausted, the team agreed to stop most talking and walking for a while to simply meditate and rest.

Meditating during part of this period on relationships between physics, psychology, and martial arts, the explorers experienced special realms of Mind manifesting in the building. In front of copies of many famous murals, they experienced aspects of Mind symbolized by the following passage:

"Paralleling 'Psychological Testing's Relation to Martial Arts Mind vs. The Turing Machine' and 'Another Way of Modeling Probability Waves Collapsing Into Observable Particles'" by An Author Choosing to Temporarily Model Himself by the Moniker 'Unknown-then-Known-then-Unknown'

(Modeling under 'Unknown')

…

(Temporarily modeling as 'Known-as-MJB')

What if someone taking a psychological test thought to him- or herself something like the following?

"This question asks me to choose between many categories, yet as a practitioner of martial arts I see the value of using behavior patterns reflecting both answers. I may choose behavior reflecting the one answer when activity of the universe presents it as more effective, and I may choose behavior reflecting the other when activity presents the other as the more effective tool. This applies to each question I now face in some way. How, oh how, may I choose to answer?

"Aha! Although my mind may be called otherwise unbound by the rigid structures of The Turing Machine model, I may choose to temporarily model 'a mind boundless as zero and infinity' as 'temporarily relating to a rigid behavioral pattern symbolized by a Turing Machine Model.' Because the psychological testers are seeking to model expectations of how I would act in contexts that concern them, I will attempt to create a Turing Machine Model symbolizing and communicating behavior patterns in their context with reasonable accuracy, to the best of my knowledge as of the present time. Of course, though, as soon as I choose 'a Turing Machine Model' for them to observe 'my boundless mind' as 'being,' and transfer this model to them, right afterward 'The Martial Arts Mind' returns to what could be called 'the transcendental-zero-and-infinity wave.'

"One could imagine in this a parallel to the quantum phenomena of observing probability waves…

(Returning to Modeling under 'Unknown')

…collapsing into the observation of 'particles with definite locations,' then returning to manifesting as 'analog probability waves with a range of locations in potentiality.'

"On the other hand, though, what if you someday felt 100% sure that through observation and testing you had completely and totally and undeniably eliminated any uncertainty in interpreting any parts of this document paralleling psychological testing and models involving quantum wave-versus-particle manifestations? What then, might you ask?

"There may be two or three more questions for you, such as: 'Would you be certain that your certainty would remain certain across every future observation?' …and… 'Are you certain that later observations will always confirm your present sense of certainty, and if you think you are, then why?'"

Zarlowe Nike thought to himself, *Some interpret high percentages of many types of Mysticism as indicating that verbal concepts generate many false impressions unless and until consciousness uses sufficiently esoteric methods to upgrade them into generating true impressions.*

After the meal adventure and meditative recess were over, their surroundings again vanished, this time replaced by a return to the cosmic roundtable-within-a-pyramid setting. Stars, galaxies, and terrestrial settings again pulsated and waved beyond the mostly invisible walls and floor of a giant pyramid. Vivid colors again evolved and revolved with lightning patterns around the perimeter of their room. Smoke, fire, steam, and fog again mysteriously came into being and vanished repeatedly.

The Great Reverberating Voice now announced, "It is now time for you to choose names for the majority of your upcoming missions. You will be known from time to time by the names you entered here with. Still, you need to choose secret names that will serve as your identities as you face your future challenges." The Voice paused, giving the crew an opportunity to make a question or comment of their choice.

Zarlowe decided to use this opportunity to ask a question he had wondered since the Great Reverberating Voice first announced "The End of Time," a question he eagerly wished to ask. "If we have already experienced 'The End of Time,' and if consciousness involves a sequencing of consciousness, then what could possibly be next?"

The Voice answered, "A new experience of all things under and over the sun and stars!" As the answer began to sink in within the minds of the explorers, they felt even deeper emotions of awe and wonder and even greater heights of curiosity.

About twenty-one seconds later, the Voice continued, "You will now have the opportunity to choose secret names with which to explore worlds beyond time and carrying out missions of your choice. When I say 'your choice' I mean this in a way where you meet environments and choose any agendas, even agenda-less agendas. Although you have much freedom, as with choices from before you came here, one could say that actions have consequences, even when you're adventuring beyond time."

The voice paused for seven seconds, then said, "Dorothy Webster, what family name would you wish to be known by as you venture into other worlds?"

She answered, "'Webster' because that is what my late, loving husband knew me by. I figure that if I'm beyond time and he's maybe somewhere out there beyond time, I would love for my secret name to be my real name. That is, if this is possible in this arrangement. Would it be feasible?"

"Yes, your secret name will be your non-secret name, Dorothy Webster," answered The Voice. After a five second pause, it continued, "Though you have told this to each of your crewmates, may you announce in my presence, how your name remained 'Webster'?"

"Yes, of course, I'd love to," she answered. "Though Gregory Gary's family name is Garrison and I was willing to change my name, he insisted that I remain 'Webster.' This was because of the impressive professional reputation I was already beginning to build. It was so sweet of him to think of me in that way. We were both willing to yield and we found a compromise solution: my name remained Webster for almost everything, though I sometimes referred to myself as 'Gregory Garrison's mistress,' which was really fun!"

"Thank you for telling us a wonderful story," said the Great Reverberating Voice, somehow sounding gentler than it had previously.

"Thank you, Great Voice! Thank you," said Dorothy.

About this time, Stewart played a slightly different version of the conversation through his mind, trying to comprehend another angle on what transpired. He imagined in his mind's auditorium a dialogue consisting of "You can even keep your whole name as your undercover name in this special situation." and "Thank you, Great Voice, thank you so much!"

Stewart imagined this in his mind as the Voice and other participants remained silent for about twenty-three seconds. After this, The Great Voice requested, "Zarlowe Nike, it is your turn to choose a secret name."

Zarlowe answered, "I've studied many religions and philosophies, and I would like to use the family name 'Kalkin' or the family name 'Kalki,' determined by the powers that be. This is in honor of the ancient Hindu idea of an avatar of Vishnu carrying that name. I would leave it up to you or the powers that be or whoever is behind all this stuff to decide when and where and how my name should appear."

The Great Voice said with great reverence, "Beings who choose Kalkin or Kalki upon entering this realm face great challenges, and they encounter wondrous opportunities. Kalkin or Kalki your secret family name it shall be!"

The Great Voice and other participants then paused about twenty-seven seconds. Sooner, the biology PhD, would be next.

"Teddy Sooner, it is your turn to choose a secret name."

"I request the secret agent family name De Soto, in honor of the ancient, second millennium explorer. You or whatever powers you are with may choose my secret agent first name," said Dr. Sooner.

"This is hereby granted," announced The Voice.

After seventeen seconds of silence, it became computer expert Scarington's turn.

"Stewart Scarington, what alias name may you wish to choose for yourself?"

"This whole bizarre, transcendental experience thing has made me think more about Buddhism and Taoism, and I did some reading about these philosophies and many areas of mysticism in general when we were at The Higher Dimensional Library. It's led to my decision that I'll resign my will to you with respect to the choice of secret mission family name. I will leave the choice with you, Honorable Voice," said Stewart kindly and gently.

"Thank you, Stewart, and thank you all four of you: Scarington, Sooner, Nike, and Webster. Thank you again," said The Voice, pausing eight seconds after saying this.

Next, the Voice mentioned something bizarre. "Dorothy and Stewart, you will have a relaxation period for a while now; meanwhile Zarlowe and Teddy will need to travel through The Division Multiplier." With this announcement, Zarlowe and Teddy disappeared from the presence of Dorothy and Stewart.

Zarlowe Nike and Teddy Sooner found themselves in separate portions of a large labyrinth.

Teddy asked The Voice, "What is happening?"

Zarlowe asked, "What is this?"

The Voice announced to Teddy and Zarlowe, "Super-agents to be, there is a great war in progress with the futures of many worlds at stake. The very survival of countless multitudes of universes is at stake. Power-hungry humans and aliens are seeking wide-scale destruction for personal gain, and are even seeking self-deification at the expense of trillions of other intelligent beings.

"Nike and Sooner, you have entered The Division Multiplier. As you walk through the labyrinth, each of you will transform.

"Zarlowe will become two super-agents, one code-named 'Ezra Kalkin' and one code-named 'Jacob Kalkin.' In some future circumstances they may also use the variations 'Ezra Kalki' and 'Jacob Kalki.'

"Teddy will become two super-agents, one code-named 'Simon Rosemont De Soto' and one code-named 'Victor Juan De Soto.' In some future circumstances they may also use the variations 'Simon De Soto Rosemont' and 'Victor De Soto Juan.'

"As you travel through the labyrinth the activity of The Division Multiplier will transform you. Begin your journey."

The two explorers wandered through the labyrinth called "The Division Multiplier," encountering what appeared to be ghosts of people from many different centuries and millennia. Zarlowe Nike became two persons, The Zarlowe Nike code-named "Ezra Kalkin" and The Zarlowe Nike code-named "Jacob Kalkin." Teddy Sooner became two persons, The Teddy Sooner code-named "Simon Rosemont De Soto" and The Teddy Sooner code-named "Victor De Soto Juan."

Ezra Kalkin and Simon Rosemont De Soto emerged from The Division Multiplier before the other two and began the missions involving what would become The War Beyond Human Comprehension and The Alpha Conference.

Jacob Kalkin and Victor Juan De Soto emerged a while later and rejoined Dorothy Webster and Stewart Scarington. These versions of Zarlowe Nike and Teddy Sooner explained to Dorothy and Stewart what happened through the technologies of The Division Multiplier.

The Great Voice suddenly made a new announcement to the four beings still present at its cosmic facility, "You are hereby granted one special request each just before beginning your journeys. Dorothy, may we hear your request?"

As the group waited to hear her response, a twilight region between the conscious and the subconscious portions of Victor J. De Soto AKA Teddy Sooner's mind's auditorium played a recording of a slightly different announcement from the voice: "They each get a special request just before starting their missions." As Victor AKA Teddy, Stewart, and Jacob AKA Zarlowe awaited Dorothy's request, they started contemplating what they might like to ask from the mysterious Voice and pyramid.

Then came the request of Webster: "I would like to just sit on the beach relaxing… We could share a deserted beach free from other beachgoers, free from buildings, boats, or docks, and free from the kinds of animals and rocks that might be threatening. We could watch home videos of good times shared that my husband Gregory Gary Garrison and I had together and these videos of us could be transformed into huge holograms filling giant portions of the night sky."

"Would you like to have music during part of the experience?" suggested The Voice.

"Yes, how about if you choose the music that my late husband would choose for this occasion, please," she asked.

"Get ready," said The Great Voice. Almost immediately after the voice said this, the four soon-to-be secret agents witnessed the entire environment again instantly transform.

Enjoying the moment thoroughly, Dorothy and company witnessed a beach without boats, docks, boardwalks, or buildings. Part of the time, the sounds of 1960s beach music and 1950s rock and roll came across through the air. Gentle winds and tides accompanied them on this beach in the night. The moon and stars provided background light, and visions of Dorothy and her loving husband danced across the sky.

After over an hour of this experience, it became time for the next request.

"It is now time for Zarlowe also-known-as Jacob Kalkin to make a recommendation," announced the Great Reverberating Voice.

"May we receive hints providing insight into the U.S.A.'s mid- to late-1960s era and how it affected history and the future?" requested Zarlowe Nike.

The explorers found themselves floating in the middle of a large, hollow spherical room, seemingly free of gravity. Looking around themselves, they figured out that it was very similar in image to the surface of the Earth, though turned inside-out, with the North Pole directly below them facing up and the South Pole directly above them facing down. Mid- to late-1960s psychedelic music began playing. As the music played, the inside-out spherical room surrounding them changed into resembling many different planets and moons, from both The Milky Way and other galaxies.

After about fifty-nine minutes of this, their environment changed into an underground bunker where they could hear bombing, explosions, and machine guns above them. They did not see other people in this underground bunker area, but they could hear German conversations in which the speakers sounded to have reached the greatest depths of disillusionment imaginable.

*****

A while later, they found themselves in a library that featured a set of eight portions, which had the labeling:

- The Philosophy of the Psychology of Science
- The Science of the Psychology of Philosophy
- The Science of the Philosophy of Psychology
- The Psychology of the Philosophy of Science
- The Psychology of the Science of Philosophy
- The Philosophy of the Science of Psychology
- The Religion of Technology
- The Technology of Religion

*****

The extraordinary experiences and changes continued for quite a while. The being using the voice and conducting the activities at the pyramid revealed that the human explorers would soon go on missions that would span many universes and many timelines.

Eventually, while still at that facility, Zarlowe Nike split into two new versions of himself, one who would use the mission name Ezra Kalkin and another who would use the mission name Jacob Kalkin. Similarly, Teddy Sooner split into two new versions of himself, one with a for-the-purpose-of-missions name of Simon Rosemont De Soto and one with a for-mission-purposes name of Victor Juan De Soto.

Dorothy Webster kept her old name to be her name to use on missions. Stewart Scarington chose to let the ultra-mysterious being with the great, reverberating voice choose what his name or names would be on his missions.

The ultra-mysterious being sent them on their way onto a variety of missions.

*****

Jacob Kalkin soon encountered one of the many manifestations of Charr Naerroan in an interdimensional prison. Jacob arrived there to serve as an interviewer, while Charr had been there for a while as a prisoner. Both of them, together with a group of others, soon received an assignment to exit the prison and arrive into a rather strange variation of Earth.

*****

The assembly of to-be-fully-released former prisoners, to-be-left-to-their-own-devices former guards, and reporters suddenly found themselves teleported out of the interdimensional prison and into a grand ballroom within a building.

A banner above a stage proclaimed to them:

"WELCOME TO THE YEAR 3534 ON A PECULIAR VERSION OF PLANET EARTH. The date is January 24th. The location is Occidental Mansion, 357 W. 48th Street, El Paso, Illinois."

A gentleman walked out from behind the curtain and stood silently for ten seconds, gazing at his audience, which consisted of the thirteen aforementioned beings who had just teleported from an inter-dimensional prison, plus 650 other beings, of whom 457 were heavily armed mansion guards. The "mansion" was a 28-story building that covered an entire city block of a town that had been extremely rural in the early Twenty-First Century, yet managed to become a bustling city by the early-to-mid Fourth Millennium A.D. It usually featured one of the most intense security details of any building on the planet as of the first half of the Thirty-Sixth Century, often having guards numbering over 7,000. It was a transition zone between a) a set of interdimensional facilities featuring diverse, temporally ambiguous relationships with the totality of reality itself and b) the "normal world" in which it found itself.

The gentleman began to speak to the assembled 663 audience members. "Greetings guests, mansion security team, and anyone else within earshot or other observability. To let those in who did not already know this on what would otherwise be several secrets, this is a version of Earth in which the Eurypterids reemerged from the waters about one-fourth of the way into the Twenty-First Century, wreaking havoc on both the ecosystem in general and, of course, on human life. People who had grown accustomed to having extremely limited fear of walking along beaches, swimming in natural waters, and scuba diving soon found themselves taking gambles when engaging in these types of activities. Picture this: a family of five gathered together in the year 2024 on a stretch of popular coastline, unaware of scientists having kept the rediscovery of living Eurypterids under wraps since mid-2022, at first enjoying their vacation. Suddenly, the three children in the family start screaming, and before the parents can do anything, it's too late. The three children are bleeding to death, butchered by the sea scorpions also known as Eurypterids. Next, the mother and father rush over in a desperate attempt to save the young ones, and they too get butchered and start to bleed to death. Scenes like these started unfolding all along many coastlines from 2024 onward, and things became so dangerous by 2029 that the human race had to radically reinvent its whole relationship with the waters of its home planet."

Although the speaker had not announced his name or the names of any of the audience members, he suddenly made eye contact with Charr Naerroan. They had already recognized each other at multitudes of levels of consciousness before this new instance of making eye contact, yet there was an extra level of knowing between them at the instant of looking somewhat into each other's souls again. Within less than half a second of time, they shared a partially-nonverbally-visually-cued and partially-telepathic inter-personal transmission recapping some highlights of their past interactions.

They both remembered being part of the collective transition from nothingness to somethingness at the creation of reality itself, one of them being Dimetrioskis Elbankovic and the other being Charr Naerroan, while trillions of other beings were also of that transitional process. As good as their memories were of that process, there were still degrees of uncertainty within the streams of their consciousnesses about the degrees of unity versus the degrees of non-unity in the very dawn of creation itself.

****

(Thus concluded *The Waters of Oblivion, Revisited*; that documentary's credits soon began to scroll onto the screen amid eerie synthesizer music. Dimetrioskis Elbankovic and Charr Naerroan were, in fact, two of the producers listed. The credits also revealed that Robert Stack, Jack Palance, and William Blake narrated, with Stack performing most of it, including the very beginning, most of the middle, and the very ending. Blake and Palance had performed a few strategically-chosen spots of the narration brilliantly, and, indeed, there were even a few portions that featured a combination of two of the narrators speaking in unison, all three of the narrators speaking in unison, or even an entire choir of priests, monks, nuns, lamas, and computers speaking in unison. A note explained that it had been recorded from actual life, and that even its inclusion of silent thoughts had either utilized emanations of the actual minds' subvocalized statements or had otherwise proven translatable into audible representation via advanced technologies that found ways to transfigure these from within the very minds of those whose thoughts became represented in that manner, even taking minds' nonverbal patterns and faithfully generating a semblance of what they had expressed. The film had recorded actual events via higher-dimensional space, higher-dimensional time, higher-dimensional mind, etc., conducted by a team of Transcendentals, featuring Dimetrioskys Elbankovic, Charr Naerroan, and others. Although they had often fought each other, they would also on some occasions collaborate on efforts toward shared goals. In this case, they had agreed that this documentary would serve Soteriology well, whichever way the vast arrays of possible futures might unfold.)

Chapter Three: Dimension Dimestore Revisited

Consider the fact pattern, "At the Dimestore, she felt and saw much of the otherworldly. She silently wondered several times about what was beyond the horizon of her knowledge. After she left, she felt, saw, and heard much additional oddity. She entered a series of daydreams at some stage. The daydreams went on and on for a while. Were there extraterrestrials present? She snapped back to regular reality from the last of that series of daydreams, and again she noticed the unusual change of weather and an ominous feeling."

Not only did the entire category of that specific fact pattern happen to a woman named Florence in 1967, it also happened to a woman named Laverne in 1998 and a woman named Jennifer in 2258.

In each case, a set of gray extraterrestrial aliens and other intelligent beings extracted them from their original timelines as part of how those grays recruited them.

PART TWO

Chapter Four

Regarding Charr Naerroan's interactions with Caesar Nero

After Florence and Elias together watched both *The Waters of Oblivion, Revisited* and *The War Beyond Human Comprehension, Revisited*, the extraterrestrial Double-Forty-One introduced them to two other gray aliens, specifically, Triple-Twenty-One and Double-Sixty-Eight. The group of five intelligent beings then dined together in part of the facility where they had gathered. They contemplated the vastness of the many universes, and the extreme vastness of the many multiverses, each of which housed a great many universes.

A few hours later, they went to their designated quarters to sleep for the night, and the extraterrestrials presented no restrictions to the possibility that the human couple might spend the night together, as they had done on a few occasions prior to being abducted by the aliens. Intermittently, they felt reverential awe at how they had become enlisted into an intergalactic and multi-universal war.

Just before the extraterrestrial Triple-Twenty-One fell asleep, he gathered a variety of thoughts about the history of the version of Earth that the human couple had come from, as well as multiple alternative versions of Earth that were very similar to that one.

One of the main sets of thoughts that raced through his mind immediately before drifting into sleep was to contemplate what he knew about the interactions between Nero and Naerroan in one sample version of Earth. That set of thoughts triggered related thoughts about what he knew regarding the interactions that happened on that planet between Hannibal and Naerroan. Triple-Twenty-One had actually performed surveillance on when the transcendentals Yadier Horowitz and Charr Naerroan had paid Hannibal Barca a visit way back when. Although he remained powerless to influence the proceedings of that visit, he keenly observed what happened from a safe distance, via rather extraordinary engineering technology.

Although legend has it that Nero played fiddle while Rome burned, the truth was much more elaborate than that oversimplification. Charr Naerroan projected himself on many occasions into the minds of many dictators throughout the histories of multitudes of worlds, providing those tyrants with an archetypal inner vision of the ultimate strongman. Hitler, Nero, and others became lured by Charr's archetype.

Other destructive-energy-harvesting-oriented Transcendentals did this, too, competing with Charr for influence over the power-hungry.

Charr's timing would prove impeccable in one case after another. Sometimes on such occasions that a given tyrant would see the writing on the wall and know that a complete downfall was imminent, it would be the case that a com-bination of at least one Destruction-Oriented-Energy-Contract Transcendentals and at least one of the Preservation-Oriented-Energy-Contract Transcendentals would pay a visit. Whether a male human dictator, a female human dictator, an AI computer dictator, or any other type of tyrant, such a final downfall-in-progress meeting would prove illuminating to anyone observing it, and it would have a huge impact on the trajectories of the possible futures.

In contrast with those with heavily-destruction-orientated ways of relating to the harvesting of energy, Dimetrioskys Elbancovic, Yadier Horowitz, and a varying percentage of other Transcendentals consistently chose to be among those with the heavily-preservation-oriented ways of relating to the harvesting of energy. They tended to project into the minds of dictators, liberators, and many everyday folks a variety of archetypal visions of beings who care deeply about finding ways to preserve both their own lives and the lives of others.

Energy harvesting, energy utilization, and energy transference were among the primary activities of the Transcendentals.

Their transcendence over space, time, space-time, and virtually every normal notion of observable reality afforded them to be perfectly poised to manipulate the fluctuations of quantum mechanics, gravity, light, electromagnetics, and even how the laws of physics would operate within given ranges.

Much of this functioned along the lines of how Gérard Encausse (as Papus) and Pyotr Demianovich Ouspensky (as P.D. Ouspensky) wrote in portions of the second millennium A.D. about the Tetragrammaton relating to reality through static and dynamic patterns of active force, resistant force, balance of force, transfiguration, unity, nonunity, and new transitions. When sufficient quantities of forces imposed by them would unify and synchronize, in many cases mere mortals would perceive the awesome, imminent presence of The Abrahamic Lord God, The Adibuddha, Divinity In General, and/or virtually any other of the concepts and/or names with which they would strive to symbolically express Absolute Reality and The Origin(s) of Absolute Reality.

When a sufficient quantity of the forces imposed by them would prove at odds with one another in a state of extreme disunity and conflict, the mere mortals would easily perceive Measuring Glitches, Electromagnetic Anomalies, All Hell Breaking Loose, Crime Sprees, Extremely Demonic Behavior By The Masses Within A Given Nation, Spiritual Interference, Inexplicable Spatiotemporal Discontinuities, Extreme Stock Market Bubbles, Extreme Stock Market Crashes, Other Manifestations Of Chaos, etc.

Sometimes there would arrive an extremely volatile admixture of synchronicity, unity, fission, nonunity, tension, duality, multiplicity, fusion, nonduality, stasis, stability, instability, and changes. In such cases, people would witness what they would later characterize as Biblical Events, Miracles, The Fulfilment Of Prophecies, Astounding Wonders Of The Dharma, Awesome Divinity, The Supernatural, and Examples Of Proof Of The Spiritual Order Triumphing Over Chaos.

Fortunately for many of the "mere mortal intelligent beings" living in what seemed to be "ordinary reality," the balance of the active and the resistant forces between the competing factions of Transcendentals helped to, in the vast majority of conscious occasions, provide what usually appeared at the macro scale to be an extremely stable reality with extremely stable physical laws.

Beneath that comfortable veneer, though, the sometimes-competing, sometimes-cooperating factions of Transcendentals were, in fact, often a seething brew of paranormal potential; they virtually always teemed with energies way beyond what virtually any mere mortal would even begin to suspect present.

To reiterate this from another angle, when the balances of the forces would get outside of normal, almost unlimited mayhem could and often would ensue, including experiences seeming to completely defy the limits of scientific reality. This became much of the basis for the development of the major religions and many of the minor religions. This is also part of the origin of a high percentage of the most truly-bizarre-and-seemingly-inexplicable human behavior.

Additionally, the ancient ideas about gods or the godlike teching other beings with profound madness, profound genius, often emerged from the competition vs. cooperation among diverse Transcendental factions.

Chapter Five: Dorians, Mycenaeans, Teutons, Germans, Russians, Americans, and Others, Revisited

Another set of rather illuminating details relevant to The War Beyond Human Comprehension and much else concerns the weavings of the Dorian, German, Russian, and American developments on the Earth where Elias Artino and Florence Smith grew up. This revisits some of the scenes presented earlier, yet here with skipping over some of what the earlier recounting presented, adding a few details that the earlier recounting had omitted, and lightly editing several spots.

* * * * *

It was over three thousand years before Apollo 11. Anticipation among some residents of the Mediterranean grew. A multicultural gathering was about to take place, and many singles and many married couples were considering whether to attend it.

Sure, there were reasons to expect to have fun there, yet there were also reasons for trepidation. Reasons for an abundance of caution, that is, in at least the minds of a few of the many prospective attendees.

Petrus asked his girlfriend Pattyla, "Oh come on, it would be so much fun to have sex with many different partners! Also, I am confident that the risks that something terrible happens to either of our bodies or that we drop dead in some painful way or catch some terrible disease is tolerably low. Besides, you have to fight inhibitions and take some risks sometimes to truly get to have fun with great partying!"

Pattyla said to her boyfriend Petrus, "If we go to that event, or if you go to that event without me, either way, this is going to be like volunteering to swim with sharks and barracuda and extraterrestrials while skinny dipping. Or maybe that's not the best analogy.

"How about this one: Someone's built a large straw house next to a large wooden lodge. Then a bunch of folks are invited to a séance to be held there, and it's BYOC: bring your own candles. So you have lots of people carrying candles and some even carrying full-blown torches into highly-flammable buildings.

"What could go wrong?!" she said, smirking with sarcasm. She was left-handed, whereas Petrus was right-handed, by the way.

She immediately bit down somewhat hard on the middle finger of her left hand, then released, revealing intentional slight imprints from her teeth.

"I love it when you do that!" Petrus said with a grin. "And that's part of why I believe that you should relent and not only give me a blessing to go there, but join me over there! Sure, we've had our thrills with each other, and so far so good, but I feel that we could do better with the consistency of pushing the envelope of pleasure and pain and thrills! You're a great gal, and I love you, but about three-fourths of the time, you're more inhibited than I want you to be!"

Pattyla shook her head slightly, then performed a half-nod. She then partially shook her head again before looking him right in the eyes and presenting a heartfelt message. "Yes, and about two-thirds of the time, I find you way too uninhibited!!

"You're a great guy, truth be told, fun to be with, and I love you, yet you're often about one misstep away lately from getting destroyed. Maybe partway or totally destroyed…

"It's one thing to be brave, but it's another to be so thrill-seeking that you play Russian roulette with your soul, your heart, your mind, and everything else you've got."

Petrus inquired, "What's Russian roulette?"

Pattyla answered with a long discussion about when she and several of her sisters wandered around one fateful day and encountered a very strange man who had reasonable fluency in the version of Greek that the Dorians spoke. The strange man somehow showed them fantastic technology. After a while he informed them that he was an American soldier who had picked them up in 1968 somewhere near Angkor Vat.

She had been confused about the meaning of what he meant by "the year being The Year Nineteen Sixty-Eight," and she had been astounded by the mechanical flying machine with an overhead rotating blade and a tail rotating blade with which the soldier transported them to an American military camp.

After a while, she was able to arrive at the nitty gritty of making it clear to her boyfriend exactly what she had meant by metaphorically alluding to Russian roulette. Sgt. Norman Petty presented an audio-visual recording to them. She described it thusly, "There was this machine, it had reams of still-frame images on miniature things, all lined up. It ran through a thing with a lamp in it, and out from the lamp-thing with the spinning reams came a shining light. That light shone upon a screen in the distance.

"They called it 'a projector.' There we saw part of what those folks were calling 'a motion picture film.' In that film, we witnessed people sometimes speaking our language and more often than not, speaking other languages.

"At some stage of that film, two soldiers and three civilians, facing a grim situation, passed around a small, hand-held metal device. Each, in turn, would squeeze a lever with their right index finger while pointing the barrel of it at their head. Some toward their right temples, some pointed it into their mouths, etc. They did this one after another.

"Also, once in a while, one of them would spin a cylinder inside the metal device, randomizing something about how its contents would line up. After about five times of people doing this, it arrived in the hands of a female civilian among them.

"She aimed it at her chest with her left hand and pressed the lever with that hand's index finger.

"Again, nothing seemed to happen except a light clicking sound. The people in the film kept laughing and drinking and taking turns.

"Someone paused the film. Our main host, the elderly guy we met in the forest, finally revealed that the device is called a 'revolver' and its lever is called a 'trigger.' Someone resumed rolling the film.

"One of the men then pointed the revolver right at his groin and pulled the trigger.

"It did not seem to do anything. The group laughed uproariously, and the other three guys in the group started giving him high fives and congratulating him. The lady blushed. All of a sudden, two ladies who entered the scene and initiated foreplay with the guy who'd just finished taking his turn in that game.

"That guy handed the revolver to another guy, a man who was taking his third turn in this game. That other guy pointed the gun right at his own right temple with his right hand, then squeezed.

"We heard a loud bang. Oh God, the humanity, that guy's head partially broke apart, and there was blood all over the place. The females in the film were screaming. The men were wailing. The last person who pulled the trigger lay motionless on the ground, with his head broken open and bleeding profusely.

"The film soon ended. *Norman then let us know that this was a secret military training video,* and that he had *authorization to show it* to us because we were four women of *unknown origins* speaking some subdialect of Greek, *mysteriously wandering* around a rural part of Cambodia not far from *Angkor Wat Temple,* and *it would serve his intelligence gathering operation to really get to know us better. He asked what we knew about Russia, China, Vietnam, Laos, and Cambodia.*

"We answered truthfully, attesting to the fact that we had no idea that those were even the names of places, though those names did sound familiar: Those place names sounded similar to the entity names of some of The Transcendentals, many of whom we at times attempt to attune with via the chanting of mantras and the wielding of iron.

"Sgt. Norman Petty was taken aback at our answer. He decided he better record a brief interview with us on tape. He asked one question after another about how we met him, why we met him, what we knew about this, what we knew about that. The interview went on and on.

"At some stage, he asked what year we thought it was, what calendar we normally use, and other such questions about measuring time.

"At times he looked at his fellow soldiers in sheer disbelief, and they looked the same way right back toward him. On several occasions, quite literally, their jaws dropped.

"They clearly had super-advanced technology, but much of what we had to say seemed earth-shattering to them.

"When it was our turn to ask questions, at some point I asked Norman, 'What's the name of that very dangerous game that we saw those blokes playing with that thing you call a 'revolver?' He answered, 'Russian roulette.'

"I asked him to explain the word 'roulette.' He said, 'You really don't know, do you?' I said, 'Yes, I positively, totally clearly confirm that I do not know what roulette is. What is it?'

"He said something like, 'Imagine a gambling place. Some people there are gathered around a huge spinning wheel. Hmm… Better yet, I'll see if you could stay a little while longer before we try to send you back from whence you came. Would that you be fine with that?'

"I said something like, 'Yes, I believe we can stay as long as it takes to appease the transcendentals, and for my sisters and me to have a good chance of going wherever we should go, whether that would be to 'from whence we came' or somewhere else entirely.'

"He said, 'You're priceless. I don't know if you're on an acid trip or what, but I've got the distinct feeling that you're the real deal, not tripping at all in terms of LSD or what-have-you, but literally time-traveling through our reality in an ultra-mysterious way.'

"Brenda, just looking at you, I can tell that you consent with staying a while longer. Well… What about you and you, Karyellenyia and Suellena?' Those remaining two took turns affirming their consent to stay a while longer.

"Sgt. Petty walked out of the room while two men stood guard silently. I looked at my sisters, and we had devious thoughts of possible attempts at seduction, yet felt that something about aggressive flirtation just didn't seem right for the situation. We did mildly flirt via the motions of our eyes and the ways we smiled at those guards. The two guards stood totally impassive, all business and no pleasure.

"When Sgt. Petty returned, we watched another video. 'Video' is another way to call motion picture films and other things that present motion video displays. That can be of stuff that actually happened or stuff that's an illusion of things that look like they happened, a very sophisticated legerdemain.

"He prefaced that next video by saying that it contained actual footage from a gambling casino. Soon we watched people gathered around a horizontally-oriented wheel that would spin while a small ball would bounce around. The ball would eventually settle into a slot with a specific number. Half of the numbered slots were black, and the other half were red. People would gain or lose small coin-like objects called chips, de-pending on what they wagered for what the wheel and ball would turn out to show. He explained that the game is called roulette. That game features a roulette wheel. He stopped the video.

"After that, he took out an empty revolver, something that he called a Colt '45. He demonstrated the way of spinning around the thing in it that could hold multiple instances of things he called bullets.

"There was a silent pause in the room for a while. Then he said, 'Earlier you saw actual footage of people playing Russian roulette. In a place called *Russia*, people at some point *invented a game in which the participants do something similar to the casino game of roulette,* but instead of winning or losing chips, *they randomly set up whether they kill themselves or not.*'"

There was silence between them for a very long time. Pattyla could tell that Petrus had been listening closely and that several of his most heavily-relied-upon paradigms had been shattered.

Petrus' cognition had turned to stone, rendering him catatonic.

Pattyla took him by the hand, lovingly looked him in the eyes, and initiated a slow, gentle, heartfelt kiss. His cognition snapped out of the catatonic state, and he started to fully engage in the romance again.

Soon, they shared the full physical intimacy of making love with each other. They proved even more passionate in their coital bliss than they had ever been before. Their hearts, minds, and souls positively glowed with completely loving each other.

After about an hour of intense sex featuring profound romantic love, featuring greater acts of lovemaking than they had previously thought were humanly possible, they resumed speaking with each other in the manner of ordinary life. Petrus said to his mate, "You know what, I've changed my mind. I'll decline to go on the trip to that big spiritual-sexual extravaganza after all."

Pattyla said, "Great!"

******

Elsewhere, there were sixty-five other cases of men and women among the Dorians considering whether to go to that big shindig, with thirty-eight of them choosing to take that journey. Several of the couples who had seriously considered the offer and yet chose to turn it down soon found themselves having rougher and more exciting sex with each other than ever before.

A few of the singles who thought about going to the orgy and yet ultimately turned it down also chose to immediately let go of their most youthful hedonistic impulses and aim to find their way to more meaningful, stable, committed, monogamous romantic relationships. That is, they set out to establish holy matrimony with suitable partners, to form lasting, outstanding marriages built on solid foundations of true love and genuine compatibility.

A group of people known as the Remians had a substantial presence in a few places in Europe back then, yet they would eventually fade into a near-total oblivion, disappearing from all but the most obscure of the annals of history, cloaked somewhat into the Romans' fable of the mythical brothers Romulus and Remus.

A group of people often known in those days as the Hebrews had a major presence in a few locations back then. They would eventually transition into becoming identified as Jews, rather than Hebrews, and perhaps few if any Post-Industrial-Revolution people would prove to have any more than a trace of an idea of exactly why.

Did that name change have much to do with Jesus of Nazareth, the emergence of the Christian church, some huge changes that occurred in the great beyond, something else, or some combination of factors?

Many a scholar and many a casual observer of culture would wonder why. Whatever the case might be, the Hebrews and Remians who had originally considered going to the event proceeded to prove unanimous in declining to participate in it.

In contrast, some of the Teutons decided to join the Mycenaeans and Dorians in getting together for the big shindig featuring intense sexual and spiritual festivities.

The event started auspiciously enough, it had seemed. After a while, though, a sharp conflict emerged between one wealthy Dorian couple and one wealthy Mycenaean couple. Unexpected problems and some arguments back and forth led to several escalations. Although during and after the event the tensions grew and grew for a while, several Mycenaeans made a trip to visit the Dorians and see if visiting could lead to a peaceful resolution to the conflict.

Visiting Mycenaeans heard a Dorian high priest in a temple say, "It is of the utmost importance while here to be respectful toward the mysteries of the planets, the plants, the animals, and the humans, and, especially, all cycles and all anti-cycles. Failure to do so in ordinary places can have terrible consequences. Failure to pay that respect here can be *immediately* lethal. *Energies here ramp up to infinity and beyond and all the way to the absolute, or very, very, very, very, very-very close thereto. See the metalwork, the woodwork, and the composite tablets? This place channels other dimensions and times.*"

****

The meeting continued for quite a while. The high priest was candid about many facts, yet he withheld sensitive information that he considered restricted. After his main presentation, the gathering included a brief question-and-answer session. It proved to be an amicable meeting between the priest and the three visitors.

The visitors went on to meet with the high-class Dorian couple who had engaged with and subsequently disputed with a high-class Mycenaean couple during the aforementioned Dorian-Mycenaean-Teutonic extravaganza hosted by Mycenaeans. The two couples were able to work out their differences after all.

* * *

Peace between the Mycenaeans and the Dorians started to flourish, better than ever before. Years went by.

* * *

On the island of Crete, one fateful day, three ships of extraterrestrials landed and interacted with many humans, including a few Dorians and a great many Mycenaeans. The visitors came from a combination of distant solar systems and interdimensional realities beyond normal notions of regular reality's here, there, everywhere, and/or nowhere.

The visitors were a mixture of grays, greens, blues, reds, yellows, and others, of varying shapes and sizes, some very humanoid, others very nonhumanoid.

They seemed like unto the legends of gods. Extraterrestrials then and there demonstrated materialization, dematerialization, teleportation, spontaneous combustion, temporary reversals, looping of time itself, the disappearances of inorganic physical objects, the reappearances of inorganic physical objects, the disappearance and reappearance of animals, and the transfiguration of plants.

The technologies with which they dazzled included high-definition motion picture films, including the ultra-bizarre comedy documentary *Heraclitus' Multiversal History, Whether Anyone Decides To Believe Any Of It Or Not.*

They presented that film multiple times, once each in several different languages, including several languages of that period and two of the languages that had not yet officially come into existence in the normal versions of the history of that world. The "new languages" were, specifically, English and Navajo.

Although those two would, in the most regular sense, wait until circa 1,500 years later to emerge in terms of that world's timeline's history, the advanced extrateresstrials had already interacted with trillions of humans in other timelines and other worlds.

A few lucky primitive humans there even boarded spacecraft and ventured into outer space with the aliens.

After the extraterrestrials flew back into the heavens aboard their starships, a few of their artifacts remained on Earth, for the earthlings to possess and to experiment with.

The artifacts repeatedly caused strange effects on the minds of many sentient beings who would come into their proximity. Item number twelve was both a Vajrakila dagger and an obliocera chronometer. The obliocera chronometers telepathically and psycho-kinetically interact with minds such as to allow for instant teleportation across different universes, timelines, and even multiverses. Item 12's design made it a conjunction of Vajrakila dagger properties and obliocera chronometer properties. Its use could and would prove especially beneficial when chosen wisely, yet its use had to remain sparing, as the few who dared to overuse it found that the device would act in a manner of having a mind all its own and punish such overuse by unleashing hellacious time travel torture adventures unto them, in some cases featuring a human being seeming to exhibit Alzheimer's Disease, Schizophrenia, Bipolar Disorder, or Coma less than one minute after seeming to be a perfectly healthy human being, whereas that human had actually become plucked from all normal reality and thrust into thousands of years of entering and exiting many battlefields, many concentration camps, many gulags, and many political prisons, including experiences of becoming tortured to death only to instantly reemerge somewhere else with an intact memory and intact body, then to become brutally starved or tortured to death, with a repeat cycle, before all-of-a-sudden becoming plopped back into the normal reality where bystanders would be clueless as to how any of this happened at all.

Such a person might in physical form appear to have simply been there all along, yet such a person might during that have gone through billions of times as much drama and difficulty as any of the bystanders would have ever imagined to have been possible.

Things seemed for a while to continue to move along peacefully between the two sets of people. However, one year later, tensions between them flared up again. Disagreements over dignity and honor were such that the Dorians stood strong with valuing the bearing of true witness better than the Mycenaeans did, yet both sides had their rationales about why to reject the other side's choices and actions.

The Mycenaeans declared war upon the Dorians.

The Dorians responded by declaring war upon the Mycenaeans.

The war was very one-sided. In addition to whatever esoteric spritiual-magico-religious advantages that the Dorians may have had from the outset, they had iron weapons, whereas the Mycenaens had bronze weapons.

At the beginning of the first battle, many Mycenaean troops had confidence and great hope. That soon evaporated, as an anatomical demolition derby of many of the parts of many of their bodies ensued. Excruciatingly painful.

Repeatedly, the same type of scene unfolded: The bronze weapons would fail to withstand impact with the iron weapons, and the wielders of the iron weapons would successfully smash and break the arms, legs, testicles, bladders, livers, ovaries, kidneys, glans, ribs, lungs, skulls, and brains of many of the wielders of the bronze weapons and many of the nearby civilians. No one was off limits. The Dorians had premeditated to feel a completely clear conscience with unleashing total war, to include smashing infants, prepubescent youths, teenagers, the elderly, and even pregnant women and their fetuses to death, showing absolutely no mercy for any of the Mycenaens, whether they would happen to be military personnel or civilians. The Dorians truly believed that the other side had crossed enough redlines that there could be no limits to what they should do to completely and utterly break the spirit of the Mycanean people and their culture. This in many respects foreshadowed many of the most brutal scenes that happened in North America, Asia, Africa, and Europe during the nineteenth century and multitudes of the most horrific scenes that happened in

South America, North America, Africa, Europe, and Asia during the twentieth century.

Mycenaean trauma from the experiences imbued perceptions of the Dorians with their having been godlike monsters with supernatural powers with which to punish humans.

At a key juncture near the end, the mysterious transcendental beings Charr Naerroan and Dimetrioskys Elbankovic chose to materialize and speak with some of the Mycenaean leadership. Charr urged each of them to consider suicide as a way to allegedly make things better. In contrast, Dimetrioskys urged each of them to consider seeking to allegedly make things better by refraining from suicide.

Both had energy agendas in presenting this to them.

Eons earlier, many of the destruction-oriented-energy-contract sets of Transcendentals had learned that edging sentient beings toward acts of suicide tended to amplify their powers and accomplishments. Also eons earlier, many of the preservation-oriented-energy-contract sets of Transcendentals had learned that influencing sentient beings away from acts of suicide tended to amplify their powers and accomplishments.

Meanwhile, some high percentage of the gray, extraterrestrial aliens philosophically pondered regarding the Transcendentals whether the destruction-oriented or the preservation-oriented were more ethical or if they were both of them fully ethical in their own ways, depending on exactly how it was that which would fit into the ecosystems of the consciousnesses and energies of each of the realities.

As mentioned earlier, there were different factions among the grays, with some siding with the destruction-oriented Transcendentals, with others siding with the preservation-oriented Transcendentals, and with yet others still choosing neutrality and/or taking sides on an ad hoc basis regarding this set of otherworldly warfare.

Some of the Mycenaean leadership did indeed commit suicide, and Charr inherited much of their life force in the process. He also, with that, inherited an ability to frequently, by the sheer force of his will together with his powers in general, reanimate those whom he had influenced into committing suicide, murder, or both. Indeed, he found the choices by human beings to commit murder-suicides to be, from his cruel, ultrabizarre perspective, somehow very ethical, as he found them very useful to his chain reactions of generating the deaths of many universes.

Others of the Mycenaean leadership did indeed refrain from committing suicide, and Dimetrioskys teamed up with much of their life force in the process. Also, they proved able to sometimes appear and disappear in the great beyond, teaming up with Dimetrioskys and others who generally favored life over death, the preservation of universes over the destruction of universes, etc. Dimetrioskys shared what some high percentage of mature living humans considered the general model of the ethics of favoring compassion toward life and the preservation of well-being, with death and destruction usually held as paths of when necessary to preserve conscience, justice, love, wisdom, compassion, and life.

Both Elbankovic and Naerroan understood rather well each other's positions on this mystery of destruction vs. preservation, yet each also knew very well how the energies of Reality tended to interact with his own specific niche thus far. Many of the humans upon whom they had telepathically poured influence had no idea that they and those who teamed up with them had energized their mixtures of impulses to kill one another, impulses to heal one another, impulses to kill themselves, and impulses to heal themselves.

The remaining living leaders among them soon agreed to the Dorians' demands for an unconditional surrender. The Dorians were now the rulers of the lands that were previously governed by what had been the Mycenaean leadership.

Choosing limited amounts of analysis of what went wrong with the Mycenaean culture, after having defeated them, the Dorians chose wholesale annihilation of over 95% of it, replacing it with much of what they considered best from both cultures and a few portions of other cultures as well.

However, as several centuries came and went, tales emerged that weaved together elements of what had happened between the extraterrestrial aliens, the Teutons, the Mycenaeans, and the Dorians, with many embellishments, sup-pressions, and exotic fable components drawn together in short stories and epic poetry.

The high preisthood of the Dorians left only a minute percentage of themselves in the Mediterranean region. Most of them immigrated elsewhere, including to portions of Africa, the Middle East, and the Himalayas. A few of the most warrior-oriented among them set up secret societies in places that would later be called Norway, Germany, and Finland.

* * * * *

Seemingly eons later, secret society members of unbroken lineages dating back to the ancient Dorian priesthood found themselves on both sides of World War II. Some of the highest-level British, American, German, and Japanese elite were among these.

Theological, ethical, and philosophical differences pervaded them, and such differences led very easily to tectonic fault lines in the tensions between them. Regular-world individuals, groups, organizations, and nations would sometimes serve like cards or chess pieces, often manipulated for purposes of which they were nowhere near consciously aware.

In the runup to that tragic war, multiple transcendentals, including both Dimetriosys Elbankovic and Charr Naerroan, chose at times to telepathically influence elite movers and shakers and to occasionally materialize as anonymous conversational partners such as to influence them.

Many of those who served in combat on either or both sides of World War II were in fact descendants of some combination of various of the Ancient Dorians, Ancient Hebrews, Ancient Romans, Ancient Ionians, Ancient Africans, Ancient Desi Indians, Ancient Native American Indians, Ancient Chinese, Ancient Australian Aborigines, and more. To Dimetrioskys Elbankovic much of it had seemed a heart-wrenching tragedy, yet to Charr Naerroan much of it had served perfectly fitting into his plot to steer patterns of events toward amplifying destructions of universes. To Naerroan, every Gentile who died in the 20th century and every Jew who died in the 20th century, no matter how gruesome the death, was part of the collateral damage that served part of his big quest for the annihilation of many universes such as to convert them into energies that he could utilize. To many of the beings who had the pleasure and/or displeasure to meet him and directly interact with him, many of his words and actions seemed utterly inscrutable.

Although many of the dead who had dedicated themselves thoroughly to a given religion and faithfully lived lives filled with enough honor and duty to wisdom, compassion, and love had escaped his clutches in the great beyond, there were many others who had found themselves, sooner or later, reanimated in his presence, witnessing him to wield godlike powers right in front of them, with ruthless force and precision.

Elsewhere, when the situations would become right for them, one or more of the transcendentals fighting in general to support the chances for the preservation of life, liberty, and the continuation of universes would recruit beings who had experienced thousands or even millions of years of peaceful heaven realms in accordance with their respective faiths, yet who had become ready to let go of their comforts and join in on the fight to find reasonable paths of preservation amid the great multi-multiversal warfare.

Of course, there were also some rare cases in which at least one representative from Naerroan's side and at least one representative from Elbankovic's side would jointly present information to a given recruit, as, in those instances, the two sides reached some mutual agreement about conducting that way of introducing others into the wonders and horrors of The War Beyond Human Comprehension and the related events and ongoing challenges.

One of the ways that some of the introductions would take place, whether with one side presenting, the other side presenting, or both of the sides mutually presenting, was to screen *Revolutions: An Alleged Secret History of the Creations of Several Worlds, the Lives and Deaths of Many Species, and Some of What Has Happened in the Great Beyond* and to screen *The Waters of Oblivion, Revisited, or: An Abridged, Revised, Reimagined Variation of All Things under and over the Sun and Stars.*

Sometimes such screenings would precede lengthy question-and-answer sessions as part of preparations for the next set of challenges.

Although those leading those Q&A sessions would often tell the audience members that it was generally best to refrain from asking the types of questions that would identify specific public figures and specific historical events of the timelines of their origin worlds, once in a while an audience member would ask such a question anyway.

Three of the most common such questions were:

- What are you at liberty to say about whichever version or versions of Napoleon Bonaparte ascended into becoming, for a time, The Emperor of France?

- Did any of The Transcendentals attempt to influence the behavior of the Napoleon Bonaparte who took over France in my timeline until later became deposed, and who, oddly enough, became deposed not once but twice?

- My timeline included both a World War I and a World War II, and would you be so kind as to comment on some of what happened there from The French Revolution to The Cold War?

Chapter Six: Regarding Some Attempts to Influence Napoleon

Another set of key facts involving the Earth on which Mister Artino and his girlfriend Miss Smith were born: interactions between public figure Napoleon Bonaparte and a group of The Transcendentals.

Before Napoleon Bonaparte was even born, multiple Transcendentals had manipulated and transfigured the events surrounding the pregnancy that, in due time, would result in his arrival on Earth. They competed with one another over whether his life would have more of a militaristic trajectory, more of a scientific trajectory, or more of something else entirely, or some major mixture thereof.

As time went by, Charr Naerroan came to dominate the events leading up to and including the French Revolution.

Afterward, as Bonaparte became the new leader of France, Naerroan started to telepathically influence him to a very substantial degree.

However, Dimetrioskys Elbankovic worked hard elsewhere to greatly influence the developments in England and North America. Although many of the Transcendentals competed with each other for influence over the mid-17th-century-to-early-19th-century events in North America, South America, and Europe, Elbankovic became especially effective with using telepathy and other means to influence Scotland, England, and North America to trend toward what he believed best for the future of Reality.

In contrast, during much of the same period, with a similar competition among Transcendentals raging to influence Eastern, Central, and Northern portions of Continental Europe, Naerroan repeatedly had his way with succeeding to steer those regions to trend toward what he believed best for the future of Reality.

The active and resistant forces applied by the total of all Transcendentals and all other beings, as well as portions of Reality beyond being specific beings per se, combined to make for horrors to escalate during much of the Napoleonic Wars. Eventually, Naerroan pushed in the direction of expanding Napoleon Bonaparte's conquests, whereas Elbankovic pushed in the direction of limiting those conquests.

Prior to the Battle of Waterloo, it became clear to Naerroan that the energy costs of boosting Bonaparte's war efforts much further would be intolerable. Therefore, he changed strategies, looking for ways to steer Bonaparte himself toward thought patterns conducive toward Naerroan's reaping a colossal energy harvest the next couple of times that he could induce widespread war in Europe.

In the twilight of his life, Napoleon Bonaparte received a visit from an unusually tall man with the most piercing eyes and spirit he had ever witnessed. Napoleon became filled with a surreal dread that he had seldom felt before, as he looked into the eyes of Charr Naerroan, visiting incognito as a mortal man bearing the name Charles Northern.

Charr, in the guise of Charles, inquired of Napoleon, "If there is an afterlife, and you become asked by the Heavenly Entourage or the Hellish Entourage or both to go on a mission, a mission of extreme warfare, then do you believe that you will be up to the task?"

Napoleon responded, "I would do my utmost to win again there in the beyond much as I often succeeded in battle here in this worldly life."

Charr then stated, "Yes. Great! Yet, what if you still faced major uncertainty about alliances and ethics, much as you faced while in this life. Many people assume that death will bring them The Lord God Almighty resolving the most difficult questions about ethics and metaphysics, but what if things do not turn out to be so tidy? What if in the Great Beyond it continues much as it is in this life, with huge unknowns about what is right and wrong about questions of religion and the ultimate reality? Would you still be fully confident about your abilities to serve a helpful role in intense warfare in that Great Beyond?"

Napoleon was unequivocal. "Yes, I still would."

Charr answered, "Great! Thank you, military legend extraordinaire for sharing this conversation, no matter what the mysteries of the Great Beyond might happen to turn out to be!"

Napoleon answered, "Yes, you are welcome. Also, thank you, too. You seem to remind me of what I was like when I was younger."

Charr concluded by saying, "Yes, believe it or not, I find that comment from you to be both sensible and a profound compliment. Take care, and here's a wish for the best for you to have a good journey to wherever you might be headed next, whether in this worldly life or beyond."

As Charr Naerroan, in the guise of Charles Northern, departed from visiting that retired military leader, he thought ahead to planning for how to steer the likely courses of events toward generating 1857-1870 and 1908-1945 A.D./C.E. extreme horrors for a great many of the inhabitants of Earth.

Chapter Seven: Multiple Influences

Terry Owens had skipped alcohol for nineteen years. However, escalating and at-times bewildering paranormal experiences had led to his decision to walk into a local Bar.

It was June 28, 1728, and the bar he entered was Easton Corner On East 37 North. He lived in a world where the ancient Persians as led by Xerxes had been abducted by extraterrestrials soon after the 480 B.C.E. burning of Athens in their military campaign against the Greeks. Also, in that world, England never emerged as its own country in the time after the emergence of Christianity, because the Romans, Scots, and others fought in such a way that eventually a large version of Scotland occupied the entirety of what people in many other versions of Earth associated with the combination of England, Ireland, and Scotland. Therefore, also, there never emerged the United Kingdom often associated with much of that in other worlds, as it would have become superfluous to call it such when it could simply instead be called Scotland.

Seemingly miraculously, that alternate timeline still wound up with Christianity, Manicheanism, Islam, and the widespread use of the Gregorian Calendar, and its Gregorian Calendar date of June 28, 1728 corresponded on an astronomical level directly to the same date of that same calendar in a great many other worlds. Some countries in some worlds as of that time were still labeling dates, months, and years according to the Julian calendar, yet this does not lead to excessive confusion in this case, for Terry and the tavern into which he had walked on that date both used the Gregorian Calendar for most business purposes of tracking time. The Easton Corner On East 37 North Tavern was located in a North American colony known in that world as Multarempo. Some pro-nounced that like, "MULL-tar-EM-poe," whereas others pronounced that like, "mull-TAR-em-POE" or "MULL-tar-REMP-oe."

Its name's pronunciation would often rhyme with intuitive ways to pronounce the phrase, "Skulls Star Hemp Poe."

Technological advances in that world proceeded at a similar clip up that point as they had in the universes that featured Benjamin Franklin achieving prominence as one of the founders of the United States of America. One technological difference was that locomotives developed in Scotland, Multarempo, and other places of that world by the early 1700s, whereas they took a while longer to develop in most worlds that featured the U.S.A.

That World of Multarempo, as some interdimensional travelers have called it, never saw the birth of either the United States of America or the famous early American statesman Benjamin Franklin. Not on the historico-scientific realm of reality, that is, whereas that world did feature some fiction that depicted that Franklin and that U.S.A. in some fine storytelling.

Instead, in that world's timeline Scotland peacefully granted independence to Multarempo, which was a large nation led by many Eurasian immigrants (from Northern Europe, Western Asia, the Middle East, Central Asia, the Mediterranean, and elsewhere) and many Native Americans. The Republic of Multarempo as of June 28,

1728 occupied portions of North America similar in size and scope to the June 28, 1820 version of the United States of America (as witnessed in most versions of the U.S.A. as of that date).

Other twists were: 1) that North America and South America had the same names there as continents as they had in many universes that included the emergence of the U.S.A.; 2) extremely little slavery had become present in that version of 1728 North America, in contrast with rampant slavery in many other versions of 1728 North America; and 3) a major religion featuring a mixture of atheistic, polytheistic, and very scientifically-rational thinking had emerged there to compete with the beliefs and practices of Christianity, Islam, Judaism, Hinduism, and other religions. 4) A popular comedy sign posted at some of the improv theaters would display, with diverse artwork and font patterns, "9x19. Thursday, 9/19. Thor's Day, 9/19. The Fourth Weekday, 9/19. 9x20. 10x20. 11.21. 10.18. 12x18. Wednesday, 12/18. Odin's Day, 12/18. The Third Weekday, 12/19. 12x20. 12x21. 12.21. 12.22. 12/23. January 1. March 31. Each of the days of the week. Each of the days of the year. December 30. January 2. September 19. December 16. June 5. December 31. Bingo!" That become a source of much speculation.

A man who became popularly known in that world as Multar Zinko was born as Desmond Thanassos Hel Killings. His parents, Ronald Jacobi Killings and Loretta Cynthia Killings (née Jones-Smith), sensed that their son would be destined to be one of the greatest of the destroyers of worlds, and they therefore resolved to grant him a legal birth name suggestive of such. They chose "Thanassos" for the first of his middle names based on making a hybrid between "Thanatos," which is the ancient Greek name for "The Grim Reaper," and "Thasos," which is the name of a specific Greek island. "Hel" for his second middle name was a straight lift from the female Scandinavian name for "The Goddess of Death." The couple loved each other and their son, and they loved danger, thrills, and the risk of serious injuries and death. They also felt a strong love for Death Itself, and that was a large part of why they wished for their son to have both a masculine way for his full name to strongly suggest death and a feminine way for it to strongly suggest death.

Their world's timeline would also never know the Nazi scourge of anti-conscience, wanton cruelty, Anti-Roma-ism, and antisemitism.

Unknown to virtually each and every interdimensional traveler was what degree, if any, the 590 B.C.E. establishment of the Scottish town Swastikaville played in 1) why some gray, ultrapowerful extraterrestrials abducted Xerxes and the rest of the Persians soon after their military victory at Athens in 480 B.C.E., 2) how and why the nation Multarempo emerged with much peaceful negotiaton and little conflict between European settlers and Native Americans, and 3) how and why there was much less antisemitism, Islamophobia, Anti-Roma-ism, wanton cruelty, and anti-conscience during the 465 B.C.E. to 2027 C.E. period in that world than in most versions of the world in which World War I, World War II, the September 11, 2001 Al Quada Attacks on The United States of America, and the October 7, 2023 Hamas Attacks On Israel occurred. In that world, the very ancient and very sacred symbol known as the Swastika was able to remain free from traumatic associations with what the German National Socialists (i.e.,

NSDAP members and collaborators) known as Nazis did during much of the 1925-1945 period in many of the other versions of Earth.

It was in the city of Swastikaville that Multar Zinko was reputed to have first said to his many followers, in a deep voice, "I vow that our religious movement, Multarzinianism, shall, whether in this universe or any other universe, find a way to throttle each and every excess of each and every version of Monotheism. If there exists any true version of Monotheism, which I seriously doubt to be the case, then it shall emerge in the long run from all the attacks that we and others unleash onto all monotheisms, emerging like those who survive baptisms of fire. Meanwhile, our movement shall aim toward either annihilating or otherwise greatly curbing the influence of each and every monotheism insofar as they have shown a repeated tendency to outgrow their britches and to be in need for people like us to give them a hard kick in the pants!"

His followers cheered and laughed, lovingly and approvingly. That was on May 17, 1681. Later, at noon on November 27, 1724, tired and knowing that he would soon be dead, Multar Zinko said to several of his most adoring family members, friends, and other faithful followers of the Multarzinian religion, "This lifetime's journey for me is about to end. However, if there is an afterlife, something of which I do not know the answer and I'm not so sure that anyone knows for sure the answer while still alive in the regular, historico-scientific reality, yes, if there is an afterlife, as per any of the many magico-religious claims allege about a larger reality, then I vow to devote my afterlife to fighting for the truth and fighting for accuracy of mind, for the benefit of everyone who has a mind, as well as any who have lost their minds, for the benefit of the future, I vow to fight against each and every false illusion that ever has or ever will be brought into the worlds of humankind by distorted versions and distorted perversions of the monomaniacally-twisted versions of what many people believe to be monotheism. I vow to fight each and every falsity that anyone has instituted, institutes, or will institute on the basis of any false monotheism. I vow to fight on behalf of everyone against such falsehoods. I vow to fight for the truth." After he uttered that, he closed his mouth and closed his eyes, drifted off into sleep, and uttered his last breath.

Several Multarzinians transcribed for posterity that vow, that last spoken testament, that concluding promise from Multar Zinko's life on Earth. Earlier, his written last will and testament had reached official completion on August 14, 1701. The combination of his famous last words and his will supercharged the mystique about him.

Easton Corner On East 37 North Tavern was a popular place for men of diverse religious and philosophical backgrounds to gather, drink beverages, and share conversations. It occupied a building on East 37th Street, a modest distance north of Main Street, in an Appalachian town in Multarempo.

The United States of America in many universes had The First Amendment to The United States Constitution: "Congress shall make no law respecting an establishment of religion, or prohibiting the free exercise thereof; or abridging the freedom of speech, or of the press; or the right of the people peaceably to assemble, and to petition the Government for a redress of grievances."

In a similar vein, The Republic of Multarempo had Article III, Section I of The Republic of Multarempo Constitution: "Neither the federal government nor any of the other levels of this governments of this republic shall establish any religion or prohibit the free exercise of religion. Each government of this republic shall refrain from abridging freedom of speech, the press, the right to peaceably associate, and the right to petition any and all levels of government for a redress of any grievances."

Eighteen men and eleven women were in The Easton Corner Tavern, which was located at 1 East 37 North Street, on June 28, 1728 at the precise instant that Terry Owens ventured in. Within three minutes, eight entered and two left; more specifically, three more men and five more women walked in, and one man and one woman walked out.

Ten minutes later, a despondent twenty-three-year-old man walked out, did not stay very aware of his surroundings, and became struck and killed by a locomotive. By then the religious demographics of the people in the bar had arrived at about 10% Jewish, 20% Christian, 30% Multarzinian, 10% Agnostic, 10% Atheist, and 20% Unaffiliated.

The town was named Asheville, and the people there spoke one of the many variations of English, even though their world had no country known as England. In that world, the act of calling the language "English" was mainly thought to have an etymological connection to legends that it is the language primarily used by the angels among the heavenly host. Many people in that world had said many times, "The Language That Came To Humanity From The Angels, in other words, The Angelish Language, is much easier for people to call The English

Language, and, therefore we often call it English and only rarely do we call it Angelish."

Nearby, a man drunk out of his mind rambled in what those around found to be incoherent gibberish, including how he suddenly said out loud for no particular reason, "Imagine Stephen Colbert portraying Representative Mike Johnson and vice-versa, imagine Chuck Norris portraying Lee Greenwood and vice-versa, yes, also, imagine Rush Limbaugh portraying Meatloaf and vice-versa, and more, yeah, and war and golfers who yell out 'fore' are good for advances of yonder shores, oh yeah. Seven impersonators and nine impersonators sitting out tailgating for college football and erotic flings, getting ready with the others to get with the partying. Working, working, playing, working, working, partying!"

The man seated next to him to his right silently looked at him with a mixture of pity and an edge of ominousness. That man had a feeling that something about hearing that statement, despite how it registered at the conscious level as total and complete gibberish, filled him to the brim with a distinct feeling of tens of thousands of hours of déjà vu arriving into his mind and soul all at the same time. His subconscious mind somehow intuited the reality of how it could serve as a portal into other timelines and universes.

Terry silently observed the drunk and the guy seated to the drunk's right, meditatively accepting and acknowledging the mystery of how the two of them had just interacted with each other and the rest of the worldly beings who were present in that tavern.

Terry felt very attracted to several ladies there, but he sensed that he would not be at all likely accepted by any of them, and he believed that his days and nights of romance were most likely over. He decided that he would avoid flirting very much at all with any ladies on this occasion.

The lovelife he had experienced had included modest success, and he had been married for about one year to a very charming young lady, yet she became brutally murdered by a sandwich shop owner whose heart and mind had been overcome by lust and jealousy.

Most disturbingly, the sandwich shop owner had cut the young woman up all over the regions between her waist and her knees with chops from a butcher knife while the lady was wide awake and screaming for him to stop. As approved by local custom, after the shop owner's conviction, the community stoned the shop owner to death.

This perfectly accorded with some methods described by portions of ancient literature.

Terry himself was allowed to be the one to cast the first stone with which to start the public execution of that shop owner. Although Terry Owen was a very devout Multarzinian and believed that each and every version of Abrahamic religion was probably total malarkey, he had studied *Leviticus* very carefully from beginning to end in an English translation, and he had decided to abide by the commandment to avoid taking pleasure in performing the execution of another human being, not based on obeying an omnipotent god whom he did not happen to believe to even exist, but based on a sense that there was some je ne sais quoi about the principle emanating from some primal and ineffable reality, and that there should be few, if any, exceptions to that principle. As he cast the first stone with which to commence the execution of that shop owner, whose name was Theodore Bundy, he felt a strange caring toward everyone, even the Ted Bundy whose face he ended up plunking with that stone. In the years that followed, Terry Owen did wonder to himself how it sure seemed more than coincidental that each of the people who had shown visible signs of taking pleasure in stoning that Bundy to death had ended up dying in tragic ways, whereas only about half of the people who had shown no visible signs of taking pleasure in stoning that Bundy to death had ended up dying in tragic ways. *Could my beliefs be wrong?* That was something that he silently wondered many a time about this and many other imponderables.

Many of the Transcendentals also wondered to themselves and each other from time to time, *Could my beliefs be wrong?* One of the most shocking of the multitudinous synchronicities was that both the Theodore Robert Bundy who was born as Theodore Robert Cowell on November 24, 1946 and who died as the infamous Ted Bundy serial killer on January 24, 1989 by electrocution in some universes and the Theodore Robert Bundy who was born on April 28, 1667 and who died as the infamous serial killer Theodore Bundy on June 24, 1709 by stoning in other universes had been incredibly similar men, though born and executed in completely different timelines than each other. Usually, the more omniscient that a given Transcendental was in one way, the less omniscient that Transcendental was in some other way. Even as much as their sets of awareness seemed to exceed that of the most brilliant historical figures of regular reality, the full awesomeness of reality remained plenty mysterious and wondrous to a great many of them.

Terry sat down at the bar and thought back to the incident that had made him famous in some parts of Spain in July of the previous year. The version of Spain in that world had bullfights up until July 18, 1727. On that fateful day, Terry Owen and hundreds of other attendees were in the crowd when some-thing inexplicable happened: The matador and the bull seemed to be performing smoothly when all of a sudden the bull traveled with acceleration upward into the heavens, accel-erating such that within a few seconds it reached the speed of Mach Three. Meanwhile, every human in the stadium, except for Terry Owen, died of spontaneous human combustion. As the lone survivor, Terry told people exactly what he had witnessed, bearing true witness for the sake of posterity. The forensics corroborated several key details, yet many a person had spread rumors that Terry was either extremely holy or extremely demonic. He had not sought out fame, yet fame had found him. This was one of the main drivers of why he started to decide to let go of skipping out on drinking alcohol. Not long after he had performed as one of the executioners of the Ted Bundy who had brutally mutilated and murdered his young wife Anna Provolone Owen (née Bundy), he had decided to become a teetotaler unless and until he might change his mind. The tragedy of it all had been enorm-ous, not the least of which was that at the trial Ted Bundy had blamed a com-bination of the influence of booze, Satan, lust for his sister Anna, jealousy to-ward his brother-in-law Terry, rejection by the five women toward whom he had felt the most sexual and romantic attraction in the two years before he had started to go on his killing spree, some Christian preachers' allegedly neurotic compulsion to condemn all human sex acts except for those between husbands and wives during marriage as part of marital fidelity and for the primary aim of procreation and neither pleasure nor recreation, and whichever medical professional had performed circumcision on him when he was an infant. That peculiar Multarempian serial killer Ted Bundy had chosen to represent himself in court while on trial, much as the American serial killer Ted Bundy chose in a different century in a different world to represent himself in court while on trial.

Although that case had been infamous and had resulted in a small amount of fame going to that Terry, it was nowhere near as shocking to the public as the incident in Spain that had catapulted Terry Owen into celebrity. That Mr. Owen wondered in the bar silently about the strangeness of it all, both how his own brother-in-law murdered his wife and several other women in gruesome ways and how the bull had seemed to defy the laws of physics just before nearly every person in the stadium succumbed to death by instant combustion. Nevertheless, he steadfastly chose to embrace the faith of Multarzinianism, one of the few faiths that included an explicit escape clause. That clause specifically stated, "If thou via thy experience and reason someday findeth sufficient proof or other plausibility with which to depart from Multarzinianism, then thou shalt depart from Multarzinianism of thine own recognizance. Thou shalt use thy critical thinking and judgment not only with respect to other religious movements and scientific movements, but also to evaluate anything thou may knowest about Multarzinian beliefs and practices."

Although there had been many times in his life that Terry Owen had proven highly talkative and outgoing, on this occasion he felt it best to mostly exercise the right to remain silent. He listened carefully to his surroundings, and he looked around to gather visually various cues about what might be going on beyond the polite social veneers of society.

Nearby, a Christian and an Atheist chose to completely avoid any discussion of religion, focusing instead on some recent weather developments.

The Christian in this case was a 6'2" man and the Atheist a 6'1" man, both of them towering behemoths for their day. The Christian said, "You know, I saw the clouds and the rains gathering more ominously yesterday. The pattern from the last ten days is quite a concern. What do you think?"

The Atheist said, "My logic tells me that this is not way too different from what I've seen in several previous years, but my gut tells me that there may be something really different this time. Who knows? What do you think about it?"

The Christian answered, "Well, I do have some intuition that something much bigger is brewing this time. Time will tell."

Much more of this sort of small talk permeated the room. Terry wondered if anyone might dare to make the first move and try to get him to say something meaningful. He also wondered if anyone would go over to him and recognize him for the seemingly-paranormal event that had happened a little less than one year prior over in Spain.

After the bartender brought out a Stella Artois, a drink which happened to exist both in that timeline and in a great many very different timelines, the bar-tender asked Terry, "Is there anything you might want to get off of your chest?"

Terry picked up the Stella Artois, tilted it, placed it back down, and answered, "I used to drink alcohol in moderation, decades ago. Then some stuff got weird and I decided to quite. Time went by, and more weird stuff happened. Now I've decided to go back to drinking alcohol in moderation."

The bartender, who was named Rob, said, "Well, we're all adults here. Be safe, now."

Terry responded, "Thanks. The idea of what's safe and what's not, that's one for the ages. Safety is fleeting in this world we live in. Also, risk is helpful some of the time. What do you think?"

Rob said, "Yes. You are wise beyond your years."

Terry said, "Beyond my years? You can already see just from looking at me that I'm either middle-aged or old. Who in this room do you think might be wiser than I am? If you know of one or two or five such individuals, maybe you could introduce me to them, and maybe they could elevate my wisdom even further."

Rob said, "Well, I'm not too sure about that. I am not entirely confident that anyone in this room is wiser than you are."

Terry retorted, "Oh, please. Spare me the flattery."

Rob said, "It is not so much flattery as it is uncertainty. You see, as the years go by, I seem to be getting more and more agnostic about almost everyone and everything."

Terry exclaimed, "Oh! So you've decided to become profoundly agnostic, have you? I dare you to present me a hypothesis that is totally outlandish. Yes, aha. Something that many people would think only fruitcakes and crackpots would ever dare say to anyone." Terry pulled out seven bills of paper currency, totaling an amount sufficient to buy six drinks. He continued, "Rather than pay you these bills to give me more drinks, besides the beer and the water that I'm already in the process of drinking, I am going to offer it as a tip to you if you can satisfy me with a conversational partner who proves able to give me such a seemingly-bonkers theory."

Rob said, "I'll see what I can do. Oh! I think I've got the ticket to that tip that you're offering. Just now, Roger Edward Evans walked into this tavern. I'll see if I can introduce the two of you to each other."

Within a couple of minutes, Rob did just as he had intended, introducing Roger Edward Evans and Terry Owen to each other. They established good rapport with each other via a little small talk about local events, then they started to go further.

Terry asked, "I'm very curious about the sorts of theories that many people might think are totally ridiculous or really crazy. I'm not going to just plain jump to the conclusion that you're off your rocker if you give me at least one such theory. In fact, I'd like for you to tell me a tale, a tale that you will enjoy telling me and anyone else here who happens to overhear you, a story that will be so outlandish and shocking and weird that some normal people might laugh hysterically at what they find absurd about it. Would you do that?"

That Multarempian Roger Edward Evans responded by intentionally twisting his accent such that he matched 20th-century American Comedian Curly Howard's way of saying, "Certainly." He then paused for a few seconds. After that pause, he proceeded to speak in his normal voice, which many of those in that version of Appalachia considered to be free from any accent.

Roger said, "Yes, certainly, indeed. What I am about to say is probably merely a story of fiction, yet I hypothesize that maybe, somewhere in the great vastness of Reality, some of it might actually be similar to some stuff that has actually happened or will actually happen.

"In ancient times, multiple Buddhists, Taoists, Jews, Christians, Hindus, and others discovered some of the most powerful insights ever, yet much of the most powerful ways to communicate the most stuff with the smallest sizes of diagrams and words were kept hidden. Some of the beings beyond our realm have enforced that bringing too much of the hidden into the open is often way too dangerous to all but the most enlightened. Thererfore, sometimes communities have become keenly aware of super-secret knowledge and maintained enough secrecy and thrived for centuries, even millennia. However, other of such communities were not able to maintain enough secrecy, and they paid the price of the extinction of their communities."

Although this was in some ways the same as many other timelines in many other worlds, in this very version of reality, a set of five gray, extraterrestrial aliens immediately abducted that Roger Evans from that world, leaving a glowing, multicolored hologram in his place for ten seconds, to the chagrin and shock of onlookers. After that period of ten seconds elapsed, the hologram, too, disappeared. Several of the onlookers wondered whether they had hallucinated what they had just witnessed with their own eyes and their own minds.

After abducting that R.E. Evans, they gathered him together with 2,700 other abductees, informed them of a few introductory pointers on The War Beyond Human Comprehension, then screened the same two documentaries that they had shown millions of other abductees: *Revolutions: An Alleged Secret History of the Creations of Several Worlds, the Lives and Deaths of Many Species, and Some of What Has Happened in the Great Beyond* and *The Waters of Oblivion, Revisited, or: An Abridged, Revised, Reimagined Variation of All Things under and over the Sun and Stars.*

Afterward, they participated in a one-hour free-form question-and-answer session as part of preparing for their next set of challenges.

They came from many different universes and many different time-lines, and, therefore, the moderators announced to them early in the session, "Please try to minimize the sort of questions that directly anchor to specifics of the timeline of the history from the reality from which our team abducted you. This shall minimize confusion and help to maintain our focus on the upcoming missions. For example, say you come from Timeline X, the person to your left is from Timeline Z, and the person to your right is from Timeline Y. Now, suppose in your timeline Celebrity A was born in a given year, went on to become the leader of a nation, grew to become elderly, and died in another given year. Suppose, in contrast, that the person to your left came from a place where that same celebrity only made it to his or her early 30s, then suddenly died, never becoming the president or prime minister or similar leader of any nation. Imagine, also, that in the history that the person seated to your right experienced, that celebrity was never born as an actual person, yet you, too, were never born as an actual person, and, even more astoundingly, both Celebrity A and you yourself appear as fictional characters in portions of some popular movie franchise that virtually everyone there categorizes as fiction."

Chapter Eight: The K-Pg Mass Extinction, Revisited

About two billion years before the initial publication of Einstein's papers on The Theory of Special Relativity and The Theory of General Relativity, Elbankovic, Naerroan, and many other Transcendentals agreed with each other to adjust the trajectories of multiple celestial bodies and the fluctuations of many quantum processes such as to arrange for major likelihood—yea verily, virtual certainty—that not one, but two major cosmic impacts upon Earth would devastate life on that planet causing one of the mass extinctions of that planet.

Eons later, as the instant of the first impact approached, that same group of Transcendentals convened to bring many of the living Earthlings to greatly expanded levels of consciousness.

In the year 65,895,250 BC, the ghosts and various other spiritually-beyond transitional beings of the dimetrodons and other organisms of the pre-Triassic periods of the Earth witnessed as, in the twinkling of an eye, millions of dinosaurs and mammals and other living earthlings achieved super-powerful telepathic attunement with them. Most of this was at a semiconscious level for the living, and most of this was at a conscious level for the dead and semi-dead. Interspecies telepathy among dinosaurs soon ramped up exponentially.

This became especially noticeable on the areas in and near what the humans would later call The Yucatan Peninsula. It was there that a large omnivorous bipedal dinosaur, with a brain small in physical stature compared to the higher-dimensional capabilities it possessed, experienced a revelation. That being was a somewhat hermaphroditic dinosaur, about 68% male and about 32% female. As conventional for some dinosaurs of that time, it did not choose to conceive of itself as having a name, rather it conceived of itself in a manner of, "I am what I am, it is what it is, and ideas like 'I' and 'it' have their own ways of transcending. The energies of presence can be self-evident of who we are, without overt over-structuring."

It gathered with a group of dinosaurs, proto-birds, birds, mammals, and reptiles, who sensed its awesome presence of mind. Welcomed and telepathically invited by the others, it went into an extended telepathic story supplemented with intermittent gestures and vocals. Many of the living, multitudes of the dead, and flocks of semi-dead gathered to listen closely as that hermaphroditic dinosaur presented a fable or a theory.

That sentient thus proceeded, "We live in something called a universe. This universe is one of many, or perhaps infinitely-analog-style sliding ranges of universes. We can transition from one universe to another, and perhaps many of us do this from time to time, whether we are consciously aware of it or not.

"Although I do not know for sure whether the following is just exactly how we've arrived where we are, nevertheless, I shall present a vision I've had as a hypothesis for the history of our universe from its inception to the present.

"Within a fabric of ambiguous spatiotemporal relations, five primordial beings spontaneously arose from sheer nothingness. They soon induced an intense explosion in which nothingness-&-potential became everythingness-&-all-potentials. Boom!!

"This eventually led to this place we live on, a giant place within many much larger places, themselves within a vastness beyond all conceivability. Long ago, the large orbiter of reflective light, which some have called 'the moon,' orbited a realm in which the first intelligent being was born. The first being was a bird, which the transcendental primordial five beings (who were and are 'super-intelligent beings' rather than merely 'intelligent beings') induced into becoming alive by charming an inanimate stone into becoming animate.

"That stone was somewhere on this planet that we now live on, long before a collision between Proto-Earth and Proto-Moon resulted in Earth and Moon and many changes. That stone hatched from being a stone to being the first bird. Therefore, if we consider the animated stone to qualify as an egg, then the first bird egg came before the first bird; whereas if we consider the animated stone to have been something other than an egg, then the first bird came before the first bird egg. That bird became capable of laying a living egg after the electromagnetics of the suddenly-conscious planet, which in that instance chose to act as a male planet, though it more usually acts as a female planet.

"The first bird, an intelligent-though-not-yet-super-intelligent being, a few years after its hatching from an animate stone, became impregnated by the Earth, during an instance in which that planet we live on chose to act as a male for a while. The bird subsequently laid an egg, which hatched into a male bird. After the first bird cared for that male second bird sufficiently, the Earth chose to act as a female for a while. The planet then engaged in telepathic and psychokinetic sex with the second bird, and the result of this act of transcendental mating was that the Earth was ready to have many independent instances of inanimate matter transitioning directly into animate biological beings of spatiotemporal, conscious, semiconscious, and subconscious energetic statics and dynamics. And Earth, for millions of years, proceeded to generate much life in a feminine mode."

That dinosaur then proceeded to expound a strange hypothesis about the emergence of bipedal humanoids within a continuation of the seemingly-absurd Planet-Earth-creating-and-then-mating-with-the-birds cosmology that he had just described. After that, he segued into the idea of what some would find a seemingly-even-more-absurd cyclic recurrence of the destruction of the planet by some set of a bunch of supernatural beings.

"Over time, the peoples and animals and plants developed profound symbiosis. However, some prior version of a being who was in some ways what became me and who in some ways was not at all what became me, a being I sense was a powerful male humanoid, foretold that all humanoids and most non-humanoid sentient beings of the planet would vanish in the flash of an eye just before a planetary total or nearly total extinction event. Soon thereafter, Earth and Moon collided, and although life did not go totally extinct, it was almost total extinction for life there. That resulted in the New Earth and the New Moon. Alternatively, we could say that Proto-Earth and Proto-Moon collided, resulting in Earth and Moon.

"A similar cycle repeated some untold number of times as divine punishment for the inhabitants having gone too far astray. Each time,

The Powers That Be chose to *manipulate* the fabrics of *All Realities* to make scientific evidence lead humans of a future cycle *lull themselves and others* into *thinking that no such cycles had ever happened* before. *Yet, happen before they did.* Eventually, a class of beings that some humans refer to as dimetrodons, kind of resembling what spinosaurs transformed into quadrupeds might look like, did something about this weird cycle of death. Through their development of embedding eleventh-generation wireless means of telecommunication into their very biological systems, they achieved sufficient power to stand toe-to-toe in battle with The Powers That Be, just enough to break our planet free from the earth-moon-collision repetitive death trap. This came at a great cost, though, as within our timeline, the dimetrodons went nearly extinct about 206 million years ago, then went totally extinct relative to worldly life 180 million years ago."

"That being said, many of the dimetrodons achieved advanced soteriological methodologies prior to their worldly deaths, with which their consciousnesses are in our very presence today as among the transcendental and semi-transcendental retinue of the great beyond.

"I do not know for sure, but I sense that we may be about to go extinct. Whether or not that happens soon, take heed, if we can tap into the cosmic consciousness of the dimetrodons and the primordial beings, we may have hope for something of the beyond."

This speech received celebratory telepathic applause, together with visible and audible foot stomping and jumping for joy. In the distance, looking up to the heavens, though, they soon saw it rapidly approaching in the upper atmosphere. An asteroid—the first of two preordained hundreds of millions of years earlier to arrive such as to end the Cretaceous and begin the Tertiary—hit Earth in the region of their gathering, generating a Richter-13-magnitude earthquake, the vaporization of over ten-thousand square miles of the surface of the Earth to significant depths, an extreme quantity of airborne particles that would blot out most sunlight from reaching the surface of the planet, and other mass-extinction-inducing consequences.

It hit in a region that human beings would later call Chicxulub, and, therefore, many of the human scientists would proceed to call the resultant geological evidence of it The Chicxulub Crater.

Individual Transcendentals and groups of Transcendentals would soon compete and negotiate with each other over many facets of how best to manage the aftermath of that K-Pg Extinction Event Impact.

PART THREE

Chapter Nine: Korchnoi, Payton, Rather, and Eisenbaum;
Aye, Aye, Captain Double-Forty-One

A web of interactions entangled CIA officers, KGB officers, Viktor Korchnoi, Walter Payton, and Dan Rather during portions of the twentieth century. This could be said truthfully of many alternate timelines.

Some of those timelines had crossover interactions with one another when extraterrestrials would extract select individuals from them.

In many of the timelines, some version or another of a man named William Tager would wind up becoming either a villainous and rather deranged criminal or a generally-law-abiding, courageous hero.

In several of those timelines, William Tager became abducted by extraterrestrials one day within the span of three seconds while driving alone on a deserted stretch of upstate New York.

Although only three seconds went by in terms of the regular, real-world, historico-scientific realm as observable in normal life, and although the region manifested his body not going anywhere out of the vehicle, the extraterrestrial aliens abducted his mind and soul nevertheless. They took his conscious experience out of his body, out of his car, and out of normal space-time, slipping through the higher-dimensional folds of reality. There he experienced a strange odyssey spanning the hidden history of five different versions of Earth, each with its own timeline.

First, they took him to 1921 in Russia, visiting both the pro-capitalist forces and the pro-communist forces of the time. Second, they took him to 1952 in the city of Washington, D.C., United States of America.

Third, they had him visit the year 2048 in some timeline where a man named Kenneth Eisenbaum served as Vice President of the United States. There, President Hugo Franklin and V.P. Kenneth Eisenbaum won reelection in the general election, it was early December, and some Americans were in a festive mood. However, the aftermath of the U.S. intelligence community's enhanced capabilities of conducting domestic surveillance of American citizens with the 2001 passing of the Patriot Act had eventually snowballed. Tager felt outraged at what he had witnessed there while the aliens accompanied him in vehicles invisible, inaudible, and in other respects undetectable to the five basic senses and scientific equipment of the regular-world humans. Fourth, they took him to a 1985 version of the Kremlin, where he again observed regular-world people while they could not observe him. Fifth, they held him in orbit, geostationary high above Manhattan, and there they showed him a series of twenty-two photographs, eleven of Dan Rather and eleven of Kenneth Eisenbaum, revealing a moderate degree of resemblance. After that, they deposited his mind and soul back into his body as he was driving along in the vehicle. Much of his conscious mind registered it as a strange daydream.

Elsewhere, the next day, they took a young Nigerian, three young Germans, and five elderly Russians on an extremely similar higher-dimensional odyssey.

Three days later, the extraterrestrials extracted William Tager, the five Russians, the Nigerian, and the three Germans from their entire universe. The very sudden disappearance of that set of ten individuals, happening to occur at precisely the same instant and not directly witnessed by any of the remaining, living human beings led to it appearing on an episode of *Unsolved Mysteries*. Meanwhile, in a whole different realm, two of the extraterrestrials explained some of why they found themselves set aside from the rest of the world.

Extraterrestrial Alien Captain Double-Forty-One announced, "We gather you here, extradimensionally beyond the world you came from, in order to enlist you into The War Beyond Human Comprehension. What war is that, you might ask? Well, as a prelude to providing an exact answer, having removed you at what was 2:42 P.M. as measured by Greenwich Mean Time on July 4, 1986 from the universe where you were born and where you grew up, we shall show you an incident from an alternative universe.

Emanating a commanding and serious presence, he stated, "In your universe, the U.S. participated in the 1980 Summer Olympics, and the U.S.S.R. participated in the 1984 Summer Olympics. However, in the universe that we are about to show you scenes from, there was a boycott from the 1980 Summer Olympics by the U.S. and multiple other nations that were at odds with the host nation of those games, namely the U.S.S.R. Four years later, in that other universe, there was a boycott from the 1984 Summer Olympics by the U.S.S.R. and multiple other nations that were at odds with the host nation of those games, namely the U.S.

"Now, without further ado."

The video *Which Timeline Is It, Anyway?* proceeded, starting with showing highlights from the 1980 Winter Olympics that occurred in that universe, including hockey, skiing, figure skating, and other events. Next, it showed American political developments. After that, it presented news reports leading up to and including the aforementioned boycott by many nations from the 1980 Summer Olympics. Then came a few highlights of political developments that happened in the U.S.S.R., East Asia, Northern Europe, the U.S., Canada, Brazil, and Australia. Suddenly, the video jumped forward to news coverage leading up to and including the 1984 Summer Olympics, including the boycott by quite a number of nations from participation.

Next, it cut over to showing Ted Turner sitting alone silently for a while in the aftermath of those two boycotts.

Things became very uncomfortable for William Tager right after that, because the video showed the William Tager of that other timeline, a look-alike with a very different lifepath, walking up to Dan Rather on October 4, 1986, hitting him repeatedly, and furiously inquiring of him, "Kenneth, what's the frequency?!" over and over again. Another man accompanied Tager and assisted in physically assaulting the famous news anchor. Lo and behold, paralleling the Tager spectator's dismay, one of the Germans watching the video recognized that accomplice as none other than another timeline's version of himself!

The video wound down soon thereafter, yet it threw in one more event from that timeline's history for the attendees to consider: the July 13, 2024 assassination attempt on President Donald Trump. It showed this from several alternate angles, including a slow-motion presentation of the would-be assassin, Thomas Crooks, becoming shot and killed. Some of those in attendance groaned as they saw an extreme closeup view in extreme slow motion of a side-by-side of President Donald Trump getting shot in the ear and getting down and Thomas Crooks getting mortally wounded by the return fire from the U.S.

Secret Service.

Immediately after that, the video showed news coverage by CNN, Fox News, and CBS News. Finally, the video closed out with showing a vacant parking lot in Area 51 as displayed in a freeze-frame while ending credits flashed onto the screen, one set after another. Some of those in attendance found that style reminiscent of the ending credits portion they remembered seeing in early 1960s *Twilight Zone* episodes.

The extraterrestrial Triple-Ninety posed a question to the ten human attendees. "The vacant parking lot at the end, would anyone dare to venture a guess about its whereabouts?"

The people remained silent. The grays appeared totally impassive as a nonreaction type of reaction to the humans' silence.

Extraterrestrial Alien Admiral Triple-Ninety followed up, stating, "Let me sweeten the pot for you. Whoever guesses right first, if anyone guesses correctly, then that first correct person in this exercise will get to choose what style of diner you will get to dine at when we feed you in a little while. Also, there is no penalty in this case for wrong guesses. Do we have anyone willing to venture a guess?"

One of the Russians guessed, "Poland."

Triple-Ninety said, "Wrong. Any more guesses?"

The Nigerian guessed, in a voice belying uncertainty, "Switzerland?"

Triple-Ninety again said, "Wrong."

A second Russian ventured a stab at this, also sounding to have little confidence in the chances of turning out to guess right, "Oklahoma?"

Rather than speaking, Triple-Ninety chose to cast a glance over at his gray alien teammate Double-Forty-One, who said, "Wrong answer. Do we have any other guessers? Will there be another guess?"

William Tager had been analyzing the situation very carefully. His attention had become laser-focused after the shock of witnessing an alternate version of himself attack a famous newsman in an alternate universe. He remembered the rumors that had circulated for years about secret U.S. government research into extraterrestrials. He made a calculated attempt, saying to everyone present, "Area 51."

The extraterrestrials looked mildly and pleasantly surprised, and they announced in unison, "Correct!"

Triple-Ninety told the group, "After William here, who correctly identified that place shown at the end of the video, chooses the style of diner for which we will supply you with a meal menu, you shall meet additional humans who are in this facility. William Tager, what style of restaurant's food do you wish for us to present you?"

Tager thought for a moment. An idea silently pulsed through his mind for a little bit: *Consider diverse perspectives that people have had about Jesus of Nazareth, Shakyamuni Buddha, Lao-Tzu, Padmasambhava, and other thought leaders.*

Thoughts shifted over to a related notion, and he said it out loud as his initial response: "I'll be diplomatic, and put it up to a multiple choice vote. We'll have each human present get one vote count. Four choices: Italian, Mexican, Chinese, and International Cuisine. By a show of hands, now, how many of you vote for Global Variety?"

Oddly enough, all nine of the other human beings in the room started to vote for that, and William soon joined them by raising his hand. "Wow, that's an immediate unanimous vote. Wow!" he said.

The gray alien, Triple-Ninety, said, "We shall bring you to the dining facility. Follow me as we walk over there."

Follow him they did. Upon arrival, they met sixteen other humans, consisting of three men and thirteen women.

Triple-Ninety resumed speaking, "Of these sixteen, there is a married couple, namely Mr. and Mrs. Elias Artino. The rest of the group are singles. We shall do our best to train you into becoming an elite team of agents to help our side of the war. Next, I shall let Elias Artino tell you a little bit about how he and his wife, Florence Artino, became involved with us." He nodded toward Elias.

There was a brief pause as Elias gathered a few final thoughts before diving right into introducing himself and his wife, whose surname used to be Smith.

A look of profound gratitude and kindness started to positively glow from his face, and he reminisced, "Long ago, I stopped by a Chinese restaurant in a shopping mall when I was eighteen years old. A woman who was about twice my age suddenly looked to me like she was the sweetest, most beautiful, and sexiest woman in the world, and she smiled lovingly toward me. Some might say they don't believe in love at first sight, but to me this was the real deal. I was smitten, whether you want to call it puppy love or genuine love or a fool rushing in. I started small talk with her, and she and I escalated carefully together, eventually leading to a series of dates. We watched some of the greatest movies of all time, such as *Psycho* (1960), *La Dolce Vita* (1960), and *Who's Afraid of Virginia Woolf?* (1966). However, we were being very careful in those early months not to go further than kissing and hugging as far as physical intimacy was concerned. By the time that I was 20 years old and she was about 38 years old, we made a special trip to El Paso to watch a film that an insurance dude informed us about via a cold call.

"That guy said he knew someone who knew someone else who gave him a tip that there was this totally rad new film about to be screened out in the West Texas area over near the Franklin Mountains. We were a little skeptical at first, but we then decided to make the trip. Well, the movie turned out to be rather terrible in many ways, but it also turned out to be truly sexy in some twisted ways involving both female domination and male domination. Yes, my lady and I are both very versatile about domination and submission and kink. Maybe that part is too much information for some of you, but it shall help gear you up for the intensity of the documentary that you will be watching in a little while, a documentary that I am helping to introduce to you as part of your orientation.

"That movie screening in El Paso was very peculiar, and it aroused my partner and me profoundly. Our passion grew and we went much further with physical romance with each other than we ever had before. After that one thing led to another, and while we were away from each other a group of gray extraterrestrial aliens abducted the both of us. They initially brought us up to speed on the situation separately. After that they brought us together to watch a documentary that they believed might best serve as the next phase of the orientation. We watched the documentary together with the extraterrestrial we met of the name Double-Forty-One. After that we went on two successful war missions together. During the second of those two military operations, believe it or not, I chose to propose to my girlfriend, and she said 'Yes!' We have since that time gone on a third successful military operation, and now here we are in front of you, helping you to adapt to this new lifestyle that the gracious aliens have decided to involuntarily enlist you into!"

William Tager voiced skepticism. "Yes, the technologies they have demonstrated are astounding, but why the involuntary abduction and enlistment m.o. Doesn't that seem a tad bit extreme?"

Elias answered, "It is extreme, I admit that, and I believe they would be the first to admit it as well. However, once you see the documentary that Florence and I watched long ago, I think you'll start to understand why this war is of such critical importance to everyone's future, and why it made sense for them to enlist you as they did."

Tager started to relent. "Well, I know that many human nations have had a mandatory conscription program or two, and by the way things have gone so far, these grays and you and your wife probably very much know what this is mainly about. Are we going to watch the video after our meal?"

Elias stated, "That is part of the plan. However, there will also be a brief break after the meal, to allow those who wish to stop by the restroom, perhaps floss and brush their teeth, and perhaps meditate to do so. I'll invite my wife to add a few more comments." He nodded over to Florence.

For about two seconds, she silently composed herself while attempting to accurately gauge the mood in the room. She then explained to them, "I know that you may have many reservations at this time. Be assured, though, the true intentions of the enemy are threatening not only to your lives but to the lives of everyone everywhere. Whether you have firmly held beliefs, one person you care deeply about, five people you care deeply about, or, for that matter, anyone or anything you care deeply about, then, believe you me, the enemy's schemes are jeopardizing all."

The ten new initiates silently held mixed emotions upon hearing such a dire warning. Within a few minutes they gathered around in what looked like a traditional diner with an international theme bringing together dishes from many regions of the world. Next, they together watched a documentary double feature, consisting of, first, a screening of *Revolutions: An Alleged Secret History of the Creations of Several Worlds, the Lives and Deaths of Many Species, and Some of What Has Happened in the Great Beyond* and, second, a screening of *The Waters of Oblivion, Revisited, or: An Abridged, Revised, Reimagined Variation of All Things under and over the Sun and Stars*. Afterward, they participated in a two-and-a-half-hour free-form question-and-answer session as part of preparing for their next set of challenges.

Here is an example of how part of what silently went through the minds of a few of the attendees of one of those sessions:

One bored attendee at one of them drifted into a daydream of visions of evildoers meeting imprisonment in prisons that resembled a hybrid of traditional notions of hell and science fiction expressions of what nightmares might come to the bad. Another bored attendee of the sex opposite of that first one drifted into an identical set of daydreams even though the two of them were oblivious to this at the conscious level. Meanwhile, eighteen members of the audience shared numerical thoughts of a pattern that started with, "4 X 45," "8 X 21," and "9 X 19."

PART FOUR

Chapter Ten: Aspirations, Parties, Changes, and More, Revisited

In Houston, TX, a young man named Josh started to cough about the time that Tropical Storm Imelda reached its zenith of activity in September 2019. He had contracted a Martian microbe, which had slipped through a shortcut in the fabric of space-time to go directly from Mars to Earth.

That microbe had special abilities, despite its lack of what people would normally think of as 'a brain,' to remotely influence other microbes and the humans in closest contact with them to act in a more pro-microbe manner.

Jupiter and Mars had conducted a joint biological attack on Earth.

Technically, though few knew it, the involvement of Jupiter and Mars in the spread of Covid-19 was only true over some ranges of universes. There were also ranges of universes in which the consciousnesses of those two planets refrained from instigating the Covid-19 onto Earth, yet the 2020 Covid-19 pandemic still reared its head. Only in some exceptionally rare timelines did Earth somehow avoid that mayhem. In one of the universes in which a large coalition of beings in the beyond convened in September 2019, those beings chose to wait until December 3, 2021 to perform the full, main opening up of Pandora's boxes and similarly-named Pandara's boxes. Gathered together at 2 A.M. Central Time in downtown Houston, they then, invisibly to most of the living, walked toward the hospital district. While there in that district, they telepathically linked their minds with a similar gathering that was taking place in Fresno, California, then opened a telepathic link to all of Earth's Ponderosa pine trees. Soon, via the powers of quintillions of beings, they opened the floodgates to the full brunt of the paranormal.

*　*　*　*　*

Noon on August 23rd, 2022, 40 nautical miles from the east coast of Japan, fishermen lifted their nets from the depths of the ocean.

Shocked to see a sea creature that looked like a ten-foot long scorpion, they arranged for scientists to haul off the creature. In a secret underwater government facility off the coast of Japan, cryptozoologists, paleontologists, and others from several Asian countries gathered and analyzed the specimen.

Japanese high-ranking military biologist Dr. Yamamoto called his American counterpart Dr. Sagovia to say, "Remember how earlier this month you shared footage of how your team acquired a living Eurypterid? Well, we've acquired a living one ourselves, only this one seems to be a twelve-foot long *Jaekelopterus rhenaniae*."

Dr. Sagovia exclaimed, "And I thought the one we caught was huge! The official fossil records showed eight feet as the most likely limit from way back when, and our nine-foot specimen was quite a shocker. And now a twelve-footer from a part of the Pacific almost half a world away from where we found ours. The Eurypterids are back.

"God help us all!"

Meanwhile, over five thousand extraterrestrial aliens pondered the *The Geneva Bible*'s version of *Revelation*, especially the fifth verse of the twenty-second chapter: "And there shalle be no night there, and they need no candle, nether light of y sun ne: for the Lord God giveth them light, and they shal reigne for evermore."

* *

Flashforward now to that same version of Earth, over 1,500 years later.

* *

Within a colossal building there stood a banner proclaiming:

"WELCOME TO THE YEAR 3534 ON A PECULIAR

VERSION OF PLANET EARTH.

The date is January 24th.

The location is Occidental Mansion,

357 W. 48th Street, El Paso, Illinois."

* * * * *

Although El Paso, Illinois in that world had been an extremely small town as of January 2022 C.E., it had grown tremendously from then through December 3533. As of 3534 C.E. / JAN / 24, it stood as quite a respectably-hustling-and-bustling, medium-sized city.

No longer would most listeners on that Earth automatically assume virtually any random, out-of-contextual-clarification reference to "El Paso" to be references to El Paso, Texas.

A few *Pace Picante Sauce* commercials had, by that time, started to generate three-way schtick coordinating comical perceptions of New York City (i.e., New York, NY), The Illinois Version of El Paso City (i.e., El Paso, Il), and The Texas Version of El Paso City (i.e., El Paso, TX), whereas their old-time, twentieth century and early twenty-first century schtick had most often poked fun at varying perceptions of New York, NY vs. El Paso, TX.

* * * * *

Dimetrioskys Elbankovic walked out onto the stage and stood

silently for ten seconds, gazing at the audience of 663 members in attendance. He started out by announcing, "Greetings guests, mansion security team, and anyone else within earshot or other observability. To let those in who did not already know this on what would otherwise be several secrets, this is a version of Earth in which the Eurypterids reemerged from the waters about one-fourth of the way into the Twenty-First Century, wreaking havoc on both the ecosystem in general and, of course, on human life. People who had grown accustomed to having extremely limited fear of walking along beaches, swimming in natural waters, and scuba diving soon found themselves taking gambles when engaging in these types of activities. Picture this: a family of five gathered together in the year 2024 on a stretch of popular coastline, unaware of scientists having kept the rediscovery of living Eurypterids under wraps since mid-2022, at first enjoying their vacation. Suddenly, the three children in the family start screaming, and before the parents can do anything, it's too late. The three children are bleeding to death, butchered by the sea scorpions also known as Eurypterids. Next, the mother and father rush over in a desperate attempt to save the young ones, and they too get butchered and start to bleed to death. Scenes like these started unfolding all along many coastlines from 2024 onward, and things became so dangerous by 2029 that the human race had to radically reinvent its whole relationship with the waters of its home planet."

Charr Naerroan looked on silently from the audience. He and the speaker had interacted with each other before, sometimes while near each other, at other times by remote influence. Their interactions spanned trillions of years of conscious experience. They also did not know how many variations of each other were out there, and both had met dozens of alternative variations of themselves.

They knew Reality Itself to be an awesome reality, including multitudes of multiverses and numerous alternative versions of either all or nearly all.

* * * * *

After the orientation speech was complete, the interdimensional travelers were each given a modest amount of money, clothing, and supplies and sent on their way, a set of visitors who were not of that world.

On his way out, Charr Naerroan had a flashback to how several humans with whom he had interacted in the late decades of the period before the com-mon era and the early decades of the common era had synthesized their im-pressions of him and several other beings by composing a religious document that they attributed to a being named Charron. That text was and is known to some as *The Gospel According to Charron*.

PART FIVE

Chapter Eleven: The Gospel According to Charron

Although The War Beyond Human Comprehension waged on and on in many variations of the multiverse, each time it became resolved into one side or the other—at least temporarily—seeming to have achieved a total victory, a set of vital artifacts and their competent wielders became central to the outcome.

In some such universes a mysterious sacred stone tablet—somehow identical in every material sense in each and every instance, except for its context—served key spiritual and technological roles in the climactic battle of that war.

Different beings created the tablet in different universes, yet in each case the resulting text had all the same characters and all the same punctuation, with the same alignment and spacing.

To some, it seemed perhaps an artifact to end all artifacts; to others it seemed a grand portal into a group of items to team up together as the artifacts to end all artifacts.

Across many realms, its craftsman forged it from the combination of competing influences, whether spiritually, telepathically, scientifically, or whatever else, that came from all of the mere regular-reality-level intelligent beings, all of The Transcendentals, and The Rest of The Totality of Reality Itself. It made reference to by legend and tradition having been authored by the boatsman who would carry the recently dying to cross over from the realm of the living to the realm of the dead. In defiance of those who would wish to keep the idea of what would constitute gospels away from alleged authorship by any-one associated with paganry—as many associated that boatsman with a few of the pagan traditions—it combined calling itself a "Gospel" while using that very boatsman's legendary, mythical name, "Charron" as the alleged author of attribution.

The document dated from circa the tenth century A.D./C.E. in each universe where it appeared. Sometimes its creation occurred in 908 C.E., other times in other years, for example, 924 A.D. In nearly every universe where it occurred, the living members of the human race on Earth had by around the middle of the 18th century C.E./A.D. completely forgotten how to speak, write, and understand the language in which it was written.

Here are translations of a few of its highlights:

- In the most ancient of days, beings knew. Today, beings continue to know.

- Some of the same pattern happened with the early Buddhists, the early Christians, and the early Muslims, and that pattern had previously happened among the ancient Dorians: Beings channeled some mysterious and awesome forces, and a group of humans revolutionized the world, using those forces. However, those people were focused on taking care of business by getting goals accomplished to such a degree that they often used a minimal amount of writing during some early phases. As their revolutionary activities progressed, though, they flipped the switch at several key junctures, producing voluminous writings. In the case of the Dorians, though, in some sense they were no longer Dorians per se by the time they fully went over to producing voluminous writings, they were a mixture of the progeny of the Dorians, the Mycenaeans, and other people, and that set of the descendants of the Dorians could in some sense be called Dorians, yet it is easier to call them the Greeks.

- Although the Persian Ruler Xerxes failed to conquer Ancient Greece, the highly syncretic religion known as Christianity includes elements of the Zoroastrianism that many Persians had advocated, as well as elements of Mithraism, Buddhism, Taoism, Judaism, and virtually anything it can cross-pollinate from diverse cultures into becoming a new creation.

- Manicheism has attempted to take the Christian syncretism to a whole other level, yet with Mani as the central figure. The entirety of that religion known as Manicheism shall appear to go totally extinct in many realities, because it winds up seeming to oppose the vitality of each and every other religion, in a manner lacking sufficient primal energy to stand up for itself. However, a rivalry between Manosism and Manicheism—in many respects, diametrically-opposed syncretic religions—shall in the long run lead to the merchants of the world developing store display models of humans, usually stationary, sometimes posable into different positions for advertising and marketing. Some shall call those mercantile display models, "mannequins."

- Tax collectors shall in the future become much better organized, and some future rulers of nations will embrace the temptation to sic tax collectors onto their political foes. However, when the tax collectors and political leaders have spiritual flaws at their cores, they will carry with them the seeds of their political destruction, because their flaws will deflect them away from correctly choosing the times, seasons, and purposes of when to write, how to write, how much to write, and how and when to refrain from writing.

- Absolute power tends to absolutely corrupt, yet enlightened absolute power presumably emanates from an uncorruptible source. Such total, infinitely-wise, infinitely-ethical, genuine absolute power is what many believe to be the province of THE LORD.

*   *   *

That artifact would remain hidden from the living for many centuries. In some universes its discovery and translation would occur about one-third of the way into the Twenty-First Century.

Competing camps of experts differed on estimates regarding to what century—or even what millennium—the artifact most likely dated. As far beyond their reality as its context was, different answers were, in fact, correct in different universes and different timelines.

Some versions dated to Before the Common Era, others to the early centuries of the Common Era, and, yet others still, to medieval times.

Those who succeeded in translating it with great accuracy found a sense of poignancy about it, and, in many cases much of the time, a feeling of heightened empathy in the immediate wake of succeeding in deciphering portions of its meanings.

Little would they have suspected that Charr had been involved in serving both as part of the inspiration for that document's creation and as part of the inspiration for many horrific acts of war, cruel acts of genocide, and cold-blooded murders in the history of the world. As he said, though, it was "nothing personal" at the root of the destruction.

CHAPTER 12: SEQUELS TO ALL THINGS

Very near where Dimetrioskys Elbankovic spoke at a most peculiar gathering on January 24, 3534, a group of seven, specifically the attendees Jacob Kalkin, Vivian V. Orion, Napol Ray, Charr Naerroan, Roger Evans, Chen Su Luo, and Sarah Rubinstein, walked together to embark on exploring cuisine at an exquisite local diner.

Chen Su Luo ordered a vegetarian meal, including a veggie steak, brussel sprouts, spinach, brown rice, whole wheat bread, tofu salad, and mixed fruit. He usually stuck to a strict vegan diet; in his most recent two decades of life—spread over portions of twenty-eight universe's timelines—about 92% of his meals had been vegan, and, besides how those were among his vegetarian meals, another 3% had been vegetarian without being vegan.

Vivian Orion chose to only order a combination of soft drinks, coffee, a smoothie, and a blackberry martini. The smoothie was high in protein, medium in carbohydrates, and low in fat. The soft drinks were moderately low in calories. The blackberry martini as crafted by that establishment blended blackberry juice, Finlandia Vodka, blueberry juice, pineapple juice, blackberry syrup, Central Market 1877 mineral water, elderflower liqueur, and fresh lemon juice. Vivian chose to put only half a creamer package, a little bit of purified water, and a few sprinkles of nutmeg into her coffee.

Charr Naerroan ordered a full-size Lumberjack-themed break-fast plus a T-bone steak dinner made with real beef, one cup of 2% milk, a veggie steak dinner made with a blend of mycoprotein and soy protein, two apples, an a la carte order of Bratwurst, a New Belgium Beer, a large bottle of Topo Chico mineral water, and three extra slices of French Toast. The other six in his party at the table were unsurprised by the magnitude of his order, given that he had chosen to manifest in the nine-foot-tall, very muscular version of himself that he had previously used when visiting Hannibal Barca way back in 183 B.C.E. He looked and sounded as if of identical biological age at the table there in 3534 C.E. as he had been while in Barca's Villa in 183 B.C.E., though he had gone through several trillion years of interactions with the rest of Reality in the interim. That was, in term of his personal journey.

Three of the others at his table knew from past experiences that he could sometimes materialize and dematerialize at will.

Those three were Jacob Kalkin, Vivian Valerie Orion, and Sarah Rubinstein. Jacob, Valerie, and Sarah were also aware that Charr could sometimes shape-shift his physical appearance. Charr and Sarah had even made love with each other on a yacht in a version of nineteenth century Earth where the timeline included neither the United States of America nor Russia having ever existed, yet the United States of Philsatlan was one of the prominent nations, and it occupied much of the same territory that people from many other worlds would have associated with the United States of America. Philsatlan usually had a pronunciation that basically equated to taking the "phil" from "philosophy" and followed it with the "-zatlán" from "Mazatlán."

Sarah Rubinstein had been born a nineteenth-century Jewish mortal, yet she transformed into a Transcendental while experiencing intense tantric sex with Charr Naerroan. She subsequently proceeded to serve a double agent in The War Beyond Human Comprehension.

Both Charr Naerroan and Dimetrioskys Elbankovic had earned her respect, and both of those transcendentals knew her to be a double agent. Useful to both, she had found a niche within which to thrive.

Dimetrioskys had avoided making any more profound physical contact with her than the occasional handshake and the rare pat on the shoulder. In contrast, Charr had an intuition that she could make for a great transcendental, and he had set out to transfigure her on a yacht through the act of physical intimacy that they shared on a fateful voyage. Across many different timelines and thousands of years of personal experiences, she had experienced much more from Reality than she had ever dreamt of as a schoolgirl. Charr first met her when she was 23 years old, whereas Dimetrioskys first met her when she was 26 years old. Sometimes she grew jaded from the weight of memory from the large amounts of death, destruction, and intrigue. *The entire war made little more sense to her now than it did when she first became aware of it, and she sometimes wondered whether the war actually made genuine sense to anyone anywhere, even the mightiest of the leaders conducting it.* Silently looking over the menu items and reflecting on her life and the lives of others, she let out a sigh. The others declined to ask what the sigh was all about, and she declined to volunteer to bring up just how weary she was feeling about everything. She ordered a kosher meal that included carefully prepared chicken, lettuce, bread, tomatoes, kale, cheese, arranged as a medium-sized sandwich, and she chose to have an orange in lieu of waffle fries.

Napol Ray ordered Eggs Benedict, French Toast, Liverwurst, and an unusual dinner meal that the diner called The Avalanche. Napol was not quite sure of it, but he sometimes wondered whether he might have been born a 24th-century reincarnation of Napoleon Bonaparte, a person of heightened telepathic interaction with the ghost of Napoleon Bonaparte, or a hybrid of partway both.

He contemplated many times about how Alan Watts had long ago explained to people the idea that Dharmic religious ideas of people going through reincarnation might best be understood as thought gateways into opening the mind to possibilities transcending sets of basic, stereotypical Western ideas about life, birth, death, and the great beyond and the various, stereotypical Eastern ideas about birth, life, death, and the great beyond.

Roger Evans also ordered The Avalanche, adding, a la carte, two fried eggs over medium, a vodka martini, a well-seasoned fried pork liver appetizer, and a small pepperoni pizza. He had attained the rank of being a 22nd-century chess grandmaster via participation in FIDE, and mysterious beings recruited him into the War Beyond Human Comprehension after a while.

That recruitment started with seven gray extraterrestrial aliens, including Double-Forty-One and Triple-Ninety, abducting him. The ensuing orientation was something else.

The enigmatic Elias Artino served as a primary instructor at that, and it included a screening of *Revolutions: An Alleged Secret History of the Creations of Several Worlds, the Lives and Deaths of Many Species, and Some of What Has Happened in the Great Beyond*, an in-depth, 600-person-room Q&A session, a screening of *The Waters of Oblivion, Revisited.*

Despite having attained extraordinary mental fortitude in connection with both his chess training and his dealing with difficult family members, FIDE GM Roger Evans found one hundred twenty of the facts involving The War Beyond Human Comprehension to be profoundly disturbing.

Jacob Kalkin ordered both The Avalanche and exactly the same type of vegetarian meal that Chen Su Luo had ordered. Jacob had been 51st-cen-tury space explorer Zarlowe Nike, and in some ways he continued to be that Zarlowe Nike, though the concept of identity had attained the complication that Zarlowe Nike passed through a device called The Division Multiplier, and emerged from it as two twin beings, agent Jacob Kalkin and agent Ezra Kalkin, both of whom served diligently beside Yadier Horowitz and Dimetrioskys Elbankovic. Jacob had served now in that epic war for over two thousand biological years of his personal journey through the mysteries of the realities. However, his physical well-being had not seemed to age a bit since he and his twin had emerged from The Division Multiplier.

The meal that the thirty-sixth-century diner there called The Avalanche included for its main entrée laboratory-grown pieces of flesh in the shapes of steaks, nuggets, and tenders. Those pieces had resulted from research and development that included fantastic advances in biochemistry.

That meal simulated bison, turkey, alligator, and crocodile meat, all without requiring the birth, growth, and death of any actual, complete living specimens of any of those animals. The earliest breakthroughs in this sort of technology had started in the early 21st century. Put the proper ingredients together, have the machines simulate how a living organism might grow some of its muscles, monitor the process, and voila, the lab can produce animal flesh without stripping it from the body of an animal.

By this time, about one-third of the way into the 36th century, this type of technology had become very good. It had already become good by the latter portions of the 21st century, but as the centuries went by, it became better and better.

* * * *

"Nutritious, delicious, great for protecting the environment, plus no animals killed!" That very advertising slogan appeared in many places for lab-grown meat.

The restaurant had run TV commercials in which a zoo at the base of a large, snow-covered mountain gets hit with an avalanche. Here is a description of how that commercial would go:

A crew of five workers digs through the mess and finds the corpses of the animals, which happen to include bison, crocodiles, turkeys, and alligators. Two workers start to speak with each other about it.

A tall, handsome, muscular black man says to a handsome, chisel-jawed, tall white man, "Hey, isn't it a shame that the meat from these animals has to go to waste?"

The tall handsome white man replies, "Yeah, I mean, we need to bring all the corpses back to law enforcement as part of the evidence. A real shame, isn't it?"

Two additional workers suddenly appear on camera and join in on the conversation. Both of them are women.

A beautiful, joyful, medium-height, medium-complexion woman of ambiguous racial background and hour-glass figure says with a flirtatious lilt to her voice, "Hey guys, they wouldn't know the difference if we took a few pounds of flesh from these dead critters, cooked them up, and ate them, would they? And what they don't know in this case probably won't hurt anyone, would it?"

A tall, beautiful, medium complexion woman of ambiguous racial background says to them, "Well, that could pose some moral issues, and we could get into some deep trouble for that. Hey, I've got an idea, let's get the zoo officials and law enforcement folks on the phone and see if we can get full authorization to cook up the critters! We can offer that they can join in on the festivities!"

The scene jumps forward to showing a huge gathering of police, zoo administrators, zookeepers, and sports stars gathered together to party and eat the remains.

Suddenly, the screen changes to narration accompanied by a large-print rolling text of the narration. The narrator and the print both state, "No animals were harmed in the making of this ad. In fact, the meat shown in the meal scene grew in laboratories without requiring the births, lives, or deaths of any individual, complete animals. The labs grew muscles in much the same way that individual complete animals grow their muscles, using advanced technology that first really got going over 1,500 years ago. This dramatization is a reminder that The Avalanche is available in El Paso, Illinois at The Hannibal Cannonball Café. See you there!"

* * * *

The main entrée came with a choice of two sides and dinner bread.

After some small talk, including basic introductions, their conversation pivoted toward more serious subjects. At the meal, Sarah was one of the first to openly pursue some way to gauge what each of them might decide to do next with their lives. She said, "Some of you I met before several of us were together in some recent times at that Temple 894723 Gateway Prison. Others of you I first met at that inter-dimensional, beyond-all-normal-notions-of-time, amazing facility. And then there is Valerie." Sarah looked over directly toward Valerie in an ostensibly friendly manner. "You are quite an interesting lady, and it was neat to first meet you as a fellow audience member at that big speech that happened a little while ago." Next, she looked away from Valerie to look toward Jacob, then toward Charr. After that, Sarah cast glances rotating through each of the other dinner guests. "It's that classic question all over again, that same question that's been around for about as long as beings have been able to use language to ask it: Where do we go from here? What do we do next with our lives? I have several ideas about where I might go next and what to do next, but I'd like to invite you to share a few of your ideas now, and I'll plan to wait until a little later to indulge you with some of what my plans under consideration might be. Anyone wanna speak up?"

* * * * * * * * * * * *

Next came what seemed to them like half an eternity, as no one at all bothered to say anything.

Charr then spoke resolutely, "I don't know about the rest of you, but I'm going to make a bee line for the nearest place that sells to the general public lethal weapons. Then, rather than speak much at all, I plan to quietly observe how the people act, how they talk, what sorts of stuff may be on their minds, how the salesfloor folks present their products and services, what sorts of clothing each of the people are wearing, etc. This will be one of the best ways to get a better handle on what in the world is going on in this world, as well as what in the world our options might be about what to do about the situation here."

Ezra Kalkin, Yadier Horowitz, Paragon East, Satan, and Paragon West all immediately materialized about six feet away from Charr Naerroan.

Satan spoke first, "First of all, as you are probably aware, Charr, I do not exist. I am an illusion, Also, no one exists, not any single being anywhere at any time. Time and space are also illusions. So, too, are all of the angels, devils, demons, gods, creators, destroyers, preservers, humans, animals, ghosts, mountains, rivers, oceans, plants, and everyone and everything else. Yes, to some degree, as reflected by portions of Esoteric Christianity, Buddhism, Kabbalist Judaism, Sufi Islam, and The Occult, everyone and everything does share a degree of reality. Therefore, although I do not exist, it is also true that I do exist. Although I am an illusion, I am also a real, actual reality. Everyone exists, every being everywhere every place every time. Time and space are also realities. I am God. I am not God. God is you. God is not you. We are God. We are not God. Now, if everyone else here would kindly shut up, I request that you, Mr. Naerroan, one of the great Transcendentals, that you may respond to what I just said."

Charr said, "Mu."

Satan responded, "Then you recognized that much of what I said has that sort of Zen transcendental complete balance, with every way of condemning it and every way of praising it confounding logic with more logic, until it becomes best to simply shut up. Well, then, Charr, I dare you, I dare you to simply continue the plan you placed into motion eons ago, a plan that I, too, have sometimes been daring to work on. You know which plan I am talking about."

Charr answered, "Oh, yes, indeed."

Satan said, "Great!"

Charr Naerroan and Satan together then vanished into thin air, leaving the rest of them there to ponder what just happened.

* * * * * * * * * * * * * * *

Several weeks went by, then several months. Ezra, Yadier, Jacob, and others who had arrived from regions not of that world chose to explore, study, interact, and plan.

Eventually, a small charter airplane, as fate would have it wound up including Vivian V. Orion, Jacob Kalkin, Charr Naerroan, and several other passengers. Hijackers diverted the flight, though. It landed in a hyper-militant organization's lair.

Unseen to virtually all was a five-way war that affected all of this: several versions of Satan and several versions of Charr Naerroan had formed an alliance, and, meanwhile, The Patriarch Moses, The Prophet Muhammad, Jesus Christ, Krishna, Shakyamuni Buddha, and a great many others led a variety of factions, some of which formed alliances with each other most of the time while fighting against each other a small amount of the time. Over the eons, it largely coalesced from time to time into what ranged between a three-way war to a twenty-way war. It happened to be the case that as of the time of the diversion of the airplane that Vivian Orion, Charr Naerroan, Jacob Kalkin, and seven other passengers had been aboard, that huge transcendental soup of cosmic conflict was in the state of a five-way war.

The ariel hijacking proved a shock, yet Jacob and Charr remained calm. Both felt at ease with dying at any time, staying alive for a while, killing others, and refraining from killing others, as long as perceiving to be on track to properly honor reality and to properly fulfill spiritual duties. As explained earlier, they perceived quite different versions of what would constitute honor and duty. Both remained unperturbed, amid the extreme dangers of the situation.

In contrast with that, Vivian V. Orion and the seven remaining passengers felt at least some anxiety. A plane hijacking combined with landing at a remote facility, followed by transport seemed an exotic form of kidnapping.

What are those hijackers and their accomplices after? wondered each abductee, in his or her own way.

****

"Visions of Assassinations, Part Fact, Part Fiction, in the Mind of a History Teacher Seeking to Think About Something Other Than The Predicament He Was In, Part One"

One of the other seven passengers was a high school history teacher. He decided to let go of thinking too much about his current predicament, believing that either too much or too little thinking about it would be less ideal than some middle way of how much.

He decided to silently imagine back to portions of ancient history, going on a brief mental adventure mixing some of what he clearly remembered correctly, some of what he vaguely remembered and might have mixed up, and some straightforward conjectures on what might have happened long ago.

At first he though back to what the historical accounts indicate to have been September 18, 96 B.C.E. He thought back to how one Roman emperor suddenly became assassinated on that day, and another Roman emperor would emerge via a vote by the Senate of Rome. Specifically, Titus Flavius Caesar Domitianus Augustus, a man also known as Emperor Domitian, had been running an array of government efficiency initiatives and other controversial pro-grams amid a bunch of political tensions.

The day continued moving along for a while. He had pleased some of his most militant of constituencies and had served some of the populist interests, yet he had alienated much of the aristocracy. At his palace chambers, he suddenly felt oddity in his central nervous system. He saw that a palace worker appeared to have sustained an injury, and, therefore, he went to see if he might help. Suddenly, he felt a sharp pain in his side. Several of the people in the palace then and there launched into a furious stabbing spree.

They stabbed him between the ribs to slide their blades into his lungs, they stabbed him in the throat to get his blood to gush out from it, they stabbed him in the groin to take out their frustrations with anything that had ever bothered them as their awareness and observation of mutilating his genitals made them feel that they had found and cruelly punished an appropriate scapegoat for all that they thought was wrong with their lives, and they stabbed him in the eyes. After all that was left of him was an almost-dead, aching, squirming, bloody mess, they simply walked away. One very young palace woman who was fifteen years old and who had gone straight for Domitian's corpus cavernosa with her blade, cutting both his left corpus cavernosum and his right corpus cavernosum right open, decided to briefly walk back to him after the others left.

****

"Visions of Assassinations, Part Fact, Part Fiction, in the Mind of a History Teacher Seeking to Think About Something Other Than The Predicament He Was In, Part Two"

She said to him as he whimpered in agony, "You asshole! I hate you! I hate you! Your policies contributed to how my parents died in the street! You also chose policies that led to how an ugly, creepy monster of a man one day lured me with a bunch of money into prostituting myself to him! I was only thirteen years old, and I had just hit puberty at the age of eleven, and he got really rough; he really hurt me between the legs, but since he had paid me so much money, I held back from telling him to stop until I knew that he had really enjoyed himself, and he really damaged me!! My parents would not have died as a pair of homeless, penniless people if your policies had been better! You Jupiter-damned evil emperor! With my parents dead and with myself living on the street, that old, ugly, creepy guy with the big bucks lured me into becoming a prostitute, and, although I have become a wealthy palace prostitute, the lifestyle has probably re-moved from me what had been my dream when I was a little six-year-old girl: The dream that I might save up myself for one man who would be a great man and who, one day, might propose to me while I would still be a very pure young lady. A few months into my new profession of being a hooker, there was virtually no purity left within me, and I blame you! You forfeited your right to live a very long time ago, you greedy, conniving, power-hungry evildoer!" With that, she spit on him as he was bleeding out. She then went one step further, picking up one more dagger, turning it around, and then using the handle of it to bludgeon the bleeding man repeatedly in the groin that she had already cut open.

He squealed, squirmed, writhed, groaned, and screamed in extreme pain and agony.

Several times during the ordeal, he wondered about how the young woman had made him into such a scapegoat, presuming his public policy decisions to have somehow been the primary cause of her family's recent misfortunes.

****

"Visions of Assassinations, Part Fact, Part Fiction, in the Mind of a History Teacher Seeking to Think About Something Other Than The Predicament He Was In, Part Three"

Domitian felt pain such as he never previously imagined to be even humanly possible. Pain that shot through his entire body, an agony that kept throbbing through from head to toe, and he knew he was about to die.

Amid such pain and agony, he wondered if it might have been better if he had never been born, and, instead of having been born, he could have gone straight from the mysterious beyond into being a weird, fictional character, transcendental being very much beyond the regular bounds of space and time, in some ways less real than the people of the regular, worldly life, though in at least a few ways, paradoxically, somewhat more real than the regular, every-day people of the worldy life of being born into the real world, living, and dying. Also, in the combination of all the ultra-extreme physical pain and agony that he was experiencing and all the psychological reality he was dealing with of how his group of assassins clearly showed themselves to despise him and the way that he had been running the empire, he wondered about if life might have gone much better in some alternate path in which he would never risen to the rank of emperor.

After the young prostitute felt that she hurt him enough to make him pay for what she perceived he had done through his public policy decisions to her parents and herself, she suddenly had a huge change in her voice and body language. She yelled out, "Jupiter, of Jove, what have I done? Emperor, please forgive me, they told me you were to blame for almost everything wrong with this empire, and they told me about their plot to kill you, and I decided to join them in the conspiracy to kill you. Oh, Jupiter, oh, Mars, oh, Venus, what have I done to you, Great Emperor?! Even if you deserved to die, you probably didn't deserve to die like this! What have I done? Can you ever forgive me?"

****

"Visions of Assassinations, Part Fact, Part Fiction, in the Mind of a History Teacher Seeking to Think About Something Other Than The Predicament He Was In, Part Four"

Emperor Domitian thought to himself, as he subvocalized in his mind's auditorium, audible within him, yet inaudible to the young lady who , "Maybe the Christians are right. Lord God of the Christians, Thou Who Art Perhaps Identical to The Unknown God whom a few of our Greco-Roman pantheon at times honor, Thou Who Art Perhaps Identical to the Corresponding Ultimate Creator and Destroyer Entity or Entities at the core of many other religions and philosophies, Thou Who Art perhaps the energy of consciousness as working from the beyond mysteriously even through the ideas of those who might think that humankind invented you instead of you having any reality other than in the human imagination and the imaginations of any other intelligent beings who might bother to, in that theory create you as a hoax, I know not whether Thou truly existeth or not, but as I am about to die, I choose full faith in You, as well as in that basic amount of core truth that I heard the East present through Easterners, that basic truth of Buddhism that suffering and trouble are real, that much phenomena are interdependent, whether absolutely all is interdependent or not, there is a major degree of nonduality between all sorts of apparent opposites within our minds, and if we recognize a major amount of nonduality, interdependency, and helpfulness of middle way approaches, then we can let go of feeling bothered by pain, suffering, agony, and the troubles of life and death.

****

"Visions of Assassinations, Part Fact, Part Fiction, in the Mind of a History Teacher Seeking to Think About Something Other Than The Predicament He Was In, Part Five"

"I am choosing full faith in You, The Christ-Channeled Trinity: The Father, The Son, and The Holy Ghost of What Christianity Doth Expresseth. Yes, and I now understandeth, knoweth it through the proof of experience and believe in the basic core of Shakyamuni Buddha as irrefutable in the regular sense no matter which religion or religions are true or false, yet I also take a leap of faith right now with all that is true in whatever might be true, out an abiding love of The Origin, Destination, and Core Foundation of Reality Itself, whether called this or that or the other. I recognize now much better the legend of Jesus of Nazareth having said to His Heavenly Father that his killers knew not what they were doing and that He requested His Father to forgive them, for they knew not what they were doing, and they should get a way to chances to heal. To The Ultimate Reality I commit my soul."

***** ** *****

THUS CONCLUDES PART FIVE (OF FIVE) OF THAT CAPTIVE INSTRUCTOR'S IMAGINED JOURNEY THROUGH HISTORY, SEEING IN ONE ASSASSINATION SEVERAL WINDOWS INTO ALL ASSASSINATIONS. (Thus concludes that fellow's flight of the imagination involving "Visions of Assassinations, Part Fact, Part Fiction, in the Mind of a History Teacher Seeking to Think About

Something Other Than The Predicament He Was In."

********* ** *******

**************************** **************************

The history teacher returned his attention to his immediate set of surroundings. He wondered why life had led to the airplane flight that he had boarded, why hijackers took over the flight, why he was now a captive, and what might happen next. For a little while, he became extra uncomfortable, as this made him associate the current predicament to parallel.

"You have been abducted through a variety of means, and we shall decline at this time to disclose to you how many of you come from where, as well as whether we are acting on the authority of Atlantis, Vinland, or another nation-state."

Thus was the announcement from a 6'5" man of medium complexion, ambiguous ethnic facial features, and a baritone voice, speaking with a midwestern American style of speech. The audience consisted of exactly one thousand individuals, each of whom was ostensibly human.

They had come from all of the eight continents of the globe, of that version of Earth's globe—Antarctica, Australia, Asia, Africa, South America, North America, Europe, and Zealandia—as well as from nearly all walks of life.

He continued, "Over one-and-three-fourths millennia have passed since the American Declaration of Independence, yet The United States of America is still a nation of global relevance, we have decided it in our nation's best interests to subject each of you to a peculiar test, right here and right now. To reiterate, though we decline to inform you of our nation's identity, we have conscripted you to help us analyze the U.S.

"Specifically, you shall put together a list of all U.S. Presidential general elections from 1792 to 2020 and place one vote to categorize each one into one of three categories. Category "Yes:" it was a reasonably, fair and free election that happened with integrity, and you deem that certain beyond a reasonable doubt. Category "No:" it was an election that lacked reasonable fairness and/or reasonable freedom and/or reasonable integrity, and you deem that certain beyond a reasonable doubt. Third, and finally, category "Maybe:" you, for whatever reason or reasons, deem it to have had reasonable doubt on both the side of fair, free, and with integrity and the side of unfair and/or unfree and/or lacking in integrity.

"Also, you shall look at a list of one hundred twelve celebrities from the Nineteenth-through-Twenty-Second Centuries and hypothesize in writing at least one transcendental karmic theory of just what *really*, primarily caused death, *beyond* conventional medical diagnoses.

"One more thing: Bear in mind that the nation on whose authority we are acting has authorized us to subject any and/or all of you to religion-based human sacrifice at the conclusion of the test, based on a combination of your answer choices, our secret dossiers on each of you, and any and all other relevant factors.

"Good luck."

The one thousand test takers represented a demographically diverse microcosm of Earth in the year 3536. They took all manner of different approaches to how to fill out their answers. Also, it soon became apparent to those involved that the test administrators had exited the room and left everyone there to their own devices. Many wondered how long they had to complete the exam; most wondered what, if anything, they could do to improve their survival chances. A very small fraction of them felt a clear inner calm amid the bizarre challenge of it all.

By the time the administrators came back, three hours had passed. The same master of ceremonies, who never identified himself to the test-takers by name, began to speak again, "Time is up. We shall now pick up your papers, and you shall remain where you are. We will then start to send several of our agents to interview you in sequestered settings—that is, in offices away from this ballroom."

Within minutes the agents indeed started to walk up to individuals, tap them on their shoulders, and walk them out to life-and-death interviews. By the time the ordeal was over, only fifty-two of the original one thousand test takers were still alive. Over six hundred had been slowly tortured to death by gruesome methods reminiscent of the most painful deaths that had ever happened before to any humans anywhere.

Three of the survivors were Vivian Valerie Orion, Jacob Kalkin, and Charr Naerroan. They also so-happened to have been among those who had maintained the greatest equanimity through the ordeal.

However, their routes to survival had been... shall we say... quite different.

Vivian Valerie Orion fully completed her written test with very fleshed-out answers. On the elections issue she wrote, "Based on the historical records and other factors, I deemed the elections of 1796, 1912, 1948, 1960, 1972, 1980, 2000, 2016, and 2020 to be in the category of Maybe. Though none of us today can really and truly know very directly about those moderately-ancient events, I believe that there is enough evidence to deem all the other elections in the range specified to be in the category of Yes. Although I decline at this time to place into writing further description on the elections issue, I will gladly discuss this out loud with the test administrators if and when they deem it appropriate." On three of the celebrity death issues, she wrote: 1) Regarding the first celebrity, "Here is A Hypothesis: He should not have chosen to participate in the motion picture film *Children of the Corn V: Fields of Terror* (1998), a movie in which he portrayed a weird Luke character; had he refrained from doing that, then, according to this hypothesis, he would have likely lived at least five years longer." 2) Regarding the next one, "She should have revealed more in her autobiography. Had she and her publisher together chosen to reveal more in that work, then she would have likely extended her lifespan by at least three years. Perhaps closely tied to this or perhaps unrelated to this was the public knowledge that Burt Reynolds unsuccessfully tried to hit on her at least once early in the 1970s. Either way, after the combination of starring in both the movie *Toomorrow* (1970) and the movie *Xanadu* (1980), she and her accomplices on those two projects had really startled a bunch of WASP nests, i.e., White Anglo-Saxon Protestant nests of intentions to get Western societies to not deviate too much from conformity to their sensibilities and thereby nest for their young-uns in a way paralleling how hornets and wasps have colonies whose nests would best not usually be disturbed by people.

The energy patterns had things precarious for her, and, per this hypothesis, if she had stated point blank more information, then that might have offset enough the set of the blowback from the WASP nests who had found alternate reality presentations in the aforementioned 1970 movie and the hybrid alternate reality of the aforementioned 1980 movie abhorrent to their ideas of what The Lord God of Abraham imposes on people in general. This was kind of like a scene from some episode of *Police 24/7*, in which that reality-based TV show with actual police footage showed the cops catch two guys who were stealing a vehicle in the state of Washington or somewhere else in the U.S., and the first guy rat-finked on the second guy, but, once they caught the second guy driving the stolen vehicle, he would not rat-fink on anyone else, even going so far as to say that he simply does not snitch. One of the police officers said to him, either verbatim or nearly so, 'Fine. You don't want to snitch, you pay the toll.' There is a time to tell more via things like autobiographies and there are times to tell less with things like autobiographies. Also, there are times to totally shut up, like some Buddhist monk or some Catholic monk, either way, as a monk in some weird monastery with a vow to be totally silent sometimes and often times reticent, leaning toward silence even in cases without requiring total silence. Finally, there occasions to be as vocal as vocal can be, like when a politician in the United States Congress might best perform an intense filibuster. She may have leaned a little too much toward being like one of those monks with a vow of silence, and leaned not enough toward being like a politician conducting a filibuster." 3) About the third famous person, Valerie noted, "It was a combination of at least two of his last few main creative projects trapping him between spiritual walls that started to close in on him. With *Enter the Dragon* he became hero-bound to steer clear of insufficient exhibition of the value of The Buddha Dharma, whereas with *Game of Death* he became hero-bound to steer clear of excessive exhibition of the value of The Buddha Dharma. They caused cosmic forces to converge on him in such a way that he had little or no escape route from threats that came from at least three different sides, the two main sides and one everchanging, ultra-mysterious, super-unknown side. Perhaps if he had the luxury of having watched *Indiana Jones and the Temple of Doom* (1984) and/or *The Natural* (1984) and/or *1984* (1984) prior to that encounter, then he would have, as per this hypothesis, had a much better chance of navigating the surreal situation he faced. Up to immediately before his fateful choice to take a combination-of-Aspirin-&-Meprobamate tranquilizer (i.e., the soon-thereafter-to-become-infamous Equagesic) to which he had an adverse reaction, that is. Also, perhaps if he had the luxury of watching any one or four or more of the other 1980s movies before that death by a weird pharmacological misadventure, then his chances of survival might have been enough to lead to his survival until at least reaching the age of 80."

Valerie had a great deal of past experience writing government reports, and she knew that in some cases overloading a document with probably-irrelevant-though-plausibly-relevant details in order to flesh out the writing would improve the chances of keeping a government job in many cases, as the weight of printed reports often had more of a check-the-box psychological effect than the actual quality of what was in the writing. Even if a given government report writer happened to be a Hemingway fan during leisure time, and even if the person subscribed to Jefferson's idea of generally best using fewer words when it could still communicate essentially the same thing, many a government worker knew, as suggested by the movie *Looking for Comedy in the Muslim World* (2005), huge verbosity and mind-numbing extra details are sometimes the way.

She also knew that with this high level of danger, it might save her life to give the judges both more fodder with which to seek to ridicule her and more fodder with which to adore her. Anxiety hit as she knew that any small misstep could prove fatal. Even if she performed perfectly, they still might be about to torture her to death. She then remembered long ago being a member of an espionage team that discovered a female espionage coworker not only dead, but the victim of acts of the cutting up and ripping open of much of the flesh from thighs to chest. The perpetrator had used razor blades, an ice pick, an X-Acto knife, a scalpel, ten matches, and 120 needles. The attacker waited until near the very end, as his victim was in bodily agony from her inner thighs to her nipples from mutilation, before he chose to ram the ice pick between her left eye and the part of her left eye socket between that eye and her nose, to then hit it with a hammer to break through into the frontal lobe of her brain, and to then perform a prefrontal lobotomy on her by wiggling the ice pick side-to-side, diagonally one way, diagonally the other, up and down, and round and round, stripping away much of the white matter of her brain, shredding apart much of the frontal lobe of her brain. Although many lobotomy patients have been known to reasonably fully regrow and restore the frontal lobes of their brains after a set of psychosurgical lobotomy, the female spy whom the ski-mask-clad male murderer tortured to death in this case was a woman whose brain would not have any more than a few minutes of life left, as her killer waited until she was nearly dead from blood loss and other effects from the massive thigh-to-chest mutilation that he had performed on her before he bothered to lobotomize her. Finally, after he had mutilated her from just above the knees to the nipples, then psychosurgically lobotomized her, he poured hydrochloric acid onto portions of her groin, face, and chest. Finally, atop her corpse, he placed one sheet of laminated paper, which stated in all-caps: "BEHOLD, HERE LIES A SPY ON THE WRONG SIDE OF THE WAR, AN EXAMPLE OF THOSE WHO DESERVE DEATH BY TORTURE, NO MATTER WHAT THEIR DEMOGRAPHICS ARE. NO JUSTICE, NO PEACE! THOSE ON THE WRONG SIDE OF WAR DESREVE NO MERCY WHATSOEVER, ABSOLUTELY NO MERCY AT ALL!! DEATH TO THOSE WHO STAND IN THE WAY OF THE LOVE OF GOD!! THOSE ON THE WRONG SIDE DESERVE TO BE TORTURED TO DEATH AS PAINFULLY AS POSSIBLE! THE SOVIETS, THE NAZIS, THE MAU MAUS, THE WORST OF THE ANCIENT HEBREWS, THE WORST OF THE ISLAMIST JIHADISTS, THE MOST CRUEL OF COLONISTS, THE TOWER OF LONDON EXECUTIONERS, THE MEDEIVAL CHRISTIAN CRUSADERS, THE KU KLUX KLAN, THE BLACK

SUPREMACISTS, THE WHITE SUPREMACISTS, THE DRUG CARTELS, THE SICILIAN SYNDICATES, AND OTHERS WERE TOO DISCRIMINATORY AND NOT VICIOUS ENOUGH! WE ARE THE FUNDAMENTALIST AND JUSTIFIED GUILLOTINE BRIGADE. GOD IS ON OUR SIDE! ANYONE ON THE WRONG SIDE CAN DESERVE TO BE PAINFULLY TORTURED TO DEATH! DEATH BY TORTURE CAN PROTECT THE TRUTH, TEACH THOSE EXECUTED A LESSON AS THEY PREPARE TO MEET THEIR MAKER, AND SERVE AS EXAMPLES TO THOSE WHO FIND THE CORPSES!! THIS HERE CORPSE SERVES AS TESTIMONY TO OUR LOVE FOR OUR NEIGHBORS, AND IT PROVES THAT WE LOVE THE LORD!!!"

A computer analyzed the corpse, especially its neural network, and provided glimpses into what the deceased had experienced: A man wearing a dark ski mask, a trench coat, gloves, dark trousers, and steel-toed boots suddenly attacked the female spy, whom he considered an enemy. Although he refrained from exposing his genitals, it was clear from the video that he experienced sexual arousal, as he went back and forth between not sporting any profile of having an erection to sporting an erection between his legs, from soon after commencing the attack onward. He tied her up, then used one hundred of the needles to repeatedly stab her inner thighs and her genitals. Next, paralleling some Extremist Islamist Jihadist horrors that some Hamas-affiliated Muslims had perpretrated onto some Israali Jews on October 7, 2023, he stabbed an ice pick repeatedly into her groin, causing unspeakable pain while mutilating much of her reproductive system. *He was one of the members of the group that called itself The Fundamentalist and Justified Guillotine Brigade. That group had a very twisted belief in what they thought to be the true version of Chistianity. Many Jews, Muslims, Jains, Agnostics, Christians, and others denounced that group as an example of Christofascism.* Vivian V. Orion wondered whether the ghosts of Jack the Ripper and some of the earliest and cruelest of the Roman Catholics might have somehow demonically possessed that group. *She knew that if she would fail to impress her captors well enough, then they would almost undoubtedly torture her to death, and she had a degree of concern that they might actually be members of the aforementioned group. How strange, she thought, about the capacity for brainwashing via language. If a group puts the word "justified" in its name, then it does not necessarily make the group justified.*

She thought this to be very similar to how the act of naming a son Jesus does not make any guarantee that he will live a life that closely parallels the life of Jesus of Nazareth, also known as Jesus Christ.

She also thought this to be very similar to how the act of naming a son Muhammad does not make any guarantee that he will live a life that closely parallels the life of The Prophet Muhammad.

Additionally, she thought similarly about when people might give any of the possible names to any of their possible descendants. She thought long and hard while waiting to stand in front of a panel of captors and face what might prove to be the toughest test of her life. Would they consider her a failure and proceed to hurt, rape, torture, and kill her? Would they consider her a success and add her to their ranks? Would it even be ethical to join their ranks if offered the chance? If offered to join them, then would it be better to agree and probably survive a while longer or disagree and probably die soon?

Again, she returned to thoughts on the mysteries of names. Many of the organizations that The United States of America and Israel chose to label as terrorist organizations during portions of the Twentieth and Twenty-First Centuries were of this sometimes-disconcerting pattern. She thought about how the U.S. of back then, the Israel of back then, and she herself as of that analytical instant all agreed on much of this. Just because some organization calls itself something that is justified to do what it does is not a reason for jumping to a conclusion that the organization actually is justified to do what it does. She wondered who in the world had hijacked the plane and exactly to what her predicament could be leading. She thought even more about how names can, at a minimum, to some degree on some occasions have effects, yet how reality often does not have to match what people try to impose upon it by their most carefully chosen acts of naming people, places, things, and ideas.

She thought to herself silently, *Hm, a more expansive version of an old saying, and it is extra relevant right now, how well do I really understand it? It is much of what it is toward which a bunch of this stuff is probably headed: "The best laid plans often pass by those who put them together, such that those who made those plans might look at them with crestfallen eyes, hearts, and souls, looking askance as passengers in a vehicle that passes by the dead corpses of those plans, as those skeletons of those plans that never came to fruition lie dead by the side of the road and those vehicles simply pass on by, with the passengers having to move on with their lives and accept it that they were not able to get the jobs done of turning those plans of which they had been fond into actualities." That was an old idea that, as expressed in a nearly identical vein with more of an economy of words, took the form, "The best laid plans o' mice and men / Gang aft a-gley."* Let me interpret that famous Burns quote: The "mice and men" in that could encompass women, girls, boys, teenagers, men, extraterrestrials, bats, deities, demons, tigers, lions, dinosaurs, mice, fish, frogs, orca, oracles, and anyone or virtually anyone else. The "gang" was an archaic way to state "go" or "go past" or something rather similar to that. The "aft" referred to "aside or going from in front to somewhere behind or going from the unknown future to the known present and past." The "a-gley" had to do with "looking askance, perhaps sadly." Hm.

Continuing, she thought, *Did I really remember and understand that quote well, or is there, perhaps, something amiss? I have come a long way from my youth, but maybe besides progressing a bunch, maybe I have also regressed a little, or maybe, could it be, I might have regressed a bunch, could this be so? I don't know for sure. If I survive much longer, then what changes should I make to my life?*

Next, she thought about how one night she had a strange nightmare in which a male piano instructor wearing a pink necktie was teaching a young student how to improve on that male student's set of music-making techniques. The six-year-old student's mother complained to the instructor, who then argued back. Seconds later in the nightmare, Vivian Valerie Orion witnessed the instructor, the boy, and the woman all go through several new phases in their lives, die, and then get reincarnated as enemies in a war in Europe. The three of them had by then changed into manifesting as adult men armed with a combination of 9mm "Parabellum" / "NATO" / "Luger" rounds, .45 rounds, large artillery shells, bombs, grenades, and other instruments of death and destruction. Next, it arrived that she suddenly found herself running naked in the very middle of crossfire, running for her life. Finally, she experienced in that nightmare herself getting shot with many bullets within a five-second interval, shot in the front from the shins to the armpits, all of a sudden bleeding out from many bullet wounds, experiencing a sheer agony like she had never felt before. Then she woke up, felt astonished be in good health, relieved to know that she had merely experienced a grim nightmare, not real life.

When she arrived at her interview, her background in espionage influenced her word choices; she remarked to the interviewers, "I have decided to take an agnostic approach toward whether or not you folks are justified to be conducting this entire project with us, yet if any of the men present inflict upon me a most painful and slow death, I understand that it is what is expected of you."

She then giggled affectionately and flirtatiously while looking at several of the male interviewers, alternating between looking them in the eyes and peeking down toward their genitals, which, though fully-clothed, obviously were both vulnerable and excitable.

Her heart, mind, and soul felt trepidation, yet each of them also felt the thrill of the ultra-high-risk, ultra-high-reward prospects that the situation presented. Throughout her erogenous zones, she felt passion for the all of the good, bad, terrible, and wonderful erotic possibilities that might soon present themselves, and she silently theorized that mentally influencing her reproductive system into going into strong arousal—maybe even elevated into going into heat—just might attract at least one male captor into caring for her and loving her enough to save her from soon experiencing her body suffering rape, torture, mutilation, and death.

Her use of the classic strategy of, "throw many things against the wall and hope something will stick" worked like gangbusters. Not only did the administrators deem her worthy of survival, they tentatively earmarked her as very likely tough and savvy enough to be potential professional-interrogator-executioner material. They now considered her to have passed the tests with flying colors; to them, she seemed among the best of the best candidates to prove very useful to their organization in the short run, the medium run, and the long run.

As part of an interrogation process, males and females among those ranks would be instructed at times to mate with male and female inmates and proceed to sexually mutilate them as part of extracting the maximum information. Such interrogators would also at times be required to be left very vulnerable to becoming captured and tortured to death by enemy organizations. They knew that some would divulge information when captured, yet selectivity when deciding whom to let into their ranks would minimize such risks. She was used to this sort of lifestyle from when she worked in an intelligence organization earlier in her life. Her conscience did indicate to her a grave uncertainty about whether it would be best to remain loyal to these people for very long or to find an exit strategy, but she decided that she would cross the most difficult bridges if and when getting there, rather than doing way too much contingency planning.

She decided a moderate amount of contingency planning would be best. Of course, the vast majority of such planning would be kept totally to herself, until if and when it might become prudent to share it with at least one other sentient being.

Her captors were already very impressed with her composure under pressure and her willingness to communicate with them firmly.

They believed with near certainty that if push would come to shove with a c.o. commanding her to do so, then she could mate with a male inmate and then use a knife, needles, her fingernails, or her teeth to butcher him. In this case, they also had great confidence that, if given the orders to do so, then she would be willing and able to play with a female inmate and then use a knife, an ice pick, needles, her fingernails, or her teeth to butcher her. Also of mighty importance, they believed her ability to withstand torture and mutilation during interrogation by enemies in a P.O.W. camp while refusing to divulge anything other than her name, rank, and serial number would have a good chance to be great, maybe even perfect. (Regarding that perfection, for example, legends indicated that one U.S. military man was able during a torture interrogation session in Cambodia during the Vietnam War to hold the line, and, by the end, he had successfully refused to tell the captors anything more than his name, rank, and serial number; all the remains found post-mortem: a green military shirt and a huge bloody mess.)

All around, they found her to have great chances of becoming a highly valuable member of their country's intelligence community.

*   *   *

Jacob Kalkin took a vastly different approach. On the elections issue he wrote, "That was so long ago, and there are so many uncertainties all over the place. I am voting for every U.S. general election for the presidency in the range of years covered by this test to be in the Maybe column." On the celebrity death theories issue he wrote, "At this time,

I decline to place any such hypothesis here in relationship with specific celebrities and their circumstances. However, I shall now write a general hypothesis covering all one hundred twelve of them, namely, that some had excessive attachments that led to premature deaths, others had excessive aversions that led to premature deaths, there were yet others who had insufficient caring about situations that led to dying either prematurely or suboptimally late, and, there were at least a few who died exactly in the correct manner at exactly the correct time with respect to soteriology." At his interview, when prompted to provide an opening statement, he responded aloud, "Frankly, I believe that much of what you are doing is, most probably, unethical. However, given that I do not know the full situation of what is going on with you, I shall decline to reach a firm judgment on the degree of ethics or lack thereof involved with these activities that you say that you are conducting. If you interact with me in such a way that I live with honor, great!

However, I am also prepared to die with honor, and I am prepared to kill with honor, if the times and purposes are ethical for me to die and let live, live and let die, or die and let die. Of course, live and let live might be a course of action available to us, at least some of the time." The administrators immediately reacted by judging him worthy to live, yet they noted that he might pose a medium-to-high risk of later becoming a major troublemaker.

*   *   *

Seven females and three males attempted to allege the causes of some celebrity deaths to have involved making political leaders into objects of excessive hate, excessive love, or a mixture of both. Each of those ten made statements, both in print and by spoken word while being interviewed after taking the written test, along the lines of, "Many of those celebrities died sooner than they otherwise would have. Some died prematurely because of excessive hatred toward conservatives, others died prematurely because of excessive hatred toward liberals, and yet others still had mixtures of excessive hatred toward multiple public figures and excessive love and veneration toward multiple public figures. Think about this detail from eons ago, as an example: Republican President Trump won a U.S. general election over Democratic Vice President Harris in 2024, a result which many Republicans and some Independents considered to be an apocalyptically good outcome, yet also a result which many Democrats and some Independents considered to be an apocalyptically bad outcome. Many foreign observers also had very mixed reactions. It can be all too easy in such situations for people to feel excessive attachments and aversions in the wake of such cataclysmic events."

Two of the seven women who chose this approach survived the evaluation and its immediate aftermath; the other five women died during gruesome interrogations that included the nonconsensual puncturing by needles and ice picks of each and every portion of their flesh from the top of the head to the soles of the feet.

One of the three men who chose this approach survived the evaluation and its aftermath; the other two men died during gruesome interrogations that included the nonconsensual puncturing by needles and ice picks of each and every portion of their flesh from the top of the head to the soles of the feet.

* * * * *

Charr Naerroan declined to write anything at all down on the paper tests presented to him.

When the interview started, one of the interviewers, a 6'9" man wearing enough clothing and other coverings, including a thorough mask, such that it might have seemed anyone's guess what racial background he might have had (unless someone had previously met him in circumstances conducive to knowing what he would look like in normal settings), appearing to be very muscular, started screaming with a deep, forceful voice at Charr, "What the hell do you think you're doing?! Who the hell do you think you are?! To dare to not write anything on the test after we posed those conditions upon you? Are you kidding me?! What do you say to this, I sentence you to be cut up, vivisected to death, starting with the soles of your feet, then the ankles, then moving upward, inch by inch, what do you say to that?"

Charr responded by looking at the hostile interviewer with a beyond-basilisk-civil-war stare, psychokinetically raged in fury at him in the spirit of *Leviticus*, Chapter 26 (a sacred text), *The 54 Wrathful Faces of Divinity at Angkor Wat* (a set of sacred sculptures in Cambodia), and all other expressions of allegedly divine wrath, and, instantly, the hostile interviewer died of spontaneous human combustion. "SHC" is in some contexts an acronym for that cause of death, a cause that some consider to be paranormal and that others consider to be a very bizarre scientific mystery best to leave uncertain as to whether to classify as paranormal or merely paranormal-esque.

Whereas the vast majority of documented cases of such SHC involved the vast majority of clothing and footwear remaining in-tact, Charr chose to burn up every part of the rude test administration captor's body, all of his clothing, and 95% of his footwear.

He did this to make an example of that disrespectful chap. The other test administrators were stunned speechless.

Charr then proceeded to say to the other administrators, "I invite the leadership of your nation, whoever they might be, to meet me in the near future. However, if this is too inconvenient to arrange, then I might as well depart from these premises soon, with or without your consent."

After five more seconds of speechless shock, one of the remaining interviewers, *a 27-year-old woman wearing military fatigues yet neither a mask nor any head coverings,* (and, who, oddly enough, suddenly found herself turned on by how off-the-charts of an alpha male Charr had shown himself to be), *said to him slowly, "Although you have demonstrated great power right in front of us, I'm not sure how long it might take to arrange for you to meet with them. That said, I'm intrigued about how it is possible for you to do what you just did. I'll tell you what, we can offer that you can meet with some intermediate-level government types from our country, and we'll see where we go from there."*

Charr Naerroan answered, *"Great, let's get started."*

* * *

After Charr rose through their ranks and engaged in many intense interrogations and combat situations, he knew from billions of years of past experiences that the time would come for him to depart from them. Before leaving, he influenced many potential dominoes into ar-ranging into exactly the pattern he intended, fitting grander schemes.

On a fateful day in the year 3798, he simply dematerialized from a platform in the Arctic Circle. Traveling through the seams between multiple universes, he arrived at a universe where extraterrestrial aliens had instigated long-term, total-world tyranny on planet Earth as of the year 4005. Ripe for an exegetic wipeout, within the twinkling of an eye, that entire reality phased out of existence.

To Charr, this was an opportunity that he was familiar with and had been long waiting for recurring. In many other realms, he had previously witnessed such a phasing out of existence of an entire reality, and he had exploited it adroitly and repeatedly. He was great at utilizing his extremely bizarre niche within reality and exploiting it to the max.

He transferred the consciousness of the beings, one by one to other universes and other times, to partially merge with the minds and hearts and souls of the troubled beings in many worlds, sort of the opposite of when Jesus cast the "Legion" set of spirits out of an afflicted person and cast them into a pig.

Rather, Charr Naerroan cast the spirits of those left without any existent universe to partway merge with the beings of other realms, then strategically visited many of them, one by one, to telepathically influence them to make a deal: Extreme destruction for extreme reward. In many cases, as he had done previously in dealing with Hannibal Barca and Adolf Hitler, he offered for a person in a final stage of downfall to commit suicide at his encouragement. Some took him up on that offer, others declined. The general trend, started to break heavily in his favor. Ramping up his energies and the energies of others, his situation escalated and escalated, taking the energies beyond anything fathomable to much of anyone. He had done this sort of thing before, but never with quite this much momentum and acceleration. Although many had resisted him, the sheer force of the situation peeled away one type of resistance after another, flipping one source of resistance after another to the side of letting go and then joining on the side of letting go of what had been.

However, as transcendental as he was, and as transcendental as his accomplices and rivals, such as Dimetrioskys Elbankovic were, there were entities at work that were at several orders of magnitude beyond them. There were those who transcended virtually all other trans-cendentals, and for them the interplay between Naerroan, Elbankovic, and others was a proxy for what they, the most imminently and transcendent of the transcendentals, the holiest of the holies, were involved with.

As Yadier Horowitz, various manifestations of Kalki sometimes also known as Kalkin, many manifestations of the Elohim, extraordinary transformations of the alternative versions of Trinity and Trinities, and more engaged in a huge, cosmic tug of war over whether REALITY ITSELF as a totality would soon be encountering either some sort of COSMIC RESET and/or COSMIC TOTAL OBLITERATION, there came the recurrence of the edge of the first emergence and fission, yet with several twists.

Within one universe, in a region several hundred million light years away from Earth, The Ultimate Lord of That Universe chose to mani-fest as a Giant Transcendental Pyramid Speaking with a Grandiloquent Voice, while The Wheel of Oblivion chose to manifest as a Huge, Serrated, Circular Saw With An Arrangement of Graphene, Diamonds, Skulls, and Skeletons, Spinning Quickly, Speaking with a Grandiloquent Voice.

The Ultimate Lord of That Universe said to The Wheel of Oblivion, "We meet again. As it was in the beginning, here it is now again."

The Wheel of Oblivion responded, "However much transcendence any of us ever achieve, we still have the way we fit in with absolutely everyone and, yes, absolutely everything. In some ways I am a thing. In other ways I am a being. You know and have known from your beginning that your universe is but one of many, and, though you are in some ways 'The Lord,' in other ways, you are a microcosm of 'The Lord' at some yet higher, more transcendental level of reality. THE END IS NIGH."

The Ultimate Lord of That Universe answered, "Yes. The tide has turned to such a degree, there is no stopping it now. *I can no longer hold back your obliteration of my universe and myself, though I had held on for such a huge amount of space-time and transcendental duration.*

"One living and conscious cell within one living, conscious, and biological multicell organism will often sooner or later become unable to hold back the tide of events from resulting in its own demise, yet the organism as a whole goes on in most cases. I renounce my will and I let go of the last vestiges of resistance to the inevitable, and as I commit my soul to the yet greater levels of being. I hope for the best. *To the Yet-More-Transcendental Levels of Reality, to YOU I release my spirit."* With that utterance departed the last resistance to THE END OF THAT COSMOS.

The Wheel of Oblivion proceeded to utterly obliterate that cosmos.

The chain reaction was off to the races. The Wheel of Oblivion proceeded to confront one universe after another, with a nearly-identical reenactment of that same dialogue and scene, over and over. Yes, some versions of The Lord of the Universe chose to manifest in other ways, sometimes as a colossal, bipedal, human body of one type or another, other times as a colossal, bipedal, superintelligent robot body of one type or another, and at yet other times still as an entire galaxy within its cosmos. Yet the main essence of the pattern remained the same, as The Wheel of Oblivion proceeded to share one last embrace with Its main original partner of a given universe, The Ultimate Lord of That Given Universe, and The Wheel of Oblivion then proceeded to grant the kiss of death, loving each of those Lords God even while serving to obliterate each of those Lords and each of those Lords' Universes.

There came to be three camps of transcendentals traversing the many universes as this cosmic chain reaction continued. There was the camp seeking to take the obliteration of universes to the maximum. There, too, was the camp seeking to minimize the obliteration of universes. Finally, there was the neutral camp. Also, there had emerged the trend of a peeling away of transcendentals from the resistance to cascading extra obliteration of universes. More and more were choosing to side with Charr Naerroan and the others who sought to burn absolutely everything down, with the odd faith that this would somehow serve the greatest good in the long run.

There then emerged a critical juncture as The Wheel of Oblivion confronted The Ultimate Lord of An Entire Multiverse.

The Wheel of Oblivion respected this Lord God even more than It respected each of the subsidiary Lords God whom It had just finished annihilating, and It said to That a different variation of executioner's speech to the soon-to-be-executed: The Wheel of Oblivion said to The Ultimate Lord of That Entire Multiverse, "Although Thou Art The Ultimate Lord of An Entire Multiverse, Thou Knoweth as well as I Knoweth that Thou Art Not Quite At The Level of THE ABSOLUTE, The Great Good Lord Of The Absolute Total Totality. The cascading chain reaction has blast its way through the gates that had held me back from reaching You. Here I Am. You know as well as I do the fact that I do what I do as an ultimate executioner."

The Ultimate Lord of That Entire Multiverse responded, "Yes, and I saw You coming.

"Thou Art A Marvelous and Extraordinary Executioner that Brings that Mysterious Extra Equality to All, yet there is more. Although You and I, yes, whether 'tis best in a given instance to stylize this as Thyself and Myself, Thou and I, or You and I, yes, indeed, although We are in many ways Omniscient, there is an Omniscience far greater than me, and that omniscience may yet be about to prove far greater than even You. I love You, and I love my creations in my multiverse, and I love That Lord Who Is Even Greater Than I Am. Normally, I refrain from advising anyone to do what anyone wilt, as most beings are not yet spiritually mature enough to handle that advice. However, you and I are about as ancient and spiritually mature as can be. Go for it! Do what Thou wilt!"

The Wheel of Oblivion mirrored back, "Yes, although We are in many ways Omniscient, there is an Omniscience in at least a few ways far greater than the Full Combination of Thyself and Myself.

"NEVERTHELESS, THE END IS NIGH."

The Ultimate Lord of That Entire Multiverse answered, "Yes. We both knew that this, The Last Day of This Multiverse For Which I Serve As Lord, would almost undoubtedly eventually arrive. Here We Are. Yet, Here We Are Not For Much Longer.

"BEWARE, THOUGH, ALTHOUGH WE BOTH REMEMBER WELL THAT TRANSITION FROM THE GREAT PRIMORDIAL ABSOLUTE NOTHING INTO THE PRIMORDIAL AWARENESS BEYOND ALL NAMES AND ALL NUMBERS OF INDIVDUATION, WHICH NEXT BECAME THE PRIMORDIAL SELF-AWARE REALITY THAT WAS IN-SOME-WAYS-NOTHING AND YET, YEAH VERILY, IN-OTHER-WAYS-TRANSCENDING-NOTHING-&-SOMETHING, WE HAVE NOW ENTERED UNCHARTERED TERRITORY.

"You have obliterated entire universes and the lords of each of them before, but only now are you crossing over into obliterating An Entire Multiverse And Its Lord.

"As omniscient as You and I are, We cannot know with complete certainty or anywhere near it what will happen once We cross the line of this next step. Will the Ultimate Destination that will occur during the next portions of THE ENDS OF THE MULTIVERSES eventually result in the absolute, sheer obliteration of the complete entirety of reality?!

"Will it lead to something else?

"Will it lead to *a mixture* of the total singularity obliteration of absolutely all *and* something other than that total obliteration?! *What will that something else even be, if there is that something else?*

"Will there be multiple versions of that something else, with all of them occurring simultaneously?"

The Lord of that multiverse paused briefly. This was as bittersweet as bittersweet could be.

The Lord of that multiverse resumed speaking to The Wheel of Oblivion. That Lord stated, "Well, in every scenario there is at a minimum the consolation prize, the bare minimum of shunyatic, ultimate interdependency, by which, no matter how much absolute death happens to the totality of reality, at least the most microscopic trace of all that ever was and everyone who ever was can and will blip ever so slightly on at least the rarest of occasions. It might not be the stereotypical visions of heaven, but it is also not the stereotypical primal fear vision of absolute, total death with not even the slightest trace of any blip of any trace of anything whatsoever of us after we are gone. Not 72 virgins, not gathering around a campfire and singing 'Amazing Grace' and other songs for all of eternity, not even a basic sitting around in a calm neighborhood, but at least that microscopic trace, something to which a few manifestations of writers in each multiverse have alluded to, at least that is something in which we can find solace.

"To reiterate, we are in uncharted territory, and, as far as I know, we might be on the cusp of a chain reaction that shall obliterate absolutely everyone and everything except for the most minimal of a subtle, rare, intermittent trace of interdependency of all that ever was.

"I do not know. You, too, probably do not know. Does anyone anywhere, yeah verily, even the manifestation or manifestations of THE ABSOLUTE,

The Ultimate Lord Beyond Even Myself And Thyself, does even that Ultra-Transcendental Ultimate Lord or Set of Ultimate Lords, doth even THAT knoweth for sure what will happen next?!"

The Wheel of Oblivion responded, "I know this relevant fact: Here is this end." Upon completion of that utterance, The Wheel of Oblivion annihilated both The Ultimate Lord of That Multiverse and that Lord's entire multiverse.

***** ~~~~~~~~~~~~ ********* ~~~ ~~ *****~~~~******* .... ***~~~~*****

In the face of a cascade of annihilation the likes of which that none had ever witnessed before, series of dilemmas, trilemmas, quadrulemmas, quintelemmas, and beyond emerged.

Tensions escalated as multitudes considered tough options.

For a brief instant, Ezra Kalkin and Jacob Kalkin remerged with each other to become a combination of a hybrid of both of themselves and the Zarlowe Nike from which they had fissioned into twinhood.

The reemergent entity of them manifested as all three—both as the fissioned pair, Ezra and Jacob, and as the fusioned and reemergent Zarlowe Nike. Whether conceived as multiple beings or as one being, consciousness flashed back to the memory of how on an elementary school playground a physical education instructor had the class participate in tug of war.

The male P.E. coach set up the friendly competition to have all the girls on one side and all the boys on the other side, although the girls numbered twenty-two and the boys only numbered nine. Predictably, in the first round the girls won the tug of war convincingly. However, as the two teams separately huddled in private to strategize the next round, the boys came up with an innovative strategy: They would simultaneously let go of the rope near the very beginning of the contest, and, thereby, although losing in some regular sense, they would control how the loss would occur, and it would prove to be a Pyrrhic victory for the girls, who would fall over onto the ground. As the two teams gathered together, ready to struggle, the P.E. coach announced, "On your marks, get set, go!" The boys team acted out their planned strategy. It worked to perfection: they let go simultaneously almost exactly when the girls started to pull the rope, and the entire girls team fell over, winning the contest yet looking ridiculous in the process.

Ezra, Jacob, and Zarlowe telepathically communicated this memory to the other remaining resistance-to-obliteration-camp transcendentals, layered with the idea that they could outflank the seeking-obliteration-camp transcendentals by transfiguring themselves from resisting obliteration into becoming, in essence, a set of seeking-carefully-navigated-and-controlled-obliteration-camp transcendentals.

A great acceptance happened: a cascading resignation of will.

An eeriness set in, spanning all universes and all worlds.

Suddenly, Vivian Valerie Orion, Yadier Horowitz, Jesus of Nazareth, THE ENERGY-REGULATING SUPER-ENTITY BEHIND THE VEIL OF THE TETRAGRAMMATON, The Adibuddha, Ezra Kalkin, Jacob Kalkin, The Prophet Muhammad, Green Tara, Shakyamuni Buddha, Lao-Tzu, THE FORM-REGULATING SUPER-ENTITY BEHIND THE VEIL OF THE INTERDEPENDENT CO-ARISING OF PHENOMENA, Adidharma, The Mysterious Firsts, The Mysterious Lasts, The Egyptian Primordials, Hermes Trismegistus, The Abrahamic Primordials, The Egyptian Ultimates, The Dhyani Primordials, The Transcendental Selves of Multitudes of Ordinary Human Beings, The Abrahamic Ultimates, The Dhyani Ultimates, and All

Others Of Sufficiently-Awake Consciousness transitioned away—in some realms one by one, in other realms myriad by myriad—from putting up any trace of resistance to the end of all of the universes and multiverses.

A combination of The Primordials, The Firsts, Yadier Horowitz, Io, Ezra Kalkin, Simhamukha, Charr Naerroan, Dimetrioskys Elbankovic, The Lasts, and All Others of Sufficiently-Awake Consciousness merged enough of their minds and their wills into arriving at the brink of Ending All.

They then converged All Powers and Channels At Once, Spanning All Universes, and They Detonated The Total Destroyer of All Worlds.

* ~ # * ~ # * ~ # * ~ # * ~ # * ~ # * ~ #

A flashback to just before that detonation: Although Charr Naerroan did not know with certainty how much of what would happen next would be sheer oblivion, sheer transcendence, or something else, both he and the popular author H.P. Lovecraft had long ago become aware that at least a trace of all variations of the mystery of death and life would emerge from such an endeavor.

Compared to the way that reality was before, would the new reality become an incomprehensibly-minute, faint ghost of a trace, or would the new reality turn out to be a cosmically complete reality, maybe even augmented? They did not know the answer to this, but there was at least a little reassurance about the prospects of how the aftermath might be. Awareness that there would reemerge and remain at least a microscopic trace of all of that led to a core peace of mind that no one could take away from Charr and H.P. Multiple beings had flashbacks to having read or heard embedded statements to this effect somewhere within the lines and between the lines of literature, songs, and film.

Charr let go of any and all specific, tangible emotional states, going over into a deep meditative samadhi in the last few instants that led up to detonation. Septillions of other highly-intelligent beings also entered samadhi in those last few instants.

Then came that huge mega-detonation.

* ~ # * ~ # * ~ # * ~ # * ~ # * ~ # * ~ #

With that Alpha-and-Omega Detonation, The Strong Force, The Weak Force, Gravity, The Will to Life, The Will to Death, and All Other Forces suddenly ceased, and with their dissemblance into sheer nothingness came The End of All Universes Known and Unknown, as well as The End of All Beings and All Things Known and Unknown.

* ~ # * ~ # * ~ # * ~ # * ~ # * ~ # * ~ #

All of a sudden, *after* that, Charr found himself back in an old familiar place. Some talk about a feeling of déjà vu, yet for him this was way beyond déjà vu: *He was in exactly the same setting he had found himself in a thousand times before.*

Jacob Kalkin sat in front of Charr Naerroan in an interdimensional realm—specifically, where Charr found himself imprisoned again in Temple 894723 Gateway Prison. Charr looked again at the badge on the person preparing to interview him. Again, as in the previous times, it read, "Name: Jacob Kalkin / Role: Investigator / Reason for Visit to Temple 894723 Gateway Prison: To Help With the Charr Naerroan situation." Charr thought things would be different this time, that he would find himself having broken out of the recurrence of arriving here. However, much to his consternation, another recurrence it was.

The detonation had been beyond the imagination, certainly beyond anything that this version of Charr Naerroan had ever experienced before, yet, somehow, quite mysteriously, he was back at the place he had revisited the most often.

Sure, he had found himself stuck in time loops before, for example, he had been stuck in a loop that returned to the aftermath of The Battle of Hastings twenty times, but never before had he seemed anywhere near this stuck in a time loop. Nevertheless, he continued to have both inner peace and a frenetic energy ready to wage war. Early in his development as a Transcendental, he had achieved this core competency, and its presence within the fibers of his being was part of business as usual in his roles *within* the many multiverses *and beyond* the many multiverses of REALITY. Although he, like Ezra Kalkin, Sarah Rubinstein, Jacob Kalkin, Vivian Valerie Orion, and most other Transcendentals were in many ways and in many situations of lesser stature than each LORD of each UNIVERSE and each LORD of each MULTI-VERSE, they were in other ways more agile. For they were capable of IMMIGRATION BETWEEN DIVERSE UNIVERSES AND MULTI-VERSES WITHOUT A CLEAR-CUT DEATH. In contrast each LORD of each UNIVERSE or MULTIVERSE would have to undergo a death akin to the death of a mere mortal before achieving that kind of im-migration capability. THE LORDS OF THE UNIVERSES AND THE LORDS OF THE MULTIVERSES WERE NEARLY OMNIPOTENT WITHIN EACH OF THEIR OWN JURISDICTIONS, YET EACH HAD EXTREMELY LIMITED ABILITY TO REMOTELY AND DIRECTLY INTERACT WITH THE MANY REALMS BEYOND HIS OR HER OR

ITS JURISDICTION. Conceived another way, this could be expressed thusly: Each of those Lords was an amazing Transcendental, yet more complete omnipotence of one type would come at the price of less omnipotence of another type. Each such Lord's own awesome powers over each such Lord's own jurisdiction proved to seriously limit the ability to become imminently present outside that jurisdiction. That is, it would limit such an ability for as long as such a Lord's jurisdiction were to remain alive. Once The Wheel of Oblivion would come around after some gargantuan stretch of eons upon eons to execute a given universe and its Lord, that Lord would become liberated from the mixture of authority and responsibility that had been part and parcel of the situation, and that Lord would then become free to fully migrate from one universe to another and from one multiverse to another. Similarly, the tandem execution of a multiverse and the Lord of that multiverse would result in liberation of that Lord from being tied down to His or Her or Its Authority Over and Responsibility To That Multiverse, freeing that Lord to wander both the vast blackness of the darkness of the stars and the oases of the shining brightness of the white, blue, yellow, red, green, and other-hued lights of the suns and stars. Similarly, hitherto-unseen magnitudes of cosmic death brought with them hitherto-unseen magnitudes of cosmic liberation for a great many of the rest of the beings who had been living within The Reality That Had Been.

Extreme transfigurations and transmigrations of beings in the wake of the annihilation of universes had long been a source of time loops, and the present version of Charr had experienced an incredible number of them over the eons. He now faced a set of time loops that he started to suspect to be part of an inescapable trap, perhaps the fruition of karma for inflicting gargantuan amounts of death and destruction.

He knew that he could not rely too heavily on himself or any one specific other being to find an escape from this loop, basing this knowledge on how he had succeeded in orchestrating his previous escapes from time loops. A relaxed, neutral, Zen approach to it all entered his mind-stream.

More tangible, basic details became less important than attempting to tune in to how to manage whatever might be happening way beyond the tangible senses; he felt the energies of how to manage intuition. Naerroan wondered what he might do differently this time around, what others might do differently, and much more.

He silently thought to himself, *What could it be about reality that leads to how I keep arriving back here in this interdimensional temple gateway prison that is in a realm that transcends all normal notions of time—somehow outside of all normal universal and multiversal timelines—and, each time, again finding myself about to be interviewed by Jacob Kalkin as the Transcendentals running the temple prison facility work on determining what to do with me next? Why do the many lives and deaths experienced always sooner or later return me to this exact setting?*

He considered options and reached out with his heart and mind and soul toward whoever and whatever might transcend the entire combination of the other beings ostensibly at the facility, himself, and the gateway temple prison itself. Ideas energizing the fields of consciousness stirred both within himself and beyond himself. Patterns of mind effervescently traveled at high rates of speed between many beings telepathically.

THE TRANSCENDENT, THE END, THE BEGINNING, THE NEW END, THE TRANSITION, AND THE BEYOND. That pattern flashed through multitudes of sentient beings.

Energies escalated beyond the imagination.

~ * # ~ *   *   *   *   *   *   * ~ * ~ # * ~

A critical convergence of conscious energies then detonated The Total Creator of All Worlds.

~ * # ~ * # ~ * # ~ * # ~ * # ~ * # ~ *

Was it old, was it new, or was it somehow both?

~ * # ~ * # ~ * # ~ * # ~ * # ~ * # ~ *

One or many? Or both or neither? Or beyond?

~ * # ~ * # ~ * # ~ * # ~ * # ~ * # ~ *

Some of those present to experience it coalesced into calling the unified and absolute Creator by the name, "Gegawndon," whereas others, indeed chose to call That Creator by other names.

Pronunciation of "Gegawndon" often was similar to how the phrase "get gown dawn" or the phrase "get gown don" might intuitively be spoken in English; exactly if dropping the "t," dropping the first "n," and speaking continuously from one syllable to the next. Other times, its pronunciation would include the last syllable sounding very much like many would pronounce the word, "done," name, "Dun," and the name "Dunne."

Much primal energy from all ultimate acts of The Creation of Reality occurred with that, as it had with what had seemed to be the previous creation of universes that featured at least one version of writer Evelyn Waugh creating at least one *The Temple at Thatch* manuscript. Much of that energy converged through intense telepathy to bear down on and for a while stifle that Waugh about twenty-and-a-half centuries after Nyatri Tsenpo ascended to the throne of Tibet. Waugh's destruction of his manuscript for *The Temple at Thatch* granted him a new lease on life, It was also a primal energy that in various universes and multiverses bore down upon the ancient Egyptians, ancient Hebrews/Jews, the Dorians, Jesus of Nazareth, the Gospel and Epistle writers among the founders of Christianity, the early founders of Islam, Shakyamuni Buddha, members of the early Buddhist sangha in general, and a variety of 20th-Century C.E. founders of syncretic religions. This was part of what led in at least some of the realities involving what some would call "The 20th Century A.D." or "The 20th Century C.E." to the strange twin manifestations of the peaceful path of Thich Nacht Hanh and the wrathful path of Pol Pot. Various motion picture film studios harnessed portions of that energy to create movies, with greatly varying degrees of success, in terms of their critical impact, commercial impact, and spiritual impact. Even some of the mysterious transcendental beings conjectured on some occasions about whether the given big bang creation of one of the universes originating in a big bang had in fact emanated from one explosion that transcended all universes and multiverses and of which this "new big bang" was simply another "beyond-old-and-new, beyond-before-and-after, a great, transcendental, creative explosion within a much larger, transcendental, ultimately original big bang explosion," one of an infinite series of smaller subsections of some ultimate big bang to encompass all creations of all universes and all multiverses.

It was an ultra-supermassive explosion, creating many multiverses, each of which included the creation of many universes.

Its scope, its scale, and its relationships remained mysterious to all or nearly all of those who subsequently contemplated it. Some of their thoughts took the forms of, *Was it new and separate from any previous extreme creations of many multiverses?*

Was it simply part of one ultimate, transcending-all-temporal-relations-to-all-multiverses creation of all multiverses?

Many beings shared a multipart, consensus hypothesis about this:

1) Among the many timelines of universes and multiverses, a multitude of them have both their beginning and their ending occurring simultaneously at the instant of the detonation of The Total Creator of All Worlds.

2) Quite a multitude of the remainder of them have both their beginning and their ending occurring simultaneously at the instant of the detonation of The Total Destroyer of All Worlds.

3) The complementary nature of those two sets of timelines can be thought to closely parallel two or more interlinking mobius strips.

4) Each time that two or more beings arrive or arrive again at either or both of those exordia-et-termini, alpha-and-omega singularities, the beings arriving there experience a judgment day.

5) Although in some senses "judgment days" do sometimes occur

elsewhere, the extremities of the exordia-et-termini, alpha-and-omega judgment day experiences are total: Within them, all beings, for at least one shining moment, reach total omniscience of all whom they had ever interacted with and total omniscience of themselves in terms of the core energy essences of all choices and actions in their individual journeys of conscious, semiconscious, and unconscious experience leading up to those judgment days. Each and every thing that they had ever wished to keep hidden from either other beings or themselves no longer remain hidden, and all beings, for at least a few fleeting instants stand fully naked in their totality in the presence of both themselves and all other beings with whom they had ever directly interacted. The sheer force of this totality leads many of them to die and become re-born with a near-total amnesia of anything that had ever occurred before, yet others find a way to achieve liberation, escaping that trap of re-birth and re-death.

6) However, each such escape from a given trap also serves as a forerunner to new challenges.

Many versions of Charr Naerroan traveled over eons of experience, sometimes stripped of powers, other times armed with powers, killed repeatedly, reconstituted to be alive with memory intact after death repeatedly, etc. The Powers That Be imposed on him on an ad hoc basis to be a Gentile, a Jew, dark-skinned, light-skinned, etc. at times. This included that he learned what it was like to die many painful, gruesome deaths in many of the most horrifying places in many places on many worlds and across virtually every era imaginable.

In a new world within a new set of heavens, the apparitions of three beings emerged from having just experienced a total-destruction-of-reality judgment day paired with a total-creation-of-reality judgment day. Gathering together after mysteriously rediscovering each other's presences, they shared a telepathic conversation:

Geronimo Watts asked, "How do you believe we arrived here, with our memories somehow intact, after the extremity of what just happened?"

Cheryl Nobel gave a part-hypothesis, part-knowledge, part-logic, part-emotion, part-beyond answer: "Love."

Ezra Kalkin then stated to them a longer response in a similar vein, though longer-winded: "Wisdom, compassion, willpower, loving-kindness, respect, and sheer and utter transcendence."

Geronimo at first felt great, but then looked as pale as pale can be.

Cheryl asked him, "What's come over you? Is something wrong?"

Geronimo Watts answered, "I suddenly had a sinking feeling about the idea from *Ecclesiastes*, 'There is nothing new under the sun,' as all of a sudden alongside the idea from *The Buddha-Karita of Asvaghosha*, 'This is the final end of all living creatures...' and two other ancient, primal idea patterns."

Cheryl inquired, "Which couple of other ancient sayings?"

Geronomo remained silent for a few seconds, then spoke slowly, firmly, and clearly, introducing them thusly, "They both come from the most ancient of antiquity."

After pausing again, he proceeded to announce the first, with the timbre of his vocals seeming to have reached about halfway from their normal pattern to something akin to an emanation from The Absolute, stating, "Alpha: There is a first time for everything."

After another brief pause, the voice that came from him somehow, next, resonated as a merger between his normal self and The Entity of The Great Voice Of The Ultra-Transcendental Meta-Grand Pyramid That Nike, Webster, Scarington, And Sooner had visited. It sounded like what many might have imagined THE VOICE OF GOD to sound like, announcing clearly to any and all who might listen, "Omega: There is a last time for everything."

EPILOGUE

After Jeremy Oppenheim and Charr Naerroan experienced ten trillion additional years of the hells, heavens, and ordinary worlds, they both found greatly enhanced, heightened awareness. They both let go of their old priorities, choosing to do their utmost to be fully ready to adapt to whatever might happen next.

However, nothing could have prepared them or much of anyone else for what happened next.

On many versions of Planet Earth, multitudes marked the date, "June 10, 10000." Early that morning, on each of those worlds, at the location known as Megiddo, multitudes witnessed Zoroaster, Stanley Kubrick, Jesus of Nazareth, John of Patmos, The Patriarch Moses, Benjamin Franklin, The Prophet Muhammad, Shakyamuni Buddha, Mary Baker Eddy, Yeshe Tsogyal, Padmasambhava, and others whom many considered long-dead suddenly materialize into full physical presence, live. *An eerie calm befell each of the worlds.*

All who had already consciously figured out the elegantly simple secret narrative that had many a time preceded doom suddenly revisited it, as did the entire remainder of the rest of the sentient beings, as THE LORD chose to announce it to All. THE GOOD LORD, THE GREAT ARCHITECT CREATOR OF ALL, chose then and there to present that narrative to each being in whichever language or languages that each would best understand. THE LORD declared to each and every sentient being, "Imagine a beginning in which there was absolute nothingness, and time and sequence had no meaning then and there. Now, something quite different, yet not entirely different: Imagine a beginning in which there was absolute nothingness except for a pervasive consciousness that the consciousness was alone within Reality. If considering an oscillating sequence between the two states, with both timelessly present, then every sequence of them is ambiguous for which came earlier or later. They are also two ends of a continuum of degrees of consciousness vs. unconsciousness sharing that timeless origin and timeless destination." THE LORD then added, *"THAT was where we all came from repeatedly, and THAT is where we now return." REALITY THEN ENDED. ALL ENDED. EVERYTHING ENDED. PERHAPS THERE ARE NO LOGICAL, QUANTIFIABLE, MEASUREMENT METHODS FOR WHETHER THAT HAPPENED IN THE PAST, WILL HAPPEN IN THE FUTURE, AND/OR IS HAPPENING NOW IN THE PRESENT.*

THE END AND THE BEGINNING OF ALL, BELIEVE IT OR NOT!

About the Author

Maurice James Blair demonstrated the ability to excel in the STEM fields early in his life, but by the mid-1990s he perceived several trends of the philosophical and scientific academia of the era to downplay the role of consciousness. Tribulations and changes led to a very different career for a while: teaming up with others to provide professional tax services. Unbeknownst to many, he worked on Comparative Religion, Philosophy, and Science on the side. During much of that period, he analyzed the minds and motives of IRS agents, business colleagues, clients, and various lawmakers while performing professional tax services. He also researched and explored science, arts, entertainment, and spirituality during much of his leisure time on the side of that.

Eventually, after overcoming many challenges, he returned to dealing directly with science, religion, the sciences, the religions, ethics, and metaphysics in the process of authoring an array of literary works. During the 2022-2025 period he participated in many book projects.

Since circa January 5, 2023, upon finding out that the fourth and final of the four original format versions of his novel *All Things under and over the Sun and Stars: Enigmas in Various Stages* (2023) had become available for sale on the Internet, he has often felt fully prepared for eternity. *That is, he has consistently felt ready since then for the possibility of encountering any of the many scenarios in which THE ENTIRETY OF REALITY ITSELF were to go away. If reality were to cease in any of a vast array of possibilities of what it might mean for reality to cease to be. That is, whether The Entirety of Reality Itself would return from whence It came or to go away in any other way, anywhere or nowhere, or somehow both anywhere and everywhere and nowhere simultaneously, or wherever else, instantly. That is, also, whether by any means or by any other means.*

He has fired bullets from firearms manufactured by Beretta, Walther, Sig Sauer, and Glock.

He has resided in Montana, Taiwan, South Korea, New Hampshire, North Carolina, and Texas; dated women from New York, Texas, and elsewhere; visited Hong Kong, Louisiana, New Jersey, Indiana, South Carolina, Pennsylvania, Nevada, Mexico, Connecticut, Utah, New Mexico, Oklahoma, Wyoming, California, Missouri, the skies over North America, the skies over the Pacific Ocean, and elsewhere.

www.ingramcontent.com/pod-product-compliance
Lightning Source LLC
Chambersburg PA
CBHW060606300726
48975CB00005B/1467